SUMMER SESSION

SUMMER SESSION

A Novel

Kelly L. Frey, Sr. & Kelly L. Frey, II

iUniverse, Inc.
New York Lincoln Shanghai

SUMMER SESSION

Copyright © 2007 by Kelly L. Frey, Sr. & Kelly L. Frey, II

All rights reserved. No part of this book may be used or reproduced by any means, graphic, electronic, or mechanical, including photocopying, recording, taping or by any information storage retrieval system without the written permission of the publisher except in the case of brief quotations embodied in critical articles and reviews.

iUniverse books may be ordered through booksellers or by contacting:

iUniverse
2021 Pine Lake Road, Suite 100
Lincoln, NE 68512
www.iuniverse.com
1-800-Authors (1-800-288-4677)

Because of the dynamic nature of the Internet, any Web addresses or links contained in this book may have changed since publication and may no longer be valid.

This is a work of fiction. All of the characters, names, incidents, organizations, and dialogue in this novel are either the products of the author's imagination or are used fictitiously.

ISBN: 978-0-595-34218-1 (pbk)
ISBN: 978-0-595-78988-7 (ebk)

Printed in the United States of America

For Faye, wife and mother, respectively.

Acknowledgements

The authors wish to thank Margaret Ashley Anderson Frey for her insights and contributions on prep school life.

CHAPTER 1

❦

What a difference a few hours can make in a life, Scott Greenwood thought as the ancient yellow school bus pulled into the roughly graveled parking lot behind the high school. He took his football jersey and wiped away the condensation that had formed on the inside of his window in the cool of the early September night. He scanned the small crowd that always gathered in the parking lot after an away game. Cheerleaders waiting for one last finale before they changed into their street clothes and went back to being part-time waitresses and baby-sitters. Girlfriends jockeying for the status that comes from claiming a varsity athlete still in uniform. Mothers and fathers, waiting patiently for sons that were usually too battered and exhausted to be trusted to safely drive home.

The other players began to gather their equipment and slowly make their way down the narrow aisle of the bus, down its creaking steps and into the night.

Twelve hours ago he had been invisible, he thought. Just another undersized sophomore boy blending into the routine that was high school and life in a small town. Too small to actually do anything for the team but return kickoffs. But too fast for anyone to catch.

Now he was a hero.

Just like that.

In one night.

After touching the football only twice. Each touch turned into the magic that a Friday-night touchdown creates in Texas.

Two touches, two touchdowns, enough to win the game.

Scott waited patiently for the other boys, the older boys, to exit first.

He was thinking of the moment when the reporter had taken a picture of him after the game. A picture that would be on the front page of the sports section in the local paper the next day. A picture of him handing the game-ball to his father, his mother and sister holding each other in the background, tears in their eyes. A picture he would frame and carrying with him for the rest of his life, he thought.

He was happy, now, he thought, following the other boys off the bus. Content in a way he hadn't felt since he was a small boy. Content and tired. All he wanted to do now was go home to his own bed and fall asleep.

He pulled his gym bag from the overhead compartment at the front of the bus and balanced his helmet and shoulder pads with his free hand.

Tomorrow was Saturday, he thought. He could sleep late. And then, in the morning, his father would make pancakes.

It was a tradition.

Strawberry pancakes.

Or chocolate pancakes.

Maybe giant granddaddy size pancakes.

Or little silver dollar pancakes.

Pancakes wrapped around link sausage—pigs in a blanket.

Or, pancakes with his initials in them.

It was a game, of sort, his father played. Surprise pancakes on Saturday morning.

There was a large street light above the door to the cinderblock locker room. He closed his eyes, slightly, as he walked from the shadows of the bus into its uncertain flicker. The other players were lined up in front of him, in slow procession from the bus to the locker room.

What was taking so long, he thought?

Peering over the bigger players, he could see two police officers standing with the coach at the door to the locker room, and as the line in front began to move forward, he tried to give the three of them a wide berth.

"Scott," the coach said as he came even with the door. "These men need to talk to you."

He felt his heart begin to race and his stomach churn.

He hadn't done anything.

But in the damp cool air, he could feel his body began to tremble. And the ever present panic that he so carefully concealed from everyone begin to gnaw at him.

"I'm afraid there's been an accident, Scott," said one of the police officers. "A car accident."

"It's your family, son," the other officer finally added. "They've been in a car accident."

Scott felt oddly relieved. He wasn't in trouble.

But, then, he thought, his family might be.

"Well, is everyone okay," he asked. "I mean, did you guys come here to take me home?"

"No, son," the shorter officer said. "I'm afraid it was a bad accident. Your family is at the hospital. That's why we're here. We've come to take you to the hospital."

"Yeah, but they're all OK. Right?"

"We don't know, son. We're just going to take you to the hospital so you can find out. Is that all right with you?"

"Sure," he said, stumbling slightly as he turned too quickly toward the police car. "Let's go!" his voice now with a rising since of urgency.

"You can leave the equipment here, Scott," the coach said, as he laid a slight hand on Scott's forearm.

Scott realized that he was still clutching his helmet and shoulder pads. He smiled nervously at the coach and dropped the equipment on the concrete steps.

It was only when he heard the equipment hit the concrete that he realized how quiet it was.

All of the other players were still there in the parking lot, staring at him.

There was none of the usual banter or cheering.

None of the celebratory activities he would have expected after a big football win.

Only hushed voices in private conversations.

Mothers sadly smiling at him.

Fathers holding their young children close to them.

He tried to think clearly. He tried to think about his father and mother. About his older sister. Had they been wearing their seat belts? Who was riding in the front seat? Had they taken the interstate or the back way? Were they in the old Lincoln? Which one of them was really hurt?

No one spoke during the drive from the school to Buena Vista hospital. Only the shrill siren and the flashing lights outside the window of the patrol car. Cars and trucks quickly pulling to the side of the two-lane, country roads as he sped pass them. Neighbors and friends, strangers in transit, disappearing into the blackness of the desert night, as Scott tried to understand what was happening.

It was after midnight by the time they arrived at the emergency room. He jumped from the patrol car before it actually came to a complete stop and ran toward the large sliding glass door. The waiting-room lights had been dimmed and he searched frantically in the cool blue hue of the corridor for his family. A young doctor in surgical scrubs was standing against the admitting desk. He was talking to Doc Simpson.

Scott was glad to see Doc's familiar face.

"Dr. Simpson!" he shouted as he rushed toward the old physician. "What happened? Who's hurt?"

"Scotty," Dr. Simpson's voice had none of the friendly tone to which Scott was accustomed. It was a voice tempered by professional discipline and practiced detachment. "It's … it's not good, Scotty."

The old doctor put his hand to his forehead and rubbed it gently. "A drunk ran the car off the road. It hit a concrete post on the old river bridge."

Scott knew the old river bridge. It was narrow. And dangerous.

"There's no easy way to tell you this, Scott, so I am just going to tell you straight out," the doctor's practiced voice cracked slightly as the professional tone faded. "Scotty, your sister died. She … she died before they could get her to hospital."

Scott heard the words, but they had no meaning for him.

Ashley. Dead?

It wasn't possible.

She had just been annoying him a few of hours ago. Complaining about how badly he smelled after the game. Poking him in the ribs. Hanging on him and embarrassing him as only his older sister could.

She was just too young to be dead.

This was just some terrible mistake, he reasoned. A bad dream from which he would suddenly awake.

"And your mother," the old doctor's voice cracked slightly as he spoke the words. "There wasn't anything anyone could do for her."

His sister? His mother?

Scott's body was trembling, again. He searched for words.

"Where's my dad?" he managed, silent tears flowing down over his crimsoned cheeks.

"He's hurt pretty bad, too," Dr. Simpson paused. "Your dad has some brain damage," the old man continued. "He is stable, now. And the hospital has called for a med-evac helicopter to take him to the Park Hospital in Amarillo."

"I want to see them," Scott's voice was firm. "I want to see my sister. I want to see my mother."

"Scott, you don't want to see your sister or your mother. Not now. You don't want to see them, to remember them ... like that."

Scott realized that he was crying. But he didn't care. He couldn't help it. Sobbing in spasms, his whole body numb, his knees buckling as he grabbed to brace himself against the admitting desk.

At the far end of the room, the double doors to the emergency room stood wide open and one of the maintenance staff was slowly mopping blood that had splattered here and there on the tile floor. Silhouettes loomed large behind one of the curtained stalls and cryptic commands were being shouted by a young doctor to nurses that could not move quickly enough.

It was their blood on the floor, Scott realized.

His mother's blood. His sister's blood.

Doctor Simpson tightened the grip on Scott's shoulder and pulled him away from the horrible sights and sounds of the place.

"Is there anyone you would like to call? Someone you need to contact?" Dr. Simpson asked.

It was all too much for Scott. He couldn't think.

Someone he should call?

Who?

All of his grandparents had died when he was young.

His mother didn't have any brothers and sisters.

His aunt! His father's sister in Massachusetts. He needed to call Aunt Macy.

"I ... I need to call Aunt Macy," he managed. "She lives in Massachusetts. I need to call her. She's my dad's sister," he said. "But, it's long distance."

"That's all right, Scott," Dr. Simpson said, leading him down the hall away from the emergency room toward a small antechamber. An old black phone sat on an undersized end table strewn with out-of-date magazines.

"I am going to tell the hospital operator to give you an outside line. You see if you can contact your Aunt. I am going to check on your dad. Then I am coming straight back. And I'll go with you on the evac when it comes, if you want."

He looked blankly at the old man. "Yeah, sure."

He sat down on the worn fabric of the chair next to the phone table as the old doctor shuffled back toward the emergency room. He rubbed the tears away with the palms of his hands and tried to think clearly.

What was his Aunt's number?

What was the area code?

The small desk phone rang softly and he picked up the receiver.

"Honey, Doc Simpson said you needed to call a relative," came a sympathetic female voice over the phone. "You just tell me the number and I'll dial it for you."

"439–4908" the number came slowly as he choked back the sobs. "Area code 508."

There was a brief pause before the line began to ring. Five long rings, then a click and a tape-recorded message from his Aunt. Scotty waited for the beep.

"Aunt Macy. This is Scott," he tried not to cry, not to sob, as he searched through the chaos of thoughts and feelings for the right words. "There was a car accident," he said. Strange how the description sounded in his own voice, he thought. "Dad is hurt real bad and you need to call me back," he said, trying to think about where she should call. "I guess we will be at the Park Hospital. In Amarillo. I don't know the number, so you'll just have to call there and find me," he paused. "Mom and Ashley are dead," he said abruptly. "You need to call me," he managed to mumble before he started crying again and brought the receiver down hard into the phone's cradle.

What was he going to do, he thought? He had always been able to count on his family. What was he going to do, now?

Then it hit him.

It was his fault!

It was his fault that they were dead. His fault that his father was now in the emergency room fighting for his life.

If it hadn't been for the stupid football game, they would all be safe at home. All of them in their own beds. All of them safe.

If they hadn't come to the game to watch him. If they hadn't been there to see him play, they would be okay now.

It was his fault.

My God. It was his fault!

"Evac's here," Dr. Simpson tapped him on his arm. "Time to go. Time to see your dad."

He jumped up and followed Dr. Simpson quickly through the waiting room and up the short flight of stairs to the helipad. The stretcher carrying his dad was fifty feet in front of them, headed toward a circle of lights and the deafening sound of a helicopter. His legs could not be contained. He bolted for the stretcher in sprinter's fashion, and was standing by his father's side before anyone knew what was happening.

"Dad!" he shouted over the noise, trying to keep pace with the medical team that hurried the stretcher along. "Dad! Can you hear me?"

His father was motionless on the stretcher, the thin white gurney sheet wiping in the wind. A large bare section of his father's skull lay where his graying brown hair had been shaved away. There were crudely sutured cuts across his father's face. One his father's arms was splinted and secured to the side of the stretcher. And there were tubes and monitor leads everywhere.

Then, for just an instant, he thought he saw his father open his eyes. For an instant, he thought that his father looked at him and tried to smile.

Dr. Simpson pulled him away toward the passenger section of the helicopter as the hospital staff positioned the stretcher in the back for the journey to Park hospital.

"I think he smiled at me," he shouted to Dr. Simpson over the noise. "I think I saw him open his eyes and when he saw me, he smiled at me," Scott tried to express the joy that came from knowing he still had his father. That he wasn't alone.

"That's good," Dr. Simpson nodded his head sympathetically. "That's a good sign," he said.

CHAPTER 2

It is difficult to say which is harder, the beginning or the end of a journey. To lose someone you love in the blink of an eye or to see a loved one slowly waste away. To know, with certainty, your absolute guilt in their passing or to be haunted simply by the specter of your inadvertent complicity.

Scott buried his mother and sister three days after the accident. But it took his father nine months to die from the injuries from the car accident. Nine months during which he learned the terrible rituals associated with the slow death made possible by medical progress. Morning blood draws that left a perpetual greenish discoloration to his father's forearms. The afternoon suctioning of the lungs that caused his father's whole body to convulse. The weight loss, despite the feeding tubes, that left only a skeletal shell of a body that peered out through unblinking, vacant eyes.

Scott tried to live through those months as best he could, alone except for the occasional stopover in Amarillo by Macy on one of her cross-country flights to visit her pharmaceutical company clients. His only diversion the daily run he allowed himself around the lake in the park next to the hospital. Running in circles, a mile and a half around the artificial lake, under the constant shadow of the hospital.

He had been a sprinter. His future once measured in hundredths of a second under the watchful eye of coaches whose careers were made by such things.

But during those nine months he measured his life in miles—six miles in the morning, six miles in the evening, twelve miles a day, eighty-four miles a week. Always ending at the same place where he had started—the hospital room he shared with his father.

A journey of two thousand, five hundred, fifty-four miles for him. A journey that finally ended when he returned one evening from his run to find his father peaceful, at last.

🍁 🍁 🍁

Had it been his decision?
Scott didn't think so.
It had just been what was expected of him.
But the decision had been made.
He was going to live with Macy in Massachusetts.

And so, on the appointed day he loaded his car with what few clothes still fit him after nine teenage months, a box of trophies and pictures of the family he no longer had, and the small fuzzy bear that had slept in the crib with him when he was an infant carefully hidden away at the bottom of his old footlocker. He locked the house for the last time, dropped the keys off with the realtor as he had been told to do, and drove east out of town.

It took him three days. Driving through the flatlands of Texas, Arkansas, and western Tennessee before turning north through the mountains of Virginia. Three days of isolation in his old Buick, continually tuning the car radio to find local stations and trying his best not to think about the past. About a life that had slipped away from him. About a future he could no longer imagine.

Three days in the car. The first night in Dickson, Tennessee at a small discount motel. The second night in the back seat in the parking lot of a truck stop just north of Winchester, Virginia. Three days of junk food and soda from whatever convenience store was adjacent to the gas stations when he filled up the car with gas.

The drive becoming more difficult as he left Virginia for Pennsylvania. Continuously checking the map and the directions he had printed from his computer. Finally, on the third day, carefully navigating his way around New York City onto the Merritt Parkway and through Connecticut toward the Mass Turnpike.

It was getting warmer. He had driven through patchy fog most of the morning and then clouds. But the sun was burning off the moisture, now. And as the last of the clouds disappeared, he kept glancing at the sky. It was so incredibly blue, he thought. Not at all like home. Brilliant blue, he thought. Not like any sky he had ever seen.

Perhaps this place wouldn't be so bad, he thought, trying to convince himself.

It was slightly past four in the afternoon when he turned north off of I-495 onto less traveled roads. The roads framed by large white farmhouses and pastureland.

It seemed that each house had a small placard or sign announcing its ancestry. 1798. 1803. 1780.

It was hard for Scott to imagine these houses sitting here, in this place, over two hundred years ago. He had known more ancient architecture from his world travels with his parents. But in Texas, everything had been new. New subdivisions. New strip malls. New office towers in the cities.

What must this place have been like in the 1700s, he thought? Before asphalt roads and automobiles. Just dirt cart-paths cut through woodland and the occasional seasonal river passage.

What had possessed people to settle in this particular place? He noticed that the soil was thin and gave way at each parcel to massive rock walls. Mere decoration now, he surmised. But not back then, he reasoned. Back then these same rock walls represented the toil of the early farmers trying to wrest a living out of the land. Those stone walls were born of necessity, not of fashion, he thought.

He pulled onto a small side-road that meandered through overhanging trees just beginning their late spring bud. He slowed the Buick to a pace consistent with the place. It was like an early American painting, he thought, remembering back to the scores of art books his mother had kept strategically positioned on the coffee tables throughout the house—not for show, but for easy access for him and his sister.

He missed his mother.

He missed having a family.

He moved the back of his index finger across the corner of his eyes to clear the moisture.

The forests began to thin as he reached the boundary of the town, where the houses turned sideways, their narrow shoulders abutting the street.

How odd that the houses didn't face the street, he thought. It was as if each house offered its own rebuff to the outsider, a cold-shoulder to uninvited intruders. Why would anyone build a house in that orientation, he wondered?

He was tired. He had spent too much time in the car over the last three days. His eyes hurt. His right leg hurt from holding down the accelerator on the old Buick. His shoulders ached from holding the over-sized steering wheel on its course. And he was mentally exhausted from having to continuously deal with the memories of the last nine months through the monotony of the journey.

He noticed a small string of shops, as ancient as the houses around them, to his left and pulled into the only available space at the very end of the angled parking row in front of the buildings. There was a florist shop at one end of the small commercial center, then a post office, then one of the Dunkin Doughnuts stores that seemed to be ubiquitous since leaving the South. Then a pizza place flanked by a convenience store and a newsstand. As he got out of the car, he noticed a low-rider at the far end of the lot in front of the newsstand with three teenage Hispanics lounging on the car.

The image of the low-rider and the Hispanic boys seemed an odd juxtaposition in this place. It was a cultural intrusion he had not expected in this place of Colonial white houses. But, after traveling so far, it seemed like home to hear the boys bragging and trading insults in Spanish.

He maneuvered his way around a group of bright orange bicycles hastily abandoned on the sidewalk and walked past the post office toward the convenience store. He passed the indifferent cashier, walked to the back of the store, and pulled a couple of cans of his favorite soft drinks from the tepid cooler.

"Could you tell me how to get to Federal Street?" he asked the cashier as he placed the two soft drinks on the front counter.

The man eyed him strangely.

"Not from around heah, ah ya?"

The wizened cashier's raspy voice seemed an indictment and the lack of "r's" in his words struck Scott as odd.

"No," he admitted sheepishly, lowering his eyes, "I'm from Texas. I'm looking for my aunt, Macy Rutherford. She lives on Federal Street."

"Rutherford, heh?" the old man shook his head knowingly and moved his thumbs to rest behind the red suspenders he wore. "Yeah, know Rutherford. Macy Rutherford," he reflected. "Lives on Federal Street."

"Yes. Federal Street. Can you tell me how to get to Federal Street?"

"Yeah," the old man continued to nod his head up and down. "Just down the street, bear off to the left at the rotary, then take your first right where the sign says 'bridge out'. If you come to the Academy, then you've gone to fah," the old man offered, making change from the five dollar bill and returning to reading his newspaper without another look in Scott's direction.

"Thanks," Scott politely offered, thinking how funny the word 'far' sounded without an 'r' in it and wondering what a 'rotary' was as he walked out of the store.

Better to just follow the computer directions, he thought, than the ramblings of the old man in the store.

Scott looked at the directions, once more, as he veered off to the left at a strange circular intersection where cars slowed, but didn't stop. And within half a mile he actually did see the "bridge out" sign and made the right turn onto Federal Street. He labored to read the house numbers as he drove slowly down the street. 147. 149. Then, finally, 151 lettered on a huge mailbox with mallards on it.

Scott pulled into the driveway. He hadn't really known what to expect, as he had never visited Macy and she hadn't thought to send him a picture.

It was a huge old Victorian house. Painted red, with a green porch and green shutters and green shingles on the roof. Three stories high, with a circular turret at one edge. There was a carriage house adjacent, but separate from the old Victorian. He could make out a light in the upper floor window of the carriage house. As he stopped his car at the end of the driveway, he noticed a piece of notebook paper tacked to the carriage house door.

Scott walked to the door and pulled down the note.

Scott—Sorry I wasn't here when you arrived. Had to go into Boston on business unexpectedly. But know you will be tired and just want to sleep anyway. Left the door to the carriage house open. There are cold cuts in the refrigerator and some ice cream in the freezer in the main house. Get your things put away and make yourself at home. Will be back late Saturday night or early Sunday morning. Macy.

A note.

After driving for three days, almost two thousand miles, to come to live with the only family he had left, what did he get? A note tacked to the door. And apparently, he wasn't even going to actually live in the huge Victorian house with Macy. His new home, a room above the garage—a place you would rent to strangers.

How could she, he thought, his disappointment quickly turning to anger?

How could she force him to leave Texas, to bring him to this place, and then treat him like this?

He crumpled the note and threw it on the ground.

He could just get back in the car and keep driving, he reasoned. It wasn't as though he had any real relationship with Macy and she obviously didn't plan to have much of one with him.

Maybe she blamed him, he thought, for her brother's death. Maybe the only reason she took him in was because of some residual obligation to his father's memory.

Or maybe she was just being cruel, he thought, his anger getting the better of his guilt.

Leave or stay?

It was the first time he really felt that he had any say in what was happening to him since the accident.

The cool spring breeze stirred the huge oak trees that lined the driveway. He drew a deep breath of the fresh air, sweetened by the blossoms of the dogwoods and the flowering shrubbery that framed the main house, moistened by the stream that he could hear in the distance behind the property. It seemed the first full breath he had allowed himself in nine months.

There were probably worse places to live, he tried to reason the rage away.

Perhaps this place wasn't so bad.

It was certainly as good a place as any for new beginnings.

And what real choices did he have left?

Maybe the garage apartment wasn't so bad. In fact, perhaps that is exactly what he needed. His own place. Space and time to try to sort through what he was going to do.

After all, he was on his own now, he thought, swallowing hard.

He walked back to the car, grabbed the first box from the backseat, and climbed the stairs at the side of the carriage house to the small second floor apartment. He turned the key in the lock, pushed open the door, and stepped into his new home … his new life.

CHAPTER 3

Scott woke suddenly, gasping for air, his body covered in sweat and shivering. The room was lit only by the last angled rays of the late evening sun. He was laying in a strange bed, in a strange room, the sound of his heart beating wildly in his ears.

And then, slowly, he reasoned it out.

He was in Massachusetts.

At Macy's.

In the room above the carriage house.

The thought was not particularly comforting, but the recognition was sufficient to calm the panic within him that had finally escaped during his sleep.

It had been a long three days on the road. Trying to follow the map and the instructions. Never quite sure he was headed in the right direction.

And way too much junk food, he thought, listening to the rumblings of his stomach.

He flipped on the light next to the bed, made his way to the small bath at one end of the room, turned on the shower and waited for the hot water while he relieved himself.

A shower. That was what he needed. A long hot shower.

And something to eat. Something hot to eat.

He stepped into the shower and let the water run over him, trying to steady himself. Letting the water wash over him. Trying to relax his stiff muscles. Standing there until there was no more hot water left.

He toweled dry and pulled his favorite jeans and t-shirt from his duffel bag. Jeans now almost too short after the four inches he had grown over the last nine months. And a t-shirt washed too many times.

Tomorrow he would have to put his things away and try to find a store where he could buy some new jeans and shirts, he thought. Clothes that fit this new place and the more slender body that he had developed. But right now, he needed something to eat.

Tonight, his first night in the town, he was going to treat himself to a hot meal. He remembered the pizza store next to the market in the center of the small town.

Pizza. Fresh hot pizza. It sounded good to him.

The sun had completely set by the time he pulled out of the driveway onto Federal Street. And as he came to the intersection with the main road, he was surprised at how much traffic there was coming from the small town. A continuous stream of expensive imports heading away from the town. Perhaps there was more to the town in the direction the cars were heading, he thought. Maybe that part of town was where the rich people lived. If so, they must be really rich, he thought, shaking his head as a huge stretched limo passed.

Then, from out the darkness and the glare of the oncoming traffic, he caught a glimpse of a short, fat kid on an orange bicycle barreling down the main road, headed straight for him. There were no lights in the rear view mirror of the Buick, so he threw his car in reverse and gunned the engine. It was just enough so that the bicycle and its rider merely grazed the Buick's front bumper. But the impact sent the bike into the field at the edge of the road and left its rider tumbling head over heels along the apron of Federal Street.

Scott carefully pulled the car to the edge of the street so that its lights were on the boy and rushed over to check on him.

"Are you all right?"

The young boy was whimpering, and blood was flowing from his nose, but at first glance all of his limbs appeared to be at their correct angles.

"My nose hurts," the young boy said. "I think it's broken."

Scott took the boys head and forced it back, pinching his nostrils together.

"Shit! That hurt's!"

"Your nose the only thing that hurts?" Scott asked, ignoring the boy's resistance to his first aid.

"I fucking hurt all over!" the boy cursed loudly.

Scott couldn't help but chuckle at the level of language chosen by the fat, little kid.

"Hold still. And hold your head back. Your nose isn't broken. We just need to stop the bleeding," Scott tried to sound confident.

"How do you know? How do you know it isn't broken?"

"Because I've had a broken nose. And believe me, it's a lot worse than what you have."

Scott loosened his grip on the boy's nose. The blood was already slowing.

"Do you live around here? I think you totally destroyed your bike. And I'm not so sure you are in any shape to ride home, even if the bike was," Scott offered.

"I go the Academy. *Stewart Academy*. And it's not my bike. It's a piece of orange crap that the Academy makes us use."

Scott remembered the oddly colored bicycles on the sidewalk in front of the pizza parlor in town.

"Why don't I pack your bike up in my trunk and give you a ride back to," Scott paused, "the *Academy*?"

"It's against the rules for me to ride in someone's car without permission," the boy said.

Scott helped the boy to his feet.

"But, this is a *special circumstance*," the boy said, sniffling. "So, yeah, you can give me a ride," the boy said. "But as far as I'm concerned, you can leave that piece of crap where it is in the field!"

Scott helped the fat boy to his car, then walked into the field and picked up the heavy, old-fashioned orange bike and threw it in the trunk of the Buick.

As soon as Scott got under the driver's seat, the fat kid started talking.

"This is your car? It sure is old, isn't it?" the boy said, holding his nose.

Scott reached into the back seat and grabbed some clean paper napkins left over from his last fast-food stop.

"Here," he offered. "And stop bleeding on my car," he tried to make the comment sound humorous.

"Thanks man," the boy said, dabbing the white napkins on the cuts across his cheek and the small stream of blood still oozing from his nose.

Scott had noticed a strong Bronx accent. And how funny the kid's voice sounded with his nose pinched so tightly.

"You're strong aren't you? I saw you pick up the bike like it didn't weigh anything. I bet you can bench 200 pounds."

Scott started the car.

"You talk a lot, don't you?" Scott offered.

The boy chuckled slightly.

"Yeah. I got a big mouth. Everyone tells me so," he said. "You aren't from around here are you?"

The question was one that Scott was becoming accustomed to.

"Which way to the Academy?" Scott asked

"Turn right," the boy said. "It's on this road about a mile. Just follow the limos. It's parent's weekend. That's why there's so much traffic. I was late for assembly. That's why I was going so fast."

There was a moment of silence as Scott finally caught a break in the long line of expensive cars and pulled out onto the main road.

"My name's Dennis. We had a big snow in March," the boy droned on, non-stop it seemed to Scott. "When it melted it flooded everything. It washed out the bridge," the boy pointed to a roadside sign confirming a bridge closure nestled neatly under the words "FEDERAL STREET".

"Really, how much do you lift?" he asked, changing subject. "I bet it's over 200 pounds, isn't it?"

"Do you ever shut up, Dennis?" Scott asked.

The boy giggled in a high, prepubescent pitch.

"No. Like I said, I got a big mouth. Quick!" the boy's voice grew animated. "Turn here!" he shouted, pointing at an entranceway guarded by two huge brick columns, each sporting an enormous black, cast iron gate. "This is the back way."

There was a large stone drive that led off to the left, encircling a grassy field, with cars parked on either side of the drive. Big new cars. Expensive cars. But the road the boy had pointed to ran behind the large brick buildings that ringed the circular drive.

"That's the freshman dorm, where I live," the boy said, pointing to the first building. "And that's the old School House. They have lots of old stuff hanging on the walls. From Presidents and important people. And that's the Chapel," he said, pointing to a Gothic stone building with huge buttresses supporting the walls and the vaulted ceiling that gave rise to a bell tower.

Scott noticed a small group of finely dressed men and perfectly coiffed women milling around the entrance to the building.

"And that's the library and that's the headmaster's house," the boy's index finger pointing out each building.

"Don't stop there," he cautioned, ducking lower in the seat. "Go around to the back ... there, take that road ... it goes to the infirmary. I need to see the nurse. It's a rule. If you get hurt, you have to see the nurse that is on duty."

Scott was impressed. The buildings were huge, some with large marbled columns and others with stone dental-work at their corners, all covered with ivy. Here and there on the large circular lawn there were kids walking with their parents. But not like regular kids, he thought. They didn't look like kids, at all, in fact. They looked like adults, in miniature. It was a strange sight, even for this new, strange place.

"There," the boy gestured excitedly. "Stop there. That's the infirmary. They used to send boys there during epidemics, before antibiotics, to quarantine them," he offered more useless information. "Now you go there if you get hurt and the nurse takes care of you on the weekends. And if you get hurt during the week they have a doctor there."

A school with its own doctor, Scott thought. Well, apparently it was a place for rich kids. Makes sense the place would have its own doctor, Scott thought. To take care of the rich kids.

Then, it hit him. To take care of the rich kids, because their parents weren't around to take care of them most of the time.

Parent's weekend.

The one time when the kids actually had parents around them.

The kids lived here. At the school. On their own. Without their parents. So, if they got sick, there wasn't anyone to take care of them. Except the nurse or the doctor.

Scott's attitude toward short, fat boy with the bloody nose and the funny accent suddenly changed.

Dennis was hurt. And as alone as Scott was.

"Oh, shit," the boy's voice was overly loud in the confines of the Buick. "It's Mr. Phillips, the headmaster!"

A slight man with thinning hair dressed in khaki slacks, blue shirt and tasseled shoes headed straight for the car with measured stride. His expression was somber and severe.

"Mr. Mordelli," the man's voice was as stern as his demeanor as he approached the passenger side of the Buick. "Perhaps you and I should have a chat about certain regulations of the Academy regarding automobiles?" he said disdainfully, opening the passenger-side door and literally pulling Dennis out of the car.

"I had a wreck on my bike. I hurt my nose. I couldn't ride the bike back, so this guy gave me a ride," the boy offered, his Bronx accent made stronger by his state of agitation. "I couldn't ride my bike."

Scott stopped the engine, shoved the stick-shift into park, and got out of the car.

"He had a little trouble and needed some help getting back to school," Scott tried to come to boy's aid once again. "So, I gave him a ride."

"And you would be ...?" the man said arrogantly, lifting his head so that his nose pointed down at Scott.

"Scott Greenwood," he replied, offering his hand to the headmaster.

The headmaster saw the hand, but ignored it.

"Well, *Scott*," the words came out now with a slight English accent. "I am the Headmaster here at Stewart. We have very strict rules here. Rules that Mr. Mordelli is very familiar with. Rules against accepting rides from *non-Academy* members," he said, glancing in boy's direction. "Rules which Mr. Mordelli and I will discuss at some length later this evening," his tone was both condescending and threatening. Then, glancing back at Scott, "And rules concerning unauthorized automobiles on Academy property."

What an asshole, Scott thought. What a pompous asshole.

"So, Mr. Mordelli," the man's tone became directive. "Perhaps you should complete your objective of seeing the nurse," he said, gesturing in the general direction of the building the boy had identified as the infirmary. "And, *Scott*," the headmaster said, "I am sure you have other important matters with which to attend," his phrasing grammatically correct, but stilted. "*The Academy* appreciates your efforts."

"Mr. Mordelli," the man said, taking the boy rudely by the arm. "Perhaps I should accompany you to the nurse and we can discuss not only rules, but your physical condition?"

Scott stood by the car, watching the poor boy being tugged along by the headmaster.

Despite his six-foot frame, Scott felt suddenly small. Against this backdrop of wealth. Against the boys in their tailored blue blazers talking to the girls in their pink cashmere sweaters. Against parents who were chauffeured to see and be seen with their children. Against the arrogant and condescending headmaster.

He had only tried to do the right thing in helping the boy, he thought

But apparently, the right thing didn't count for much around here. At least not at the Academy.

Dejected, he slid back under the wheel of the Buick and made his way as quickly as possible through the maze of narrow passages and parked cars, out through the brick columns and heavy metal gates of the Academy, back onto the main road toward the town's center.

CHAPTER 4

His appetite seemed to have waned, but he still had to eat, Scott reasoned. And pizza still sounded as good as anything.

Now, his was the only car on the road. Traveling in the darkness. Guided only by the headlights of the old Buick and the irregular lane-markings on the unfamiliar road.

He hated feeling small. And sad. And guilty.

He hated being alone, he thought, driving around the rotary and toward the strip mall.

The fragrance of the fresh pizza dough and oregano drifted out of the screen door of the pizza parlor as he pulled into the parking lot. It was not even eight o'clock on a Saturday night, but his was the only car in the lot. The small grocery he had visited earlier in the day was closed and the pizza parlor appeared to be the only commercial establishment opened in the whole town.

The first thing that Scott noticed when he walked through the door was a huge glass deli case just inside, then a lower counter next to the cash register.

But the most striking thing, the thing that captivated him, was the young girl standing behind the counter. Long blonde hair. Fiery green eyes. Full lips, pursed. Standing akimbo, with a freshly floured apron wrapped tightly around the most perfectly proportioned female body he had ever seen, the girl just standing there staring at him.

For a moment, all Scott could see, all that seemed to matter, was the girl.

"Can I help you?" she said, smiling at him as she tilted her head to one side.

Suddenly his heart was racing and his mouth had gone dry.

"Ah, yeah. Ah, pizza," he finally stammered. "I came to get ... some pizza," he said, glancing down at the floor, his face beginning to flush.

What an idiot I am, he thought, not daring to look up from the floor.

He ventured a brief glance back in her direction.

"My God," the girl said, giggling.

She's laughing at me, he thought. His heart sinking in his chest. The prettiest girl he had ever seen was laughing at him.

"Where did you get that accent, cowboy?" she smiled, winking at him.

Well, maybe she wasn't laughing *at* him. Maybe she was just flirting with him, he thought. Sometimes girls did that. When they were flirting with him.

But he felt incredibly self-conscious. He had been talking Texan in this strange new place. And not only did he look foolish in front of this girl, now, he obviously sounded it, too.

"I'm ... I'm from Texas," he managed, unable to take his eyes away from the girl. "I'm not from around here," he offered, remembering the earlier comment of the convenience store clerk.

"Well, Tex, what'll it be?" she asked, in imitation of his Texas drawl.

OK. She is obviously flirting with me, he thought.

And she seemed to like the idea that he might be a cowboy.

"Pizza, ma'am. Pepperoni pizza" Scott tried to mimic the girl's exaggerated impression of his own accent. "Two slices, if you please."

The girl reluctantly broke their gaze and twirled around to the counter behind her where the fresh pizzas were laid out on a large butcher-block table. As she turned, the open back of her apron revealed a cropped cotton t-shirt that made it only to her mid-drift and cutoff jeans below which were a pair of incredibly long legs. Scott suddenly realized how tall the girl was—she was almost as tall as he was. And most of that height had to be in those legs, he thought.

The girl turned back too quickly and caught Scott staring at her backside.

"Gets pretty hot in here," she offered, laying the slices on a fresh waxed paper on the counter in front of them. "So I wear shorts and a tank top. Even in the spring," she offered, still smiling, without a bit of awkwardness. Then offering her hand in a broad gesture, "I'm Allie. Allie Regis. Actually, *Alexandra*" she said brushing a wisp of the blonde hair away from her fact, trying to make her voice sound very formal as she said the name. "But everyone just calls me Allie."

God she was beautiful, he thought.

"Ah, Scott," he managed only his first name as he took her hand. It was soft and covered in the same white flour that pervaded the place. And so deliciously warm. "Scott Greenwood."

The girl's eyes suddenly lost their flirtatious twinkle and the corners of her lips turned down as her mouth fell open a bit.

"You're Scott Greenwood?"

The smile was gone. Now her face bore only the image of condolences. The type of face he had become accustomed to seeing on most people that knew him.

"Of course, you are. The Texas accent."

Her smile was so soft, he thought. Tender and genuine.

"I should have known it was you. I'm sorry ... about your parents ... about your family," she said quietly.

Scott was astounded. This was the first time he had ever seen this girl. How could she know?

"How ... how do you know about ... about my family?" he withdrew his hand and assumed a more guarded posture.

"Oh, I'm sorry. I didn't mean ... I didn't mean anything ... I just ... I'm just sorry ... that's all."

It was plain that now it was the girl's time to be embarrassed.

"I work for Macy. Part-time. I work for Macy part-time. Helping her. She told me. About your family. About you. About you coming to live with her ... for a while ... until...."

He could tell that the girl was having a hard time trying to get her thoughts out. And for some reason he couldn't stand to see her in distress, unable to say the right thing, to try to find the right words. It was actually endearing, he thought.

"She told me. That you were coming. And I'm sorry."

The girl's eyes were darting between the floor and Scott. Her cheeks were now reddening. And he thought he saw her eyes begin to form small tears, just at their edges.

She was just trying to be polite, he thought. Like all of the others.

"I just got here. I drove from Texas. In my car. I left Wednesday from Texas. I just got here," he said, his young voice now filled with the weariness of the journey. "Guess I'm just tired," he offered. "You surprised me," he said. "A good surprise, though," he quickly added.

"Guess you are kind of tired of surprises by now, though. I mean ... bad surprises."

She was trying. He knew it. But her words were coming out all wrong.

"It's all right," he offered, smiling. "I know what you mean. Sometimes ... sometimes, it's just hard to find the right words."

The girl wiped away tears that she could no longer hold back.

"I'm so stupid! I didn't mean ... I didn't ... I ... I"

The tears were now flowing down her cheeks and words were replaced by sobbing.

"And now ... now ... now I've cried all over your pizza!"

It was the stupidest, most absolutely adorable thing she could have said, he thought.

"So, maybe, we could start over again?" he offered, as he brushed away one of her tears with the back of his hand. "Fresh pizza. And fresh introductions," he said. "I'm Scott Greenwood," he said.

"I'm ... I'm Allie Regis," she managed a smile between sobs.

They just stood there, looking at each other.

The phone rang. And rang. Until finally the girl turned away from Scott and picked up the receiver.

"Stewart Pizza. Pickup or delivery?"

She was working now, he thought. And he needed to get back to Macy's in case she came home. Now wasn't the time for any more talk. Not now. But most certainly later.

He pulled a napkin from the dispenser on the counter and picked up a purple crayon from a large wooden box.

'What's your phone number?' he wrote on the napkin.

The girl was feverously scribbling down a pizza order on her order pad, but took the crayon from Scott and wrote down a number under the question. Then below the number, the words 'Call me in the morning.'

The second line on the pizzeria's phone began to ring.

Scott picked up the napkin and put it in his pocket.

"I'll call," he mouthed, without really saying the words.

The girl smiled back at him, waved, and went back to trying to scribble orders on her pad.

Scott turned and walked out, smiling now himself.

The first day in town and he already had a girl's phone number. And what a girl, he thought, pulling out of the parking lot and heading back to Federal Street.

It was all he could think about. Her face. And those incredible legs. She had to be, he thought, perfect.

It was only after he had pulled into the driveway and turned off the car that he realized he had walked away without his pizza.

But he did have a phone number.

And now, thinking about the girl, he definitely wasn't hungry any more. At least not for pizza.

CHAPTER 5

Scott pushed open the back door of the old Victorian adjacent to the carriage house and walked into a small pantry area. There was an ancient double porcelain laundry sink against one wall and what appeared to be a little used washer and dryer against the other. The floor was painted a dull, military gray, which seemed completely out of place against the colorful red and green exterior of the house.

He poked his head through the open doorway into a small breakfast area centered around a soap-stone stove. The only furniture in the room was a small round table, with two place settings on it. A gas stove was to his left, positioned in front of some sort of small pantry with built-in shelving filled with dishes behind glass doors. There was a hole cut in the wall to the right of the stove into an adjacent room, which also looked like a kitchen. He guessed that you cooked the food on the stove, then shoved it through the hole in the wall into the other part of the kitchen where you put it in serving bowls. The whole place looked old and not particularly impressive.

But as he walked through the door of the adjoining kitchen area, it was like walking into a different world.

The adjoining room was huge, the walls covered in embossed leather. The ceiling was made out of some kind of metal, also embossed, and a huge crystal chandelier was hanging at the exact center of the room. There was a stone and carved-wood fireplace at one end of the room and he could almost see his own reflection in the glossy hardwood floor. The room was entirely taken up by a huge mahogany table with elegantly carved legs and over a dozen fancy chairs carefully arranged around it.

He turned around to look back through the door into the kitchen area.

Slowly it dawned on him.

He had entered through the back door. Through the servant's entrance. Into the kitchen, where the staff worked. A place of labor, not of repose.

The huge room in all of its elegant detail was reserved for the owners of the house.

He chuckled.

Guess things hadn't changed that much since the house was built over a hundred years ago, he thought. The only question that remained seemed to be which side of the door did he belong on—the kitchen side or the dining room side?

He quickly toured the rest of the first floor. An oversized entry-way with circular stairs leading to the second level. Another huge room at the front of the house with what looked like velvet wall covering, where the circular turret provided a designer setting for carefully arranged cushions on a low bench that looked out onto the large porch and another fireplace sporting a carved-wood enclosure. A back room, larger than any room in his old house, also with a fireplace and an entrance way arranged as a library. And at the back of the entry-way a bathroom the size of his garage apartment, with a less formal sitting room, as large as the dining room.

Scott made his way up the stairs to the second floor and roamed from bedroom to bedroom. He counted six in all. Each with a different style of furnishing. Each with a different type of wood accent. Macy's obviously the front bedroom, the one with the upper level of the turret—a place dominated by what his mother would have called a "fainting couch". And three large bathrooms, one shared by each set of bedrooms.

There was more than enough room for him in the main house. As large as it was, if he had one of the bedrooms at the far end of the hallway he probably would never even see or hear Macy or she him.

So why was he sleeping in the carriage house?

No reason, he figured, except that she had things just the way she wanted in her house.

And she didn't want him there.

"What a bitch," the words came out of his mouth as he thought them.

"You're a bitch Macy!" he shouted into the empty house.

He shrugged his shoulders, listening to the echo of his profanities, and continued up a flight of smaller stairs to the third level.

He stopped on a small landing at the top of the stairs to open a stained-glass door with a small brass plate that read "Ballroom". He pushed the door open and walked into a large open area, as large as the entire house. There were mirrors along most of the walls and the floor had the look of a basketball court—only without the painted lines. There was a grand piano at one end of the ballroom and a stereo system that seemed to take up an entire wall at the other end.

Macy must be rich, he thought, making his way down to the kitchen. It had never really occurred to him before. She had always just been some distant relative to him that occasionally showed up at family reunions. An occasional embarrassment at such events to his father, because she always smelled of whiskey.

Rich. And a bitch, he thought, taking the back stairs, the servant's stairs, down to the kitchen on the first floor.

He rummaged through the fridge in the kitchen area until he found a soda and some deli meat and put together a triple-decker sandwich. He grabbed a bag of tortilla chips from the pantry and made his way into the back room on the first floor—the only room in the house that seemed to have a TV. He flipped on cable and searched for a baseball game while he ate.

He defiantly put his feet up on the glossy finish of the hardwood coffee table.

The only game he could find was the Red Sox against the Yankees. It figured, he thought. Why should he expect to see the Rangers? Or the Braves?

The sandwich quickly disappeared, as did the soda and the chips. He pulled a quilt from the back of the couch over him and tried to concentrate on the game.

What am I going to do?

It was a question that kept running through his mind.

What am I going to do?

Over and over again.

Until finally, sleep came.

❦ ❦ ❦

Scott heard a door slam and he jumped to his feet, the quilt still wrapped around him. An infomercial was running on TV and the first hints of daybreak were visible through the huge floor-to-ceiling windows of the room.

"Macy?" he shouted, walking toward the front entry-way. "Is that you?"

"Shit, honey," the female voice carried through the doorway. "I didn't know you were in here."

Scott stopped in his tracks as he walked into the entry-way.

There was Macy, at the front door, hanging on a man in a dinner jacket. Her dress was too short and the strap on one side had fallen off her shoulder, revealing more of her breast than Scott cared to see. Her heels were dangerously tall and she was having trouble maintaining her balance, even with the support of the man next to her.

And he could smell the whiskey on them a room's width away.

"This is Rob," she said.

Her words were heavily slurred.

"He's … he's … a client of mine."

Macy tapped the man on his chest with her forefinger, and giggled.

Scott felt his whole body tremble and the hair on the back of his neck began to stand on end.

Despite everything that the had been through, he had never felt so disgusted as he did in that moment, the sickening smell of the alcohol on Macy and her male companion filling his nostrils.

Scott turned without saying a word and walked out of the room, out of the house, pausing only once to wretch in the driveway as he made his way back to his apartment in the carriage house.

CHAPTER 6

Allie lay quietly in bed looking at the red glow of the digits on the clock. The curtain on the window fluttered slightly as a chilled morning breeze swept through the room. She pulled the down comforter closer under her chin and rolled over on her side to face the clock.

7:28 the numerals read.

She thought about the boy from Texas. About Scott.

He was not at all like she had expected from the stories she had heard, from the description Macy had given her. She had expected a slim boy, weighed down with the grief of being recently orphaned. Saddened and stooped by the vigil she knew he had kept for the last nine months in the hospital there next to this father.

But he wasn't at all like Macy had described him.

He was tall. With huge, muscular shoulders.

And incredibly cute.

What must that be like, she thought? To be an orphan? To be all alone? To see your father die?

The slight blonde hairs on her forearms began to stand on end and she shivered slightly.

She couldn't imagine what he must have gone through.

But, he was so cute, she thought, her mind quickly shifting. Such deep, blue eyes. And his smile. She had never imagined that he would be able to smile, given everything that had happened to him. But he had. He had smiled at her, she thought. Last night. In the pizza parlor. Right before he had asked for her phone number.

He had smiled at her. An incredible smile, she thought, imposed upon his square-set jaw. She thought about the wisp of blonde hair that had fallen over his forehead. She recalled the scene in all of its infinite detail. The first time she had seen him smile at her.

7:29 the numerals shifted.

Oh, Allie, she thought. You are in trouble with this boy. He was ... different. Not like the others. Not like the pimply-faced boys in school or the haughty rich boys from the Academy. Not even like the weekend collegians with their freshly laundered khakis and designer shirts or the young married men who always looked at her a bit too long when their wives' backs were turned.

She imagined she could still smell him, drawing in a deep breath. Male. With a slight citrus sweetness from his aftershave. Intoxicating, she thought, her eyes closed trying to concentrate, to recapture the smell.

This was silly, she thought, her face beginning to warm in the solitude of her embarrassment. He had just smiled at her. That was all.

And boys were out of the question.

She had her future to think about. And a boy, now, added complications she just didn't need.

But there had been something in that smile, she thought. And in his sudden awkwardness. Not knowing what to say to her.

He had liked her, she thought, smiling to herself. He really had, she thought.

7:30 the numerals shifted again.

It was time to get up now, she thought, reluctantly letting go of the image of Scott stumbling out of the door of the pizza parlor.

Time to start the day, the routine, again.

Allie threw back the covers and sat on the side of her bed while she quickly pulled back her long hair, wrapping it tightly in back. She undid the top two buttons of her sleep shirt and pulled it off over her head. The room was cool against her exposed skin and she walked to the window to lower it a bit. She paused briefly, looking down on the small lawn in front of the house and then at the cloudless sky. It was going to be a good day, she thought, her bare feet padding across the linoleum floor to the bathroom. She went through her morning rituals and pulled on the slight pink leotard that hung on the back of the bathroom door. She pulled on her dance slippers as she sat on the closed seat of the toilet and made her way back to the opposite wall of the bedroom, to the mirrored wall where a short wooden bar was securely anchored slightly above waist level. She pushed a cassette into the tape player and assumed her position at the bar.

As soon as the tape started, she went through the mental task of transforming herself. From what she was ... into what she wanted to be.

Her long neck straightened even further as she raised her chin. The arch of her back became accentuated as she repositioned her feet in the perpendicular and straightened her legs. She grasped the bar lightly with her right hand as she gracefully lifted her left in a broad arch, fingers properly positioned, above her head. Then turning her hand upward, retracing the arc in a downward motion. She repositioned her stance to the other side and repeated the motion with her right hand. Slowly, deliberately, a mimicry of two hundred years of classic dance. To the pace of the steady sound of the recorded metronome on her tape player. Under her own watchful eye in the mirrored wall.

She synchronized her breathing to the motion, then began to alternate the motions with measured stretches of her calves, her thighs, her abdomen, her shoulders, her arms, her neck. It was a stretching routine requisite for the dance moves she really needed to practice, and it lasted for over twenty minutes. Not that she was conscious of the time anymore. She knew exactly how long the stretching tape lasted. How many times each motion was required. How long each motion took. What each motion should look like, in perfection.

The beating of the metronome ceased.

She relaxed, her shoulders stooped, her breathing deepened by the exertion, her posture relaxed. She suddenly looked out of place in the thin pink leotard and worn shoes, an imitation of the dancer she aspired to be reflected in the mirror.

It was a brief thought, allowed only until the French accent of her dance instructor from the cassette called her to attention again before the bar.

Each move, practiced one hundred times, her constant eye looking for any deviation from the form. A slight under extension corrected, in repetition. An awkward finger position, remedied, in repetition. An appearance of strength over grace, un-forgivingly dismissed, in repetition. The reflection of her sparsely furnished bedroom in the mirror giving way to the images of a grandly lit stage of an immense auditorium filled with an expectant, appreciative audience.

Her mind slipped into the dream of performance, willing her body into the unnatural and painful postures of the great dancers. The mental exercise did nothing to dull the pain of a newly spawned blister on her right foot or the sprained left knee that was too recently healed. She merely practiced through the pain, as she knew she must.

By a little after nine o'clock the cassette had run its course. She stood before the mirror, sweat dripping from her forehead into her eyes, her leotard marked by the moisture of her body, her breathing labored. She collapsed, cross-legged, on the floor. She pulled a towel from the bar and wiped it across her face, clearing her eyes.

She was pleased with her morning practice. She gave herself two minutes of reflection. Imagining perfection, then over-layering her performance on that abstract.

9:22 the glow from the clock warned her.

Practice was over. Time to move on, she thought, jumping up and heading for the bathroom.

She went through her schedule for the day as she quickly showered. She had the 12–8 shift at the parlor. That wouldn't be too bad, she thought, rinsing the shampoo from her hair. Then, about two hours of homework, she estimated, combing out her hair as she sat at her table, the towel wrapped around her. An hour on the English paper due next week. Half hour of algebra problems, no more. Half hour of biology review for the test on Tuesday. That would give her time for another hour at the bar tonight, she thought, pulling on a tank top and yesterday's cut-off jeans. And then she had Macy's house to clean, she thought.

Then she remembered Scott. In the carriage house apartment.

She imagined him in the bedroom she had prepared for him. She had talked Macy into making that his room. She had known that a boy would like that. Having the carriage house all to himself. Having his privacy. That's what boys liked. And, she thought, that way he wouldn't have to be in the main house when Macy was home. When she had ... company. When she was drinking, she thought, recalling the way the main house looked after Macy had been entertaining male friends.

She hadn't mentioned that part to Macy. But, she was sure that had been in Macy's mind, as well. What to do with the boy when Macy was there at the house ... entertaining.

It had been more work for her. Cleaning out the musty room. Hauling the old newspapers and boxes full of junk down the narrow stairs. Washing the floors half a dozen times to get the grit and grim from two decades of inattention from the hardwood, then layering the wax on the floor. Washing the windows and shutters as the last of winter had visited town. Then fitting the curtains she had found in one of Macy's closets to the windows—not frilly or dainty, just right for a boy's room.

How funny, she thought, looking back at herself in the mirrored wall, that she would have done all of that before she had even met him.

Suddenly the tank top she had picked out didn't look right and she saw a dirty spot on her cut-offs. She switched to her favorite t-shirt, last year's City Ballet t-shirt that came down just above her navel. Another pair of cutoffs? Or jeans?

She had caught Scott looking at her legs, yesterday, she thought smiling. And she did have great legs, she thought. She really liked her legs these days, taut from all of her hours at the bar. And the flat stomach that showed between the t-shirt and the low-rider cutoffs.

But not her nose. She didn't like her nose very much, she thought, turning her head back and forth in front of the mirror. And her ears. They weren't even, she thought, pulling her hair back from her face to cover them.

She tried to put her nose and ears out of her mind.

Her legs. That's what he would be looking at.

She pulled open a dresser drawer to look for a fresh pair of cutoffs. She rummaged around in the drawer looking for the Calvin's that had been just a little too-long her favorites last fall before she turned them into shorts. She squirmed into them with a little effort.

A bit tight, she thought, looking at her body in the mirrored wall. And a little short, she thought, seeing one of her hips peek ever so slightly from below the raveled leg of the cutoffs when she turned around and leaned forward a bit. But not trashy. Just a little tease, perhaps, she thought, thinking about Scott calling her, about Scott stopping back by the pizza store to see her.

10:02 the numerals glared from behind her into the reflection in the mirror.

Shit, I'm going to be late, she thought, grabbing her keys and racing down the stairs and out of the back door before her father had a chance to make any comments about what was inappropriate about what she was wearing today.

"Be back around 8:30 tonight," she shouted back through the closing door to her breakfasting parents. And then she was in the car, out of the driveway, onto her day. Thoughts of the boy intruding upon her usual preoccupation with her future.

※　　　　※　　　　※

Scott found himself sitting on the edge of the small bed in his room above the garage, his bare feet on the planks of the cold hardwood floor.

It had been a long night and he was still trying to get the image of Macy and the man out of his mind.

He sat in the dimly light room, trying to orient himself.

The room was large, but had only two small windows on the opposing walls. A large, shallow closet stretched along the facing wall. An overstuffed maroon leather chair and ottoman sat slightly off-center of the room under a floor lamp with an amazingly ornate, fringed Victorian share.

Old furniture, he thought, trying to forget the stench of the alcohol on Macy.

Pieced together rather than thrown away, he thought, trying to forget how slutty his Aunt had looked.

An oak night table, its surface ringed with the stains of glasses left unattended, supported a tiny lamp and a clock radio with a faux wood face next to the bed.

The room smelled musty, even with the chill of the morning air sinking in through one of the slightly raised windows.

He didn't want to go back into Macy's house. He really didn't want to ever have to see her again, he thought.

But he didn't want to just sit around in his room.

It was time to run, he thought. The one thing that he knew that would take his mind off of even the worst of situations.

He pulled on a pair of gym shorts from the small bag next to the bed. He fumbled for a pair of matching white socks and a well-worn t-shirt. He pulled on his running shoes and laced them tightly. He placed his hands against the wall at the top of the stairs and began stretching his legs, alternating the pressure, first one leg, then the other. Bending from the waist, touching the floor with his palms. Arching his back. Twisting to either side. Pulling his elbows behind his head. Rotating his neck, first clockwise, then counterclockwise.

He was procrastinating, he thought.

Another deep breath, almost a sigh, and then down the stairs and out of the driveway.

The sun was shining through the tall trees that surrounded the property. It was cold for April, he thought. Well, cold for April in Texas. But, he wasn't in Texas anymore, he thought. The weather was just one more thing he would have to get accustomed to.

It was a good morning for a run. The wind was still and the chill in the air was refreshing after the closeted feeling of his room above the carriage house.

He didn't know where to run, so he turned left out of the drive and began to retrace his route back to the center of the town. He ran for a mile without seeing any people, any cars. Only the sound of the birds and insects intruding on his run. Another mile and he was at the rotary, turning right this time onto the main road. Keeping to the sidewalk on the right side of the road, now. He inspected each house that he passed. White clapboards with permanently unshuttered windows. The small historical markings of pedigree proudly displayed in some of the yards next to the road. They were a chronicle of survival, Scott thought, smiling. The people who lived in these houses might have changed—but the houses hadn't. The houses added a pleasant sense of permanence, of stability.

He saw the strip mall up ahead. And the pizza parlor.

Would it be open?

Would she be there?

He was thinking of her eyes, of how green they were. Of her smile. And those legs, he thought. Those long, beautiful legs.

She was a runner! Her legs. They were so sculpted. She must be a runner, too!

He slowed his pace as he approached the parking lot and wiped the sweat off his brow with the back of his arm.

Or a dancer, he thought. She could be a dancer. That was it! She wasn't a runner. She would have been wearing tennis shoes when she worked if she was a runner. If she was a serious runner. But Allie had been wearing clogs. Not tennis shoes.

She was a dancer. Clogs were what dancers wore.

The way she stood behind the counter. The way she turned. The way she moved.

She had to be a dancer, he thought, smiling, pleased that he had reached this conclusion on such minimal examination.

And then, there she was, standing in the door of the pizza parlor, in a short little t-shirt and cut-off jeans that seemed to be painted on her body. Smiling at him.

God, she had great legs, he thought, his brief confidence shattered by the sight of how incredibly beautiful she was.

"Good morning Scotty!"

He felt his face begin to burn and knew it was turning red.

"Hey … hey Allie."

"You're up and at it early this Sunday morning."

He noticed that she let her eyes fall from his to check out his body. And her voice seemed to have just a hint of a tease to it.

"I go running every day … I'm a runner."

Shit! That sounded stupid, he thought.

"I can see that you're a runner, silly."

How could she be make those words sound so sexy, he wondered?

"Want to come in while I open up the store? No one usually shows up this early. I just have to get the tables set and get the ovens started. Come on in. You can run later."

And like that, with one simple invitation, Scott's new daily routine changed.

He followed her into the store, trying not to make it too obvious that he was staring at her legs.

"You want to help me?" she asked.

"Sure, ah, yeah, ah, what do I do?"

She giggled. Not like she was making fun at him. Not like that at all, he thought. It was … like she was nervous and he had said something funny.

"Here. Take these napkin holders and put one on each table. And then make sure there is one cheese and one pepper shaker on each table."

He began to pull several of the stainless steel napkin holders from the shelf.

"You carry them," she said, pilling more of them into his folded arms, until they were in a formidable heap. "And that way I don't have to make so many trips back and forth."

He tried to balance all of the heavy metal containers as he obediently followed Allie from table to table.

"So, are you all settled in? Do you like your room? I mean, it isn't much, but I thought you would like to have some privacy. You know, like a guy thing. Not being stuck in the big house with all of the frilly, lacy stuff that Macy likes so much."

"What do you know about my room?" his voice came out overly loud and accusatory.

"Oh, I work for Macy. I clean up her house for extra money. For my dance lessons. And … well I thought you would like the apartment over the carriage house. You know … like a bachelor apartment."

Allie had moved on to another table, but he froze where he stood.

So it was Allie that had decided that he would live in the carriage house. Not Macy.

And she was a dancer.

And she worked for Macy.

It was just too much to sort through and suddenly, the napkin holders in his arms came unbalanced and begin to crash, one at a time, onto the concrete floor, his frantic attempts to juggle them in mid-air a disastrous failure. Left standing there, napkins flying everywhere around him.

"Oh My God!" she shouted, breaking into laughter. "You are such a klutz!"

She punched him lightly in the stomach and scrambled to try to piece together napkins and holders from the mess on the floor.

"So, you … you fixed up my room? You did it?"

"Sure. Don't you like it? I mean, its not much. But its yours. And you can do whatever you want to it. Fix it up just the way you want it."

He didn't know what to think.

She was obviously so pleased with herself. And she was so cute, looking up at him expectantly.

Hell, he thought, trying to sort through his feelings for Allie and his feelings about Macy. This is just too complicated.

"I … I better get back to running."

He noticed that the smile on her face disappeared. Now she looked a little hurt.

"Oh, sure. Sure. I … I have lots of stuff to do here. It's all right. I … I usually have to do this myself, anyway. You … you go on."

Great, he thought. Not only did I manage to make a mess that she has to clean up, I didn't even think about her feelings. About how hard it must have been for her to make the old room above the carriage house presentable.

"I … I like the room," he said, backing toward the door. "It … it was nice of you to do that for me."

The smile was back on her face.

"I knew you'd like it!"

"Yeah, I do," he managed the lie, as he stepped onto the sidewalk and began to run away as fast as he could.

CHAPTER 7

Ben paused briefly to wipe the smudge from the brass name plate on the door to his private living quarters.

Benjamin Franklin Phillips, IV.

Despite his best efforts, it always seemed as though the name plate was tarnished by the incessant fingerprints of his juvenile charges at the Academy, after whom he was continuously tidying up.

Just one of the less auspicious elements of his tenure over the prepubescent boys, he thought.

He strolled through the outer room that he had converted into a combination receiving room and library into the back bedroom that faced the river and began to replace his Sunday headmaster's attire with his running clothes. Outside the window he heard the shouts of the Academy boys breaking into play after the long morning's Chapel.

Ben had never really enjoyed being a student at the Academy. It always seemed like he had to study harder than the rest of his classmates and train harder than the other boys on the squash team, just to be able to compete without embarrassing himself. And even when he did excel in his studies or receive some recognition for his athletic abilities, it seemed as though the students he wanted to be his friends were all more interested in associating with the football players or the day student girls who had finally gained entry to the former all-male bastion his sophomore year.

So he took particular pleasure in finally having returned to the school, now as headmaster.

He also took pleasure in his appearance these days, he thought as he caught a glimpse of himself in the full length mirror next to the cherry dresser at the end of the bedroom.

Sure, his hair was more gray than brown these days, but then the majority of his former classmates had lost most of their hair.

Perhaps his skin was beginning to thin into the parchment texture he had come to dread, but his body still had the lean appearance of an athlete. A leanness that was both envied by other more portly men his age and appreciated by their wives, he reasoned.

Running. And a commitment against indifference. That was what made the difference, he thought as he pulled on his Academy jogging shorts and laced his running shoes. That is what set him apart. He had learned that the glory his classmates had achieved at The Academy was fleeting. He had learned, the hard way, that life was not a sprint. It was a marathon. And he had perfectly adapted himself to such a competition. Outlasting, surviving and displacing those of his classmates that might have appeared more competent early in their careers, but who could not manage to sustain the pace required for success such as he enjoyed.

He caught what he considered to still be his best boyish smile in the reflection of the mirror.

He had made it. He had achieved his goal. Without family connections. Without inherited wealth. He had shown all of the classmates that had looked down on him. Now, he was headmaster. And he finally had the ability to set the type of example young men and women of good breeding, but undeveloped character, needed in order to succeed as well. Character that the rich, especially, needed, he reasoned.

He quickly tidied up the room and exited through the back door of the manse onto the circular route around the village. A chance to get away from the Academy buildings and the responsibilities of leadership. And an opportunity to get out into the community beyond The Academy, to connect in some small way with the locals.

There had always been a tension between The Academy members and the local town residents, he thought as he slid into his normal pace and headed counter-clockwise today on his route (it being an odd number day—and the clockwise route being reserved for even numbered days). Even when he was a student he remembered the inevitable fights that occurred every few years between an Academy student and a local boy.

Ben thought, however, that he may have been instrumental in bringing those difficulties to an end. Since his tenure as headmaster, not a single altercation involving an Academy student had occurred.

He saw a young boy in the distance down the straight segment of road running toward him. An academy boy, no doubt, he thought with pride, noting the maroon shirt the boy was wearing. Another competitor, like himself, out for a Sunday morning run while his classmates wasted their time in horseplay.

Ben picked up his pace a bit and waved to Halton Smyth, the untidy town plumber whose family at one time must have been substantial given the property that Halton had inherited and now tended. Halton smiled slightly and made a feeble attempt at a wave before going back to trimming the grass along the long sidewalk that ran from the road to the Federalist house that had been in the man's family since the early 1800s.

Ben had come to the ultimate conclusion that Halton was somewhat of a simpleton. But he was a valuable resource for a small town to have. And the Academy had used his services consistently over the years for the inevitable plumbing issues attendant to hundred year old buildings.

As Ben glanced back down the road, he saw the young man running toward him was getting much closer. Almost in a sprint.

It was the Hanson boy. Ben's face slipped into a much practiced smile as he came even with the boy and they jogged in place.

"Mr. Hanson, I see that you are beginning your training runs a bit early this year," Ben said, trying to make his comment sound sincere. He never quite understood this boy. The boy's father, T. Hunter, was the chairman of the board of trustees for the Academy. The son was a younger replica of the father—but in appearance only.

Ben had known the father as a classmate. T. Hunter had been the quarterback of the Academy team that had actually won the division title when Ben was only a freshman. He had been a heroic figure, both then and now. One of those rare men who were born leaders, who people naturally followed.

It was in this area that the son bore no resemblance whatsoever to the father.

Marc was lazy. He was inattentive in class. And he lacked the discipline required of a true leader. Like so many of the legacies, as a son of a former student he appeared to be coasting through his life on the name and reputation his father had earned a generation before.

"Yes, sir, Mr. Phillips," the boy managed between quick breaths. "Working this summer with the coach during the camp. Going to be in shape this fall. Guaranteed!"

In shape, Ben thought. The boy was barely able to carry on a conversation after a morning jog, it seemed.

"I'm sure your father would find that commendable, Mr. Hanson," Ben nodded. "Absolutely commendable."

The boy smiled sheepishly and then darted away, obviously trying to impress Ben with his efforts.

Ben returned to his course.

No, the son just wasn't in the same cut as the father, he reasoned, making the turn to his left back toward the village center. And he didn't see that changing ... over the course of the summer ... or during his senior year.

Marc would certainly go to Harvard, like his father. But there he would just be one of the crowd. Nothing particularly unusual to commend him.

Ben's mind wandered back to the father. And the board meeting in August. He should give T. Hunter a call this afternoon, he reasoned. Just to touch base. So that the two of them could work on the agenda. And discuss more fundraising.

That was always T. Hunter's favorite subject. Raising money. Perhaps it went with being an investment banker. Or perhaps T. Hunter shared the same pride as Ben that the Academy now had the largest endowment of any prep school in the world. An endowment larger than most colleges could boast. An endowment the two of them had grown by more than 30% since Ben had become headmaster and T. Hunter had become Chairman.

And the arts center. They needed to discuss those plans, as well. A favorite project of Margaret Hanson. A surprise that Ben and T. Hunter had been saving for the Hanson's thirtieth wedding anniversary. A new Academy arts center named after Margaret.

Ben caught a glimpse of another runner coming toward him. He knew most of the boys—but he didn't recognize this fellow

Perhaps the young man wasn't from the Academy, Ben thought, trying to concentrate on lengthening his stride.

As Ben drew nearer, he slowly realized that the young man running toward him was the same rascal that had been driving that dreadful ancient Buick last evening. The same dreadful boy who had delivered Mordelli back to the Academy, bleeding. Obviously some transient relative of a local. Not at all the sort with whom Mordelli should have been associating.

Sam. Or Smith. Some name starting with an "s", Ben tried to recall the strange boy's name.

As the boy passed, he smiled and waved somewhat overly enthusiastically.

Ben ignored the boy and ran past him.

Obviously the boy was some sort of social climber hoping that his contrived greeting would somehow convince the other locals that might be looking that the boy was somehow associated with the Academy. Somehow associated with Ben.

Ben didn't want to give the boy the pleasure of such an association.

Scott. That was the boy's name.

Scott something, Ben remembered, hearing the boy's cadence fade away behind him in the distance.

No one of consequence to him, he reasoned, trying to concentrate on the pending conversation with T. Hunter.

🍁   🍁   🍁

Scott was running as fast as he could now.

He quickly caught up and passed another boy running the same route. A boy who had done his best to stay even with Scott as long as he could, before falling behind. A boy that lacked Scott's speed and urgency.

Scott was running away again. Only this time, in this new place, he had no idea where his efforts would take him.

He ran as long as he could, as fast as he could.

Past the ancient Academy buildings and the sounds of rich boys at play.

Past the dreadful Victorian on Federal Street.

Until he ran out of road at a bridge still under construction. Gasping for breath, beads of sweat and salty tears, mixing in with the grit from the apron of the road, on his face. Doubled over until he felt the heaving start within him. Dry heaves, from deep within him. Nothing left within his empty stomach to disgorge. Nothing left inside him. In the quietness next to the bridge. By himself. At the end of the road.

Could things get any worse, he thought, trying to regain his breath and his composure?

No home. No family. No friends. No where left to go.

Then he noticed it.

Almost hidden behind the large orange barrels that barricaded the chasm over the river where the road had been washed away. Clearly visible on the single piece of old concrete that still stood at the edge of the road. A broad streak of paint, mostly embedded in huge scratches across the surface. Ending abruptly at a steel girder that twisted at an odd angle. Remnants of a shattered plastic lens cap from the car that had hit the bridge scattered here and there under Scott's feet.

CHAPTER 8

Marc Hanson knew more about Ben Phillips than any other student at the Academy.

Some of the knowledge came from his father, who as chair of the Academy's board of directors, Phillips incessantly courted. As discrete as his father was in public, he was equally as candid with Mark in private in this regard. His father held absolutely nothing but disdain for Phillips, or anyone like him for that matter.

His father had also used Phillips as an example to his son—of the type of Academy student not to emulate. The kind of classmate his father had tried to shun while he had been a student at the Academy. Someone mediocre at best. A snitch, a whiner, a ferret—just some of the terms his father had used to describe the headmaster in recounting tales of how Phillips had managed not only to screw up his own academy career, but jeopardize the careers of several of his classmates (even as a freshman).

Marc had seen it first-hand, as well.

The way Phillips refused to speak to any but the most wealthy of the students (unless the parents were on campus or the situation absolutely demanded that he lower himself to that level). The way he took credit for even the smallest of successes, but deflected any blame to other staff. The "dorm inspections" he engaged in while the boys were in class—a vague excuse for prying and insinuating himself into the students' private affairs.

Marc considered himself one of the lucky few at the Academy who were impervious to Phillips. The man was a bully. But easily intimidated by even the slightest hint of Marc calling his father into a controversy at the school.

So even the chance encounter on the road with Phillips during his daily run held little real significance for Marc.

Marc's mind was focused on one thing: football.

It wasn't easy being T. Hunter's son at the Academy, he thought as he ran past the entry gates and chapel into the practice field next to the river. His father had won almost every accolade the Academy had to offer. President of the student body. Captain of the football team and first team all-prep. Number one in his class. Early admission to Harvard.

So it seemed that regardless of what Marc did, in his own right, he could never quite live up to the reputation his father had at the Academy as a student (which now ensconced even his father's misadventures as legends).

So, Marc just tried to be himself. And would succeed, he thought as he came to a stop next to the river, if only everyone would stop comparing the two of them.

He began to stretch as he walked along the edge of the river, past the mown field into the shallow woods that led to the old bridge.

Sunday morning was his time, he reasoned. Time away from the Academy. Time away from being T. Hunter's son. Time alone, he thought, navigating the narrow passage between the water and the bank that had been cut into the earth when the river had flooded during the spring snowmelt.

His breathing was almost back to normal when he rounded the bend of the river and saw the remnants of the covered bridge that had been washed away.

But unlike other Sundays, today there was someone standing at the edge of the bridge. A boy. About his age, maybe a bit younger, a bit taller, a bit more slender. Just standing at the barricade where Federal Street now ended.

It was the boy Marc had seen earlier on the road. The one that had sped past him, despite Marc's best efforts to match him stride for stride.

Mark stopped, leaning against a large tree, peering around it, in the stillness of the forest, the shallow river rushing over the smoothed stones at its bottom.

Odd the two of them should have been on the same road, the same route this morning, he thought.

Even odder that he should now find the boy in this out-of-the-way place. This place that Marc thought of as his, alone.

Still odder to see the boy wipe his face with both hands, and in the stillness, hear the boy's muffled sobs as he lashed out at the ground beneath him, kicking the dust at the edge of the old road up in a huge plume around him. To see the boy drop, cross-legged, on the ground, his face in his hands, the boy's actions in mimicry of one of Marc's most painful memories—of a time when Marc had done the same thing, in exactly the same place, as this boy.

The sun was low, but it was still light as Allie pulled into the driveway at 151 Federal Street after her shift at the pizza parlor. Macy's car was gone, but there was an old black Buick parked at the end of the drive in front of the carriage house.

Scott was here, Allie thought, surprised at how happy that thought made her.

She pulled her Volvo behind the old Buick.

The lights were out in both the Victorian and in the carriage house and she didn't see or hear anyone stirring in the quiet of the early summer evening.

Perhaps he was out running again, she thought.

She pulled the bucket of cleaning supplies from her trunk and made her way to the main house.

Allie reached under the woven rope mat at the side door and retrieved the door-key Macy kept there for her. Allie unlocked the door and moved through the house to assess the damage she would have to undo this week.

As she moved quickly through the house, she picked up wine glasses in the den, in the living room and the bedroom. She tossed the bottles left in a row on the kitchen counter into the re-cycling bin. Both of the upstairs beds had been slept in and left unmade. The bathroom was littered with towels. There was an empty can of men's shave cream next to the sink.

That is the way Macy had left the house, Allie thought. In a hurry, probably.

It's hard to keep secrets in a small town. Everyone knew Macy had a problem. Only Allie knew how bad the problem was. She was continually reminded every time she cleaned house for Macy. Every time she collected the assortment of empty bottles Macy had left haphazardly lying about the house.

And it had only gotten worse in the last year. Since the accident.

Before, the house had been neat and tidy. Allie had almost felt guilty taking the money for the light dusting and vacuuming, for changing the sheets and wiping up the bathroom and kitchen. For occasionally washing and waxing the floors.

There had always been the bottles, and occasional evidence of the men that Macy had brought home with her. But they had been discrete reminders of

Macy's activities. Activities Macy had seemingly tried to conceal even from Allie.

Before the accident, Macy had the same schedule for the two years Allie had worked for her. A senior pharmaceutical reps' dream job, with trips to all of the major cities and even a European visit every other month.

Allie had always cleaned on Sunday. Just tidying things up, really. Many times working with Macy when she was in town. The two of them working and talking together. About the places Macy had been. The things she had done. Places and things that Allie dreamed of in a future too far distant. Talking more like … friends … hanging out together.

Allie liked Macy. She had such good taste. And the money to satisfy it. But Macy had always seemed sad to Allie. As though there was something missing in her life.

But after the accident, things had been different, she thought, as she set to work putting the house back to order. Trying to wax the circle left from a wine bottle off of the large, expensive coffee table in the living room.

At first, Allie thought it was just the changes that Macy made so that she could travel through Texas every other week. Contrived business trips to give her more time there in the hospital while her brother was dying. Macy's work schedule becoming chaotic in her quest to spend time with him. To look in on Scott. Accommodations that Allie knew had cost her a promotion and detoured her career.

Allie had started cleaning twice a week. Always trying to find a time when Macy was on a trip, so the house would be clean when she got back to it.

Then Allie began to notice the vodka bottles that had begun to appear alongside the empty wine bottles. At first, just the miniature varieties that Macy probably retrieved from her latest flight. Then their larger counterparts.

More glasses left on the tables. Magazines scattered on the floor. Twice used towels hanging from the curtain rod. Clothes, underwear and stockings abandoned in a pile at the bottom of Macy's king-sized bed.

Not that Allie minded cleaning after Macy. That was what Macy paid her to do. Allie was glad for the money that gave her an extra dance class a month and new toe-shoes every quarter.

Allie put the last of the glasses and dishes into the dishwasher and rinsed out the small particles of rice that had dried in the kitchen sink from Macy's last takeout meal.

Allie hadn't minded the additional work that cleaning house involved. She just felt sorry for Macy. And worried about her. Like a friend should.

It was just all of the men Macy had started bringing home with her. After that, cleaning up after not only Macy, but her boyfriends.

Everyone in town knew about the drinking.

Everyone in town had suspicions about the men.

But Allie knew.

And it was an intimacy with which she was uncomfortable. An intimacy all too real during the weekly cleanings.

She made her way upstairs to change the bedclothes and vacuum. Macy's king-sized bed had the same sheets from last week on them. That was another change. Macy had always had fresh sheets on her bed. Good quality sheets with high thread counts and designer labels. They never had actually needed to be changed before the wreck. Allie had just changed them as part of the routine.

She pulled the blankets back onto the floor. There were stains on the bottom sheet that she carefully avoided as she stripped the bed. More evidence of the intimacies she preferred not to dwell on.

Not that she would ever be judgmental about such things, she thought to herself. Macy was a woman. And single. And beautiful, even for her age. She had every right to have a boyfriend, to enjoy a boyfriend.

But, in her heart, Allie knew these weren't boyfriends. They weren't even friends. They were … she tried to think of the proper term. They were just … "men", she thought, pulling the sheets tightly across the mattress and spreading the comforter across them.

The sound of the door closing downstairs startled Allie.

Macy must be home, she thought, hurriedly finishing with the bed and throwing the assortment of dirty clothes into the hamper in the upstairs bathroom. Allie put the worrisome thoughts out of her mind. She was glad Macy was home. She wanted to talk to her. She wanted to talk to Macy about Scott, she thought, giggling to herself.

She took the stairs two at a time and finding the entryway empty, slid on socked feet across the waxed floor into the kitchen.

And there was Scott. Standing in the refrigerator door. Wrapped in a towel, tucked in low around his hips. His shoulders broad and muscular. His stomach flat, bronzed. A glass of milk in his hand.

"I'm … I'm … sorry," her voice overly loud in the huge kitchen. "I was cleaning. I clean Macy's house," she offered in apology. Then she realized she was staring at his body. "I didn't mean to …" she said, looking into his startled face, then stopping in mid-sentence as their eyes met. His perfect, blue eyes looking into hers.

The silence was horrible, but made worse by the shattering of the glass Scott let fall, sending milk and small shards of glass in a semi-circle around him.

"Don't move!" she screamed, her eyes making their way to Scott's bare feet. "You'll cut yourself on the glass!" she offered, dashing out of the kitchen and back to the entryway to retrieve her sneakers. "Don't move," she screamed back into the kitchen as she slipped her toes into the front of her own shoes, walking on the heels slipper-fashion, back to the kitchen as quickly as she could. "I'm coming," she screamed, as she pulled the broom and dustpan from the hall closet when she passed it.

Scott was still standing in front of the fridge, his arms crossed now, milk running outward from his feet across half of the kitchen floor now.

"I didn't move," Scott said softly, the first traces of a smile at the corners of his mouth.

Allie stopped short at the sight of him standing there in the kitchen, draped in the towel, muscled arms across his chest.

"So, you gonna help me ... or just stand there and stare at a half-naked man in distress."

The voice was laced with that thick Texas accent she remembered.

"I wasn't staring," she protested as she started to sweep the pieces of glass into the dust pan. She felt her face grow warm and knew she must be blushing. "I was just ... surprised," she struggled with the words, trying not to look up at Scott as her sweeping brought her closer to him.

"Well, just imagine how I must feel."

She stopped sweeping. She looked up into his face. At his broad smile.

Then, unexpectedly, a girlish giggle escaped.

He had such big feet, she thought, the giggle turning into a laugh that, despite her best efforts, she could not contain.

And when she finally could regain control, she found herself on her knees in front of him, with no remaining evidence of the mishap that had placed her in that position. Very conscious that only a small towel came between the two of them. A towel that, in perspective, grew smaller with every passing moment.

Scott just stood there, silent. Looking down at her kneeling there in front of him. Cinderella style, disheveled, her hair up in a bandana from cleaning, broom tightly clutched close to her.

What a sight she must be, she thought.

And then, just as suddenly as the laughter had come and gone, the tension of the moment overcame her and she started to sob, tears welling in her eyes.

"I ... I ... I," she said, trying to find words through her sobs.

God, she was crying! Why the hell was she crying, she thought?

Scott bent from his waist, placed a hand on each of her shoulders and pulled her into a standing position, her body limp in his grasp, quivering when she sobbed.

She raised her head, slowly, tentatively, the tears rolling down her cheeks. And then, he kissed her full on the lips. He had a sweet, slightly salty taste, his mouth a perfect match to her own. It was a brief kiss. That seemed to last forever.

She just let herself hang there, in his grasp, her knees weak. Feeling the strength in his hands as he held her there in front of him. Helpless in Scott's arms.

❦ ❦ ❦

For the next three weeks, Scott forced himself to do one new thing each day. He found places to shop for his food and clothes. He found the commuter rail station that could take him into Boston. He even ventured as far as Lexington and Concord in the old Buick, to the trails and monuments of the Revolutionaries that had so fascinated his father.

But he always found himself gravitating back to the same place each afternoon at the end of the local school day—the pizza parlor in the center of town and the young girl that, despite his best efforts, seemed to occupy more and more of his thoughts.

Sitting in the very back, reading from Steinbeck or Hemingway, the hot dough and spices that permeated the place adding their intoxicating fragrance as he watched Allie work and the townspeople come and go—their lives punctuated, as was his, with pizza.

It was natural enough, then, when he became a part of the place, too. Trying his hand at spinning the dough. A disastrous effort that condemned him to delivering, rather than making, the potent pies that fueled the town. Tips to cover his gas. Then finally, a paycheck when the manager realized that having the two of them there, the chemistry that they produced, the lure that they created for both the locals and the prep school crowd, more than covered the cost of keeping them together during Allie's shifts. Yankee commerce, and the syncope of a town attuned to the delicious inevitability of first love, a backdrop to the relationship that neither Scott nor Allie could have anticipated. And for which neither was prepared.

CHAPTER 9

Scott handed the flyer to Allie as he pulled into the driveway on Federal Street.

"I saw it on the board at the library," he said. "What does 'move out' mean?"

He stopped the car in front of the carriage house as Allie read through the flyer.

"When the Academy closes at the end of the year, they hire townies to help move the kids out of the dorms and clean up," Allie said.

"So, its just cleaning out the place?"

"Sort of. But the really good part is that you get to keep whatever they don't take with them. All sorts of things. TVs, microwaves, rugs, lamps, mini-fridges. You'd be amazed at what the rich kids leave behind."

"So they just leave all of the stuff that they don't want and whoever moves it out gets to keep it?"

It seemed an odd practice to Scott. But no odder than the Academy, itself.

"Yeah. Most of the stuff. Some of the stuff the kids store in trunks. There's a big storage facility at the edge of campus. So, you just sort through the stuff. The stuff in the trunks goes to storage for when they come back next year and the stuff they don't want, you get to keep if you want it. Or sell. I know a second-hand place in Ayertown. We could take the stuff over there and sell it all at one time."

He thought about the proposition. He could use the extra money. Especially now that he and Allie were spending so much time together.

The two of them began climbing the stairs to his room.

"You could find some more stuff for your room, maybe," Allie offered as he opened the door for her. "Those kids have really nice stuff," she said, bobbing her head to one side.

He chuckled. It was obvious that she wanted him to do it. And that the "nice stuff" was what she wanted.

"OK. I'll call in the morning."

Suddenly Allie grabbed him and threw him on the bed.

"Great! I'll call the second-hand store tomorrow, too. And maybe we can get enough money to go into Boston."

He should have guessed it, he thought. A trip into Boston. To the ballet.

He decided to tease her just bit.

"Oh, yeah, that's right. The Braves play the Red Sox in Boston this weekend. Wouldn't that be great! To go to the Braves' game?"

He waited for her reaction—which was immediate. First a puzzled look. Then, realizing his effort at humor, a broad smile.

"No silly! Not the baseball game! The ballet!"

She pushed him over on the bed and pinned his shoulders to it.

"Now say it! Promise me! You're taking me to the ballet on Sunday!"

He hesitated, savoring her weight on him and the light on her blonde hair as it fell over her shoulders toward him.

Allie began tickling him mercilessly.

"Alright! Alright! I'll take you!" he managed between fits of laughter.

She rolled off of him, onto her back, kicking her feet in the air.

"Yeah! We're going to the ballet! We're going to the ballet!"

He was such a wimp, he thought. The god damned ballet. Again.

"So, you know, there is this new girl on Sunday. And she just started with the company. And …"

He listened to the words, but they lost all meaning as Allie went off into her own world. Recounting the lives of ballerinas. And of the dance that seemed to pre-occupy her.

It was enough that she was there with him, he thought. Listening to her, watching her, as she shared that part of her life with him.

For some it would be a matter of fate. For others divine intervention. But mostly it was just a product of unavoidable coincidence that determined that Scott Greenwood, a boy running away from a family he no longer had, and Marc Hanson, a boy running away from a family legacy that he could not match, would meet each morning in the cool mists on the back roads of a small hamlet in Massachusetts. A dictate of the schedule they both kept to give each of them the perception that they had some control over their lives.

Simple acknowledgments the first few mornings they passed each other.

Giving way to small talk, as they chose each other's company to the solitude of their long distance run each day.

Culminating in the casual comfort and conversation that comes when two extra-ordinary people chance upon each other in a single passion that they both share.

Marc fascinated by the athleticism of Scott. Enough to read the Web reports about Scott from the local Texas newspapers before the accident had ended his career. About a talent Marc could only wish for, a gift for speed that seemed to be just beyond Marc's own grasp.

Scott equally fascinated by the easy affluence of Marc. By the stories he coaxed from Allie about the Hanson family and how Marc fit into it. By the boy who seemed to have so much, yet who, by his own admissions, always fell just short of the impossible goals that he set for himself.

They were an odd pair.

The two of them running together.

※　　　※　　　※

Scott counted the huge wooden trunks haphazardly spaced around the front of the dorm. 52. He checked the list on the clipboard. 52. At least the numbers matched this time, he thought. At least he wouldn't have to go searching the dorm for an errant trunk this time, he thought.

He opened the latch on the back of the truck and pushed the door up. He unlocked the ramp and slid it full-length, then set the hooks of the ramp tightly into the slots on the floor at the back of the truck. He wheeled the appliance dolly down the ramp.

'Move out,' he thought as he wiped the sweat from his forehead with the back of his hand, was hard work.

He checked the label on the closest trunk. Wingate. He checked the list on the clipboard. Wingate. He put a checkmark next to the name on the list, then strapped the trunk on the dolly and pulled it up the ramp and into the far corner of the truck. He un-strapped the trunk, then positioned it tightly into the corner. He rolled the dolly back to the assortment of trunks.

Over and over. 52 trunks. 52 names. 52 checks on the list. A truck full of trunks.

Then the short, bouncing ride back to the storage building. Reversing the process. Adding another checkmark next to each name on the list as he deposited the corresponding trunk into the storage room for that dorm.

He emptied three dorms of trunks. It was a full day's work. A hard day's work.

He pulled the truck back into the maintenance facility at twenty past five.

"Hey, kid," the supervisor yelled as he climbed down from the cab. "Need you to take this box of books over to Wilcot. Room 208. I'll clock you out at 6:30—should only take you ten minutes, so you get an extra hour of pay. What do you say?" his gruff voice leaving little room for negotiation. "And I'll give you the truck tomorrow to pick up all of the stuff you sorted out today that you wanted to keep."

He was tired. But it was only one box. And it was worth an extra $15. Plus, with the truck, he would only have to make one trip from the Academy to the second-hand store in Ayertown tomorrow.

"Sure," his voice cracked a bit, weary from the heat and humidity. "Wilcot. Room 208," he repeated, hoisting the box onto his shoulder and making his way back to his car. Wilcot. Room 208.

He drove back across Academy Street, through the brick pillared entrance and around the circle until he came to the large classroom building with the ionic columns. "Wilcot" was inscribed on the pedestal at the top of the building.

He parked his car in the small area in front of the building, pulling the box of books back onto his sore shoulders and walked through the oversized paneled entry doors and into the empty building.

He liked Wilcot, he thought.

He liked the smell of wood that came from the place. He liked the names inscribed on the wood panels, a panel for each class that had graduated from the school. A panel for each year since 1803. A roster of everyone who had graduated from the Academy.

He liked the autograph collection of the presidents that hung in the long corridor between the large classrooms at either end of the building. Commodities until the mid 1800's, then personalized messages to the respective headmaster of the Academy. From the Presidents of the United States!

Scott climbed the winding marble stairway. He liked the rounded feel of the marble, worn down by the decades of use. He tried to imagine the young boys whose fine leather shoes had worn the marble down. Governors, Senators, and at least one President that he was aware of. Pulitzer and Nobel Prize winners.

Even a pro football coach. All in the eclectic mix that had worn down the marble.

He turned onto the second floor and began to look for the right room. It was mid-point of the building. The door was closed. The lights were off. Scott glanced either direction down the hallway. Everyone had gone home, he reasoned. The building was empty. He opened the door to the classroom and walked in. He spotted a table under the row of windows that looked out onto the circle. He could leave the box there, he thought. As good a place as any, he thought, walking across the front of the room, depositing the box on the table.

He noticed a stack of larger sized books laying at the far edge of the table. One especially caught his eye. It was a copy of the children's graphic novel of Tin Tin. In French. *Tin Tin and the Black Island.*

He felt a lump in his throat.

It was one of the books his mother had read to him as a child. A part of the nightly bedtime ritual they had shared. His earliest recollection of his mother's native tongue.

He picked the book up and thumbed through the pages, looking at the comic-book pictorials on which the text was set. He read the words, but he heard his mother's voice, the words remembered in her voice, her accent.

"*Ah, my little rabbit,*" the sweet Parisian accent came from behind him and he froze. It was the nickname his mother had used for him when he was a little boy! It was her voice!

Scott's heart was filled with joy.

His mother!

He spun quickly to face a young woman, smiling at him.

He had actually expected to see his mother. His dead mother, alive, in the room with him. He had heard her voice. He was certain he had heard her voice.

"*Pardon, madam,*" he quickly apologized, still thinking, speaking in French. "*I meant no harm. I ... I was just reading. One of your books. Please forgive me,*" his accent a perfect match to the voice that still lingered in his mind.

"*Ah, but you are not one of my little rabbits, are you?*" the young woman's face now changed to a somewhat puzzled expression. "*No, I don't think so,*" she said. "*Your accent ... it is not a schoolboy's,*" her smile deepened. "*You are from Paris, I think.*"

Scott was still recovering. She sounded so much like his mother. Her French so much like his mother's.

"*My mother. She lived in the Latin quarter,*" he stammered. "*She grew up in St. Germain on Rue des Ecoles.*"

"*Yes*," the young woman beamed. "*I know it well. I lived on Rue Saint Jacques. Just the next block over, across the street from Maison Robert. Do you know it?*" she quizzed him.

The name was familiar. He remembered his mother's stories of the bread hearths there that tempted the neighborhood with their yeasty delights.

"*Oui, Madame*," he smiled. "*It was one of my mother's favorite places*," his voice saddened by the recollection. "She loved the *tarte aux poire et chocolat*. She would always tell me about the *tarte aux poire et chocolat*. They were her favorite," he recalled. "She said she would stop on her way to work at the Luxenbourg petite school, for fresh *tarte aux poire et chocolat* for her students."

"Luxenbourg petite school?" the woman's face was even more quizzical. "Was your mother Agnes Greenwood?" the mixture of French with the Anglican name sounding completely out of context.

How could she have guessed?

"*Oui, Madame*," he said. "*But, how would you know?*"

"*And you are 'Scott*'," his own English name equally out of character for their shared language and her rich accent.

He stood silently. The exhaustion of the day's work, the sound of his mother's voice, the apparent knowledge of this young woman, confounded him.

The young woman walked toward him gracefully, her summer smock clinging to her movements.

"*Your mother was my first teacher*," she smiled at him, placing her hand on his shoulder. "*When I was just a little girl*," she shook her head. "*She would bring tarte aux poire et chocolat to our class*," the young woman was remembering. "*She was a wonderful person. I had heard*," she hesitated, "*about the accident. About your coming here*," she withdrew her hand from his shoulder and offered it politely to Scott. "*I am Virginia, Virginia Simone*," she offered. "*I teach French here at the Academy, now.*"

"You knew my mother?" Scott asked, the vulnerability in his voice a stark contrast to the calloused hand he offered in return.

"*Ah, but of course*," the young woman beamed back. "*She was a wonderful teacher. And a wonderful person*," she added.

There was a moment between them. Of mutual love for the woman whose memory each shared.

"*And how do you find 'Massachusetts'?*" she asked, seating herself on the teacher's desk.

Scott thought a moment for an adequate description.

"*Strange,*" he said. "*Quite strange.*"

The young woman laughed, throwing her head back a bit. The gesture so much like his mother's.

"*Yes, it is,*" she said. "*Quite strange. And do you have any friends here? Have you made any friends here, yet?*"

"I know Allie Regis," he said. "*She lives in town. She works at the pizza parlor, in town.*"

"Ah! The dancer," she said knowingly.

"You know Allie?" Scott was more perplexed than ever.

"Well, but of course. I saw her dance last season. A lovely girl," she smiled. "And perhaps," she taunted pleasantly, "*more than just a friend?*"

He smiled bashfully. Was it that obvious, he thought?

"Perhaps," he replied.

"Well, then," she said, hopping down from the desk. "*You must come for dinner at my house. With your Allie,*" her pronunciation of the name stilted by the accent. "And we will speak French, together. And talk about the Dance."

"Sure. Allie and I can come over," he said. "*For dinner, if you want.*"

"Yes, that would be lovely," the young woman swept past him. "And," she said, picking up the copy of Tin Tin he had been reading, "*you will read this to Allie so that she shall know who Tin Tin is. Ca va?*"

He took the book. He liked Virginia's suggestion. He liked the idea of reading Tin Tin to Allie. Of sharing with her what Tin Tin meant to him. And he liked the idea of speaking French with Virginia. He had only just realized how much he missed hearing the language, the accent.

"*Of course,*" Scott replied. "*But of course.*"

"So, here is my number," she wrote out the numerals on a yellow sticky pad and handed it to him. "*And you shall call me to let me know when you are free. And we shall have tarte aux poire et chocolat and chateaubriand avec bearnaise. And potage bonne femme.*"

"Yes," he said, taking the yellow note and moving past Virginia to the door. "Yes," he said moving across the front of the class and out the door. "*I'll call,*" he said, leaving the room with Virginia.

CHAPTER 10

The sight of the ancient white Buick parked in front of Wilcot was enough to infuriate Ben Phillips. It's not as though he didn't have enough responsibilities in tending to the school closure. Now that upstart of a boy from town, the one from the Mordelli affair who persistently interfered with the pleasure of Ben's morning runs, just didn't seem to understand his place. A place that did not include any association with the Academy, Ben thought, bounding up the school house stairs.

What was that boy's name? Ben tried to remember as he peered down the darkened corridors of the first floor. Some kind of wood, he thought, taking the marbled stairs to the second floor two at a time.

Greenwood. That was it. Greenwood.

There was a light at the end of the second floor near the modern Romance language offices.

What was he doing there? In this building?

Ben tried to walk as softly as possible down the hallway, hoping to catch the boy in the act of whatever nefarious scheme he might have. He turned the corner quickly, standing full in the door, prepared to confront the scoundrel and deal with him once and for all.

"Ah, Mr. Phillips, hello."

He peered around the room, but found only Virginia Simone sorting through a box of books on the table next to the window.

"Good day," he managed, still scouring the room for the boy.

"Are you looking for someone, Mr. Phillips?" the young woman asked in English.

Ben wasn't quite sure why he was becoming so agitated. Initially it might have been the thought of that boy in his schoolhouse. But now the fact that the impudent young woman had disdained to speak with him in French seemed an outright affront. She knew perfectly well he was fluent. And yet, invariably she insisted in speaking in English to him.

"A boy. A young boy. Not one of ours!"

He had never especially liked the Simone woman. She had been thrust upon him by T. Hunter. In a situation where Ben had no choice but to hire the woman. Not at all a good influence on the Academy students. She never seemed to have control of her classes. And the way she dressed! Perhaps for the streets of Paris, it was acceptable. But here. Certainly not. A very bad influence on the young girls who tried to match her questionable sense of proper attire for the Academy. Equally so on the young boys, who flocked to her class not so much for the language instruction as for the sight of her, he reasoned.

It all seemed a bit sordid.

Did T. Hunter actually think that he wouldn't see through his efforts on the young woman's behalf? Did he really think that he would have hired the woman on her credentials alone?

"A boy?" she said, breaking the silence between them in the room.

Granted, she was incredibly attractive, he reasoned, the light from the window highlighting the young woman's body through her thin summer dress.

But certainly T. Hunter had other women, women more "substantial" in character and breeding, that might have filled the same need.

"Yes, a boy."

Not that it really mattered to him what T. Hunter saw in the woman. It was just the fact of having to place her here. In the Academy. A decision he had only concurred in because of the hold it placed on T. Hunter. More regular visits now by the Chairman. More opportunities to assure that funding flowed for Academy necessities. A wild-card dealt to him, which he could hold, and play, at the appropriate time.

"No. No boy. Just me."

Just you, indeed, he thought.

Perhaps she and T. Hunter could keep their little secret. Perhaps not. But he knew. And she knew that he knew, he reasoned, turning quickly back to his more urgent task.

Where was that boy? That Greenwood boy?

🍁 🍁 🍁

Scott had caught a glimpse of the headmaster racing up the stairs at the opposite end of the Wilcot as he headed back to his car.

Just as well, he thought, that the old man not find him on the school grounds, as he didn't relish another confrontation.

Besides, he had other things to think about.

Memories of a mother's voice and a better time. Thoughts of shared time with a sister as they had coached each other through the colorful adventures of Tin Tin and taught each other how to read. Moments with his father, in the sterile hospital room, as he had tried to recreate the feeling of family that had been lost by reading in French to the comatose body that stared blankly back at him.

They were all bittersweet, now that they were lost.

Made more so by his growing concern that the faces of his family seemed to be fading away.

Now, hearing Madame Simone, her voice, her accent, those faces, those feeling came flooding back.

He could almost smell the flour and the oil of the pancake breakfasts. He could almost feel the love that had pervaded the house during the quiet times when they had gathered in one room, to read, each one gently touching another, connected.

Almost, he thought, starting the old Buick and pulling around the circle drive of the Academy out onto the main road.

Almost remember a time when he was happy.

🍁 🍁 🍁

"How did you get your nickname?" Marc asked. "Why did they call you 'Gnat'?"

The question stopped Scott in his tracks. He hadn't heard the nickname since before the accident.

It took Marc a second or two to realize that Scott was no longer running next to him. When he did, Marc stopped and retraced his steps at a slow jog.

"Heah," Marc offered, seeing the surprise, the pain in Scott's eyes. "I didn't mean anything, man," he offered genuinely. "I ... I looked you up online," Marc admitted. "I looked up the newspaper stories," he lowered his eyes to the ground. "They called you 'Gnat' in the newspaper. Said that was your nickname," he hesitated, then pressed on. "Why?"

Without warning Scott started back into the run and Marc fell back into pace with him.

"Because I was small," Scott said, looking straight in front of him. "And fast," he remembered. "No one could catch me."

Scott sped up as he turned onto Academy Road, sprinting away from Marc. It wasn't until he came to the brick pillars of the entranceway that he slowed, then stopped. He bent from the waist, hands on either side, breathing deeply, watching out of the corner of his eye as Marc made up the 200 or so yards that Scott had put between them.

Marc jogged tentatively toward the entranceway, then stopped and started stretching out against the near pillar.

Neither boy spoke. Both in silence, pressing into either pillar, their backs arched, their legs extended.

"I could teach you," Scott finally said. "I can teach you how to run," he offered. "How to run faster," Scott said earnestly, still staring into the brick pillar that supported his weight.

Marc thought about the offer. About the orphaned boy standing next to him. About the impression Scott had made on the sports writers in Texas.

"You could teach me to run faster?" Marc asked skeptically.

"If you were willing to work at it," Scott cautioned.

Marc was shocked at the suggestion. That speed like Scott's could be learned.

"Really?" Marc quizzed Scott. "You could teach me to run as fast as you? By next season? By the time I graduate?"

"Yeah," Scott was looking at Marc. "If you were willing to work at it. You could run that fast," he added confidently.

"Mr. Hanson!" an annoyed shout came from the edge of the first brick building.

Scott recognized the voice. He recognized the man. It was Phillips.

"Mr. Hanson! A word with you," the stern voice commanded. "Now, if you don't mind," Phillips called.

"Got to go," Marc said hurriedly, urged on by the voice.

Phillips was still looking in Scott's direction. Glaring at him, his chin up, nose down.

Scott watched Phillips and Marc walking away into the complex of brick buildings. Talking, in undertones. Talking about him, Scott thought.

What was Phillip's problem, Scott thought? He had such a condescending air about him. How was that little man able to make other people feel so small around him? Why would he want to do that, Scott thought?

Scott felt sorry for Marc. For Dennis. For all of the boys under Phillips's thumb, who had known only life at The Academy.

🍁   🍁   🍁

Marc waited until he and Scott had almost finished their morning run before he finally made the transition to the plan he had so carefully crafted over the last week.

"Say, you got a few more minutes? There's someone I want you to meet," Marc tried to sound nonchalant, as if he had just had a thought.

"Sure," Scott said, falling in with Marc's easy pace out of the Academy stadium and toward the gym. Scott had met a few of Marc's friends. An eclectic group whose only commonality seemed to be wealth and privilege.

The boys made their way across the back of the campus toward the athletic center, then through the double doors into the small basement corridor that Scott knew led to the locker room. The place was empty now that the school term had ended and the two boys' footsteps resounded against the stonewalls.

Marc took a sharp left away from the locker room into the cage where they kept all of the jerseys and training gear. A short man, with thinning hair, in gym shorts and an Academy t-shirt was putting laundry into a commercial washer.

"Jim," Marc called.

The man looked up from his laundry and smiled.

"This is the guy I was telling you about," Marc continued, gesturing to Scott. "Scott Greenwood," Marc made the introductions in a semi-formal way, "this is Jim Roberts. He coaches third's football and does the summer session here at the Academy. He was the first coach I had when I came to the Academy."

Jim's face already had a smile on it.

"Scott," Jim said, offering his hand to the boy, "Nice to meet you at last. Marc just won't stop talking about you," he said, nudging Marc in the side with his elbow and pumping Scott's hand vicariously. "Marc says you're a runner?"

This was a man he was going to like, Scott thought immediately.

"Says you were quite a football player, too," Jim continued, letting go of Scott's hand and turning back to the table behind him to retrieve a manila folder from a neat stack. "Says you might be interested in helping us with our summer camp," Jim said, handing Scott a small booklet.

The cover of the booklet had a picture of the Academy on it. But the first page was a flyer for some sort of football camp.

"It's our summer 'enrichment' session," Jim said. "We bring in boys from all over New England, teach them a little football and give them an SAT review course between the drills."

"Ah, Scott," Marc stammered. "Forgot to tell you about the summer camps," his voice somewhat unconvincing. "But wouldn't that be great!" his enthusiasm real enough. "You and I? All summer? Doing the camps? Wouldn't that be great!"

Scott hesitated just long enough to leave an opening for Jim.

"Pays good," Jim offered. "Twice what you would make delivering pizzas," he said, knowingly. "It's easy work. Mostly just helping the coaches who run the camp. And, you could take the SAT review course, no charge," he sank the real hook.

Scott realized the opportunity. He had taken the GED to get out of classes while he sat with his father in the hospital. But now ... well now he couldn't imagine going back to high school after all he had been through. And he couldn't imagine getting into anything other a junior college with just the GED. He knew the SAT review course would add at least 100, maybe even 150 points to his college board scores next year. The course even had a guarantee—you could repeat the sessions as many times as you wanted until you scored 100 points better than your first practice exam. It might make the difference between community college and a real one, he thought, all other factors being equal.

But then, there was the football. Something Scott wanted nothing to do with.

Jim and Mark just stood there, staring at him.

"Ah, I ... I don't ... I," he tried to come up with some rational reason why he was going to turn them down.

"No rush on your decision," Jim said. "Just think about it. You can let Mark know. But I sure hope you do it!"

"OK. I'll ... I'll think about it."

It was late afternoon before Marc had a chance to get back to the athletic facility. An afternoon spent considering options. He had thought that it would be easier getting a yes answer out of Scott. But Jim had been right, again. A coach's instinct perhaps, Marc thought.

He finally found Jim in the weight room, putting up schedules and drills on the bulletin board.

"So, did you convince your young friend?" Jim asked.

"Not yet. But give me time. I've been thinking about a plan."

Marc paused, but Jim just kept working.

"Do you really think he could make that much difference?" he finally asked, trying to get Jim's full attention. "I mean, as far as I'm concerned?"

Jim finished stapling the papers on the board and sat down on a weight bench.

"Marc, I have to be honest with you," he said. "As good as you are at throwing the ball, you are never going to be any better than the receivers that can catch it. I've done the best I can to stack the cards in your favor this summer. I pulled in the best I could find for the camp. Hell, I laid out more scholarship money this year than ever. Roxbury, Revere. I even went to Nashua to grab a tight end for you. So, I would say you have a fifty-fifty chance of getting noticed by a Division 1 coach."

"But with Scott? You said that with Scott, it's a done deal."

"It's as close as you're going to get, Marc. I did what you asked me to do. I called his coach in Texas. He was really high on the boy. And my guess is that boy has exactly what you need to make you look good. Good hands. And great speed. His coach said if you could get the ball close to him, the boy would do the rest. With him ... well, with him, I would say you might be able to get a Division 1 coach to notice you."

Marc nodded.

He knew that Jim was right. He knew that he needed something more than his own talent to obtain his goal.

"Now tell me again why the hell this is so important to you? I mean, with your Dad and all ... with everything he has done for the university ... with his donations and being a Trustee and all, I thought you were Cambridge bound."

Marc felt the hair at the back of his neck stand on end and he clinched his teeth.

Even Jim couldn't understand, he thought, trying to calm himself. He was just like all of them. They all thought Marc had it made. Because of his father.

Damn! Couldn't they see? This wasn't about his father. It was about him. About what he could do. On his own. Why did it always have to be about his father, Marc thought? Always!

"Probably, probably I'll go there," Marc offered. "But I want more than that. I want to be the best. The best the school has ever had. I want to be recruited by the best schools," he paused. "By the best teams. Nationally ranked teams."

He paused.

"That's something not even my father had, was it? None of the Division 1 scouts ever called him, did they?"

Jim stood up and put his hand on Marc's shoulder.

"No, Marc. Your dad never got a call like that."

Jim turned back toward his office.

"You get the boy. The Greenwood kid. You convince him," Jim said. "And I'll do the rest. I'll get the Division 1 coaches here," he paused in the doorway. "And you'll get your shot."

Jim walked away, leaving Marc alone.

That was it, then, Marc thought. He would just have to find a way. Find a way to get Scott to say yes. To play football, again.

After all, it would be better for Scott, too, Marc reasoned. What did Scott have going for him, now, anyway? An orphan. A drunken aunt that everyone in town had slept with.

It was better for Scott, he reasoned. He would be doing Scott a favor. Maybe even one of the college coaches would take a look at Scott, make him an offer, as well.

CHAPTER 11

"Don't peek," Allie shrieked.

Scott couldn't see anything through the blindfold Allie had tied around him. He stumbled forward, trying to follow her steadying hand. He tripped over an uneven piece of pavement.

"Watch out!" Allie giggled. "Just keep coming forward. That's it ... that's it," she encouraged him.

He felt so stupid. He should never have let Allie talk him into this. She said it was a surprise. She said it was her "month-aversity" gift. Big gift, he thought, tripping again. He felt so awkward. And vulnerable.

"Wait a minute," Allie's voice was playful. "I have to open a door," she explained.

He obediently stopped, let go of her hand and stood motionless. He wasn't sure where they were any more. After Allie had blindfolded him at Macy's he had lost track of direction. The drive hadn't taken more than 5 or 10 minutes. But there had been a lot of turns and he still didn't know his way around the town. Then, the walk. Another 5 or 6 minutes. With Allie leading him, first across gravel, then pavement. The traffic sounds had died away, so they weren't close to the highway any more. But he was definitely lost. He had no idea where they were or what Allie was up to.

He heard a creaking sound and a hollow thud. A metal door echoing in a vacant room or a hallway, he thought.

"OK, now be careful and step over the landing," Allie's voice was still high-pitched and giddy. "That's my boy," she encouraged him. "Just a little more," she said, leading him again across what felt like linoleum. "Another door," she cautioned, prompting him with her hand to stop. "That's right," she said. "Now through the door," she said.

It had been a lot of fun at first. Not knowing what she was up to. Not knowing where she was taking him. But sufficient time had passed for him to begin to question what they were doing … what Allie had in store for him.

He didn't like surprises. And he only tolerated them with Allie.

"I can't see anything," his voice was a bit terse as he banged into a metal door. "Are we there yet?"

"You are such a baby," she chided him. "*Are we there yet?*" she offered in childlike mockery.

"What's going on, Allie?" he was getting tired of the game. "Where are we? What are you up to?"

"All in good time," she quipped. "Now, I'm going to lead you into a row of seats and I want you to sit down. Okay?" she explained, maneuvering him with her hand to his right.

He bumped his knee against a metal chair.

"Be careful, goofball," Allie laughed as she pushed him further into the darkness. "Just a little bit further. That's right," she said letting go of his hand. "Just a bit further. Now stop!" she screamed. "Stop. Right there. And sit down."

He reached out into the darkness. He felt a seat bottom and pushed it into a horizontal position. It was an awkward movement.

"Can I take the blindfold off now?"

"No! Not yet!" Allie's voice was loud, commanding, but further away. "Don't take it off until I tell you!" her voice growing more distant and echoing a bit.

They were in a large room, he thought. A large classroom at the Academy perhaps. And from the quiet, they were all alone.

He could hear Allie's clogs on a hard surface, then a more padded cadence. And finally he didn't hear anything at all.

"Now, just a minute more," Allie's voice was more plaintive and very far away, in front of him, very muted by the distance.

She was up to something, he thought. He could tell from her voice that she was doing something. Pulling or tugging on something. Moving something, maybe, far in front of him.

Suddenly there was a halo of light around the periphery of the blindfold, then all darkness again.

"OK. Now take off the blindfold. And don't move!"

He obediently removed the blindfold. He saw quick flashes of light before his eyes slowly adjusted to the darkness of the room.

They were in an auditorium of some sort, but much too shabby to be an Academy building. More likely the public school in town, he thought. The room sloped down slightly and there were rows of seats neatly arranged in long aisles from the front to the back of the room. He was seated near the middle of a row, a few rows back from a large stage. There was a faded maroon curtain drawn across the front of the stage. He was alone in the auditorium.

Music suddenly came from a series of speakers at either side of the stage. It was "O soave fanciulla" from La Boheme. He recognized the melody from all of the times that Allie had made him listen to the opera in his room. In the dark of his room, together, in each other's arms.

The curtain opened, revealing a dark, vacant stage. He narrowed his eyes to focus. Where was Allie, he thought?

As the music began to increase in volume the stage lights came up slowly. And from stage left, Allie emerged. She was wearing a slight pink dance leotard, with a large ruffle. And her ballet shoes.

As she entered stage left, she appeared to ignore his presence, her movements perfectly synchronized to the music. Slow, graceful, extended movements. Head erect, arms outstretched. Her hands, sculpted into classic form. She moved, as if suspended, to center stage.

She was going to dance for him, he thought, smiling. That was her gift to him, he finally understood.

He had seen her practice before.

But he had never seen her ... dance. Not like this. It was as if she were another person. Still Allie. Still his Allie. Only different. The sophistication of the dance, of the ballet, transforming her.

He sat enraptured. The music came from all directions now and engulfed him. Rodolfo and Mimi in their passionate profession of love for each other. Allie fluttering across the stage. Her long legs accentuated by her pointe. Her figure slim in the glare of the stage lighting. Every movement coordinated to the music. Every step perfectly timed. Every motion effortless.

He had no idea she was this good. He had seen dance recitals before. At home. In Texas. Awkward girls making vain attempts. And he had seen professionals. In Boston, at the recitals that Allie had insisted he attend with her.

But this was Allie. There in front of him. Dancing. And she was ... wonderful!

The music neared its conclusion and Allie slowed her pace to one of measured exit. She ended in a deep curtsy, her fully extended leg, toe toward him, hands symmetrically askew, head deeply bowed. Motionless in the final silence of the auditorium.

He jumped from his seat, clapping wildly.

"Brava! Brava!"

Allie looked up smiling. She was no longer the dancer. She was suddenly, again, his Allie.

"Brava!" he called out, still clapping loudly as he made his way from the aisle and ran toward the stage. "Bravisimo!" he shouted.

And then they were both at the edge of the stage, facing each other. Allie's exertions clearly visible for the first time. Her breathing hard, disciplined only by her endless hours of practice.

"Happy month-aversy," she cooed, leaning over to give him a slightly sweaty kiss.

He caught her off balance and pulled her from the stage into his arms. She seemed weightless there.

"Did you like my present?" she asked earnestly.

Her dance concluded, back to her natural character, he sensed her innate insecurity.

He placed her lightly on the ground, then positioned her squarely in front of him.

"It was the best present I have ever had," he said, running the back of his hand along her face. "You ... you," he struggled for word. "You are the best," he said, placing his hand behind her neck and pulling her into a long kiss.

He felt Allie's legs give slightly and he tightened his embrace to steady her.

They stood looking into each other's eyes for a moment. Then Allie smiled broadly, a mischievous expression surfacing from her face.

"Want the rest of your present?" she asked demurely, as she slowly stepped back from him and pulled one of the thin straps of the leotard down across her bare shoulder.

Marc waited in the empty parking lot next to the pizza store until he saw the light in the building go out, then stepped onto the sidewalk and made his way toward the door. He reasoned it was the only time he would be able to get Allie alone. And that was critical to his plan.

"Allie," he said, trying to sound friendly on the dimly lit sidewalk as she stepped out of the pizza parlor and locked the front door.

"Oh!" she let out a small yelp as she stepped away from him. "Oh my God, Marc. You scared me to death. What are doing out here skulking around the parking lot."

She looked as good as she always had, Marc thought, remembering the sophomore year he had spent flirting with her. Only more mature. And perhaps, happier, he thought.

"Oh, just walking around enjoying being out of school," he said. "The Academy courses were a bit harder this last year. Guess they just want to stress you out your junior year because they know that's the last time grades really matter."

"You are so right," she said, closing the screen door and turning back to face him. "Between working and dance lessons, I barely had time to keep up with classes this last year."

It was just the opening he was waiting for.

"So how is dance going? I hear from Scott that you are really getting serious," he said, leaving the comment open-ended.

Marc thought he caught a hint of blush in Allie's face.

"About dance, that is," he laughed.

"Oh, sure, about dance," she giggled, nervously. "I might even try to get into a college dance program next year."

"Really? Well, that would be great," he paused. "But didn't you want to dance in New York. I thought for sure you would want to try to make it in the City this summer."

"New York? Well ... yes ... of course ... New York. That's ... well that's simply the best."

"You know, there's a great summer dance program there. With the Repertory Company. Did you ever think about trying out for their program? Their summer program?"

She stepped back and for a moment Marc thought he had lost her.

"You know, my father is on the Board of the Repertory Company. If you would like, I could call him. I know they have scholarships. That is ... if you are interested," he tried to sound somewhat indifferent.

She seemed to hesitate for a moment.

Then she asked the right question. The one he knew she would ask.

"Any why, Marc Hanson, would you care about what *I* wanted? When did you ever care about anyone other than yourself?"

Maybe that is why the two of them had never really gotten very far in the relationship, he thought. Allie had always assumed that Marc had some agenda, some scheme. Even when he didn't. Even with her, that sophomore year they had shared together.

Only this time she was right.

But this time, he reasoned, it wouldn't matter.

"You and Scott, the two of you, you're getting pretty serious."

"And what business is that of yours!"

"None. Other than the fact that we both like him. That we are both his friends."

"Marc, I've never known you to have a friend. Or be one, for that matter. So, just this once, let's both of us not play games."

And it was at that moment that Marc knew he had her. He could tell it from her expression. From her body language. She was hooked.

"I need Scott to help me this summer. With football. At the camp. Only with you around, that's never going to happen."

"Go on."

"And you know what else is never going to happen with him around? If you spend all of your time with him?"

He waited for the answer he knew that she didn't want to give him.

"Go ahead, Allie, just say it. It's what you always wanted. Before me. Before him. Right now, right this very second."

"That's not fair Marc!"

"Think about it, Allie. How much time have you spent practicing since you met him? More than before? Less? A lot less?"

He heard her breathing quicken.

"This is it for you Allie. This is your chance. You either want to be a dancer or you don't. Think of what I am offering you. New York, Allie. It's what you always wanted."

"And Scott?"

"Scott's not going anywhere. He'll be right here. Right here waiting for you. Hell! I'll even make sure he gets down to New York this summer to see you, if you like."

Marc waited. He waited to close the deal. Waited that extra couple of seconds.

"And speaking of Scott, what about him? I can get him in, Allie. I can get him into the summer program. What's he got now? No family, unless you call that slut of an Aunt family. No future. No place to go. Are you going to be the one that holds him back? Are you going to be that selfish, Allie?"

She was wiping away the tears now. Choking back the emotions. But all the time he could tell. He knew she was just trying to rationalize the decision she had already made.

"You're a real shit, Marc Hanson. He thinks you're his friend, you know."

"I am his friend, Allie. And I'm your friend, too. I am just being a realist. I want something. You want something. And he needs all the help he can get, regardless of who gives it and regardless of the reasons."

"You're being a prick, that's what you're being. Just like you always were. Just like all the rich pricks at the Academy."

"OK. I agree. I'm a prick. Does that make you feel better now that I've admitted it."

"One condition. You have to promise me. You have to promise me one thing. You have to promise you won't tell him. You have to promise he'll never know."

"Never know that you sold him out so that you could go dance in New York?"

She slapped him hard across his face.

Then she stepped back.

"Yes," she said.

He had never heard her voice sound so cold.

"Done. He'll never know."

CHAPTER 12

Scott loved Sundays most of all. Especially when Allie didn't have to work at the pizza parlor and it left the two of them alone, working together in the big Victorian, straightening up after Macy. It was the only time Scott permitted himself in the main part of the house. It had become part of the ritual that Allie and he had developed. Almost like their house. Like playing house. Alone. Together. In the big Victorian.

She had seemed a bit distant last night after work. They had talked, briefly. She had called him. But she hadn't come over to see him. She had been too tired, she said.

And today, she seemed ... well different. Smiling. Playful. Full of herself, as they tidied away the liquor bottles and glasses from the tables downstairs. Almost giddy when she was vacuuming, running the machine up onto his toes, trying to make him jump out of her way.

Girls were like that. One day they could be sad. The next day happy. For no reason, he guessed. Just part of being a girl, he guessed.

They did the laundry and watched baseball on the big screen TV in the back room, snuggled together on the couch. Not talking. Just being close to each other. Waiting for their favorite part of the chores—folding the towels, fresh and warm from dryer. Laying them out neatly on Macy's huge bed upstairs, before stacking them away in the bathroom closet.

It was a good day. One of his best. Being there, alone, in the house with her.

They pulled the old bedcovers off of Macy's bed and began to put on the freshly laundered fitted sheet. It was always a tug-of-war for them, more of a game than work. Trying to push and pull and tug the rounded corners into place around the edges of the oversized mattress.

She had worn the cut-off jeans today. The ones that were just a little too short and that hung low across her hips, the short T-shirt she was wearing revealing her delightfully taut stomach.

Maybe it was the jeans. Or the T-shirt. Or her stomach.

Or maybe it was just that they hadn't been together in days and she had that certain look on her face.

Whatever it was, it set in motion that series of events that inevitably led to a bulge in his pants.

"I see you brought Mr. Happy with you today," Allie said, as he tried to finish his side of the bed.

"We haven't seen Mr. Happy for a few days, have we?" she said, backing away from the bed and pulling the T-shirt tight across her chest.

"Does Mr. Happy want to come out to play?"

Scott watched her as she began to sway her hips to some imagined tune, rocking them back and forth, in slow undulation.

"Oh, Mr. Happy. Won't you come out to play with me," she sang in mimicry of the ancient children's song, as she pulled the T-shirt up over her head.

"And we'll have lots of fun," she continued, unbuttoning the top of her shorts.

"Just you and me!" she shouted, as she dropped her jeans to the floor and jumped onto the huge bed in front of him, naked, smiling.

"Come on Scott! Don't tease," she said, looking now below his belt.

He wasn't teasing, he thought. He just felt a little uncomfortable in this situation. Not with Allie, so much. He loved to see her naked. And he loved that they were still new to each other, still discovering each other.

No, it wasn't that. Or standing there with a huge bulge in this pants. Not that either.

This was Macy's room. Macy's bed. And, for some reason, it just didn't seem … right. Despite that fact that Macy was hardly ever at home. One night in the last week—and then only to pass out on the couch in the front parlor, where he had found her the next day while searching for car keys after she had parked so badly that she had blocked the Buick in the driveway.

He watched Allie swaying, naked, on the bed, her finger provocatively placed on those wonderful pouting lips.

"You can't get me, you can't get me!" she teased, pulling the top sheet up around her, concealing nothing, the effort merely more provocation.

He looked over his shoulder, nervously, then slid off his shirt and stepped out of his jeans. Standing there in front of her, he heard her take a quickened breath as she dropped the cover from in front of her, repositioned herself at the edge of the bed and reached out for him. Only this time, instead of facing him, she turned around, pulling him toward her from behind.

It was a new sensation for him. Allie beneath him. The full weight of his body on hers. Not at all what it had been like with her before. None of the tenderness. None of softness.

This was something totally new. Totally unexpected to see her like this.

Was this really her? Was this really his Allie? A part of her that she was only now revealing to him?

Or was this something new to her, as well?

He had never seen a girl like this before. No coquettish pretense. Just pure desire. And language that he had never heard any female utter, urging him on.

He closed his eyes as Allie fell back into him. On tiptoes against him, suspended almost, in front of him. His hands steadying her.

When he opened his eyes, there, just beyond Allie's naked shoulder, standing in the doorway, was Macy.

Allie froze, her breath coming in small gasps, barely able to balance herself against him. Her eyes, obviously closed, oblivious to the reality that he now confronted.

All he could do was stand there. Trying to catch his own breath. Trying to hold on to Allie so that she didn't fall. Trying to think about what would happen next.

It was over in seconds. And could have been only a moment of awkwardness for all of them.

Instead, Macy stood there motionless. Her face gradually contorting into the drunken smirk he had seen so many times before.

"So, you and your little slut having fun in my room?" she said, her words slurred. "In my bed!"

He felt Allie's body lock in rigid position and knew that she had finally opened her eyes.

More seconds passed.

"Oh, God!" he heard Allie's plaintive voice as she slowly freed herself and slid away from him, down to the floor, seeking the cover of the bed between she and Macy as she clawed for the sheet to cover herself.

Ordinarily, standing naked in front of Macy, especially in his current condition, would have mortified him.

But it wasn't shame that he felt.

It was rage.

Rage that she had walked in on the two of them.
Rage that she had stayed.
Rage that Macy, that she of all people, had called Allie, his Allie, a slut.
"You drunken bitch!" he shouted, as he covered the short distance across the room to confront Macy. Directly in front of Macy, now, his fists clenched.
She was laughing.
Laughing at them.
Laughing at him.
The smell of scotch on her.
It was the breaking point.
He had been in fights before. It was just part of growing up in Texas. And in all of them, when his fist had connected, he had felt a jarring sensation the length of his arm, up through his shoulder.
This time, however, hitting a woman, a slight woman of Macy's size, all he felt was flesh giving way beneath his knuckles.
Macy crashed into furniture on the way to the floor, blood spurting from the gash just beneath her left eye.
"Scott! No! No! Don't!"
He heard Allie before he felt her, climbing across his back, trying to pull him away from Macy.
"Stop it! Stop it, Scott!"
Allie was beating him on his back.
Macy was below him on the floor, her hand pressed against the flow of blood that was dripping onto the oriental carpet beneath her.
"You little ingrate!" Macy shouted as she attempted to drag herself away from him across the floor.
"First, my brother! Now me! Are you going to kill me, too?" she screamed.
He was shaking. His whole body was shaking.
Allie still screaming at him to stop, beating on his back with her fists. Using her full weight to pull him back away from Macy.
Macy cursing, calling them both awful names.
And he suddenly realized what he had done and the full gravity of his actions.
Standing there, naked, in the bedroom.
Macy in front of him on the floor.
Allie still clawing him, pulling him back.
Standing there between the two of them.
No where to turn.

No where to hide.
No place to go.
Nothing he could do to make things right, again.
Ever.

CHAPTER 13

Scott spent most of the afternoon trying to straighten up the bedroom and rinse the bloodstains out of the carpet. Trying to put things back into place, as they had been. Waiting for Allie to call him from the hospital. It was almost dusk before the phone rang.

"She's OK, Scott. Really, she's going to be fine."

Her voice sounded tired. And strained.

He reasoned that was to be expected. The responsibility of driving Macy into Boston, to Mass General, had fallen to her. Of dealing with the hospital. Of dealing with Macy.

"She had a broken cheekbone that they had to be reset. But there wasn't any damage to her eye or eye socket. They had to put her to sleep. She's just now waking up a bit. But she's going to be fine. No scars or anything."

There was a long pause.

"The police came by. The hospital must have called them."

The police. He hadn't even considered that possibility.

"Macy told the admitting clerk when we came in the emergency room that she fell. But I don't think they believed her. So they must have called the police. They said, in a case like this, that they had to file a report. But Macy told me what to say. Before the police showed up. I guess she must have overheard the hospital staff talking. She just said to tell them that she fell, on the edge of the carpet, and hit her face on the rocking chair," Allie said. "So … that's what I did."

He recounted the toll the day had taken. His aunt, in the hospital, her face smashed. Allie, perjuring herself to protect him.

"Scott. Macy said you have to leave."

He heard Allie sob.

"She said she wants you out of the house before she comes home."

He couldn't blame Macy, he thought, for wanting him gone. She had given him a place to stay, a place to go to when he had run out of options. And what had he done? He had put her in the hospital for her efforts.

"They are going to keep her a day or two. As soon as she gets out of recovery they are going to admit her and keep her for at least a day or so … for observation … to make sure," Allie paused, "that … well … that there isn't any more damage. You know … like a concussion or something."

A day or two. That's all he had. A day or two to figure out what he was going to do now. What he was going to do for the rest of his life.

"Scott, I'm so … so sorry," Allie said.

He could hear her crying now, trying to hold it back, unsuccessfully.

"It's OK, Allie. Really. I understand. It's not Macy's fault. It's not anyone's fault. Except maybe mine. It was never going to work out, anyway. Me being there. In her house."

"I can ask my parents. If they will let you stay with us for a few days. Until you know what you are going to do."

What he was going to do?

How could he know?

"Sure. Maybe a couple of days. If they wouldn't mind. Just to finish out the week. Until I can decide, you know, what to do."

The crying had lessened and he heard Allie take a deep breath.

"You could always do the summer camp at the Academy," she said.

But now her voice was different, somehow. Different and mysterious to him.

"You know, just to have a place to stay. Just for the summer to give yourself some time to sort through things."

How did she know about that!

How did she know about the Academy's summer camp?

"I mean," she stammered, "you know Marc Hanson pretty well. You guys are running buddies and all. And Marc's dad, well, he can usually get whatever he wants at the Academy. And you would be around guys your own age. Guys like you. I see them every summer. They all show up at the pizza parlor. Not like the Academy students. Not the stuck up, rich kids. These are really nice kids. From all over. Just looking for a break. For some help."

So that's how she knew. Of course. The boys in summer camp. They would find their way to the pizza parlor in the small town. That was it. Nothing strange in that. Nothing mysterious about it. No reason to be suspicious. What was wrong with him? Why would he ever doubt that Allie had anything but his own interest as heart. That's the way Allie knew about the camp, about the other boys that came to the camp. From her job at the pizza parlor, he reasoned.

"You could stay in the dorms at the Academy. Live there. Eat there. You could help out, maybe. You knowing how to play football and all."

Help out, he thought.

That was the bargain he would have to make?

For the chance to stay in the town? To stay close to Allie?

To play football, again? Despite his vow to his dead father never to play football, again.

It seemed a deal only the devil could have conceived. But maybe, just maybe, Sunday was the day that the devil did most of his business, he reasoned, hearing the familiar sounds of the hospital over the phone, the sickening smell of the antiseptic coming through the phone's receiver.

"But I promised," he began trying to explain to Allie. "I promised," his own voice choked.

"I know Scott, I know," she said.

She was so good to him, he thought. Maybe the only one who could truly understand. The only one with whom he could share the pain that seemed to crush him.

"I promised … my father," he managed.

"I know Scott, I know," she said.

He tried to regain control. To concentrate on what had to be done.

"Call Marc, Scott. Call Marc and talk to him. He's your friend. Call Marc. Ask him. Ask him to help you. That's what friends are for. He won't mind. He likes you. He'd love having you around all summer long. You guys are buds!"

He wiped his nose with the back of his hand.

Allie was right. He knew she was right.

Marc was the only other person he knew that might help him. The only other person who might understand. A smart kid. A rich kid with connections. Maybe Marc was the only one who might be able to really help him out of this situation.

"OK. I'll give Marc a call. Tonight. I'll call him tonight. And tell him," he paused. "Tell him I can do the summer camp."

He had thought that his agreement with Allie's suggestion might ease her, somewhat. Might make her feel better.

Instead, he heard her break into tears, again, sobbing. As if her heart were breaking.

"Allie. It's OK. I'll call Marc. Today."

He listened to her sobbing.

"I … I have to go … Scott. I have to go now."

He heard the click and then silence on the phone.

How odd, he thought. That she should react like that.

Maybe it was the police, again. Or one of the doctors that needed to talk to her.

Still, no goodbye. No, I love you.

It was odd.

In context, though, just another odd event in a day of oddities, he reasoned.

He would have to do something nice for Allie. When she got back. Something nice for everything that she had done for him.

❦   ❦   ❦

It had been an inconvenience for Ben Phillips to change his favorite morning jogging route. But necessary to avoid the inevitability of seeing Marc and the Greenwood boy every morning, running together. Laughing and talking as they ran.

What did Marc Hanson see in that Greenwood boy? Certainly not someone of the Marc's station in life. A discard. An orphan. No one of any particular relevance, certainly, to a boy like Marc.

A new route. That had done the trick. To set things right again. Such that Ben could once again enjoy his morning jog. A route down to the commuter train station in the adjoining town. Not through the nicest of neighborhoods. But pleasant enough. And with the added bonus of having the townsfolk parking their cars at the commuter station for the daily commute into Boston acknowledge him. Waiving or shouting early morning greetings. All of them aware of his position with the Academy.

A longer jog. Down and back. Repeating the scenery on the return trip. The last half not quite as good, after passing the mid-point at the commuter station and the greetings there.

Maybe he needed to write an article for the local town paper, he thought on the return trip. Something about the Academy. About its history and contribution to the local economy. About the prestige it provided to the local area, he thought.

He could even send in a picture. Of himself, perhaps. To go with the story.

The weekly paper came out on Thursday. He would write the article today. Edit it tonight. Get it to them on Tuesday morning, he thought, as he turned left into the Academy gates and began to stretch against the hitching posts of the black jockeys that still stood in front of the headmaster's residence.

Something informal, so that the locals could relate to it. He went directly back to his office and began sorting through a stack of papers on this desk. A charity event, perhaps. Something the students at the Academy had done for the local community. He remembered a story in the Academy newspaper about some students who had spent last semester in a reading program at the local grammar school. Teaching some third graders to read.

Where was that paper? He knew he kept it. It should be right there on his desk.

Teaching third graders to read. Ah, what was the public school system going to do? When third graders hadn't yet learned how to read? When it was up to his own students at the Academy to remedy the inadequacies of the public education system?

As he finally made his way to the bottom of the appropriate stack and pulled out the Academy newspaper, the phone at the other edge of the desk began to ring.

Ben looked at the clock on the wall. Too early for business, he thought, as he checked the display on the phone to see the caller's number.

It was T. Hunter!

What was he wanting at this hour, Ben thought, as he lunged for the phone before the line rotated over to voice mail?

"Hunter, how nice of you to call me back. I was just going over the budget numbers. I wanted to discuss with you how we were doing on the science center improvement fund," Ben tried to sound as if he had been hard at work at his desk, expecting Hunter's call.

"Ben, I have a small favor to ask of you."

A favor? So Hunter wasn't returning his call?

"Well … of course, Hunter."

What might be on Hunter's mind so early on Monday morning, if not the budget, he thought? A wealthy investment banker friend who wanted his son in the Academy, perhaps? Or was it that French teacher? Something else for that French teacher?

"My son called me last night. He doesn't do that very often, Ben. So when he does, I pay attention."

Marc had called his father! But Marc was fine. There wasn't anything wrong with Marc. Ben and he were on excellent terms. He had seen to that. That Marc was taken care of.

"Well ... well, I hope there wasn't anything of concern," he tried to sound nonchalant. "He's a fine boy, Hunter. A chip off the old block!"

He waited as he listened to Hunter carrying on a conversation in the background about moving some funds into an offshore account. Millions of dollars. Just an ordinary conversation, Ben guessed, for someone like Hunter.

"There's a boy that Marc wants in the summer football program this year."

Ah, football! He should have guessed, given Marc's present preoccupation with the sport. If only the boy would pay as much attention to his academics, Ben thought.

"Well, of course, if one of his friends in New York would like to come to camp with Marc, I'm sure we could make special arrangements," Ben tried to reassure Hunter.

"Yes, exactly," Hunter said. "This is a special situation. Someone we would need to support. Fully."

"I am sure that we can make whatever arrangements are necessary," Ben tried to sound pleasant. "What sort of special situation are we talking about?"

"Listen, Ben, I have to go to a board meeting, now. I'll send you email later in the day. And I'll tell Marc to come by to sort through all of this with you. Does that work for you?"

What would possess Hunter to call asking Ben to admit a special needs student into the summer program, with Hunter in the middle of preparing for a board meeting? Something fairly important, Ben surmised. Something that Ben would have to take personal responsibility for ... just to make sure it was done correctly. To make sure he kept Hunter happy.

"Of course. I see Marc almost every day since the spring session ended and ..."

"Good, knew I could count on you Ben. Now, have to run. Will send the details later. The boy's name is ... let me see, I know I have my notes here somewhere. Yes. The boy's name is Greenwood. Scott Greenwood."

CHAPTER 14

Allie stopped by her house on the way from pizza shop to check her mail. The interior of the box was dark and smelled slightly of last fall's leaves. Magazines, she saw in the dimness. Some sales flyers. A postcard. And two very business-like letters.

She encircled the magazines that cradled the rest of the day's post and pulled the contents of the box out, being careful not to look at the letters. She held the mail tightly in her grasp and walked slowly to the side door of the house. She pulled the key from the clay planter next to the door and unlocked the door. She walked into the kitchen and stood at the edge of the chrome-edged breakfast table, steadying herself on the pink plastic covering of one of the chairs.

She took a deep breath in the silent house and laid the bundled mail on the table, letting the magazines fall open, exposing the two letters.

One was a bill.

The other had the insignia of the New York Repertory Company in the upper left corner.

Marc Hanson had kept his promise. She was going to New York. At last, she was going to New York to dance. Perhaps only for the summer. But that might just be the start. If she did well enough. If she was good enough.

She picked up the letter. It was light in her hands. A single sheet of paper inside. How funny that something of such importance, such gravity, could feel so weightless, she thought.

It was bittersweet. The feeling of the letter. Would Scott understand, if she told him? Would he understand that it meant that much to her? Had she betrayed him?

It had all worked out for the best, she reasoned. He didn't have any place else to go after Macy kicked him out of the house. So it wasn't like she had done anything bad. It wasn't like she had to convince him to do the summer camp with Marc. It's just the way it had worked out.

Like the Repertory Company. And her chance to be part of it. She knew she was good enough. But good enough didn't mean she would have ever been accepted.

And she would have never have asked Marc for his help. For his family's help.

It just happened that way. Her doing something good for Marc. Something good for Scott. Something good for herself. That's just the way life worked, sometimes, she thought. Sometimes you get screwed. And sometimes, just sometimes, you get what you want.

She wasn't sure how she was going to break it to Scott that she was going to New York for the summer. Being away all summer was really the only thing she felt guilty about. Perhaps leading Scott to think that she would be there in town throughout the summer. That they would have the summer together if he did the Academy camp.

They wouldn't have any more time together even if she did stay in town, she reasoned. With Scott working the camp, her job, and her trips into Boston for dance classes. They would still have the same amount of time together if Scott made trips into the City on the weekend to see her.

He should be proud of her, she thought. He knew how much dance meant to her. How much an opportunity in New York could mean for her.

He should be proud of her and happy for her, she reasoned.

New York. Dancing in New York!

It was all she had ever hoped for. All she had every dreamed of.

Scott looked one last time around the small carriage house apartment to make sure he had everything. He didn't want to have to come back here. He didn't want to have to face Macy. And she certainly didn't want to see him. She had made that clear through Allie. He was to be out of the house within ten days. Macy would stay in Boston until then.

So be it, he thought.

It had never really felt like home here, anyway. She had never really made him feel like family. Just an unexpected guest, relegated to the empty room above the garage.

He wasn't sure where he went from here.

Summer at the Academy. Living in the dorms there. Helping with the football camp. His only option on such short notice. His only option if he wanted to stay close to Allie.

Then?

Well, then, after camp, after the summer, that was just too far in the future to comprehend. The thought of going back to high school to sit through classes in subjects he had already mastered on his own, almost infantile against the responsibilities he shouldered now.

College?

Perhaps.

But the only colleges that would accept him, especially this late, wouldn't be places he wanted to attend.

He didn't even look in the rear view mirror as he pulled away from the old Victorian and made the short drive to the Academy.

Best not to look back.

Best to look forward, he thought, entering the Academy through the back entrance.

Best to think about what was in front of him, now, he thought, parking the old Buick in front of Hanover dorm.

Scott noticed Jim walking quickly from the edge of the ancient, vine-covered building, smiling at him. At least Jim could smile, Scott thought. Genuinely smile.

"Great to see you my boy," he said. "Bad circumstances, these. But what an opportunity for you! It's all here," he said, gesturing around the campus. "It's whatever you chose to make of it, my boy. That's what you have to keep in mind. Whatever you make of it."

Jim's attitude was contagious. And Scott couldn't help but feel a little better.

"Let's get you moved in," Jim said, opening the back door of the Buick and pulling out a couple of the nearest boxes. "I've got a great spot picked out for you. Right at the edge of the building overlooking the practice fields and the river. It's the biggest room in the dorm!"

Scott grabbed a couple of more boxes and followed Jim into the building through the side door. Up one flight of stairs to the second floor, then left to the end of the hallway. The other rooms deserted after the close of the spring semester. Their footsteps echoing in the stillness.

"Oh, I know it's a little quiet now," Jim said. "But you just wait until next week. When the other guys start showing up for camp. This old place gets so loud in the summer. Music. And laughter. All hours of the day and night. It's going to be great! You'll see."

Jim opened the door to the room and flipped on the light switch.

"What did I tell you? The best room in the place!"

Scott was impressed. The dorm room was larger than the carriage house. A huge first floor, with a stairway up to a second level where the bed was located.

"It's a triple during the normal school term. But, this summer, you get it all to yourself!"

The windows were open, with Academy curtains fluttered in the breeze. There was a TV at one end of the room, and a huge stereo on one of the desks against the wall.

"I took the liberty of adding a few furnishings," Jim said. "And, I'm not supposed to tell you, but apparently the boys have found a way to hook up the TV through the computer network to get cable access. You'll have to ask young Mr. Hanson about that, though," he laughed.

"Jim, I … I appreciate …" Scott began.

"Nonsense! No reason to thank me, son. Just glad to have you here with us! Part of the team, as it were!"

Part of the team, Scott thought. He didn't really feel like part of anything.

"Now, the cafeteria doesn't really open back up until next week. But I have some keys for you," Jim said, handing him a key-ring full of keys. "You'll have to sort them out yourself. I marked the dorm keys here in yellow," he said, pointing to the small dabs of paint on two keys. "And the blue ones are for the gym. The green ones there are to the bathrooms here in this building—just down the hall, there. And I know there are a couple of keys that get you into the cafeteria building and the refrigerator and freezer. Those are the important ones! The Academy keeps the kitchen stocked full for the instructors staying over between terms. You just fix whatever you want. Whenever you want. Marc even made sure that your favorite root-beer was stocked for the summer. How's that for a friend?"

A free place to stay. Free cable TV. Free food. Free root-beer. At least he had all of the essentials, Scott thought.

"Well, I'll let you get settled in. You let me know if you need anything. I've left numbers on the pad there next to the phone. And I know Marc is around here somewhere. He knows where you're rooming, so I imagine he'll stop by later to check in on you."

His new place, Scott thought, listening to the echoes of the doors closing as Jim left the building.

How odd, he thought.

To be living in a dorm-room, in a school for rich kids. Something he could never have imagined. Never planned.

"That was Marc," Allie called from the doorway of Scott's dorm room down the empty hallway toward the bathrooms. "He says he was going to come pick us up in his car," she yelled.

Scott turned off the shower and ran his index fingers over his eyes to clear them.

"He said what?"

Scott wasn't sure he had heard Allie correctly, with the water running and the echo in the empty hallway.

Allie snatched back the shower curtain, trying to look Scott in the face, but letting her eyes wander.

"That was Marc, *big boy*," she smiled lecherously, handing Scott a towel. "And he said he was going to come pick *us* up," she said, turning back to the mirror behind her to check her eye makeup. "I didn't know he had a car," she offered.

He toweled dry quickly. He had long since lost any shyness around Allie. And she certainly didn't seem to have any inhibitions in the empty dorm, even in using the more convenient boys restroom facilities.

"I didn't know he had a car, either," he offered, working his way down to his feet and then wrapping the towel around his waist. "Are you sure that's what he said?"

Allie spun around, akimbo.

"That's what he said," Allie offered emphatically, a slight pout on her lips. "He said he would be here in five minutes," she said, grabbing for Scott's towel. "So move your ass, mister," she teased, jerking the towel away and running from the bathroom playfully.

He slapped some after-shave on his face, ran the stick deodorant under his arms and rubbed a bit of gel into his still-wet hair before combing it into place.

"I'm sure Marc doesn't have a car," he said as he came out of the bathroom and started toward the dorm room at the end of the hall. "He's never said anything to me about having a car," he said, pulling on the clothes that Allie had laid out for him on the bed.

Allie was sitting cross-legged on the floor, rummaging through one of her bags.

"Well, he seems to think he does," Allie laughed. "And he seems to think that he is giving us a ride to New York."

He finished dressing and watched Allie as she settled into the chair next to the window. That would be great if Marc could give them a ride, he thought. He wasn't sure if the old Buick was up to the trip. And he had promised Allie that he would take her into the City when she moved into the Repertory dorm. That the two of them could spend their last weekend together at Marc's brownstone in the City.

"You're not going to believe this!" Allie shouted from the dorm window. "Come on," she yelled gleefully. "Marc's downstairs!"

He watched Allie vanish down the stairs, her bags swung in tow from her slender shoulders. He picked up his own gym bag and made sure he had his dorm keys and money in his pocket before following her at his own measured pace.

I guess Marc does have a car, he thought, switching out the light at the bottom of the stairs and locking the ancient door of the dorm.

"It's a limo!" Allie shrieked as he walked into the sunlight.

It was quite a limo, he thought. A wicked stretched limo.

"Well, my friends," Marc said, smiling from ear to ear as he leaned back against the polished black lacquer of the limo. "Ready for a real road trip?" he said, gesturing toward the huge length of automobile.

Allie grabbed Marc and hugged him.

"This is great!" she giggled. Then stepping back to admire the limo. "Is this really yours?" she asked.

"It's my father's," Marc admitted. "I asked him if we could use it," he explained.

The front driver's-side door opened and a large man in black coat and bowtie wearing a chauffeur's hat stepped out.

"Manson, can you get the bags?" Marc said in an overly formal voice.

"Certainly Master Marc," the chauffer replied, his voice filled with deference.

Scott watched the large man make his way around the limo, open the trunk and begin to stack Allie's bags inside.

"Well, come on," Marc urged from inside the voluminous interior. "Let's party!" he yelled, holding up a bottle what looked to be Champagne.

Allie was busying herself with the controls of a stereo laid out along the passenger side of the privacy screen, flipping through a huge carousel of CDs.

Scott shook his head and got into the back seat of the limo. The door closed behind him at the insistence of the chauffeur's hand.

"Home, Manson," Marc ceremoniously declared to the chauffer before raising the privacy window.

"Is this great, or what!" Allie squealed, turning up the volume to one of her favorite rap songs and gyrating in rhythm to the music.

CHAPTER 15

"This is it!" announced Marc as the limo turned off of Park Avenue.

"Is that the Art Museum?" Allie asked, craning her neck as the limo turned sharply away from the large stone building. "It is! You actually live across from the Art Museum?"

The limo stopped in front of one of the large brownstones.

"Yes," laughed Marc. Then mockingly, "*I live across from the Art Museum.*"

The rear door adjacent to the curb opened and Manson stood at full attention.

"Master Marc," his voice deep and formal. "I shall bring the bags up directly. Will you be needing the car later?"

Marc pulled himself out of the limo and stood next to the tall man.

"Yes," he replied. "If you could bring the car around at … "he paused. "What time is dinner tonight?"

"Dinner would be at 7, Master Marc," the chauffer intoned.

"Yes, then, well, then," he stumbled over the words, trying for the right pitch. "Yes, then bring the car around at 8:30, Manson."

Scott and Allie stood blankly next to him during the ritual.

"Very good, sir," Manson replied, swinging the door shut and turning away.

"Hey, come on," he chuckled, watching the expression on Scott's and Allie's faces. "Wait 'til you see the place!"

Scott and Allie followed him through the heavy wrought iron gate, up the half flight of granite steps and waited silently again as he hit the buzzer at the side of the door.

The oversized wooden door opened slowly and a small, slight man wearing a blue blazer, crisply starched shirt and tie nodded graciously.

"Master Marc," the man smiled in a gesture of true affection through his British accent. "How nice to have you back for a visit," he bowed and pulled the door wider for the trio on the steps to enter.

"Nice to see you again, Jaffrey," he replied, clapping the small man soundly on the shoulder. "These are my friends, Scott," he said, gesturing in Scott's direction. "And Allie," he said, throwing his arm around Allie's shoulder. "They will be dining with us tonight and staying over," he said with a wink to the small man.

"Very good, Master Marc," Jaffrey replied. "The guest suite is ready, and I think you will find that the cook has prepared something quite extra-ordinary for your return."

"You have a cook and a chauffer *and a butler*?" Allie's voice was filled with awe and resounded against the hard marble walls of the entryway before dying away over the elaborately sculptured circular staircase leading to the upper floors.

Jaffrey smiled affectionately.

Marc chuckled in feigned embarrassment.

"Yes, Allie. And a housekeeper! Want the grand tour?" he asked invitingly, dropping his arm from her shoulder and grabbing a willing hand to drag her along as he moved quickly through the foyer through the double leaded glass doors on their right.

The doors opened into a sunny greeting room. The painted panels on the walls were perfectly coordinated with the diaphanous curtains that hung from gilded rods at the bay window facing the street. A large rug both protected and accented the parquet flooring surrounding it. Antique furniture and post-modern lighting added an eclectic look to the room. And on the wall opposite the entry way hung a large impressionist painting.

"Marc! Welcome home, son," Hunter traversed the room in long strides. "And this must be Scott and Allie?" he asked rhetorically, offering his hand to Scott and a slight bow of acknowledgement to Allie.

"Scott Greenway, Mr. Hanson" Scott offered, grasping Hunter's hand firmly and looking him in the eye.

"Call me Hunter, Scott. Heard a lot about you. Quite a runner, so Marc tells me," Hunter winked at Marc, who had suddenly turned sheepish. "And you, young lady," he continued, facing Allie. "A dancer, as I recall?" he continued, hoping his meager knowledge of the two teenagers would be sufficient to indicate some level of actual interest in them.

"Why, yes," Allie said, tilting her head ever so slightly. "Ballet," she cooed, assuming a somewhat formal mockery of classical form.

"And quite lovely, I might add," Hunter's charming manner with women apparent through his innocent statement. "Marc, too bad Scott has this one tied up," he offered in an effort to both compliment and oh so slightly condescend. "Scott, I caught you looking at the Monet," Hunter quickly changed his focus to his prize possession. "One of his best, I think," he continued, his gaze now fixed on the oversized painting. "Interested in art as well as athletics?" Hunter asked the question in a somewhat undiplomatic way.

"Why, yes," Scott replied unaffectedly. "When I was growing up, my mother had all of these art books that she kept out for us," he offered the simple explanation. "I always loved the Impressionists," he paused, "because they were the ones my mother especially liked, I guess."

"Father, Scott doesn't want to look at paintings," Marc protested, real embarrassment creeping into his expression. "Want to see the guest suite?" he interjected enthusiastically, shifting the attention away from the ancient paintings.

"Yes, yes," Hunter affirmed. "By all means. Explore the surroundings a bit and freshen up. Dinner is at seven," he trailed off, absorbed in the paintings now.

Marc escorted Scott and Allie out of the room and continued the tour. The ballroom, with its mirrored walls and crystal chandelier. The dining room, china hutch displaying dozens of matched sets and crystal glasses. A brief gesture to the kitchen area and other less frequented rooms on the first floor. Then up the huge spiral staircase to the second floor bedrooms, each with its own bath the size of Scott's dorm-room, each tastefully decorated. Then up another floor to the guest suites, arranged in quadrangle around the three-story atrium above the foyer. Each of the four unique in color and furnishings.

"And this is your room," he finally escorted Scott and Allie into the largest of the third floor suites.

The sight of Scott and Allie's bags on the floor in the room added a bohemian touch to the meticulous detail of the decorator. Allie moved toward the curtained window and pulled back the sheers.

"This is incredible," Allie said shaking her head. She wandered into the adjoining bath.

"So, it's okay if we are ... together?" Scott asked the question somewhat obtusely, nodding in Allie's direction. "I mean, for the weekend?"

Marc threw back his head and laughed. Allie stuck her head out of the bathroom suite and turned her reddened face back in the direction of the boys.

"Scott!" she tried to sound surprised and exasperated at the question.

"No one gives a damn who you sleep with in this house," Marc's voice was still filled with laughter. "Better to bunk you two together than for us to hear doors opening and closing all night," he teased. "Now, get cleaned up and dressed," his expression turning more serious. "Dinner is in half an hour and the old man gets really cranky if you're late," he said, backing out of the room. "If you make it through dinner, then we can go out. I'll call a couple of friends and see what's happening tonight," he offered, slipping out of the room and closing the door behind him.

"Marc's parents must be loaded," Scott offered. "Can you imagine having a real Renoir or Monet in your house?" he asked rhetorically, the paintings still vivid in his mind.

"Wonder what his Mother is like?" Allie offered, slipping away from Scott and throwing her bag onto the elevated bed. "His Dad seems nice enough," she said, pulling her clothes from the bag. "Maybe a bit formal, but nice."

Scott followed Allie's lead and began sorting through his bag.

"So, I guess if you 'dress for dinner', that means I have to wear a tie?" he smiled as he laid his clothes out next to Allie's on the bed. "And you have to wear a dress!" the thought of seeing Allie in a dress was sufficient compensation for his own requirement of formal attire.

"Oh, like you never see me in a dress," Allie punched him in the ribs with her finger at the words.

Scott grabbed at her arm before she could fully withdraw it.

"Like I never get to see enough of you, period," Scott said affectionately.

Allie pulled away from him, throwing her head to the side.

"Down boy!" she commanded playfully, backing away from him. "We have to get dressed!" then her voice softer and teasing, "There will be plenty of time later tonight," she offered. "All night," she teased over her shoulder as she made her way into the bathroom.

"You're not going to believe this," Allie called, sticking her head back into the bedroom. She held a striking blue bottle in her hand. "Can you believe the family even has its own cologne? I saw it sitting out on the counter. It's in a huge blue crystal bottle and it has a family crest or something embossed in silver with an 'H' on the bottle."

Allie ducked back into the bathroom and Scott heard the faucet begin to run behind the closed door—a ritual that Allie insisted upon when attending to her biological necessities.

Dressing for dinner might be nice, Scott thought, turning back to his clothes on the bed. Somehow, it seemed the appropriate thing to do in this house. He couldn't remember the last time he had worn a tie.

Then it hit him.

The last time.

The last time he had worn a tie.

It had been at his father's funeral.

It seemed so long ago, now.

So far removed from where he stood, in this rich man's home, with his dancer girlfriend, in the city that considered itself the center of the universe.

※   ※   ※

"This is my mother, Anna," Marc began, gesturing to the tall, extremely thin woman wearing a long string of pearls over a perfectly black evening dress. "Mother, this is Scott and this is Allie," his voice a bit hollow in the large dining room.

"You two make a charming couple," the woman said, air-kissing on either side of Allie's face. "Marc has told me all about you," she continued. "But I want to hear first hand," she continued. "Now let's see," her voice changing slightly. "Allie you sit here," she directed Allie physically to one of the mahogany chairs. "And Scott across from Allie, there," she said, pointing him across the table to his place setting. "And Marc, you there next to Allie."

Marc noticed the sixth place setting at the table.

"Are we expecting someone else, Mother?" he asked.

"Why yes, of course," his mother's voice filled with pretentiousness. "How else could we have girl-boy-girl-boy?"

"OK," he tried to rephrase his question. "Who else is coming to dinner, Mother?"

"I asked Vanessa, of course, Marc," Anna sounded disdainful. "Oh, Allie, you will just love Vanessa," she gushed. "She and Marc have been together since they were just babies," she smiled maternally at Marc. "Her parents own that hotel chain," she said.

"Oversted's," Marc whispered to Allie. "They own the Oversted chain," he said, rolling his eyes. "You'll like her," he said winking at Scott. "She's a model for one of the French design houses," he said proudly. "We have been like best friends forever," he continued.

The doorbell rang and there were footsteps in the hallway. Hunter's loud voice echoed through the foyer.

"Vanessa!" came his father's overly loud voice from the foyer. "How nice to see you, again!"

There was a clapping sound on the marble floor, heralding their approach.

"Marc," Hunter looked around the dining room from the doorway. "Look who is here. Vanessa!" he said delightedly, as if to surprise his son.

Vanessa, all grown up, Marc thought. Thinner than the last time he saw her and now incredibly blonde, an abundance of absolutely perfect, peach-colored skin showing beneath a small black dress that looked like it had been spray-painted on her body.

"Vanessa," Hunter continued. "These are Marc's friends, Allie and Scott," he said ushering Vanessa into the room.

Vanessa gave a somewhat hesitant smile in the direction of both Allie and Scott. "Marc," her high-pitched voice a sharp contrast to her imposing physical appearance. "I haven't seen you in a while, you bad boy," she mocked him as she leaned forward to kiss him ever so slightly on the lips. "And you haven't called me once," she scolded him in front of the group.

"I … I've been busy, Vanessa," his voice wasn't at all apologetic.

"So, you're the one who has taken my Marc away from me," Vanessa teased formally looking in Scott's direction with a slight wink.

Allie moved closer to Scott and placed her hand on his forearm.

"All right everyone," Anna interrupted. "Everyone to the table. It's almost seven," she encouraged. "Vanessa, you sit there next to Scott," she said, in the process achieving the perfect alternation of sexes at the table.

"Yes, yes," Hunter said loudly. "Dinner at seven. On the dot," he said with the mastery of a drill commander as he took his seat at the head of the long table.

As Marc squeezed in between Allie and Vanessa, Hunter picked up a small crystal bell from the table and rang it quickly. The back door to the room immediately opened and Jaffrey appeared carrying a large soup tureen.

"Does your family always eat like that?" Allie asked over the noise of the evening traffic on the street. "I mean, everyone dressing up and with the butler and everything?"

Scott wanted to ask the question, but didn't. So he was glad Allie had poised it to Marc.

Marc stopped for the light at the street corner, Vanessa close at his side, holding his arm.

"It's like a ritual," he admitted, shaking his head. "I think it's because that is the only time the three of us are ever really together," he suggested. "Guess I just got accustomed to it, but it probably seems a bit funny to you."

"Oh, I liked it," Scott offered sincerely.

Vanessa giggled in high pitch. "Oh, I just loooove your accent," she smiled in Scott's direction. "It's so … cute."

"Vanessa," Marc pulled her closer. "Give it a rest, will you?"

"It's okay. We all talk funny in our own way," he retorted, the obvious reference to Vanessa's nasal, squeaky voice. "So, where are we going, exactly?" Scott asked as he and Allie continued to follow Marc and Vanessa's lead through the intersection and on to the next crowded block.

"It's a place called Boomers", Marc said loudly enough to be heard over his shoulder above the dim of the city noise. "It used to be a big arcade and then they renovated it into this really trendy bar," he continued, steering the group to the east side. "There are some people I know that usually hang out there on Saturday night."

The two couples jostled their way through two more crowded intersections before coming upon a commercial section. In the middle of the block a huge neon sign flashed "Boomers" above loud hip-hop music. There was a large crowd of people sandwiched between the street and a section in front of Boomers that was cordoned off by lengths of maroon velvet rope strategically anchored to a series of brass supports.

"Are we going to be able to get in?" Allie asked as she scanned the crowd.

"No problem," Marc smiled back over his shoulder. "Just follow me," he motioned Allie and Scott forward with a head gesture. He raised his hand above his head, waving a hundred dollar bill at the two security guards closest to them. The effect was instantaneous. The velvet rope in front of them disappeared and the guards eagerly began clearing away the crowd so that they could pass.

The music was even louder in the confined space inside of Boomers. Speakers seemed to be suspended everywhere, punctuated by the ringing of bells and digital tones of myriad video games that lined the walls and cluttered the center of the club.

"Let's check out who's here," Marc urged, leading them further into the cacophony.

"Did you see that?" Allie whispered in Scott's ear. "Marc gave those guys a hundred dollars! Just to get in!"

"Shhhh!" Scott warned. "He's just trying to show us a good time, Allie," he cautioned. "A hundred dollars is nothing to him," he said, thinking about how many trunks he had had to move at the Academy, how many pizza's he had to deliver to make that much money. "Don't make him feel bad about it."

"I'm not," Allie assured, "It's kind of nice, actually," she smiled.

"Hey, you guys," Marc shouted back at Allie and Scott. "I see some kids I know. Come on and I'll introduce you."

Marc maneuvered the group through the crowded hall toward an open sitting area where the music and crowd-noise weren't as loud. There were four young, perfectly dressed and accessorized people sitting at a large table with drinks and nachos. They all stood up as Marc neared the table.

"Marc, my man," one called out, grabbing Marc's hand and patting him soundly on the shoulder.

"Marc, Darling!" one of the girls called.

"Hey Vanessa!" the other girl chimed in.

"Guys," Marc pulled Scott by the arm closer to the table. "I want you to meet Scott Greenway. He's the guy from Texas I told you about. And this is his girlfriend, Allie. She's a dancer—she's going to be with the Repertory Company here this summer," he recited appropriate pedigrees to the group. Then, reciprocating the introductions around the table. "This is Will Sanford. He goes to Phillips and makes movies," he said, gesturing to a sandy haired boy with wire-rimmed glasses. "And this is Naveed," he said, grabbing the fragile looking short boy by the shoulder. "He got a perfect SAT score and won a Westinghouse this year. He's wicked smart," he said, with admiration. "And this is Vicky," he gestured to the dark haired girl. "She's an equestrian," he continued. "And not all of her surgeries have been for injuries," he joked, his obvious reference to the augmentation that was barely contained within the girl's small knit top. "And this is Wendy," he finished, lightly touching the very thin blonde with the wine glass. "She knows everyone whose anyone in New York," he finished the introductions.

There were handshakes and hugs around the table with each introduction.

"You're a dancer?" Will immediately pulled Allie into conversation. "I'm making a movie that has a dream sequence with a dancer in it."

"I hear you are quite the jock," Wendy purred into Scott's ear. "Marc never stops talking about you, you know. Always 'Scott this and Scott that'," she took advantage of Will's preoccupation with Allie to pull Scott down onto the seat beside her. "And I hear you have the cutest accent," she bobbed her head slightly in his direction. "Say something for me! Please?!?" she pleaded earnestly.

Scott noticed how close Wendy's body was to him, her bare knee touching his. Her fragrance in his breathe.

"*Comment allez-vous*, Wendy?" Scott teased in perfect metropolitan French.

Wendy was completely taken aback by Scott's French.

"*Bien!*" she replied delightedly in an equally appropriate accent. "*Tres bien!*" she giggled. "I meant say something in Texan, you silly goose," she chided him in English, leaning her whole body into his.

"So, you're going to be here this summer?" Will's questioning distracting Allie from the conversation between Wendy and Scott. "What kind of dancer are you? Ballet, obviously, if you are going to be with the Repertory Company," Will answered his own question. "Listen, I really need someone to do ballet for my movie," he continued to monopolize Allie's attention. "Not just anyone, because you see the dream sequence has a dissolve into another scene and the dancer needs to be almost a body double of the female lead," he was explaining in a detail that lacked the context appropriate to provide any real meaning. "But, you," Will eyed Allie from head to toe. "You could double for the female lead," he nodded his head in approval. "Right height, right shape," he continued. "Might have to cut your hair a bit," he said thoughtfully. "OK. So, you want to be in my movie or not?" he jumped ahead in the conversation. "Two days at guild rates," he offered. "No, I'll give you a credit and added comp," he said. "Maybe three days," he said. Then finally acknowledging Allie's perplexed expression. "That's a thousand dollars a day for three days work and you get a movie credit," he explained.

"Sure," Allie said. She wanted to be polite to Marc's friends. They all seemed so intense.

"Will, stop already with the fucking movie," Vicky interrupted. "God, that's all he talks about. He is so obsessive," she shook her head disapprovingly.

"Allie, that's really great you are going to be here this summer. I'm going to be in the city as well," her voice was inviting and sincere. "I know a couple of girls from school who are going to the summer program. Heather Larkin and Rosalyn Carter. It'll be hard work," she offered. "But you'll have a great time. We can hang out together, if you want," she offered demurely.

"Sure," Allie assented, finally catching Wendy's closeness to Scott out of the corner of her eye.

"So what are you guys drinking?" Naveed yelled out over the table.

Allie and Scott looked at each other.

"Two martinis for the girls and a couple of import beers for us," Marc broke in.

"Allie," Wendy caught Allie's glance in her direction as she pulled back away from Scott's side. "How long have you and Scott been together?"

The question gave Allie a chance to slide around the table to sit next to Scott, opposite to Wendy.

"A long time," Allie said, throwing her arm around Scott's shoulder in uncharacteristic fashion. "A wicked long time," she assured Wendy.

"You make such a cute couple," Wendy offered in final retreat from Scott's side.

"You're drunk, Wendy," Vicky interjected. "She's drunk," she offered apologetically to Allie. "And a bit of a bitch, I'm afraid," she laughed, falling into Wendy playfully.

"I am," Wendy agreed, very pleased with the characterization. "I am a bitch!" she said proudly, winking at Allie.

"I'll drink to that!" Naveed yelled. "To Wendy. The bitch!" he said, raising his glass just as the martinis and beer arrived at the table.

"To the bitch!" Will echoed, raising his glass.

"To the bitch!" the table of young people retorted in chorus, the first of many toasts of equally off-color nature for the night.

"Allie, will you be here June 28–30?" Will interrupted the group as he paged through his day-timer at his shooting schedule. "Because that's when we scheduled the shoot on the dance sequence."

"Shit, Will!" Marc shouted. "Will you knock it off with the movie!"

❦   ❦   ❦

"You have a very … colorful group of friends, Marc," said Allie. "Was Will serious about making a movie? About me being in a movie?" she asked, daggling one of her long legs over the arm of the chair in the den.

"Yeah," Scott continued the questioning. "Is that guy for real or just some kind of pervert who wants to take pictures of young, innocent girls?" he asked luridly stretching his arms over his head and yawning.

"Oh, he's for real," Marc slid down further into the overstuffed couch. "Haven't you guys heard of Max Sanford? I mean he's only won two Oscars and god knows how many other awards."

"Max Sanford?" Allie's voice was unusually high-pitched. "Max Sanford is Will's father?" she asked incredulously.

"Runs in the family," Marc offered. "Will grew up watching his father make movies. So I guess it was just natural that he would make them himself. He has this whole move set that he uses in an old off-Broadway theater. Kind of sad, really," Marc explained. "His father is agoraphobic. He had to give up acting. Now Will can't even get his old man out of the house. So, Will fixed up part of the old theater as a soundstage and that's where he shoots his videos. That way, his father can watch from the apartment without having to go outside."

"How does that happen?" Allie asked. Her eyes were getting very heavy. "He was such a famous actor. How do you go from performing in front of hundreds of people to being afraid to go outside?"

"I don't know the whole story," Marc tried to condense what he knew into succinct terms. "He was on a sound stage one day and had kind of a panic attack and started busting things up and that was the last time he was in public," he offered. "That was two years ago. When Will moved him to the new place, they had to sedate the old guy and transport him by ambulance. Really sad," Marc said. "And kind of creepy."

"And what's with Vicky?" Allie left the question open-ended.

Marc chuckled.

"I think Vicky likes you," he teased. "She likes girls, you know," he said, trying to embarrass Allie. Then abruptly changing the subject. "You guys want some ice cream?" he asked. "I really want some ice cream. You guys want some?"

Allie pulled herself out of the chair and walked to the window.

"Sure," Allie laughed. "How far is the ice cream shop?"

Marc picked up the receiver to the phone and pushed a bottom.

"Jaffrey," he said into the receiver. "I think we would like some ice cream. In the den," he said. Then he put down the phone. "Not far," he laughed.

"Oh, Marc," Allie said, falling into a lump on the floor next to Scott. "And you certainly had fun with Wendy tonight," she chided Scott playfully.

"I was just being nice," Scott's voice was defensive.

"Don't worry Allie," Marc assured her. "Wendy is like that all of the time. With everyone."

"Gee thanks," Scott retorted. "And I thought I was 'special.'"

"Oh, baby," Allie rubbed her body against Scott. "You are 'special.'"

"Get a room, you two," Marc shouted in mock disgust.

Jaffrey appeared in the doorway carrying a large silver tray with a half-dozen cartoons of Haagen-Dazs ice cream in assorted flavors.

"Your ice cream, Master Marc," he said formally, pacing across the room to a small coffee table. "Shall I serve?" he inquired.

"No, thank you Jaffrey," Marc's voice equally as formal. "We'll serve."

"Will you be needing anything else this evening, Master Marc?"

"No, Jaffrey. That will be all for tonight," he said. "Good night."

Jaffrey paced out of the room leaving the trio alone.

"Your ice cream," Marc offered, gesturing to the tray.

"This is sooo cool!" Allie jumped from the floor. She picked up a large ice-cream dipper from the tray and retrieved one of three silver bowls. "It's cold!" she giggled as her fingers touched the chilled metal bowl.

"But of course," Marc smiled. "Wouldn't want to melt the ice cream from the warmth of the bowl, would you?"

CHAPTER 16

It didn't feel like the second week of June to Scott. The mornings were still cool enough to warrant an Academy comforter on his bed. And even at mid-day, the sun could barely raise the temperature into the 80's. In Texas, he remembered, the humidity and heat would already be taking their toll. But not here. Not in Massachusetts.

That was one thing he really liked. The cool weather. It made his morning runs with Marc even more pleasant. And it made the work he did at the Academy with Jim in preparation for the summer football camps seem too fun to be called work.

He liked Jim, Scott thought to himself. He liked working with him. Talking to him.

Scott made his way to the vacant cafeteria, pulled some toaster waffles from the giant stainless steel fridge and popped open a bottle of root-beer. He checked his watch. 7:45. Still plenty of time to punch the clock by 8:00, he thought.

The Academy had been devoid of students these last two weeks. After move-out, only the resident teachers remained. And the omnipresent Phillips, of course.

Scott tried to be nice to the man. Every time he was with Marc, it seemed Phillips displayed a more human side to his metallic demeanor. When Scott was by himself, however, Phillips seemed to relegate Scott to the position of scenery. Even if Scott spoke, his greetings seemed to fall on deaf ears. He knew Phillips heard him. It had become somewhat of a game Scott played. His own loud greeting whenever they met, returned with stony silence and disdain by the small man.

Scott thought about Allie as he made his way out of the dining hall, around the corner of Massey and walked down the steep incline to the back of the gymnasium. He was already missing her. Two weeks had been a long time without her. But she seemed happy enough in New York when they talked. Always excited about something she had done or someone famous she had seen.

"Scott, my boy," Jim's smiling face and warm greeting broke Scott's reflections. "Well, today's the day!" he said excitedly, slapping Scott on the shoulder as he came along side him. "Check-in day," he said, brandishing a clipboard cluttered with lists. "Looks like a good crew this first term," he continued, offering the clipboard to Scott. "This guy," he continued, running his finger down the list to an Andrew Synesi. "He's from Roxbury. A really tough kid. And fast, too," he commented. "Well, not as fast as you," he laughed. "But fast for his size."

Scott scanned across the page. Andrew Synesi, 6'2", 240 lbs., 4.8 second 40 year dash, bench presses 260 pounds, middle linebacker, all league as a junior. Pretty big kid, Scott thought.

"And this guy," Jim ran his finger down the page. "This Lindsey Quinlan," he continued. "That kid is a maniac. I saw him play at Phillips. First play of the game he broke one for 70 yards!"

Lindsey Quinlan, 6'1", 210, 4.7 second 40, bench 230 pounds, running back, junior. Good stats even by Texas standards. And really impressive for the prep school community, Scott reasoned.

"You need to take that Lindsey kid under your wing," Jim's voice sounded serious. "He's a smart guy. Straight A's with four honors classes last year. But he has … a discipline problem," Jim searched for the right words. "He has a tendency to lose his head. Gave one of his own team members a concussion in the locker room after the league championship last year," he said, shaking his head and opening the locker room door with his large set of keys. "Hell, played three quarters last year with a broken finger," he chuckled. "Didn't want to tell anyone because he was afraid they would take him out of the game. Nasty break, too. Nasty!"

Jim fumbled with the light switch in the darkened hallway.

"Here's the way I see it," Jim continued, leading the way down the hallway and through the wire-mesh doorway leading into the cage, the bowels of the athletic department where uniforms were laundered and records maintained. "You check the guys in when they come off the bus and give them their room assignments. Marc can give them the tour of the campus and you can help me set up the field. You know, post the assignments and schedules, set out the water, stack the t-shirts and practice jerseys. We'll do the orientation in the stands, divide up into sections and then you can help me with equipment checkout," he sounded enthusiastic. "You can take off after the practice today for the first SAT review session and I"ll finish up on any equipment stragglers," he said, taking the clipboard back from Scott. "These are the guys I want you to take care of," he said, taking his red pencil and putting checks next to a dozen names on the list. "They're the ones with real potential," he nodded in self-agreement. "Oh, I signed you up to be proctor in Hanover. You, know, to keep the guys focused, enforce lights out, things like that. I think the boys would really respond to you," he said confidently. "And you would get to know the guys better, learn their schedules."

Scott wasn't sure what 'proctor' was, but it sounded official.

"Sure," he offered. "Why not?"

"Fine. Get things squared away back at the dorm, then meet me back at the Circle in front of chapel by 9:30."

❦   ❦   ❦

"Mr. Greenwood!" Phillips's shouted as loudly as he could when he saw the boy running across the campus toward Hanover.

He hated the fact that the Greenwood boy was there, at the Academy. Even for summer session.

But he knew how to deal with boys like Greenwood. Boys that used their connections to reach far beyond their station in life. He had learned how to deal with them.

He stopped, forcing the boy to make the run across the Circle. To come to him. And when the boy was there, standing in front of him, he forced him to wait again.

"I understand that you will be joining us for the summer as an *employee*," he said, trying to make the word employee as disdainful as possible. "Well, quite a change of circumstances for you, I am sure. Being here this summer. With the *students*," he said, once again trying to draw the distinction between being a student at the Academy and merely hired help.

"Yes. I am going to be staying here. At Hanover. As proctor. For the summer session," the boy offered, trying to catch his breath.

Some runner, Ben thought. Winded after such a short sprint. He would have expected more.

"Well, if you have a minute, I have some forms for you. Personnel forms. Just follow me," he ordered.

Yes, he knew how to handle such boys, he thought. How to keep them in their place. He directed the boy through the entrance to his study and motioned for him to sit in one of the small chairs in front of his carved wood table.

He had always liked that table. It had been a gift from the class of '99. A class project of sorts from the mandatory woodworking class. Something the class had made especially for him. A little odd in dimensions, surely. The legs slightly too short, such that he was continuously banging his knees against the desk's well. And slightly angled, such that ovoid objects tended to roll across the desk if not secured. But he had been gracious in accepting the present from that class in particular. It had been such a rowdy class. And it had needed all of the discipline that he had measured out to them.

The boy sat silently in front of him. Dripping small drops of sweat onto his carpet.

"You will have to fill these out," he said, pushing the W-4's, I-9's and other employment forms toward the boy. "Bring them back this evening, with two forms of identification."

If he had two forms of identification, he thought. Orphans were like that. Never having the right credentials, he thought.

There was a long silence.

"So is that it?" the boy asked.

Ben let him sit there a few seconds longer. Waiting. Enjoying the unpleasantness the boy seemed to feel in the ornate surroundings.

"Just one more thing," he said, turning to his credenza and pulling out a parcel wrapped in cheap brown paper. "Something from the Academy for you this summer," he smiled, handing the parcel to the boy.

The boy took the package, ripped open the paper, and sat looking at the stack of starched green work-shirts.

"I took the liberty of making sure that you had something appropriate to wear this summer while you were helping us out," he said, watching the boy's face.

The boy separated the shirts and held one up in front of him. There was a label neatly sewn to the breast pocket of each shirt. The name "Greenwood" in block letters.

"We prefer for our staff to dress similarly and to make sure the student and faculty have no difficulty with the staff names," he said.

That's right, my boy, he thought. You might be able to fool young Hanson. Perhaps even to fool old Hunter, himself.

But I am no fool. I know you for who you are. And for who you will always be.

An hourly wage earner, destined to wear your name on your work-shirt for the rest of your life.

"That's all," he said, waiving off the boy as he turned to Academy matters. Important Academy matters.

CHAPTER 17

Scott hated Phillips. And he was fairly sure that the feeling had to be mutual. So, it was a surprise when Phillips had given him the work-shirts. Scott kept trying to figure out why the man had been nice enough to give him the new, laundered shirts, after being so nasty since the day they had met.

Maybe Phillips didn't have a choice. Maybe the Academy was required to give all employees their uniforms.

Didn't matter, he thought, as he buttoned the freshly laundered shirt over the ragged "Alien Abduction" t-shirt he had bought when he visited Roswell. He wanted to make a good impression when the players arrived. Good thing Phillips had caught him before the buses arrived, he thought. Although, it did seem dorky to have his last name on the shirt. His first name would have been much better, he thought as he raced down the stairs to find Jim and Marc waiting in the shade of the large oak at the corner of the dorm.

They both started laughing at him. Uncontrollable laughter.

"What's so funny?" he asked.

No answer. Just laughter. Side-splitting laughter.

"Really? What's so funny?"

"Where the hell did you get that shirt, son?" Jim finally managed.

"My work shirt?" he said, as he pulled at the crisp, overly-starched surface of the shirt.

"God, Scott. What's up with that shirt?" Marc said, holding his side.

Both Jim and Marc were still smiling. Enjoying their laugh.

"Phillips. Phillips just gave it to me. Said it's what I was supposed to wear. Said its what all employees wore," he said, suddenly realizing that neither Jim nor Marc were dressed the same way.

"Phillips!" Jim was barely able to utter the name before breaking into laugher again.

"It's a joke, Scott," Marc offered. "A really, really bad practical joke that Phillips was playing. On you, I'm afraid."

Scott wasn't really sure what the joke was. Perhaps the shirt was just for when he moved boxes around campus. Maybe he should have saved it and just worn a t-shirt and some shorts, like Jim and Marc, when he helped with the camp. Well, shit, he thought. How stupid could he be. Of course, it made sense to wear athletic gear when he was working with the camp. He was supposed to save the shirts for other work around campus. He should have known that.

"Oh, I get it," he said. "I'm only supposed to wear the shirt when I'm not working with the football camp," he said, trying to join in the joke. "I get it," he said, trying to muster a laugh.

"Well, not exactly, son," Jim offered, his smile as genuine as ever.

"No one wears those shirts except the groundskeepers, Scott," Marc said. "Phillips was trying to make a point with you. A very sad, very cruel point. That you don't belong here at the Academy. That you are just a laborer. He's an asshole, Scott. Just get used to it."

Scott could feel the anger begin to rise within his body. It was there, just below the surface, and he tried hard to keep it inside. He tried so hard to keep it from showing.

"Oh," he said. "Yeah … I get it," he said, unbuttoning the shirt. "He was just being an asshole to me."

He struggled trying to get the shirt off as quickly as he could, before anyone else saw him in it. Before it became the joke that Phillips had intended.

"Yeah," Jim smiled. "He's a real professional at that, I'm afraid. Best just to get accustomed to it," he said, shaking his head. "So, let's get on to real business," he said.

Scott threw the shirt on the ground against the oak tree, making sure the name on the shirt wasn't visible.

"Here's your list," Jim offered him another clipboard filled with names and room assignments in Hanover. "Just sort through the boys and try to get everyone settled in by 12. Let's keep to the schedule, if at all possible," he said as the first chartered bus made its way around the Academy's central drive and pulled to a stop in front of them. "And Scott, ignore Phillips. Just listen to me and Marc. We'll take care of you," he offered.

The doors to the busses hissed opened and a column of boys emerged.

"Hello, welcome to the Academy," Jim began the ritual greetings. "Hello, welcome to the Academy," he progressed to the second boy. "Hello," he said offering a hand to a third.

The ritual ended in a mass of oversized boys and over-stuffed baggage at the side of the road.

"All right! Quiet! Quiet!" Jim shouted over the din of the young voices. He retrieved his coach's whistle and blew a short blast. The sound brought the desired silence to the assemblage.

"Boys, welcome to the Academy and the 22nd annual summer enrichment program," he began. "We're going to be practicing hard for the next couple of weeks, and you're going to get the opportunity to go through some rigorous drills. We will divide up into two teams, both with offensive and defensive squads. Marc Hanson, a senior here at the Academy and our captain and quarterback next year will be proctoring in Smith dorm. That's where we're going to put the Green Team," he said gesturing in Marc's direction. "And Scott Greenway," he said, pulling Scott forward by the shoulder, "will be proctoring Hanover dorm. That's where the Red Team will be staying. Now Marc and Scott have a list of room assignments, so check with them and they will get you all moved in. We'd like to get everyone settled in by 12, so we don't have much time," Jim continued. "We will be having an early dinner tonight in the dining hall," he said, pointing in the direction of the service building. "And your first SAT study session will be from 7–8:30."

The mention of the SAT study session initiated a groan from the group.

"All right, all right," Jim laughed. "Now I know you guys are interested in football," he said, turning serious. "But, football is only part of the story. When the college coaches come rolling in here to watch our scrimmages and make out a recruiting list, you can bet that they are going to be just as interested in your SAT score as your forty-yard time or your bench press. So, I want you to apply just as much discipline, just as much effort, to the SAT study sessions as you do in practice," he said. Then, in mock threat, "And if I catch any of you boys slacking off in class, you can bet that there will be extra laps in store for you."

There was another groan from the group of boys.

"Now, let's get this place policed and get out on the field!" he shouted as he turned away from the group to make a graceful exit toward the field house.

"John Webb!" Marc quickly shouted the first name on his list as if on cue.

"Here!" a burly black boy raised his hand, picked up his gear and sauntered over to stand next to Marc.

"Room 103," Marc said, handing the boy a room key.

"Joshua McGuiness!" Scott followed Marc's lead, reading from his clipboard. "Room 240," he said, offering the room key to the Irish kid who answered.

The group parted into two sections under the direction of interlaced exhortations from Mark and Scott. When no more names were left on the lists, the Green team began its trek to Smith, the Red Team to Hanover.

❦   ❦   ❦

"So, how is Allie doing?" Marc asked.

Scott preferred silence on his jogs, but had become accustomed to Marc's incessant chatter during their regular morning runs.

"Fine, I guess," he offered. "I tried to call her yesterday and but they only have one phone in their dorm. And they have a rule against having cellphones at the Repertory. I must have called half a dozen times and when I finally got through, all I could do was leave a message for her."

"Girls!" Marc scoffed. "They're always on the phone talking. Guess there must be a couple of dozen girls in Allie's class. Better get used to leaving messages. Is she coming up this weekend?"

"Well, I thought I might go down to see her," Scott explained. "It just seems easier for me to drive down than for her to take the bus up here."

Scott noticed the expression on Marc's face change abruptly.

"You can't go down there this weekend," Marc sounded surprised at the suggestion. "This is a 'closed weekend' at the camp," he said.

"'Closed weekend'?"

"Yeah. The first weekend at every camp is closed," he explained as they turned right into the center of town. "Jim wants to make sure that everyone keeps focused on studying for the SAT and on the drill schedule, so the first couple of weeks no one is allowed to leave and there are no visitors from outside."

The news came as a complete shock to Scott. Jim hadn't said anything to him anything about 'closed weekends' and Scott had just assumed he would have his weekends to himself like he always did.

"So, I have to stay at the Academy over the weekend?" he asked sheepishly.

"Oh, yeah. You can't leave. You're a proctor. And besides, we have a full weekend of practices. And a surprise fieldtrip!" Marc tried to make it sound like an adventure. "And," he said cautiously, "you and I have to keep to our training schedule. Right?"

"Oh, sure," he reassured Marc.

He owed a lot to Marc, he thought, and he didn't want to disappoint him. Or Jim.

They ran in silence for a few minutes.

"So, what is this 'field trip' you were mentioning?" he asked, resolved that he didn't have a choice but to be away from Allie for the weekend.

Marc laughed.

"OK. I'll tell you," Marc chuckled. "But you can't tell anyone!"

"Sure. Just between us. Just between proctors!"

"Jim's nephew owns the franchise for the state's women's professional football team," Marc's delight was obvious, even over his labored breathing. "So, Jim got us all tickets to see Saturday afternoon's game in Boston! Can you believe it? Full contact, hard ass, professional football," Marc continued. "Only women!"

Scott couldn't help but smile.

"You've got to be kidding," he said. He couldn't imagine it.

"No shit!" Marc's voice was a mixture of enthusiasm and delight. "And we get to go into the locker room to talk to them after the game! Can you imagine what type of women play professional football?"

OK, Scott thought. So he wouldn't see Allie this weekend. That couldn't be helped. But, the field trip might be fun. Women … playing football. Two of his favorite things!

"Must be some big girls," he tried to downplay his enthusiasm.

The boys had passed the pizza parlor and were ready to turn onto the road that led back to the Academy.

"Yeah. I checked out their web site. Some of those girls are a little scary," Marc offered. "But, the quarterback and a couple of the receivers are pretty good looking women. Guess good looks just go with the skill positions," Marc joked, referencing the two boys' own positions on the team.

"Can't say much about quarterbacks. All of them look alike," he joked back with Marc as they neared the entrance to the Academy. "But receivers, well they are definitely good looking!"

Scott changed from his running shirt into his practice jersey and headed out of the dorm toward the football field. He herded the stragglers from Hanover in front of him.

"Quinlan, you are the slowest running back I have ever seen," he taunted the large boy lumbering down the sidewalk.

"Hey, Scotty," Lindsey smiled. "Saw you out running this morning with the 'golden boy,'" Lindsey's reference to Marc an obvious insult. "So, you guys friends or what?"

"Yeah," he said as he came alongside Lindsey. "Marc is the reason I'm here at the camp. He was the first guy I met when I came here," he offered in Marc's defense. "He's really a good guy if you just get to know him."

"I know him," Lindsey shot back. "We went to the same day school in New York. He was a little weasel back then," Lindsey's comment was filled with contempt. "Always getting in trouble and his dad was always bailing him out. Have you met his father? Hunter? Did you know Hunter has the league record for most passing yards and most total offence in a single season? And that was from almost twenty years ago," Lindsey added shaking his head. "Hunter must have been something. But Marc," Lindsey huffed. "Just doesn't live up to the old man."

In the last twelve hours Scott had learned three things about Lindsey Quinlan. First, that he had no sense of tact. Second, from news reports on the internet that Lindsey was probably the best player at camp. And, three, that Lindsey had developed an affinity for him for some reason.

"Really, Marc's an okay guy," Scott offered in Marc's defense. "Just give him a chance. You wouldn't believe how hard he trains."

"You guys going to make it to practice or what?" Andrew Synesi shouted as he came running past them. "You white boys are all alike," he offered running as fast as he could toward the field. "S-L-O-W!"

"That guy is good!" Lindsay said after Andrew was out of earshot. "Our team played Roxbury in a scrimmage first of last year. Andrew was nasty! One of the strongest kids I came up against all season."

"His stat sheet puts him at 240, but he must have put on at least another twenty pounds."

"Steroids," Lindsey explained. "He started taking steroids spring break. His bench went from 210 to 260 in a month."

"That doesn't mean he's taking steroids," Scott didn't like Lindsey's off handed accusations. Not about Marc. And not about Andrew. "Lot's of kids bulk up the end of their junior year. Creatine loading will do that. A guy at my school did that. Spent lots of time in the weight room and did creatine loading."

"That shit ain't creatine!" Lindsey said, gesturing in Andrew's direction. "I mean, I don't care if he does steroids. If the guy wants to screw with his body chemistry, it's his life. A poor kid like that, from Roxbury, this is his big chance. Come to a football camp like this on fee-waiver. Kick ass here on the field. Get a few recruiting directors to notice him. If he can even manage high 500's on the SAT, with minority status and football, he's in at any Division 1 school he wants," he said matter-of-factly. "Hey, I like the guy. He's a real hard-ass. If he can play the game and make it out of Roxbury, good for him! So what's your story? You obviously aren't from around here."

Scott laughed at the observation.

"No," he said. Lindsey was such an oaf, he thought. It was hard for him to imagine the guy being a straight A student in the New England prep league. "I'm from Texas. My parents died. So I came to live with my aunt here in town."

"So why are you here at the Academy? You a rich kid?"

Lindsey was so blunt.

"No. I don't go to the Academy. I'm just doing the camp this summer as a job."

"No one does the camp "as a job"!" Lindsey scoffed. "This is the place to be if you want to get recruited at the top tier schools. And proctors *always* get recruited. *Always*! Someone must be looking out for you," Lindsey shouted back over his shoulder as they entered the field and trotted off to where the Red Team was stretching.

"Good morning Scott!" Jim yelled enthusiastically. "I see you have our resident head case under your wing," he laughed gesturing toward Lindsey Quinlan. "Be careful with that guy."

"He's been crazy like that from grammar school," Marc added scornfully. "A real berserker."

"Obviously, Marc doesn't think too highly of our Mr. Lindsey," Jim said. "But I like a few crazies on my team," he said, smiling.

"What's up today?" he said, trying to focus on the tasks for the first day of camp.

"A lot of these guys are out of shape, so we are going to concentrate on conditioning," Jim's voice became suddenly serious. "Thought we would spend the first hour out on the field. We can get in a good hour and still finish breakfast before classes. Scott, I want you to take the receivers and backs from both teams. Marc says you have a couple of drills that you two do with rulers or sticks or something to increase speed. Why don't you get your group to do a couple of warm up laps after they stretch while you set that up," he said, handing Scott a small bag full of rulers. "And Marc, you take the defensive secondary guys. Put them through the drills we did first of last season. I'll take the fat boys and put them through some linemen drills. Let's try to finish up in an hour and get these boys off to the training table. Okay? Here's a whistle for both of you and the roster broken out by position," he said offering a gleaming metallic whistle strung on a lanyard displaying Academy colors. "Make sure everyone on the list shows up at practice. Mark off their names on the sheet. And keep track of any notes you want to go over with me after practice on any of the boys."

Marc seemed perfectly comfortable with the instructions. But Scott wasn't too sure about his newfound authority. It seemed odd to him that he would be putting some of these athletes through a training program. He knew how good some of these boys were. And most of the boys were at least a couple of years older than he was.

But he had promised Jim and Marc that he would help. And he would do what Jim asked him to do.

"Two things," Jim added. "The dining hall is open all day long. So tell your guys to visit early and visit often. Stuff their pockets. I want your guys to eat! And water. Can't drink enough water. The days are going to start getting hotter, so make them carry the water bottles they got with the welcome kit and tell them to go through at least four bottles a day. Now let's get going!" he yelled, blowing his whistle loudly.

❧ ❧ ❧

"You guys off to the weight room?" Lindsey asked as he wolfed down another dinner roll. "I feel like pumping it up!" he yelled as stepped back from the table and flexed. His biceps popped to attention and his chest expanded beneath his thin, ribbed T-shirt, as everyone began to heckle him.

"Yeah, man," Andrew smiled. "Let's do it. I need a break from all this SAT shit. Two hours makes my butt hurt!" he laughed as he spoke.

Scott liked Andrew. He was exactly what he represented himself to be.

"I'm in," he offered. "Can't let you boys show me up. Marc, you want to go to the gym?"

Marc came walking from behind Lindsey and Andrew. Lindsey's face contorted into a scowl and he refused to turn to face Marc.

"No," Marc replied, keeping his pace toward the cafeteria door. "I … I have to help Jim with some stuff," he said. "You guys go ahead. I'll catch up later."

"What a punk," Lindsey said, just loud enough for Marc to overhear as he walked out of the door. "What a lazy punk," he said, shaking his head.

"What you got against that kid, Lindsey?" Andrew asked as he got up from the table. "Every time you around that Marc guy, I see the hairs on the back of your neck begin to stand up," Andrew chuckled, grabbing the last roll from the platter on the table and sticking it in his coat pocket. "He beat the shit out of you or get it on with your sister or what, man?"

Lindsey suddenly pulled himself to full height and positioned himself nose to nose with Andrew.

"You want to see someone get the shit beat out of them, Synesi?" Lindsey shouted.

The dozen of so boys still left in the lunchroom were suddenly quiet. Scott jumped across the table and pulled Lindsey back.

"Andrew was just kidding Lindsey!" he tried to get Lindsey to break his stare and look at him. "He was just joking with you. Just joking," he said as Lindsey finally looked him in the eye. A hollow look, full of rage. Scott had seen that look before. Scott had felt that a similar rage inside of him.

"Yeah, man," Andrew smiled and backed away from Lindsey. "Don't get so pissed at me," he tried to sound friendly. "Marc is the dude that you have the beef with, Lindsey. Not me," he chuckled. "I'm your brother, man," he said, slapping Lindsey on the shoulder. "You and me. We're the same, man. We're both hardcore."

Scott felt the tension in Lindsey's arms ease away slowly. Maybe there really was something wrong with Lindsey. Maybe he was a bit crazy. Andrew had just been kidding. Everyone could see that.

"Yeah, okay," Lindsey smiled. "I knew you were just kidding," he said, offering a hand to Andrew. "I knew you were just kidding me," he said as he shook hands with Lindsey.

"Man, you need to get ripped!" Andrew offered as the lunchroom conversations began again around them. "Let's take it to the gym, man."

The trio walked together the short distance from the lunchroom to the weight room. There were boys laying out under the trees and lounging on the steps of buildings. But in the weight room, there was no one. Just Andrew and Lindsey and Scott.

"All right!" Andrew's voice echoed against the hard walls and metal gym equipment. "We got the place all to ourselves!" his voice obviously pleased. "I could get used to this, man," he said, resetting the bench press machine to 180 and laying down on the hard plastic platform. "Definitely, my kind of place," he said, beginning his first slow set of presses.

Scott was a bit puzzled. Jim had told the boys to spend an hour of their mid-day break in the weight room. And the schedule didn't leave enough time in the evening to do a complete circuit of the weight room. So even if you did upper body one day and lower body the next, unless you were in the weight room mid-day, there is no way you could stay on any sort of schedule for strength training. And the room was so well equipped. New machines. New everything. Why would anyone not take advantage of this, he thought?

"Where is everyone else?" he asked Andrew as he reset the bench press to 200 pounds.

"Getting weak, man," Andrew said, positioning himself under the bar for his second set. "Getting weak."

Scott walked over to the curl machine. He reset it for 2/3's of his maximum and went through one repetition. He watched as Andrew reset the bench press to 230 and did a third set effortlessly, his deep breathing the only sign of any exertion. He watched Lindsey at the squat machine as he went through his first repetition—with more weight than Scott had ever done—Lindsey's huge thigh muscles straining against the weight, his face set in maddened glare at the machine.

Scott watched himself in the mirror wall, how slim he had become, how small he seemed against the other two boys toiling at the machines. It was a good thing he was fast, he thought. He needed to be fast to stand a chance against players like Lindsey and Andrew, he thought.

Andrew reset the bench to 275 and started on a fourth set.

"Argggh!" Andrew shouted with each lift, echoing in the room his contempt for the weight he lifted.

Lindsey added another fifty pounds to the squat machine for his second set.

"Yeah!" Lindsey yelled each time he straightened his legs and locked his knees. "Yeah!" his voice a triumph of will over any physical limitation.

Scott added an extra five pounds to the curl machine over what he normally would use on his second set. An added challenge sparked by the intensity of Andrew and Lindsey.

"All right!" Andrew screamed at the top of his lungs as he pushed the last repetition at the bench into a memory. "All right!" he yelled, flexing and watching the sweat roll down his arms and across his bare chest in the mirror on the wall.

These guys are both crazy, Scott thought. Good crazy, he thought, smiling and struggling under the additional weight on his curl machine. But crazy, none the less.

It took the three boys less than forty minutes to make the full body circuit of machines. A relatively short time to push their athletic bodies to the point of exertion, to the point of absolute muscle fatigue, to the point of tremors.

"Good workout, boys!" Lindsey slapped a sweat-drenched hand on Scott's back. "Damn good workout!"

Andrew pulled a small brown plastic bottle from his gym bag and dropped a couple of large white pills into his hand, then threw them into his mouth and washed them down with a half bottle of water. He looked up to the stare of Lindsey and Scott.

"You white boys got a problem?" Andrew said aggressively as he met their stare.

"No problem," Lindsay assured him, smiling, as he pulled a towel from the stack on the floor for himself and threw another at Andrew.

"That stuff will kill you, you know," Scott tried to sound sincere. He had seen this before. He had seen what the small white pills did to young bodies. And to young minds.

Andrew's eyes narrowed as they stared right through Scott. Then Andrew relaxed and rubbed the towel Lindsey had thrown him across his face. A smile appeared from behind the towel.

"Well, we all got to die, sometime, white boy," Andrew said. "Only difference is, I plan to die rich and famous!" he said, trying to laugh off the warning. Then the smile disappeared. Andrew's face became suddenly earnest. "Are you my friend, Scott?" he asked as he turned to face Scott squarely. "Are you my friend?"

Scott knew what the question meant. He knew Andrew was asking if he was going to tell. If he was going to tell Jim about the steroids.

Scott thought about the question.

It was the first thought he had when he saw the prescription bottle in Andrew's hand. Was he going to tell Jim? Scott turned the question over in his head. Either way, Andrew was screwed. If he told, that might end Andrew's chances for recruitment at the summer camp, for the one thing he had worked his whole life for. If he didn't tell, the drugs would eventually do their damage. Either way, he thought, Andrew was screwed.

"Yeah," he said, grudgingly. He would try to help Andrew, to help him see he didn't need the pills. But, he wouldn't tell Jim. He wouldn't end Andrew's career, his chances to make a better life for himself. "I'm your friend," he said, nodding his head.

❋ ❋ ❋

Scott sat at the small wooden desk overlooking the Academy circle working through the math homework from the day's SAT classes. The huge dinner he had eaten clouded his mind. The day's heat whirled through the small window fan and rustled the papers stacked on the chest of drawers. He looked at the clock on the table. He had 15 more minutes before he had to be back in the cafeteria for the football films. And he had half a page more of math starring back at him from the workbook.

"Do you have any golf clubs?" Lindsey asked, sticking his head around Scott's half-closed door.

What a funny question, he thought.

"No," he laughed, looking back over his shoulder toward the doorway. "No golf clubs. Sorry Lindsey."

Lindsey shook his head and disappeared, the sound of his metallic golf cleats rasping against the tiled floor.

Scott went back to the homework. As he finished the next problem he heard Lindsey's voice from the room next to his.

"Do you have any golf clubs?" Lindsey asked in the same inflection.

Scott laughed to himself. What was Lindsey up to? Why was he looking for golf clubs?

Scott was halfway through the next problem when he heard Lindsey's cleats further away and a repetition of the question at the next room down.

Lindsey was a strange character, he thought, finishing the problem.

Three more problems left. Ten more minutes before he had to leave.

"You got any fruit in here?" Lindsey was back at Scott's doorway, a golf club now propped on his shoulder.

"Yeah," he called back. "I got an apple and a pear on the dresser. Help yourself. You finished with the math homework?"

Lindsey entered the small room. In addition to the golf club, he carried a small, brightly colored plastic bucket like Scott had seen children use at the beach.

"Just finished," Lindsey responded in a very determined manner.

He glanced in Lindsey's direction as he picked up the apple and pear from the dresser and tossed them into the small plastic bucket.

"What are you up to Lindsey?" he asked as Lindsey turned to exit the room.

"Fruit golf," Lindsey said, a small smile on his lips and a twinkle in his eye.

"Fruit golf?!! What the hell is 'fruit golf'?"

"You know," Lindsey said. "Golf—only instead of using a ball, you use fruit," he said. "Want to play?" he said, the infectious smile spreading across his face.

Scott looked at the clock. Eight minutes left. Plenty of time for a quick round of fruit golf, he imagined. "Sure, I'll play."

"Excellent!" Lindsey was obviously pleased to have subverted Scott's study schedule.

Lindsey led the way out of the dorm via the back door and across the small road to the edge of the freshly mown Academy lawn. He pulled a half-eaten apple from his plastic pail and placed it on the ground in front of him. He positioned himself slightly askew to the fruit, shifting his weight back and forth from one foot to the other in classic golf stance and took aim at the apple with the golf club.

"Fore!" Lindsey yelled loudly as he drew the golf club over his shoulder and swung furiously at the fruit.

The apple exploded as the club hit it, bits of pulp expelled in the general direction of Lindsey's aim.

"Fruit golf," Lindsey pronounced, obviously pleased with his shot.

Scott couldn't control his laughter. The sight of Lindsey smashing the apple juxtaposed against the solemnity of his preparation and swing was hilarious.

"You want to try?" Lindsey asked, breaking into laughter himself.

"Sure! Tee up an orange," he directed, taking the club from Lindsey.

Lindsey rummaged through the bucket, pulled out an orange and placed it deliberately on the ground.

"You have to aim a bit under an orange," Lindsey offered his expert opinion. "They're a bit tricky," he said seriously.

Scott tried to contain his laughter as he took aim.

"Fore!" he yelled, bringing the club down abruptly.

Bits of orange peel and pulp splattered across the boys' legs as a section of orange arced gracefully across the open field and landed just short of the fence.

"Nice shot!" Lindsey offered through his laughter. "But I think you sliced it a bit," offering a lame pun. "Try an apple."

Lindsey dropped an apple on the ground in front of Scott.

Scott concentrated on the apple, drawing the club back slowly.

"Drive through it," Lindsey offered more expert advise.

Scott slammed the head of the club down into the freshly mown grass and sent both the apple and a huge section of grass flying toward the fence. Scott and Lindsey both shielded their eyes with their hands to follow the fruit and grass through their arc. The apple burst as it hit the fence.

"Good shot!" Lindsey complimented Scott. "I'd say about 70 yards on that one. Not bad for an apple."

By this time, boys had begun spilling out of the dorm and were gathering at the edge of the road, attracted by Lindsey's and Scott's antics.

"Next!" Scott exclaimed, offering up the club to the small group of boys behind them.

"Hey, me man," Andrew yelled, pawing through the group after the club. "Give me an apple," he said, planting his feet perpendicular to the fence and roadway. "A big one!"

Lindsey pulled a huge yellow apple from the bucket and placed it in front of Andrew.

"Move back a little," Lindsey offered in suggestion. "Keep your front foot even with the apple," he instructed.

Andrew looked up briefly, then followed Lindsey's directions. He pulled back the club and let fly at the apple. His swing was high and only grazed the top of the fruit. But the club had sufficient power to send the greatest part of the apple whizzing across the top of the lawn and bring a chorus of cheers from the boys.

"Me next!" one of the linemen exclaimed. "Me next!"

CHAPTER 18

"I'm dying here," Katrina said, leaning against the mirrored wall and letting her feet slide forward slowly until she sat next to Allie. "I thought our break would never come. This bitch," she spoke softly next to Allie's ear in reference to the wrinkled matriarch who presided over the afternoon sessions, "must be some kind of Nazi sadist!"

Allie was trying to take long deep breaths and exhale forcefully through her mouth between sips on her water bottle. She held her side against stitches from the workout. Her blistered feet were swelling again. And her hamstrings began to tense involuntarily.

"Oh! Katrina! Leg cramp!" Allie said quickly, jerking back into a prone position and thrusting her leg forward. A huge knot began to form in the back of her leg. "Stretch me!" she pleaded. "My leg!"

Katrina immediately grabbed Allie's left leg in one hand and the heel of her foot in the other. Slowly she started to apply pressure back on the toe while supporting the heel and pushing down on Allie's knee.

"Breath!" Katrina commanded. "Deeply. One. Two. Three," she barked the cadence slowly forcing Allie to concentrate on her breathing rather than the pain in her leg. "That's it. Relax. Relax."

Allie felt the tension from Katrina's efforts began to take effect and the knotted feeling in the back of her leg began to subside. After a few seconds, there was only a dull pain where the cramp had begun.

"Do you think it will be like this the whole summer?" she asked earnestly, a small dribble of water from her water bottle blotting the front of her leotard. "I mean, just as hard?"

Julia joined them, her own leotard drenched in sweat, the afternoon repair on her eye makeup smeared and running across her cheek.

"She's just trying to weed out the weak dancers," Julia offered as she sat cross-legged in front of Allie and Katrina. "She figures if she can get rid of 6 or 7 of the younger girls, then she can manage the rest of us."

Allie looked around the room. There were two dozen exhausted girls, in small groups speaking in hushed tones. Some of the younger girls were sobbing. They looked so young, she thought. So vulnerable.

"Why is she so mean to Kirsten?" Allie asked, looking in the direction of the skinny 14 year old who sat gazing blankly out of the second floor window.

"I heard Kirsten's father paid them off," Katrina repeated the rumor. "He gave them a couple of million for the endowment to get her an audition and they had to at least let her start the program this summer. Poor girl. She just doesn't have it. Better if they just told her flat out, rather than let her think she had a chance. Better than to put her through this."

Kirsten was a very weak dancer, Allie thought. Her technique was awkwardly rigid and immature. She danced as if to a metronome rather than music. An automaton of the practice bar. Maybe with age Kirsten would get better, Allie thought. When the young girl matured a bit and her body gained proper proportion and she gained more control over her gangly limbs.

"I feel sorry for her," she said. "Kirsten tries so hard."

"Effort means nothing. Only results," Katrina was curt. "The sooner you realize that, the better for you Allie. Only a dozen of us are going to make it through. That's a fact," she said, massaging her foot through the flimsy toeshoe, "It's easy for you. The rest of us have to work for it."

Allie wasn't sure if Katrina's comment was a compliment or a criticism. Girls were like that, she thought. Like Katrina.

"It's hard for me too!" Allie protested in her defense. Her whole body ached.

Katrina and Julie both rolled their eyes.

"Right!" Julie said. "Have you seen the way Natasha smiles at you?" she asked accusatively. "It's so obvious!"

Allie's face flushed. She had seen Natasha smile at her as the old dancer had tapped out the rhythm for the class. The matriarch's only display of emotion over her entourage the whole day. Only Allie had been good enough to produce a smile on that time-hardened face.

"Allie! Katrina! Justine! Kirsten!" Natasha called from the doorway as she entered the practice room. "To the bar, please!" the matron commanded, cutting the water break short.

Natasha's voice sent the four girls scurrying across the hardwood floor.

"Kirsten! Watch Allie, if you please! And music!"

The pianist labored at the keyboard to keep pace with Natasha's routine. Time metered out by the omnipresent yardstick Natasha used for pace and retribution for any imperfection on the part of the young girls.

"One, two, three four. One, two, three, four. Arms out, Kirsten! And one, two, three, four," Natasha shouted over the music. "Keep time Kirsten!" she shouted, bringing the ruler down across the back of Kirsten's thigh. "One, two, three, four!" she counted in time to the music. "All right, all right. Enough!" she huffed is disdain. "Next four girls," she ordered, dismissing the four at the bar.

Allie and Katrina resumed their place next to Julia. Justine ran across the room as far away from Natasha as she could get. Kirsten began sobbing again as she moved to her window seat.

"Twenty bucks says Kirsten doesn't come back tomorrow," Katrina said between shallow breaths.

"You're on!" Julia said.

Julia's voice distracted Natasha and the dance instructor brought the ruler down hard across her back.

"Quiet if you please!" Natasha shouted. "And music!"

The second set of four repeated the routine. Two of the girls did well. One was weak. And one, Erin, was miserable.

"She's out," Julia whispered, referring to Erin.

Allie finally understood what was happening. Natasha was pairing the girls. Two she thought would make it. One questionable. One … well, one just going through the motions. A quarter of the girls would be gone by the end of the week, she guessed. Another quarter by the end of the first month, probably. Maybe a third of the class would make it through to the recital at the end of the term. Allie was glad she was one of the dancers that would make it.

"So, you guys want to go out clubbing tonight?" Katrina whispered.

"But curfew's at 10," Allie stated the obvious before she realized Katrina's intent in freeing them from the confines of the dormitory. "How do we get out of the dorm?" she whispered.

"I've got it all figured out!" Katrina reassured Allie in hushed tone. "I found a fire escape next to the third floor bathroom window. We throw our party clothes in a duffle, climb down the fire escape, dress in the alley and we're off. You in Julia?"

"All right!" she whispered excitedly. "Music and liquor and boys! I'm definitely in!"

"Next Four!" Natasha shouted. "Quickly!" she shouted, bringing her ruler down across the backside of one of the students who moved too slowly and too near her.

"Definitely liquor!" Katrina said in hushed tone.

❦   ❦   ❦

Allie scanned the message board on her way back from the bathroom, her wet hair dripping onto the oversized towel she had wrapped around her. That was one of the problems living in the dorm at the Repertory—no cellphones and only one pay phone at the end of the hallway on the second floor. And that was constantly in use by one of the girls. All of the in-bound messages were sorted into a haphazard alphabetic montage on the large corkboard next to the phone for the whole world to see.

"Did Scott call?" Katrina asked, scanning the board as Allie brushed through her own wet hair, producing a mist that engulfed her short silk kimono. "Any messages from 'lover boy'?" she teased.

Allie was almost two thirds through the array of pink note pages until she found one with her name on it. She pulled it from the board and reset the thumbtack that had held the message.

"What's he say?" Katrina sounded genuinely interested. "*I love you, Allie? I want your body? I can't stand it without you?*" she teased in rapid succession.

Allie scanned the note.

"He says he can't come to the City this weekend. That he has to stay at the Academy," Allie said. How strange he hadn't told her, Allie thought. Allie's face couldn't help but show her consternation.

"Well, that sucks!" Katrina said loudly. "If the phone situation is anything like it is here, you guys are going to be playing phone tag all summer long," she said, working on a particularly tangled strand of hair with her brush. "Anything else?" Katrina asked as the two girls made their way down the narrow staircase to the second floor dormitory room.

"The note says 'I love you,'" Allie said, sheepishly.

"*I love you, Allie!*" Julia's shrill voice repeated the phrase she had overheard as Allie and Katrina entered the small room the three girls shared. "Let me see that picture of Scott, again," Julia demanded, picking up the small gold frame from Allie's dresser table. "Look at those abs!" she squealed, inspecting the photo of Scott Allie had taken without his shirt on. "That boy is a hotty!" she laughed, replacing the frame and falling into her bed in fake swoon.

There was no privacy in the confines of the Repertory dorm rooms and Allie just smiled back at Julia's comment and hysterics as she undraped the wet towel she had around her and threw it over the end of her own bed.

"You know you would look great in my red dress," Julia offered as she surveyed Allie' body. "You've got great legs," she said, jumping up from the bed and rummaging through their shared closet. "Here," Julia offered Allie a very small red dress. "Try it on," she encouraged.

Allie slipped the tight fitting dress over her head and tried to stretch the fabric into proper position over her body, tugging it down across the top of her thighs.

"It's kind of tight," Allie offered, struggling to smooth the dress over her. "And short!" she exclaimed, looking at her reflection in the full-length mirror on the inside of the closet door.

"Girl, you are dangerous in that dress! You definitely have to wear that tonight" Katrina offered in absolute envy. "Here, I've got some red shoes that would match," she sorted through a bag of shoes hidden away under her bed. "Here's one," she said, continuing her rummaging. "And here's the other!"

Allie took the tall red pumps and slipped them on. They were too tight for her, but they didn't look that bad and they made her legs look fantastic. She looked at her reflection full length. She didn't dress like this, she thought. Never. Not even for Scott.

"OK, so what are you going to wear, Julia?" Katrina asked after dismissing Allie as totally prepared for their night out. "How about this?" she asked, pulling a short black skirt from one of her bags. "See how this fits," she offered the skirt to Julia who unashamedly dropped the boxer shorts she was wearing and pulled the skirt up around her, letting it fall low around the top of her hips, revealing a diminutive, absolutely flat abdomen accented by a small gold loop through her navel. Julia threw off the oversized t-shirt she had been wearing and pulled on a white tank top that came down just above her waist. The bronze skin between the tank top and the skirt glistened.

"Julia, that outfit is you!" Katrina offered.

It was fun being with Katrina and Julia, Allie thought. Just spending time with other girls. Not the vapid fluff-heads in her class at home. The jealous ones who tried to belittle her. With Katrina and Julia, she felt … accepted … and special.

"So, what time do we leave?" Allie asked, glancing at her watch.

"Lights out are at 10, so let's give them forty-five minutes or so to forget about us," Katrina went through her plan. "We go up to the third floor bathroom one at a time," she continued. "Then, when we all get there, I'll climb out the window and pull down the fire ladder," she said. "Then, we're off!"

Allie understood now why they were packing their clothes. There was no way she could climb down a ladder in the red dress or those tall pumps, she thought.

❧ ❧ ❧

The sound of ringing in her ears woke Allie. Her head was killing her. She wasn't sure if it was all of the loud music or not getting in bed until slightly before dawn … or that final margarita she had at the club. But, now, she felt horrible. Her body hurt all over.

"Can somebody catch the phone?" Julia shouted. "I have to hurl," she called out over her shoulder as she ran down the hallway toward the stairs that led to the third floor bathroom.

Allie rolled out of bed and struggled to find a t-shirt or robe in the dark of the dorm room. All she could find was last night's bath-towel in the jumble on the floor. And it was still damp.

The phone in the hall rang again urgently.

"Shit!" Allie said under her breath. She grabbed the towel and held it up in front of her as best she could as she hurried out of the room into the hallway to answer the phone.

"Second floor dorm, Repertory Company," she answered, running her tongue over her dry front teeth and trying to wrap the small towel around herself with her one free hand.

"Allie? Is that you?" Scott asked.

"Scott!" the excitement in her voice sent a sudden pain through her forehead. "Yeah, it's me," she spoke more softly and leaned her bare backside against the hall next to the phone. "What time is it? Where are you?" she asked.

"Oh, sorry," Scott apologized. "It's still early. Around 6:15 I think. I just got back from running with Marc. I tried to call you like a dozen times yesterday," he explained. "But the number you gave me was always busy," his voice clearly frustrated. "And when I finally got through some girl named Kirsten answered and said you had gone out … that you weren't there. So I just left a message for her. Did you get my message? What's going on, Allie?"

"I got the message that you couldn't come in this weekend. That you had to stay at the Academy."

There was silence from Scott's end of the phone.

"Scott, you wouldn't believe how hard it is," she spoke softly, checking to make sure no one was in the hallway. "And all of the girls here are so good. And our teacher is so strict. She actually has a yardstick that she hits you with if you screw up," she spoke in run-on sentences. "But I think she likes me. She smiled at me yesterday while I was practicing and used me to demonstrate a new routine."

"Where were you Allie?"

Allie rearranged a corner of the towel so she could sit on it and still have enough to drape over the lower half of her body.

"I went out with two really nice girls here," she said, her voice sounding too tentative for her. Could he tell, she thought? Could he tell she felt guilty about last night?

"Vicky's friends, Heather and Rosalyn?" Scott asked.

"No. Katrina and Julia. My roommates. They're really nice and we get along really well," she added. "We went out together last night," she blurted into the receiver.

I shouldn't have said that, she thought the instant after the words were out of her mouth. A good lie would have been better, she thought.

"We went to this place Julia likes," she said innocently. "It's … downtown," she tried to be truthful without telling Scott what really happened. "Maybe we can go there when you come to visit me," she added quickly.

There was another long pause.

"About visiting … this weekend. I can't come to see you this weekend. Marc says this is a 'closed weekend' and no one can leave the Academy. I can't come to New York this weekend."

Allie stomach began to churn and her head throbbed again.

"I know. That's what your message said. That you couldn't come this weekend?" her voice trembled a bit. She had been planning her whole week around seeing Scott on Friday night, on being with him this weekend. That was how she had planned to get through the week. To get through the endless hours of practice and rehearsals. Thinking about spending the weekend with Scott.

"I'm really sorry Allie. I didn't know that I wouldn't be able to come. Marc just told me."

"That's okay," Allie tried to sound convincing. "I understand," she said, glad to be talking about his problem rather than where she had been last night.

"But I can come up the next weekend. I'm sure I can come up in two weeks," Scott sounded enthusiastic. "I miss you so much," he added.

"I miss you too," Allie's voice cracked.

"Are you okay Allie? You sound ... different."

Allie's guilt over last night and, even more, over not being completely honest with Scott added more stress to the urgency she was beginning to feel in her stomach. Did she miss Scott that much? Or was it just the alcohol from last night? Or the guilt over what she had done?

"I'm fine," Allie's voice was weaker. "I'm just a little tired, I guess. Look, I've got to go. OK?"

"I'm sorry I woke you up. I just wanted to hear your voice."

"I'm not mad," Allie's tried to sound comforting. But her stomach wretched suddenly and she knew she had to get to the bathroom. Quickly.

"Scott. I have to go now!"

"What's wrong Allie?"

"Goodbye Scott. I'll call you later," she managed, before tossing the receiver back into the cradle of the wall phone and sprinting toward the third floor bathroom. In her urgency, the towel she had used to screen herself caught on the stair railing. But she was too sick to care and left it lying on the floor at the bottom of the stairs. She met Julia halfway up the stairs.

She heard the phone begin to ring again.

"Bring me some clothes!" Allie implored as she ran past Julia and up the stairwell.

"Don't use the first stall!" Julia shouted after her.

Allie burst into the bathroom and threw open the door to the second stall just in time to empty the contents of her stomach into the toilet in one violent spasm. The second and third heaves produced nothing but excruciating stomach pains.

I'm never going to get that drunk again, she promised herself, holding her forehead as her stomach insisted on one more dry heave. Never, she promised herself, her naked body shivering in the damp, stale coldness of the huge tiled room.

❦   ❦   ❦

Tuesday was hell for Allie. All of the rigors of the Repertory competing with the hangover from Monday night's escapade with Julia and Katrina. It was a miracle that she made it through the day. But she did. Allie knew that she had made a bad decision to sneak out with her two roommates. To drink. To stay out all night. To do the things she did. After all of her hard work and the good luck to get to the Repertory, she realized she could have lost it all in that one night. And given what had happened, she couldn't stand being around Katrina, and Julia any more than she absolutely had to.

So, on Thursday, when Kirsten's room turned up empty and without asking anyone, Allie moved her things into the vacant room.

By Friday lunch break, Natasha had made her first cuts. Then, there were no more triples in the dorm. Enough girls were gone to provide a double for everyone. No one mentioned the girls who were cut from the program by name. And other girls expanded quietly during the breaks in the practice schedule to fill the space those cut from the program had occupied.

Allie had three messages on the message board from Scott. She had left an equal number for him at his dorm.

She had also gotten two messages from Will Sanford reminding her about her commitment on his movie and a message from Vicky saying she was going to stop by after Saturday morning's closed recital to take Allie sight-seeing in the City.

She was happy she had made the cuts at the Repertory. And that she had a major part in the closed recital on Saturday.

But she was also sad.

Maybe it was just the physical exhaustion. Or the emotional strain of competing with the other girls for Natasha's approval. Or Allie's own anxiety about the first recital on Saturday morning, the first chance for the other instructors at the Repertory to see her dance.

All she wanted to do was crash in her room. Alone.

By Friday night she was beyond the self-control she had so carefully cultivated. And she cried herself to sleep, softly, muffling the sounds in her pillow so the few other girls still left in the dorm couldn't hear.

She couldn't help it.

She was exhausted. She was lonely. And, for the first time, she was scared she might not make it.

"I saw you dance this morning," Vicky said, taking Allie tentatively by the arm as they walked through the park. "You were the best one," she offered enthusiastically with a warm smile.

"I thought it was a closed recital?" Allie couldn't hide her puzzled expression. She hadn't seen anyone from outside the Repertory Company at the recital that morning. Just the other instructors, making notes as each class of girls went through their short pieces.

"I was upstairs, silly," Vicky laughed, pulling Allie along. "There's an observation room upstairs. Didn't you see the mirrors on the second level? They're one-way, so family and friends of the Repertory can watch without disturbing the classes."

Allie stopped in her tracks. She hadn't even considered the fact that anyone outside of the company would be looking at her dance. It would have made her much more nervous, she thought.

"Who else was there? Watching?" she asked, giving way to the slight pressure of Vicky's arm and moving with her along the trail.

"Oh, let's see," Vicky's voice was reflective. "Heather's mother and younger sister. And Katrina's stepmother," she paused. "I guess a dozen or so people. Not that many," she said. "And Hunter Hanson, Marc's dad, was there for some reason," she added. "Want to get something to drink?" she asked quickly, pulling Allie toward the curb at the south side of the park. "Let's get something to drink!"

I guess I will just have to get accustomed to people watching me, Allie thought. She really didn't mind that they had been watching behind the half-silvered mirror. She just wished she had known that other people had been watching her. Not that it would have made any difference in her performance.

"Can anyone come to watch?" she asked.

"Oh, no!" Vicky said, pulling the two of them through the stalled traffic across Central Park South. "Everything about the Repertory is very exclusive. I only got in because I'm rich," she giggled. "My dad gives shit-loads of money to the arts in this town," Vicky let go of Allie's arm long enough to catch the revolving door on the large stone building on the corner. "That's how I got in to see you. Now let's have that drink!" she said, "and talk about how wonderful you were this morning," she said, her eyes full of admiration for Allie. "Then we'll go see all of the tourist stuff! It'll be fun," she promised. "Just you and me!" she beamed as she slid over next to Allie on the oxblood leather seat in the corner booth.

Allie wasn't sure why Vicky was being so friendly. But, with Scott at the Academy for the weekend, Allie was happy for the company. She was lonely. And she did want to see all of the tourist stuff in the City. Having Vicky as a guide would be fun, she thought.

"Two cosmopolitans," Vicky ordered quickly.

"I … I haven't had anything to eat today," she whispered to Vicky.

"Great!" Vicky seemed pleased. "I have reservations for a late lunch already. At Tribe. It's the best. Everyone shows up there," Vicky said, laying her hand slightly on Allie's forearm as it rested on the table.

Lunch sounded good. Allie just needed something on her stomach if she was going to drink, she thought. How thoughtful Vicky was, she thought. To take care of her. To take her out for lunch at a nice restaurant. To show her the city.

"You are so nice. Thank you," she said, laying her hand on top of Vicky's just as the waiter brought their drinks. "You're a good friend," she said, taking a long cool drink from her cocktail.

"Let's talk about this morning," Vicky urged, sipping from her own glass. "About how good you were!" she said admiringly.

Allie relaxed a bit and leaned back in the booth. Vicky was so funny, she thought. But Allie liked the attention. It was odd to see that sort of admiration from someone outside of the dance community. Allie was more accustomed to jealousy and envy from her peers. And ignorance from all of the other girls her own age. It was nice to have someone like Vicky appreciate her, she thought, taking another long sip from her glass.

They spent almost an hour talking about the morning's recital. About Allie's dance career. About Allie's life. About her fashion preferences and what type of makeup she used and how she did her hair. Girl talk. And not a single mention of boys.

It wasn't until after she had finished her second drink that Allie realized they hadn't discussed anything having to do with Vicky.

"So, what do you do in you spare time, Vicky?" she asked, the alcohol just beginning to slur her speech.

Vicky seemed uncomfortable with the question. She glanced at her watch.

"We should go," Vicky said, emptying her cocktail. "We'll be late for our reservation," she urged, reaching into her purse, pulling out a hundred dollar bill and laying it on the check at the end of the table.

"How much do I owe?" Allie asked, trying as best she could to calculate what half of the tab would be. God, she thought as she remembered her budget, I hope that the drinks weren't twenty-five dollars!

Vicky just smiled sweetly and pulled Allie up by the hand from the booth.

"Nothing, dear," Vicky purred. "This is my treat today. You are my guest!" she proclaimed, grasping Allie's hand firmly in her own and pulling her along. "And, besides," she said, leaning close to Allie's ear, "I'm filthy rich!"

She laughed as Vicky pulled her along. It was nice to have Vicky's steadying hand. Maybe it had been drinking on her empty stomach. Or just the exhaustion from the week. But, Allie's legs didn't seem to be too steady beneath her.

"Maybe we'd better take a cab?" Vicky asked as she steadied Allie at the street corner. "You aren't walking that well, girl!" Vicky giggled.

Allie just smiled. She was plastered, she thought. On two drinks! Must have been her empty stomach, she managed to pull the thought together coherently.

"Cab!" Vicky leaned Allie against her body and threw up her free hand before forming two fingers for a loud whistle.

A yellow cab veered across two lanes of traffic and came to an abrupt stop at the curb in front of them. Vicky opened the door and tried to help Allie into the cab. But at the last instant Vicky lost her balance and the two girls fell onto the back seat on top of each other in hysterical giggles.

"Where to, Missies?" the driver said, obviously amused by the antics of the two attractive young women.

"Tribe," Vicky finally managed through her laughter. "Off of Fifth Avenue...."

"I know the place, Missy," the cab driver interrupted her as he gunned the engine and darted back into the frantic traffic.

The cab lurched forward and threw Allie against Vicky. She was just too drunk to fight the momentum of the cab and decided to lay there on Vicky's shoulder. It was nice of Vicky to take care of her, she thought through the haze that clouded her mind.

"Hungry, Allie?" Vicky asked softly, shifting in her seat so that Allie could more comfortably lean against her.

"Yeah," Allie said. "I'm hungry. Let's get something to eat," Allie said, laying her head against Vicky. "I'm just going to close my eyes for a minute. Okay?" Allie asked as she closed her eyes. She suddenly felt incredibly tired. And so comfortable leaning against Vicky in the cool air flowing through the cab's window. "Just for a minute," she said, her voice trailing off into sleep.

❦   ❦   ❦

Allie lay in her bed, the pillow over her head, trying to blot out everything. What was happening to her?

Far away she heard the phone ringing.

The one night she went out with Katrina and Julia. Well, that had been an accident. Too much to drink, too fast. Too many people around them. It was just part of the club atmosphere. Dancing together. Like that.

But Vicky! What excuse did she have? Sure she had a couple of drinks. And she was lonely.

But she knew what she was doing.

The phone kept ringing in her ears.

She loved Scott. She knew she did.

But everything was so different here. All of the other girls were so sophisticated. And adoring.

The phone! The phone was ringing!

Allie jumped out of bed and ran into the hallway to answer the phone.

"Repertory, Second Floor. This is Allie"

"What the hell is going on!"

It was Scott's voice. Angry.

"First the phone is busy for two hours. Now no one is answering the damn thing? And it doesn't make any difference when I call, you're never there!"

"No hello?" she asked. "No how are you Allie? No how has your week been Allie? How did your recital go Allie?"

"Fuck the recital, Allie. I want to know what the hell is going on with you!"

Allie slid her back against the wall, lowering herself into a sitting position on the floor. "I was one of the leads, today Scott."

"Where were you Allie? Earlier this week? All day today?"

"Do you remember Vicky, Marc's friend from Boomers? She came by to watch the recital this morning. And then we went out for drinks and lunch," she said. "She's really rich and paid for everything!" Allie said, quickly.

Best to change the subject, she thought. Best not to talk about Vicky.

"I ran into Will Sanford," she said, only having to lie a little. She had seen him. Just not today. "He was filming next to the Statute of Liberty and he needed some help, so I helped him 'crew'".

"Well," Scott's voice was reflective. "I thought the recital was closed," he said, thinking about how in a city as large as New York, Allie just happened to run into Will.

"It was ...," Allie started, then sensing her voice was too defensive, "It was closed. Only the instructors were allowed on the floor. But they have an observation deck for 'friends of the Repertory' where the patrons can watch," she explained. "And Vicky's dad gives a lot of money to the Repertory so she was allowed in," she explained. "And, Marc's father was there," she tried to make it sound like Vicky's attendance was normal.

"Marc's dad?" Scott asked. "What he was doing there?"

"I guess he gives a lot of money to the Repertory," Allie was glad to be talking about Hunter. Or Will. Anyone but Vicky. "There are so many rich people here," she blurted out. "And they all act … so strange."

"Like Will?"

"Will?" Allie began to stumble over her lie. "Yes. Like Will," she said.

Much better for Scott to be jealous of Will, she thought.

"You aren't jealous, are you? Of Will? You're not jealous of me spending time with him?" she tried to sound as if the mere suggestion was ridiculous. "Look, I just … I just …" Allie wasn't thinking as fast as she was speaking, so she tried to slow down her voice. "I got tired of sightseeing with Vicky," she tried to make the lie sound credible. "So, I was getting ready to go back to the dorm and I just happened to see Will making his movie," she stopped long enough to allow Scott to speak, but he didn't. "So I walked over and said hello and he was short handed on his crew, so he asked me if I would hold the sound boom during one of the shots," she tried to sound convincing.

"You just 'happened to run into him'?" Scott's voice came out an accusation. "Making his movie?"

"Well, yeah. Why?" she asked. "You don't think I set it up so I would run into him, do you?"

Allie heard someone shouting about a movie in the background over Scott's breathing.

"Are you going to the movies?" Allie asked, trying to sound equally indignant. Scott had told her that he had a closed weekend. That he couldn't leave the Academy. Who was he going to the movies with?

"No, of course not. One of the guys here from Boston figured out how to hook up cable so that we get the premium channels. These guys are *wicked smart*," he added.

"*Wicked smart?*" Allie found herself getting angry at Scott's use of the New England colloquialism. "When did you start talking like a New Englander?" she demanded.

Why was she angry? She was the guilty one. Scott was just watching movies. He was the one that should be angry.

"Look, I'm hanging up now. I'm hanging up now, Allie. We can talk later. When you're not so bitchy."

She hated the bitch word! And Scott knew that!

"Fuck." she started.

CLICK.

There was silence before she could get "you" out.

She had wanted to tell him what was going on in her life. About her confusion. About her fears.

She had wanted to tell him so much more.

Perhaps not the truth, exactly.

Damn Scott!

Damn him for loving her, even when she didn't deserve it.

CHAPTER 19

"Are you ready to play some football for me, boys?" Jim shouted, emptying the contents of a large canvas bag onto the ground.

There was a melee as the excited boys stampeded for the loosed balls.

This is what they had come to camp for, Scott thought. This is what they had waited for. Everyone, even the linemen, jockeying for the touch of the rough leather covering on the ball against their hand.

Everyone but Scott.

He hadn't touched a football in ten months.

Not since ... the accident.

Funny, he thought, as he watched the boys break off into small groups. When Jim had asked him to work at the summer camp, he hadn't even thought about it. He hadn't even thought about touching a football. The thought had never crossed his mind. He was just supposed to help Jim with the camp. That was all.

His only thought now was ... to run away. Far away.

Scott shifted his weight and started to turn away ... to turn away from the footballs ... away from the horrid memories of that night that flooded over him.

Then, suddenly, a heavy hand came down on his shoulder.

"Want to throw some with me?" Jim asked quietly, holding out a new football to Scott with his free hand. "I think it's about time. Don't you?" he asked almost in a whisper.

Scott looked up at Jim. Into the most compassionate eyes he had seen since his father had died. At the reassuring smile on his face.

"Sure, coach," Scott chocked on the words, fighting against the moisture that was building in his eyes. "I'll throw with you."

🍁　　🍁　　🍁

Lindsey, Andrew and Scott sat in Jim's dimly lit office talking about the football camp.

There was a knock on the door and the three boys stood up in unison only to see Marc Hanson entering the room.

"We've got a meeting in here now," Lindsey rebuffed Marc as he slid back into his seat. "A private meeting," Lindsey added.

"Me too," Marc's replied in an equally irritated tone. "Me, too," he repeated, pulling a chair up alongside Scott and as far away from Lindsey as he could get.

Jim hadn't said anything about Marc being in on the meeting, Scott thought.

The thought was cut short as Jim came scurrying into the room carrying a bankers box and settled into the large armchair behind his desk.

"Here are some playbooks," Jim began, pulling small white three-ring binders from the box and sliding them across the desk to the boys. "Notice they are numbered and marked confidential. No copies are to be made of any of the pages, and I will collect the binders at the end of camp. That means you guys have to memorize the plays and teach them to the other guys. Just enough to know their own assignments when the plays are called," he paused as he reached back into the box and produced four neatly stapled piles of paper. "This is a little literature I want each of you to read," he said, his tone of voice all business. "It is for your eyes only. That means no one else sees it and you either give it back to me at the end of camp or destroy it," he continued."

It had all happened so quickly. The boys looked blankly at each other.

"Good!" Jim smiled. "We'll start working together at the Monday morning practice. By Wednesday we'll have our timing down, and we'll pull together the rest of the offense," he instructed as he stood. "Now, I suggest you gentlemen enjoy your weekend. Because next week I am going to work you four into shape," he said genially, grabbing the empty banker's box. "Welcome to the big league," he said making an exit as quickly as his entrance.

"That was real charming!" Lindsey said quietly as soon as the door closed.

Scott sat there, holding a white three ring binder in his hands. The word "confidential" in red, all capital letters, stenciled on the front of the binder. The stapled papers Jim had passed to him lay on the floor at his feet where he had dropped them.

"Here's your 'literature', Scott," Andrew smiled and winked knowingly as he picked up the sheave of stapled copies from the floor and handed them to Scott.

The four of you, Scott thought. Jim had said 'the four of you'. Lindsey Quinlan, Andrew Synesi, Marc Hanson, and Scott Greenway, he thought, in third person. One linebacker, one running back, one quarterback, Scott thought. And one receiver who could run faster than anyone else at camp.

❦   ❦   ❦

Scott pulled frantically at the straps on his shoulder pads. They didn't feel right, today. Too tight across his chest, he thought, struggling to breathe as he fought with the straps. The shoulder pads too heavy on him, he thought, his knees weak.

Putting on his equipment had exhausted him. It wasn't at all like he remembered. Putting on his uniform. He had always felt … invincible.

Not now.

Now he felt trapped within the webbing and the foam and the plastic.

He picked up the 3-ring binder of plays again. The pages were full of small Xs and Os and curved arrows, all beginning to smudge against the retracing of Scott's forefinger.

24 split, red. 32 dive. 5, I-reverse.

He ran through the calls in his mind, closing his eyes, imagining his assignment for each play. Visualizing the route he would run. Thinking about what the defense would be doing. How he would avoid his coverage.

A head-fake here. A stutter-step there. A sudden cut to the sideline. Timing. It was all about timing. And working together. As a team.

He thought about what the other boys on the team would be doing. Where they would be on the field. How the linemen would be blocking on each play.

He thought about the split-instant that Marc would release the ball and it would begin its arc down the field. About the moment when he would finally catch the blur of the ball out of the corner of his eye and watch it fall into his out-stretched arms. He thought about how the tips of his fingers would grip the ball and bring it, ever so gently, into the cradle of his arms just before the cornerback or the safety would hit him.

It was all in his mind. All of it. Every move, every sensation, buried deeply, in his memory.

He opened the door and stepped to the edge of the sunlit expanse of green lawn that led toward the field. It was going to be a warm practice this morning, he thought, wiping the beads of perspiration from his forehead and twisting the helmet down onto his head. And full of pressure now that there were college coaches there to help Jim out with the camp.

The sounds of repetitive warm-up drills synchronized to the count of the players echoed through the ear holes of his helmet as he trotted onto the practice field. They were almost finished with warm-ups, he thought. He was really late, he thought, joining in the last of the sit-ups on the back row. Trying to blend in with the rest of the team.

The boys finished the warm-ups and broke into their two scrimmage teams, red team at the north end and blue team at the south end.

"All right men," Jim broke into his routine of pacing in front of the team as he talked. "We are going to start at the beginning of the play book and run all the way through. Marc, here, is going to quarterback us."

Scott glanced over at Marc, shifting his weight back and forth, fidgeting with his helmet. Scott was glad they were on the same team.

"And we going to destroy the blue team!" Jim shouted. "So, let's get started. Marc, let's run I-32, split, on two."

The boys fell into a well-ordered huddle around Marc, assuming the positions ordered by the game. The spot for the wide receiver was left vacant for Scott. He leaned in from the periphery and listened as Marc repeated the call.

"I-32, split, on two. I-32, split, on two," Marc glanced around the intense young faces.

In the short intense silence, only the players closest to Scott could hear him popping his knuckles.

"Break!" Marc said loudly, the single command sending the red-jerseyed young men to the appropriate X-positions set out for them in the playbook.

I-32, split, Scott thought. An "out pattern" to him, remembering the route from the playbook. Down the field ten yards. Quick right to the sidelines. On two.

He had run similar patterns hundreds of times.

But, it all seemed different now as he came to the line of scrimmage.

"I-32! I-32!" Marc shouted, first to his left, then to his right. "Hut. Hut!" the second cadence accentuated as the center snapped the ball into Marc's waiting hands.

Marc dropped back in slow motion, faking a handoff to Lindsey three yards into the backfield as the huge halfback lumbered forward from his sprinter's stance toward the defensive line. Two more yards into the backfield, Marc set his right forefoot into the soft turf, as he drew back the football and sent it sailing into the air toward the right sideline.

Scott tried to restrain his urge to sprint, jogging forward at first to disguise his speed, then made his turn just as the defensive back bumped him, and split out to the sideline as fast as he could run. It was only when he glanced back over his right shoulder that he actually saw the wobbling ball coming down.

The ball was below his knees when his fingertips finally touched the grainy leather surface. He scooped the ball before it had a chance to hit the surface of the field, lowered his shoulder and allowed his momentum to send him into a roll out of bounds. He stood up, holding the ball high over his head to confirm his catch. It was a dramatic his father had taught him. Even when he hadn't actually caught the ball, the gesture many times had encouraged an enthusiastic official to signal a catch.

"Great catch Scott!" Jim yelled from his spot behind the line of scrimmage. "All right, that's the way to start out. Intensity! Now let's run it again. A little faster this time."

Scott jogged back to the huddle that had already formed. Marc barked out the same play in the same fashion. The boys once again came to the line. Only this time when the ball was centered, the play began to take on its true sequence. The defense knew what to expect this time. But it made absolutely no difference. This time when Scott glanced over his shoulder, the ball was high, urged on by the adrenalin pumping in Marc's arm. Scott had just enough time in his last two steps to speed up and cut more down field. With a tremendous leap into the air, he was able to pull the ball down with one hand inside the end zone marker.

And Scott found himself, once again, standing in the end zone with the football.

Funny how quiet it sounded there, all alone, by himself. Funny how familiar it all seemed, once again.

His reflections were cut short as members of his team began to pile on top of him.

"Nasty catch!" Lindsey shouted, tipping the whole group over onto the turf as he jumped onto the pile.

The glory was short-lived, as the referee started blowing his whistle and pulling the boys off of each other. Until finally it was just Scott and Marc standing face to face with each other.

"Guess this means we just became a throwing team?" Marc said with a sly smile.

🍁   🍁   🍁

"Scott!" Jim yelled across the cage over the noise of the boys locker room. "Come over here a minute. I want to introduce you to a couple of guys."

Scott walked through the piles of shoulder pads and helmets and foam pads littered amongst the group of boys icing their wounds after the scrimmage, the red team hurling good-natured insults at the blue team after their win.

Next to Jim stood two hefty middle-aged men. Both had clearly been athletes, Scott thought, from their builds. The one with the thick neck had to have been a linebacker, he thought. Maybe alumni from the Academy, he thought. There had been a dozen new faces standing on the sidelines for the day's scrimmage.

"Scott, this is Harold Casey," Jim said, gesturing to the shorter of the two men wearing the maroon hat with the large white "H" on it. "And this is Richard Peabody," Jim turned slightly toward the one Scott had pegged as a linebacker, the one with the purple T-shirt with "W" neatly embroidered on the left chest. "Harold is going to be helping out next week with a couple of the backs. And Richard is going to be helping me with some of the linebackers."

Scott smiled politely and shook hands with each man.

"Scott, I hear you've been working with Marc Hanson for a few weeks," Harold said in a strong New England accent.

"Yes sir," Scott said, trying to sound forceful. "He and I train together."

Harold and Richard both smiled.

"Not from around here, are you, Scott?" Richard asked the familiar question in a good-humored way.

"He's a Texas boy," Harold volunteered, slapping Richard on the shoulder. "A *real* football player," he said, nodding his head in approval.

How did he know I was from Texas, Scott thought?

"Scott, I need you to introduce Harold to Lindsey Quinlan, if you don't mind," Jim instructed Scott. "And I would like for you and Andrew to spend some time with Richard later this afternoon, after lunch."

"Sure coach," Scott replied.

❦ ❦ ❦

"I'm serious Lindsey," Scott was emphatic. "Jim told me to introduce you to this coach, Harold something or other. You too, Andrew. There is this coach named Peabody that you and I are supposed to meet after lunch."

"Well, when are we supposed to do weights?" Lindsey resisted the break in their routine.

"Damn, I thought you running backs were supposed to have brains!" Andrew chimed in across the dining room table, tossing his accusation and a half-eaten roll in Lindsey's direction. "Don't you get it, white boys? Don't you guys know how this game works?"

Scott and Lindsey stared blankly back at Andrew.

"OK. I'm going to make this real simple," Andrew lowered his voice and leaned across the table. "R-E-C-R-U-I-T-I-N-G," he spelled out the word slowly. "You see, you got your division three schools. Rules say they can't make recruiting trips off campus. So how you think they find their players?"

Andrew paused.

"The assistant coaches work the summer camps, man!" Andrew explained. "How else they goin' see the talent? And the Ivy's," he continued. "Different set of rules, but it's the same game. They want the first look at the fresh meat before they start using up the 70 slots they got for campus visits," he smiled and looked back over his shoulder to make sure no one was listening. "Coaching staff!" he huffed. "That's bull shit man. Those guys are here for one reason. Recruiting."

Andrew sounded sure of himself and his evaluation of the situation.

It made sense, Scott thought. You couldn't really tell how good someone was just by looking at game-tapes. You needed to see them play. Even better, you needed to see them practice. Didn't make any difference how good a player was, he thought. Unless the player had good practice habits, he was just going to be average.

"So, this guy. Where's he from? Which school?" Lindsey asked Scott.

"He didn't say," Scott tried to be obscure.

"Give me a break, Scotty!" Andrew scoffed. "Lindsey's guy has got maroon ivy tattooed across his butt!"

"No shit!" Lindsey beamed. "And it's just you and me with this guy this afternoon, Scott?"

"Yeah," Scott tried to downplay his role. "Jim just said the guy was going to work with you next week."

Andrew slapped his hand down on the table.

"Work with you!" Andrew exclaimed. "Man, you are in play, Lindsey. In play in the Ivy!"

"I'm the man!" Lindsey replied proudly, his chest expanded. "I am the man!" he shouted, beating on the table and overturning their drinks. "I am the man!"

The other players had become accustomed enough to Lindsey's rants to ignore them, provided that Lindsey was far enough away from them not to inflict bodily injury during one of his outbursts.

Made sense, Scott thought. Lindsey had the best stats of the running backs. And the best grades, from what he knew. Andrew had to be right on this one, Scott thought.

"And me, man," Andrew laughed, "I love western Massachusetts! Anything to get me the hell out of Roxbury. And I do look so sweet in purple!"

So that was the way it worked, Scott reasoned.

Andrew with Peabody. Lindsey with Harold. Both of them being recruited by the best of the best.

He was glad for them.

They deserved it.

CHAPTER 20

Marc sat silently in the corner of Jim's office watching the coaches.

Harold Casey put down his cup of coffee on Jim's desk and leaned back in the chair.

"I think the red offensive unit is going to do pretty well this year. Still too early to tell, obviously. But I see some real potential there," Harold commented. "You've done a great job Jim. You, too, Marc," he said, looking back over his shoulder into the corner.

"Defense looks solid," Richard Peabody confirmed. "The Johnson kid is a good lineman. Big and strong. And that black kid. The one from Roxbury. What's his name?" he asked, thumbing through the papers on his clipboard.

"Andrew Synesi," Jim offered, smiling.

"Yeah, the Synesi kid," Richard nodded his head. "That kid is out to make a name for himself. He a scholarship kid?"

"Started looking out for him last fall," Jim couldn't suppress his obvious pleasure that Richard had singled out Andrew. "Just keeps getting better and better. His bench and squats are incredible. Maybe one of the strongest kids I've seen in a few years. If you guys don't pick him up this year, I am going to get him for a post graduate year here at the academy," Jim smiled at the mock threat, knowing that someone with Andrew's talent, his desire, would be at the top of the recruiters' lists. No chance to get him for a final PG year at the Academy. Only the pleasure of knowing that he had helped the boy out of Roxbury. Helped him into a good school that really cared about graduating him as well as putting him in a football uniform.

"And I want to see what that Texas boy can do. He one of yours too?" he asked Jim.

"Not yet," Jim squirmed a bit in his seat. "But I'm working on it."

Marc tried to contain himself.

"You know, Marc," Harold addressed him, again, making him a part of their conversation. "If you could get your arm a bit stronger, and you had one good running back to keep the opposing defense honest, you and that Texas boy might be able to do something extra-ordinary this fall," Harold offered. "Texas boy has hands I wished I had on my own team," he said, only half jokingly. "He a senior next year?" Harold asked casually, as he thumbed through his papers. "Didn't even see his name on the roster."

"He's not on the roster," Jim admitted sheepishly. "He's a townie. I got him to proctor one of the dorms this summer. Sad case. He moved up here this spring from Texas. Papers down there said he had a 4.4 forty. Saw the clipping from his first game as a sophomore—ran the opening kickoff back 95 yards for a touchdown against the prior year's state championship team His family was killed in a car crash after that game," Jim paused. "He hadn't touched a football since then. Not until he came to camp. But, he and Marc," Jim nodded in Marc's direction, "have been training together. His name's Scott. Scott Greenway."

Richard Peabody shifted in his chair.

"So, Marc," Peabody said, "what do you think about the Texas boy. Would you want him on your team?"

It was the moment Marc had waited for. The moment he knew that would come during the meeting.

"You know a good receiver can make a great quarterback, Marc."

Marc bit his tongue. He knew he was a great quarterback. But he also knew he needed a good receiver.

"Could make young Hanson look better than his old man," Harold offered his opinion. "Hunter still holding the records here at the Academy, Jim? The old man still goading you on, boy?" he said, nodding at Marc.

"He still has the records," Marc grudgingly admitted. "But we'll see who holds the records after this next year!"

The older men laughed.

"Marc, you should talk to your father about getting that kid into the Academy. If he comes in as a sophomore next year, if he repeats his sophomore year, which it sounds like he could from an eligibility perspective," Harold went through the chronology as he spoke. "Then you've still got an outstanding year for yourself as a senior. Sure, the boy will get some coverage. But only being a sophomore, none of the recruiters are going to be too interested in him other than for summer camps. Best of all worlds for you, young Hanson. If there's a problem, you write it off to the 'inexperience' of the young Texan. But if it clicks, you get the headlines."

"Harold, you know my father pretty well. Don't you think that sort of recommendation would sound better coming from you. From his old coach, rather than his son?" Marc tried to make his voice sound steady and deep.

"Hell, I think I will give him a call," Harold banged his fist down on the table. "Owe that to Hunter," he said, remembering the new weight room Hunter had funded for him at the university. "And to you, Marc," he added, belatedly. "I would really like to see the two of you on the same team this next season. Any problems getting him in here, Jim?"

"Well, of course late admissions usually end up with Mr. Phillips," Jim planted the second critical point to the strategy that Marc had devised. "You guys might want to mention it to him while you're here on campus," Jim offered, turning from Harold to Richard.

First, the word from Harold Casey in his father's ear.

Then, twisting Phillips' arm.

It was the one-two punch, Marc had reasoned.

The word from Hunter, the money-man that Phillips and the Academy Trustees depended upon year after year.

The word from Harold, the trump card Phillips used Jim to maintain to keep the college admissions statistics he had perfected as headmaster.

"Well, I guess I will just have to have a word with Phillips," Richard Peabody sounded like the issue needed immediate resolution. "You know, I would really love to see Marc and that Greenwood kid up against the league this next year. That would make for some interesting match-ups!"

"Me, too," Harold Casey said, pushing himself up from the chair.

"So, it's a done deal?" Marc asked. "Harold, you'll speak to Dad. And then both of you will talk to Phillips?"

"Hey, that is something I would like to see myself," Jim laughed. "The two of you putting the squeeze on Ben Phillips!"

The other two coaches joined in the laughter.

Marc smiled.

That was something he would look forward to as well, Marc thought.

❦   ❦   ❦

There was a slight knock at Scott's door, just loud enough to wake him. As the door swung open, a beam of light cut through the darkness of the room and shown directly into his eyes.

"Go away!" he managed. "It's the middle of the night!" he said irritably. Scott turned toward the clock. The glowing numerals read 4:30 am.

"Wake up!"

He recognized Lindsey's voice in the darkness.

"What's up," Scott tried to rouse himself from the sudden awakening. "Is anything wrong?"

"No," Lindsey laughed. "Grab your mattress and follow me," he commanded.

"What!?!"

Scott thought he might have misunderstood Lindsey.

"Grab my mattress? Where are we going?"

"Mattress luge," Lindsey explained.

"What?"

"Mattress luge. Me and Andrew and you are going to luge the stairs in Wilcot on our mattresses. Now move your ass," Lindsey commanded, pushing Scott onto the floor and throwing Scott's mattress over his shoulder. "Mattress luge," Lindsey explained again, walking out of Scott's room with the mattress.

Scott sat on the floor trying to piece it together in his brain.

He and Andrew and Lindsey were going to ride their mattresses down the marble stairs in the Wilcot, he thought. Mattress luge, he thought, pulling his jeans on over his boxers and stumbling out the door after Lindsey. Probably made perfect sense, he thought, if you were Lindsey Quinlan.

Scott trotted after Lindsey in the darkness, close to the buildings as they rounded the outmost limits of the Circle.

"How are you going to get into Wilcot?" Scott asked.

"Easy. You have the key, man," Andrew said, jumping from behind the laurel bushes at the edge of the building.

"I don't have the key to Wilcot," Scott protested.

"You white boys. You all alike. So naïve. You got the key to the dorm?"

"Sure," Scott offered.

"And you got the key to the cafeteria?"

"Sure," Scott replied.

"And is it the same key, dumb-ass?" Andrew laughed.

Of course, Scott thought. How stupid of him. He had a master key for all of the buildings.

"OK, now you guys aren't going to break anything, right?" Scott asked, digging in his yesterday's jeans for the key that unlocked all of the doors at the Academy.

"Me break anything?" laughed Lindsey. "How could you think such a thing?"

Scott turned the key in the door on the basement level of Wilcot and the lock gave way.

A master key. He had a master key.

The other two boys ran past him with the mattresses and up the marbled steps to the first floor.

Scott was more cautious, however. He made a quick check around the Circle to make sure there weren't any lights on in any of the buildings before he entered. And he tried to listen for any sounds in the building, knowing that anyone in the building was probably already aware of them from the rough language Andrew and Lindsey were using as they jockeyed for position at the top of the stairs.

Scott took the stairs two at a time until he came alongside Andrew and Lindsey.

"How did you guys dream this one up?" Scott asked.

"You don't read very much, do you, Scott," Lindsey laughed as he slapped Scott soundly on the shoulder before lowering his mattress and careening down the stairs, head first.

"What's that supposed to mean?" he asked Andrew.

"I ain't even a prep and I read that book," Andrew shouted as he followed Lindsey down the stairs on his own mattress.

Is that where you learned about such things as mattress luge, Scott wondered? From a book?

"Come on you pussy!" Scott heard Lindsey's attempt at muffling his voice in the darkness at the foot of the stairs.

Scott positioned his mattress as he had seen Lindsey and Andrew do, mimicking them, and pushed off the landing into the darkness.

❦ ❦ ❦

They made it back before dawn. And no one caught them.

Mattresses in tact. Only a few bruises to show from their early morning antics in Wilcot. Except for Lindsey, who had dislocated another finger (which Andrew had expertly popped back into position).

And it had been fun, he thought, stretched out fully on his bed watching the dawn light through the window. Real fun!

A normal life.

A boy's life.

The life he should be living, he thought.

CHAPTER 21

Did they think he was a fool, Ben thought?

Did they think he didn't know what they were up to, what they did, every hour of every day while they were on his campus?

He knew.

He always knew, he thought, inspecting the new scratches on the freshly waxed parquet in Wilcot.

Sliding down the stairs?

How un-original! How childish!

It was the Greenwood boy. He knew the Greenwood boy must be involved someway in this, he thought.

But Ben knew how to handle such boys. He had years of practicing on betters than Greenwood, he reasoned.

So Greenwood liked high-jinx?

He could provide the boy with plenty, Ben thought.

They were all pandering to the boy. Jim. Marc. And now, apparently, Harold Casey and Richard Peabody. Trying to give him the run of the place.

Well not while he was in charge. Not while Ben Phillips was still headmaster at the Academy.

Catering to the boy, Ben thought.

Yes, that was it.

Jim had been catering to the boy since he first showed up in town.

Right down to giving him the key to the cafeteria, to the treasures of its stainless steel appliances. Probably the same key they had used to get into Wilcot, Ben reasoned.

Live by the sword, he thought. Die by the sword, he thought, developing his retribution.

It wasn't enough to discipline the boy. No, Ben thought. That might just make him a martyr.

Something more clever was needed, he thought, heading toward the kitchen area in the cafeteria building.

A little high-jinx of his own, he thought, reaching into his pocket for the prescription bottle.

He had seen the new orders from food service when the boy came on campus. He knew. Nothing escaped his attention.

He walked through the kitchen to the huge stainless steel doors of the commercial refrigerator and opened them with his key.

Where were they? They had to be in here somewhere, he thought, rummaging through the cavernous refrigerator.

Then he saw them. Neatly stacked along the far side, all in a row.

Six two liter bottles of root-beer.

High-jinx, Ben thought, as he opened the first bottle of root-beer and dumped in a half dozen of the pills from his prescription bottle.

Two could play that game, he thought, reaching for the second bottle and more of the small white pills.

🍁 🍁 🍁

"Allie! Telephone!" Heather called from the hallway.

Allie jumped from her bed and ran to the dorm phone.

"Scott!" she said expectantly.

"Ah, no. It's Will."

"Oh, Will," she tried to hide her disappointment. "I … I was expecting Scott to call tonight. He's been trying to reach me all week, but we keep missing each other."

"Sorry. Listen, I was running out of money and time and had to move up shooting on the movie. I need you to stop by the studio right now and then I need to film your dance sequence tomorrow. And you can lend a hand again on the crew, if you don't mind. It's a closed set for the next three days and I'm short-handed."

Allie thought a second. What else did she have to do over the long weekend other than sit in her room and wait for Scott's call? And to tell the truth, she was getting tired of waiting. He had been angry for over a week at her. Angry for no good reason. At least not the reason that he should have been angry about.

"OK. What's the address?" Allie asked, trying to calculate the cost of a cab ride into her weekly budget allowance.

"Not to worry. I'll send a car around for you in fifteen minutes."

And that was the end of the conversation.

Allie quickly combed out her hair, changed into her best jeans and the only clean t-shirt she had and repaired her makeup. That was about all that she could do in the time Will had given her. She walked out of the front door of the dormitory just as a stretched black limousine pulled to the curb. In the front passenger window was a sign with her name sketched in a failing magic marker. In an instant she went from worrying about cab fare to enjoying the comforts arranged for her in the back of the limo. Iced Pelligrino. A silver tray of cheeses and strawberries. Air conditioning that really worked. Luxuries that made the limo ride downtown all too short.

The limo pulled off of Broadway into an alley that had once been at the center of the theater district. It stopped in front of the one building that still supported an empty marquee on its façade. The driver came around the car and opened the door for Allie, then escorted her down a well-lit sidewalk on the side of the building to a door. Above the pedestal was an ancient placard with intricate lettering that read "Stagedoor". The driver keyed the lock and held the door open for Allie to enter, then scurried away back to the double-parked limo.

From her vantage point at the far backstage, Allie could see a dozen or so people milling about. A couple of men were working on a scaffold with a variety of translucent, multi-colored gels that covered large stage lights. A grip was tugging a large dolly with camera and cameraman across a track that ran in an elliptical orbit from one side of the stage to another. A young woman was wrestling with an uncooperative boom from which a huge, furry microphone extended. A stage decorator was positioning bedroom furniture at the opposite side of the stage. It appeared to be the same type of purposeful chaos that seemed to accompany Will wherever he went.

"Allie!" Will shouted from a position that at one time must have been the orchestra pit, but which now was covered over with planking and laced with a tangle of wires and cables. "I want you to meet someone!" he motioned her toward him.

She made her way through the equipment and busy bodies to where Will stood with a young woman wearing a somewhat gaudy silk robe and a boy in jeans and a t-shirt.

"Allie, I want you to meet some people. This is Seth Madden, our leading man," he began, "and this is our leading lady."

"Emily Ros!" Allie finished the introduction for Will. "I saw you in 'Disrespect' last year. You were incredible!" she gushed.

The movie star smiled at the obvious admiration of her young fan.

"I hear you are going to make me a wonderful dancer in Will's film," Emily said, stepping back and eyeing Allie from head to foot. "Not a bad body double for me," she said to Will, nodding in approval. "How do you do it, young Will?" she asked rhetorically. "How do you do it?"

Allie couldn't believe it.

She thought Will was just another kid with a video camera. Maybe a rich kid with really good video equipment and enough cash to hire a crew, but still just a kid working on some amateur summer project.

She had no idea when Will had asked her to double in place of Emily Ros. The Emily Ros!

She was standing here talking to Emily Ros.

"I'll try," she managed to stammer. "I'll try to make it … the dance … look good," her voice nervously searching for the words.

"To hell with the dance," Emily laughed. "Make me look good!" she said, putting her arm around Allie.

Will and Seth chuckled politely.

"OK, then let's get back to business," Will quickly directed Seth and Emily back to his obsession. "We'll shoot scenes 108 and 103 first," he said, flipping through a heavily annotated copy of the scenes. "If we have enough time, we'll do 105 tonight before we wrap. Once we get the scene set for 108 and the props and lights for 103 and 105, we'll get rid of the crew we don't need and close down the set. Emily," he continued, looking up reassuringly. "I didn't think you would mind if we let Allie sit in. That way she gets some better context for the dance sequence that we are filming tomorrow," his voice, his tone suddenly very formal, mature and directive.

"Why don't Allie and I get better acquainted while you set up Will?" Emily said, taking Allie by the arm and moving her to the edge of the stage behind a small three-panel screen set out stage left. Once there, Emily climbed into one of the tall canvas chairs and pulled a bottle of champagne from the silver top-hat next to it. As soon as Emily sat down, a middle-aged woman with big hair descended upon her with a large makeup brush. Emily offered no resistance to the attentions of the makeup assistant, ignoring her in favor of her conversation with Allie.

"You know," Emily continued. "I don't think as an actress you ever get accustomed to doing love scenes. No matter how many times you do them. It's usually part of the romantic storyline these days. But, here," she gestured to the side of the screen where two burly men were visible as they adjusted props on the stage, "on the set, it's really hard to get into character. The male leads have it easy," she smiled as the makeup artist brushed her way down Emily's throat. "All they have to show is a little ass every now and then."

Emily sat complacently, her hands firmly gripping the arm-rests of the tall chair as the makeup girl smiled politely and pulled open Emily's robe to began shading on body makeup to cover the tan lines and the white triangular areas stenciled by the sun across each of Emily's breasts.

Allie suddenly didn't know where to put her eyes.

Will had said that her dance was going to be a dream sequence that was part of a love scene. But, Allie had ignored the detail that a love scene might include a naked woman ... with a man.

"It's fine, dear," Emily noticed Allie's furtive glances and reassured her. "I'm very comfortable with my body," Emily said, as the makeup girl worked her way down Emily's body in routine fashion. "Why don't you show me what you are going to do for the dance sequence? That would be fun," she said encouraging Allie to take both of their minds off the intimacy of the body-makeup process as she stood and casually pulled the bottom of her robe up around her waist for the convenience of the makeup girl.

"Ah, sure, sure," Allie stammered, standing in concert with Emily. She took a few steps back, distancing herself.

Concentrate, she thought. Concentrate!

"I thought something like this to start," she stepped into a classic position, then twirled and brought her arms upward before extending them. Her tight jeans wouldn't allow a proper flexion of her right leg, but she did manage to finish the movement gracefully. "And if there is enough room, I could chain several of these together," she continued, altering her start position, arm position and the angle of her spin momentum.

"Very nice," Emily smiled as the makeup artist finally finished. "Wish I could still do that," she said. "I used to be a dancer, you know. Before the movie thing."

"Emily!" Will's voice echoed from the stage beyond the screen. "We're ready for a walk through of 108, if you please!"

"You are going to make me a wonderful dancer!" Emily said. Then, lowering her voice, "Now, if there was just any way for you to do this love scene for me, I think we could become best friends."

Emily winked as she walked past Allie and the paneled privacy screen toward the lighted stage.

Allie shook her head in disbelief. She was actually going to be Emily Ros in Will's film. Or rather she was going to be her double in the dance sequence, she thought, as she drifted around the small screen and to the edge of the black flooring over the orchestra pit.

The stage had been set as a bedroom. Huge backdrops had been lowered at obtuse angles to give the stage the appearance of a real bedroom, with soft lighting added to the curtained windows through which Allie could see what looked to be the vista of a snow covered landscape. The furnishings of the room were sparse, but elegant. The huge four-poster, king-sized bed overpowered everything else in the scene.

Will was talking to Emily and Seth, watching and coaching them as they walked through the beginning of a scene. It was a short scene, no more than a few lines of dialogue. Will was framing the scene with his fingers, scurrying around the periphery of the lighted section of the stage. He carried a roll of masking tape from a hook on his belt, from which he would pull short segments and place in "X" patterns on the floor. An X-mark on the floor where Emily was supposed to stop and turn. An X-mark where Seth would pause near the bed and beckon Emily to him. A line of tape tracing the path Emily would take from her first pause to the bedside. Then Will backed away from the set as Emily and Seth went through the scene again without scripts and placed an X-mark for each camera position, framing the actors as they did the scene within the box he made from his index fingers and thumbs. Will and the cameramen setting up the tripods for the cameras over the last set of X-marks Will had placed as Emily and Seth repeated their lines and their movements along the masking tape directions laid out on the floor of the stage.

Finally Will seemed satisfied. Or at least resolved.

"OK! We'll take ten minutes and close down the set! This is a closed set, tonight, ladies and gentlemen! Gaffers and grips and everyone else not directly involved in scenes 103, 105 and 108—thanks for your work, this will be a wrap for you tonight. See you back here tomorrow night at eight for the next scenes," Will barked orders to the crew in a voice over-aged for him.

Emily disappeared behind the privacy screen and Seth walked to the bathroom at the opposite side of the stage. The technicians started packing up their personal possessions and made their way off the set through the stage-door which Allie had entered. Within minutes, there were only a handful of people left on the set, talking in hushed tones and sipping coffee.

"Well, what do you think?" Will asked Allie energetically. "Pretty intense, don't you think?"

"I can't believe you do this, Will," she admitted. "I thought you were just fooling around with me. I had no idea you had Emily Ros in your film. *The Emily Ros!*"

"Cool, isn't it!" he smiled. "She owed my dad a favor. He got her the first movie role she ever had. So he called her up and asked her to be in my movie. She couldn't say no," he smiled mischievously.

"It's time people!" Will shouted. "Let's get this scene down, please. Seth, Emily, if you please!"

Suddenly everyone was back to work. The cameramen hung over their cameras, adjusting focus and checking lens. The lighting tech balanced precariously in her perch behind the lighting rig. The sound lady pulled her dolly back to its start position. And finally, Seth and Emily emerged on the lighted set.

"What we're going to do, people, is let the cameras run and just go through the scene a couple of times. I want to see how it looks on the monitors and let everyone get nice and comfortable. So, Seth ... Emily if there is a problem, just keep going with the scene. We'll do pickups later if we have to. OK. Let's make some magic!" Will wheeled abruptly back to a position midway between the two cameras. "Now, cameras," his voice low as small red lights appeared above each camera. A measured pause as he waited for Seth and Emily to get into their characters. "Action," his voice soft and reassuring.

Allie lost track of how many times they did the scene. Once Seth forgot his lines. One take, Emily stumbled over planking in the stage. But what really amazed her was how comfortable they all were with the nudity. And the touching. Even she wasn't embarrassed when they finally finished the last take.

"Great!" Will finally exclaimed. "Excellent work, everyone. That's a rap for tonight. Thanks to everyone. And to our star, Emily Ros," he said, clapping loudly.

The small crew joined half-heartedly in applauding for a few seconds, then quickly set about putting away their equipment and searching for their personal belongings after a long night's work.

"Everyone back at 3:30 tomorrow," Will ordered, glancing at his watch. "We're on union rates here, so it's 3:30 sharp!"

"Allie, you want to see some of the footage?" Will called to her across the stage.

She fell into a canvas chair next to Will and opposite a large video monitor. Will passed her a pair of earphones, pulled the tapes from the cameras and shoved them into a tape deck beneath the monitor. The cameramen worked around the two of them as the screen on the monitor was suddenly filled with the scene, as filmed from stage right, from Seth's perspective. Long shots first. Then close-ups of Emily's face. The whole scene replayed again and again. Each take no more than thirty seconds. Will readjusted the toggle switches on the tape deck. This time, the perspective on the monitor was from stage left, from behind Emily. Again, long shots first. Then close-ups of Seth's face. They went fast forward, pausing to watch a dozen short takes that looked promising.

"Pretty good footage," Will's voice seemed less than confident. "But just wait until you see what I do with it in the editing room. That's where I work my magic!"

Allie smiled to Will. Emily was so good, she thought. She made it look so real. Take after take. What had looked so contrived, so trite, on stage came across on the small monitors as so real. The passion of the moment was there even in the unedited takes. It wasn't Will's magic. It was Emily's that Allie saw.

"What I plan to do," Will continued, "is to dissolve into and out of your dance sequence from the scene we were just shooting. We can block you into and out of the dance scene before you leave tonight. It's like a dream sequence. Seth and Emily lying next to each other in bed. Then it's like one of them dreams that Emily is dancing and then the dream fades," he said, both of his arms tracing a slight movement from the bed to stage left and back. "Like her spirit leaving her body to dance and then returning," he said, articulating his vision. "At least, that's what I am trying for," his voice suddenly back in the moment.

"Sure," Allie agreed only slightly reluctantly. She glanced at her watch. Almost midnight. She was going to have to sneak into the Repertory dorm again. "Sure, I can stay for a while," she said, walking onto the set.

❦   ❦   ❦

It was three-thirty in the morning before Will's car dropped Allie off next to the Repertory and she scampered up the fire escape, through the third floor bathroom window of the dormitory and down creaking wooden stairs to the second floor rooms. As she passed the message board, she noticed a large pink note with her name on it. She pulled the note from the board and opened it. It was in Katrina's handwriting. It read "Allie, Where are you? Scott."

❦ ❦ ❦

The driver escorted Allie from the limo, down the alleyway to the stage door and keyed the lock. She pulled her bag up over her shoulder as she ducked inside the dim lighting at the back of the stage. At exactly 3:30.

She walked out onto the stage and looked around for Will. One of the cameramen recognized Allie and waived, motioning her to the side of the stage where Will was arguing with the lighting technician. She stood anxiously waiting for him to finish. She glanced around her. There were only a few people on the set today. The two cameramen and a couple of young women snaking cables along the edge of the stage.

"Allie!" Will shouted as he dismissed the lighting tech and walked hurriedly in Allie's direction. "Trying to get anything done on Saturday is a bitch. No one wants to work the weekend, I'm afraid. So, you ready for your big dance number?"

"I'm … I'm kind of nervous," she admitted.

"Sure. Sure. Of course," Will took her lightly by the arm and walked her to the edge of the stage and behind the privacy screen. "We'll just run through it a few times to get camera angles and lights and by then you will be all relaxed. It will be just like dancing at the Repertory recitals. Just ignore us!" Will joked, pushing his glasses back against his nose with one finger and gesturing to the crew. "Look I'm going to get things ready. Why don't you change? I have the music we discussed up on the stereo system for you. Of course, we'll dub in the sound track later. But this way you'll have some feel for what it will sound like in the movie. Now, hurry along. I want to get everything set for the shot."

Allie glanced over her shoulder to make sure no one was on her side of the privacy screen before she started to change. She peeled off her jeans and t-shirt and quickly pulled on the leotard and tights Will's costumer had sent over to her by courier that morning, then the small ruffle over the leotard. She laid a towel on the floor, dropped into a sitting position, and laced on the new ballet shoes that had been in the same package. Expensive shoes. More expensive than she had ever bought.

She stretched her legs and loosened her arms and shoulders and neck. She went through the choreography that she had worked on. Each movement. Trying her best to mimic the posture and body movements of Emily Ros.

"Allie!" Will shouted from the center of the stage. "We're ready when you are!"

This is it, Allie thought, as she picked herself up off the floor and summoned all of her poise and grace to walk onto the huge lighted stage area.

The camera men were busy working on their equipment and the lighting tech was up in lighting rig adjusting spotlights that illuminated the bedroom setting that had remained in tact from last night's shots. No one seemed to be paying much attention to her as she stood, nervously, center stage, waiting for Will's direction.

"OK," Will finally broke away from his pre-occupation with one of the monitors. "This is the area you have to work in. From here," he said, laying out a strip of masking tape. "To here," he judged the distance and then laid another strip of tape on the floor. "Is that good for you?"

Allie glanced around. It was a relatively small space. But it would do.

"Sure. That's fine, I guess," she said, tugging at the straps of her leotard.

"Well then, let's try a few dry runs," Will paced back to his position between the cameras. "Allie, we're going to run the cameras just to see how it looks on tape, but this is just for practice. So, we'll cue your music and then you just start whenever you're ready."

Allie smiled weakly. She walked to one edge of the area Will had framed for her and positioned for the start of the music.

"OK. Now, cue music," Will spoke deliberately.

One of the young women who had been moving cable had taken over the sound system duties and started the tape deck. She turned the volume of the music up until it filled the small auditorium.

Allie listened through a few bars of the music and began her routine. A slow fluid series of movements. She ignored everything but the music. She concentrated on the movement of her body to its rhythm. She finished the dance and stood at attention, right on the final mark that Will had laid for her.

"Great!" Will shouted. "Let's do it again! Allie one more time, if you please," he said, gesturing her to the start position marked on the stage.

And so it went. Time after time. Over a dozen takes.

"OK. Let's just take a break and see what we have. Yes. A break," Will's voice sounded frustrated. "Break everyone! Allie, you want to watch the tape with me, dear," his voice more a command than a request.

She obediently followed Will to the two chairs facing a large monitor behind the cameras. Will fiddled with switches and the monitor began to glow.

"We'll just run through the tape," Will smiled weakly. "And see what we've got so far."

She watched as she appeared on the monitor in the center of the stage. As the music came up, she followed the movements of the first take. Then the second. Then the third.

"It looks fake," she volunteered after a few takes.

"Yes. Exactly. That was what I was thinking," Will pondered the lack of passion in the precision of Allie's movements. "Not exactly what I had in mind," Will's face was troubled.

"Will. If I were Emily Ros ... I mean if I were the main character. I ... I don't think I would be thinking about dancing while I was ... making love. Not dancing like I was doing."

"Go on," Will seemed intent on what she had to say. "You're a dancer. Like the main character. What would you be thinking about?" he said, tossing his annotated script on the floor. "Be honest. I want to know. Really."

Allie closed her eyes. She was a little embarrassed by the question. But Will was so earnest. He was so caught up in the movie. In making a good movie. And he was depending on her. He had given her a big chance. Dancing for Emily Ros. She owed him, Allie thought. She owed him complete honesty. One artist to another, she thought.

"First," she said, reaching back into her own memories. "It would be more like I was watching myself making love than like a dance routine," she said, the first truth opening the way to others. "I would be moving around the bed," she continued, her eyes closed, imagining the scene. "Looking at myself ... looking at the two of us," she felt her cheeks blush. "And then," she paused, reluctantly. "it would be like I was feeling his hands on me ... on my body ... even though he wasn't there."

"And how would I know that?" Will asked. "What would I see if I were inside your mind?"

She kept her eyes closed tightly.

"I would be leaning against the bed post ... or maybe against a couch ... or something," she stammered. "And ... and my hands would be running over my body," she admitted, her hands hesitantly tracing the motions as she leaned back in the folding chair.

"I see it. I see it, now. I see what you are seeing. And then what?" Will asked intently.

"And then … I would see myself in a tall mirror," Allie shared her stream of consciousness. "Standing in front of a tall mirror. Seeing myself. Just like he would see me."

"Yes!" Will's voice was giddy. "Exactly! You are so independent. And you have all of these feelings that wash over you. And you can't let go of being by yourself. But, then you realize how good it is to be part of someone else. And you don't want to just be you. You want to be with him … part of him. Exactly! That is exactly what I am looking for!"

Allie opened her eyes, reluctantly.

Will's face was beaming.

"Can you do that? What you just said? Can you … oh, I don't know … make me see that through the camera?" he said anxiously.

"Yeah," she nodded her head. "I think so. If you can give me just a few minutes to practice. And if I don't have to stay within the tape," she teased, gesturing to the scuffed pieces of masking tape littering the stage floor.

"Oh, no problem. We'll have to relight the set anyway. Around the bed. And we can pull in a couch. I have a great old Victorian couch. They call it a fainting couch. It'll look great. And a mirror. We have a mirror. A big one. So, you … you practice and we'll re-dress the set and re-light the stage," Will mumbled walking away from her in his typical manic pace.

Allie's embarrassment quickly gave way to reflection.

How was she going to do this, she thought, walking toward the bed?

Emily would be lying on her back at the edge of the bed, she thought, trying to recreate the scene from last night's takes.

She flopped down onto the bed and thought about what it would be like to be Emily Ros. How she would rise from the bed, her body following the urgings of her imagination, and gracefully move around the edge of the bed. Spinning. Spinning. Small spins. Always with her eyes on the bed. On the two of them, Emily and Seth, lying there in bed together making love. And then how she would flutter away, in quick, tiny steps to the couch, she thought, tracing out the movement on the stage as she thought through it.

"Will! You need to put the coach here!" she shouted, pulling up a row of tape and tearing it into a big "X" on the floor as she had seen Will do.

She closed her eyes again.

Lying back on the couch, she thought through the movements. How her hands would flow. Then, almost ghostlike, finding herself in front of the mirror.

"And the mirror should go here!" she insisted, laying out another X on the floor.

"Okay. Okay." Will was frantically trying to comply with her instructions.

She saw the scene in her mind. Standing in front of the mirror. Her back arched. Her body rocking from side to side. An instant on the ball of her right foot. Just like Emily. And then a mad rush back to bed. To be with Scott, she thought absently. Then, correcting herself with a smile, for Emily to be with Seth, she thought, rushing back across the stage to the bed.

She had it all in her mind now. Every movement.

"Well, this is certainly going to be different," Will admitted as he watched her step through the movements. "Much better, I think! Now, you go freshen up and I'll deal with the damn lights," he instructed.

Allie retired to the solitude behind the privacy screen. She pulled out her makeup purse and used the wall mirror to repair the damage her earlier exertion had caused. Then she brushed out her hair and sat down in the tall folding chair that Emily had used. She closed her eyes and went through the series of movements again and again. Seeing herself as she spun and glided and pranced across the stage in the lights. She opened her eyes and caught her reflection in the mirror.

The image she saw in the mirror was different from the one she saw in her mind.

What was it, she thought?

What was so different between that reflection and the images in her head?

She closed her eyes again and went through the sequence of movements.

She let out a small gasp as her stomach began to churn and her muscles tensed.

She knew what was so different. Why the reflection from the mirror looked so different from the images in her head.

The reflection in the mirror had on a ridiculous leotard, she thought.

The image in her mind was … was … naked. Just like Emily had been last night in the scene.

Her breath came more quickly.

The color rose in her cheeks.

She couldn't do it, she thought, biting her lip. Not naked. She just couldn't.

The reflection in the mirror seemed to mock her.

A petty image of a silly girl, in an outrageously gaudy recital costume, waiting for a bit part in a small town dance recital.

A 'want-to-be', she chided the image in the mirror critically. Just another dancer who couldn't quite make it, she thought.

She hated that reflection.

She wanted nothing to do with it.

She bent over in the chair deliberately and unlaced the toe shoes. She took a deep breath and stood up in front of the mirror on the wall.

She knew what she had to do.

She slipped the thin straps of the leotard off her shoulders and slowly pulled it down, letting it fall on the floor beneath her. She pulled her tights off and laid them over the back of the chair. Then she took the brush she had seen the makeup girl use on Emily Ros from the box on the floor behind the screen and began to shade out her tan lines. When she was finished, she stood in front of the mirror with her eyes closed until she had the image she aspired to indelibly fixed.

Then she opened her eyes.

The reflection in the mirror was now an exact replica of the image in her mind.

"Oh!" Will suddenly came around the side of the privacy screen. "I ... I didn't know you were changing," he stammered, backing nervously around the screen.

"Will, I think ..." her voice hesitated, but she made no effort to cover herself. "I think I should do the scene this way," she said softly. "Without the leotard," she said.

She gazed at her naked body in the mirror and waited for Will's reply.

"Well ... yes ... I can see why," Will's voice was incredibly professional coming from the other side of the privacy screen. Then his voice changed to one of excitement in a moment of insight. "Of course! Exactly! How silly of me!" he exclaimed as he came around the screen, again. "That is so obvious!" he said, keeping his eyes fixed on her face. "I mean ... if you ... if you ... don't mind ... I mean ... doing it ... this way."

She laughed at the feigned modesty Will was trying so hard to muster. She knew that he was thinking about lights and camera angles and dissolves. She knew that she was just a piece in the puzzle he was trying to sort into the movie that was in his head.

Suddenly, she didn't feel very naked at all. She just felt ... right.

"So, I'll get things set up, then," Will smiled as his mind darted back to the details of capturing the scene for his movie and he disappeared around the screen.

Allie glanced back at the reflection in the mirror. She arched her back and shifted her weight to the ball of her right foot. And, for a moment, from the neck down at least, the reflection she saw was of Emily Ros.

CHAPTER 22

Scott sorted through the vocabulary flash cards he had made.

Didactic—intended to instruct, he thought, pausing only briefly to flip over the flash card for confirmation.

Mr. Davis, the SAT instructor was didactic, Scott thought as a memory aid.

Poignant—profoundly moving, he remembered, flipping the card confidently.

Petunias were poignant, he thought, laughing at how absurd the mnemonic seemed.

Unfettered—he paused. Not something, he remembered from the prefix, tapping his finger on the card. Unbound, he thought. Set free from restrictions, he remembered, flipping the card. He couldn't come up with any aid on unfettered and that was why he always had problems with it, Scott thought. He would just have to memorize the word, he guessed, taking another drink of root-beer.

One after the other. Card after card. The cards he knew in one pile. The cards he didn't in another. Over and over. For the entire hour he had set aside. The pile of unknown words shrinking each time he went through the deck.

Why was it so hard, today, he thought? Usually he didn't have any problems with the vocabulary words they had given him to study for the SAT.

"Phone call for you Scott," Andrew yelled through the door.

Allie, Scott thought, jumping from his chair and running down the hallway toward the receiver dangling from the end of its cord. He stumbled a bit as he slid to a stop, banging against the wall.

"Allie?" he asked enthusiastically.

Through the earpiece came a familiar French accent.

"No, *my little rabbit*, I am afraid it is not your Allie," Virginia Simone's voice was both apologetic and soothing. "It is your friend, Virginia," her voice light and playful. "I promised I would cook something special for you," she reminded him.

Scott loved to listen to Virginia's voice. Her French. Her accent was almost like listening to his mother.

"Ms. Simone," Scott's French came out with obvious pleasure. "How did you find me, here?" he asked.

"Ah, you are not so very hard to find, my little rabbit," Virginia laughed. "One has only to look for big sweaty boys playing the football, I think.".

"Jim asked me to help him here at the camp," he felt compelled to explain. "I get to stay at the Academy at one of the dorms."

"Oui, and that is why I am calling you there," Virginia continued to tease him. "So you will come and have a wonderful dinner with me tomorrow night. Yes. You will come?"

"Yes. I ... I would love to come to have dinner with you," Scott smiled again at the prospect of someone, of Virginia, cooking a French meal for him. A real French meal. "Where do you live? Is it close to campus?"

"Oh, but of course. I think you know the house, already. The small cottage next to the car park. You know it? Next to the car park."

He had passed the small house many times and had parked in the adjacent lot when he had worked maintenance at The Academy. He had never realized that Virginia lived there, though.

"Yes, I know the place," he assured her. "I have practice until six, but I can come after that."

"Yes, clean up yourself for me, I think," she laughed. "No boys smelling of the football in my house, if you please," she joked. "So, you will be here at seven and we shall eat a wonderful meal and speak French together. And you can tell me all about the football, I think?"

"Sounds great!" Scott. "I'll be there at seven."

"Goodbye then my little rabbit," Virginia ended the conversation quickly, as if distracted, the sound of a door closing and a male voice in the background.

Scott hung up the phone and stood smiling in the hallway. He liked Ms. Simone ... Virginia. And he liked the idea of spending an evening with her, speaking French.

"You have any duct tape?" Lindsey Quinlan interrupted Scott's reflection as he hobbled down the hallway past the phone.

"Duct tape?" Scott considered the request as bizarre.

"Yeah," Lindsey held up his left foot to reveal a huge blister on his heel that had broken open.

"God, Lindsey!" Scott exclaimed. "That's disgusting!"

"Yeah," Lindsey smiled back impishly. "I was going to put some Band-Aids on it and then tape over them with duct tape for practice," he said. "Got any duct tape?"

"No," Scott chuckled at Lindsey's practical solution. "But I'm sure Jim has some in the cage. I'll run down and see," he offered. "And I'll grab some antibiotic ointment and NewSkin while I'm there as well. Don't want my tailback limping around on me," he smiled.

"Thanks man," Lindsey offered, hobbling away toward the shower room. "I think I'll wash my feet," he muttered, limping away and curling his nose against his own smell.

Lindsey seemed to smell particular bad, Scott thought. Worse than usual. But then, the guy never showered, he thought, steadying himself against the wall.

"Hey, Lindsey," he said, his voice weaker than intended. "I … I don't feel so … so good," he managed.

The hallway seemed to be spinning around him.

Lindsey was in front of him, talking.

But Scott didn't hear anything.

How funny it was, he thought, watching Lindsey's mouth move but not hearing his voice.

How funny it was, he thought, as everything went black.

🍁   🍁   🍁

Scott suddenly choked as his stomach convulsed and a terrible gritty texture appeared in his mouth. He spit it into a large porcelain bucket a woman in white was holding under his chin.

He threw up again.

And again.

Black, tarry material, covering the bottom of the porcelain bucket.

"It's OK," the woman in white was saying. "It's OK. We just needed to get it out of you. Just go ahead. Get it all out of you," she said, offering the bucket to him again as he purged his stomach contents.

🍁   🍁   🍁

It was dark.

He was cold.

And the sickening smell of antiseptic was in his nose.

He propped himself up in the small bed.

Lindsey Quinlan was sitting next to him, thumbing through a Sports Illustrated.

"Where am I?" he asked.

"Man, am I glad to see you," Lindsey whispered. "You scared the shit out of me! Andrew," he called out. "Andrew, he's awake."

"Can I have some water?" Scott asked, unable to right himself completely in the bed.

He watched Lindsey pour out some water from a pitcher into a plastic cup and saw Andrew walk through the door.

"Man, that must have been some nasty shit you took," Andrew said, shaking his head. "What's up with you man? Why would you do something stupid like that?"

Scott was confused. His head was pounding. And his stomach was so sore.

"What happened?" he asked. "Where am I?"

"You're in the infirmary," Lindsey whispered as he handed Scott the water. "You must have had some bad drugs or something, 'cause you passed out right in the dorm."

"Yeah, man," Andrew broke in. "I could tell it was drugs. I seen that shit before. Bad shit!"

"I ... I didn't take any drugs."

Lindsey and Andrew looked at each other, puzzled.

"Well that shit got in you some way," Andrew offered.

"I wanted to call 911. But Andrew wouldn't let me," Lindsey said, shoving Andrew.

"No 911, man," Andrew said. "First thing the hospital do is run a drug screen. And then you would be screwed, white boy."

"Drug screen? Why? I don't take any drugs."

"Look, Scott," Lindsey said, pouring more water into his cup. "Someone must have snuck something into your food or something. Because you were one whacked out dude when we got you here. The nurse gave you something to make you throw up and we made you chew up some charcoal that she gave us when you came around."

"She was going to call an ambulance," Andrew said. "But I talked her out it."

"Some talk," Lindsey scoffed. "You threatened to beat the shit out of her. And you think she's just going to forget that, you stupid jerk?" he said, pushing at Andrew again.

"No worries, Lindsey. I will use all of my charm on the lady. She'll be wrapped around my little finger before we get out of this place."

Scott rinsed again, trying to get rid of the gritty material out of his mouth.

"You made me eat charcoal?" he asked, spitting again.

"Think of it as dessert," Lindsey offered. "Nurse said it would soak up whatever you didn't throw up."

"So how's our patient?" the nurse said, as she pushed Andrew and Lindsey back away from the bed. "Feeling better," she said, taking Scott's wrist and feeling for a pulse. "God knows, child, you sure are looking better than when you came in here."

"I didn't … I don't … take drugs," he said. "I never.…"

"That's what your two friends here said, sweetie. And that one should know," she said, winking at Andrew. "That's right. You heard me. I see you there looking so proud of yourself," she said.

"So, what happens now?" he asked.

"Well, first, you tell your friends to leave you with me. And then," she said, "you tell that one," she said, pointing at Andrew, "that he owes me an apology. And some roses."

"Missy, you too sweet for roses," Andrew offered, smiling. "Chocolate. That's what you need. Fine dark chocolate."

"And just where do you think I am going to be getting that from," she laughed, teasing the boy. "Certainly not from a skinny little boy like you!"

"I didn't take any drugs," he said again.

"I heard you, darling. But your friends already convinced me of that. So, for now, this is just between the four of us. As far as I'm concerned, it was just a stomach virus. A 24-hour stomach virus," she said, making a short note on his medical file.

❦   ❦   ❦

Scott lay in bed in the darkness.

Where did the drugs come from? Who would have tried to drug him? One of the boys, trying to play some sort of prank? He doubted it. Where would they get any drugs? And why? They all liked him.

Maybe it was just bad sandwich meat from the frig in the cafeteria, he thought. Maybe it wasn't drugs at all. Maybe it was just food poisoning.

Unlikely he thought, trying to sip some more water through the straw in his cup.

The root-beer!

He hadn't remembered opening any of the new bottles of root-beer that had just come in. But the top had already been twisted off on the bottle he had used. He was sure of it.

Someone had opened the bottle and put drugs in it.

Someone had tried to drug him. Maybe even kill him!

Why?

Who would do that, he wondered, setting the cup aside?

Who?

CHAPTER 23

Scott felt better the next day. Just a little tired. Hung over a bit from the drugs, perhaps. And restless. He didn't like being confined in the infirmary. But it was afternoon before the nurse finally let him leave. Taking his pulse and blood pressure one more time before sending him on his way with an envelope for Andrew.

He went straight to the cafeteria and keyed the refrigerator door to check on the root-beers.

But where he was sure there had been five two liter bottles remaining, there was just empty space.

Someone had taken them!

He jogged back to his dorm, to his room.

No root-beer bottle. Not in his room. Not in the trash.

The person who had drugged him had come back and destroyed whatever evidence might remain.

Scott was left with only his suspicions. And a growing apprehension as to who he could, and could not, trust.

It was a few minutes before seven when Scott pulled into the parking area next to Virginia Simone's little cottage. He had dressed in his best khakis and borrowed a fancy shirt and tie from Andrew. He had even forsaken sneakers for real shoes. He was glad to be out of the dorm. Glad to be alive, actually.

He rang the doorbell and waited.

Virginia opened the door.

"Hello, my little rabbit," she offered with a half smile. "I had heard you were not feeling too well? And do you still feel like keeping me company?" she said, taking Scott by the arm and leading him into the front room.

She seemed ... sad, he thought. Not at all like he remembered her.

She seemed, sad and tired, he thought.

"I don't often have company, here," she said, falling into a well-worn chair next to the front window.

She sat on one of her legs, like a teenage girl, and dangled her shoe as she rocked the other leg back and forth. She looked so young, more like someone his own age. Only sad and tired.

"I ... I could always come back later if this isn't a good time," he offered.

"Oh, no, my little rabbit," she smiled. "I am just a little sad, today, you know, because I have a friend that I haven't seen in a long time. And," she paused, "he came to see me, but he could not stay very long, I think. And, so, I miss him a bit too much maybe."

Then she turned back to Scott.

"But tonight, we shall have some fun together," she said. "We shall speak French, only French, all night. And have some good food. And some nice Bordeaux! And so, we begin," she said, standing and motioning for Scott to follow her into the small kitchen.

It took over an hour to finish preparing the meal that she had started. Vegetables to wash and peel and cut. Meat to sauté with fresh herbs and butter and fresh mushrooms. Even fresh dough for the dinner rolls. It was all so much fun for him. Helping Virginia in the kitchen. Talking as they sipped a wonderful red wine from huge crystal goblets. It reminded him of home. Of the kitchen duties he had so begrudgingly performed under his mother's watchful eyes. With his sister and his father. All of them in the kitchen. Working together. The wonderful sights and sounds and smells all coming back to him.

They nibbled so much during the prep that neither of them were really hungry for the meal when it was ready to be eaten. And they both preferred the conversation and their shared language. So they just lingered over the dinner table. Eating the hot rolls, dripping with butter. Drinking the wine. And talking.

She must be as lonely as he was, Scott thought. To talk so much. To have so much to say.

"Was it a good day for you?" she finally asked, pushing her dish back away from her and resting her elbows on the table, holding the half-empty wine goblet with both hands in front of her. "Today. Was it a good day?"

Scott thought.

He was alive. That was good.

He had a place to stay.

And he had Virginia to talk to.

"Ah, I think that you must miss that young lady of yours?" Virginia skipped quickly from one subject to the next. "It is hard being away from the one you love," Virginia reflected. "Very hard sometimes, I think," she said, emptying her goblet.

"I think her days are really busy. And she has made friends with people in the City. So I think she is OK. But we haven't seen each other in almost a month. Our schedules just never seem to work out."

"Yes. The City is full of distractions, I think," Virginia said, as she filled her goblet from a newly opened bottle.

He thought about the comment.

"Oh, I don't think she is too distracted. She is pretty focused on doing well at the Repertory," he said. "And I think she is being in a movie."

"A movie? Really? What movie?"

"One of Marc Hanson's friends is making a movie and he asked Allie to be a dancer in it. So she is doing that and helping out as part of the crew. We haven't gotten to talk too much this week, because they are shooting her dance scene. I was going to go down to the City with Marc to see her, but … well things didn't work out."

"So you cannot watch her make the movie?" Virginia stood up and began to clear away the dishes from the table.

"I couldn't leave the Academy. And besides, Allie said something about it being a closed set, whatever that is," he explained, following Virginia's lead and tidying up the mess he had made at the table, following her into the small kitchen to deposit his dirty place setting.

"And when you do visit, when you do go into the City, you will stay with Marc? At Marc's home in the City?" she asked, taking his dishes and rinsing them thoroughly in the sink before putting them in the dishwasher.

"Yeah. Marc's place is huge. And his parents are never around. Except at supper. They have this ritual about supper. Everyone has to get dressed up for supper," the description not nearly adequate for the event.

"So, you see Marc's father?" Virginia asked, slurring her words a bit.

"Sure. I guess," he said, following her back into the front room. "He was here yesterday, at the Academy, watching Marc practice. It was really nice for Marc. Do you know Marc's father?"

"Yes," Virginia's voice had a slight tremor. "I see him, perhaps when he visits the Academy."

Virginia's voice seemed distant to Scott. As if she were far away, thinking about something else of importance to her.

The wine, Scott thought. She had had a bit too much to drink, he thought.

"He is a very rich man, I think," Virginia added. "And very powerful."

"Stinking rich!" he agreed. Then, feeling the effects of the wine he had consumed during the meal, "Uh, Virginia, where is the bathroom?" he asked bluntly.

"Right down the hall on the right," she responded, curling up into a small ball on the sofa. "Just there," she gestured awkwardly.

Scotty followed the gesture, walking down the tiny hallway to the last door before the bedroom. He shut the door behind him and politely lifted the seat cover before relieving himself. He stood absentmindedly glancing around the pink-tiled bathroom at the small pictures, the basket of bath beads and the perfumed oils. He could smell the scent of the vanilla from the half-burned candles in the window.

Everything was so neat in the small cottage, he thought, closing the toilet seat. Everything in its place. And all of the rooms were so bright. Not like the darkness of the dorm. A woman's touch in every room, he thought, as he rinsed his hands under the faucet. Light, pastel, frilly.

He turned to reach for the small hand towel on the rack behind him. Above the rack was a shelf full of bottles. As he dried his hands, he glanced down the row of bottles. Perfume. Hand cream. Moisturizer. And at the end of the row, an elegant blue bottle with a large silver medallion embossed on it. The medallion inscribed with an intricate family crest and a monogram. A single letter. H.

Then it hit him.

He had seen that very same bottle before.

At Marc's place.

It was the Hanson family cologne.

It was Marc's father, he realized. The 'friend' Virginia had been referring to. The one that she missed.

Virginia was in love with T. Hunter Hanson!

This is where they met. In her cottage. He stayed here with her. He even left his cologne here.

Hunter hadn't come to see Marc.

He had come to see Virginia.

Scott leaned back against the cold tiles on the bathroom wall.

Did Marc know?

Did Marc know about his father and Virginia?

Did he know that his father came to the Academy to see her?

Virginia. With Marc's father.

He could see it. Her easy grace. His charm. Their shared elegance.

It was just so … cosmopolitan. All very French, it seemed to him.

He walked back down the hallway into the front room to find Virginia nodding, barely able to keep her eyes open.

"I think perhaps I am not such a good hostess for you tonight," she said, her French accent now so slurred he had trouble catching the phrases. "Perhaps a little too much wine for me? And perhaps a little too much sadness for you, I think?"

"Oh, it has been wonderful," he insisted. "I had a wonderful time. I loved fixing the meal with you. I haven't done that in such a long time. And talking. I miss speaking in French."

"Well, then, we must plan another meal, my little rabbit. Just the two of us," she smiled. "But now, I am afraid that my eyes are too tired to stay awake any longer. And I find that my legs, well," she sounded sad again, "they are not working so good, it seems. So perhaps I can use a good, strong football player tonight. To help me to my bed?" she asked, trying, unsuccessfully to stand on her own.

Scott helped her up from the sofa, lifting one of her arms around him so that she could support herself, walking slowly with her back down the small hallway to the last door.

"I am not so nice, it seems," she said. "Not so nice to make you take care of me."

"Don't worry about it," he offered, leaving her grasping the small wooden chair for support as he moved over to pull the duvet back from the bed and rearranged the sheets.

She was already undressing when he turned around.

"Now, if you can just put me to bed, my little rabbit, and cover me up so that I am not so cold, I think then I will say a good night to you so that you can be with your friends. With your footballers," she said, holding out her hand for his support.

She seemed so small and fragile standing there in the bedroom, holding onto the chair, reaching for him with a thin white hand.

It would take more than a hand, Scott thought, to get her from the chair to the bed. He threw her arm back over his shoulder, then lifted her off of the ground and carried her to the bed, covering her quickly.

"Good night, my little rabbit," she whispered.

Her eyes closed. And she was asleep.

Scott stood looking at her.

Such a beautiful person. So nice to him. And so incredibly sad, it seemed.

He turned off the lights as he made his way through the cottage and locked the door behind him.

❦ ❦ ❦

What had she done, Allie thought, downing her second drink as quickly as the first? It would have been fine to do the scene for Will in the costume. That was what he had originally expected.

But no. She had the bright idea to do it in the nude! Dancing without a stitch on.

"So you want another?" Seth asked.

"Do I ever! Did Will tell you? Did he tell you about what I did?"

"Yeah. He told me," he laughed. "Can't wait to see the rushes!"

Allie punched Seth Madden in the stomach.

"You're so bad!" she shouted over the music. "Get me another Cosmopolitan, you bad boy!"

She liked flirting with Seth. Much too old for her. But he was a movie star, after all. And just about every other woman in the bar would die to have him paying as much attention to her as he was paying to Allie.

"So where is everybody? Is Will still trying to chat up that girl from Bradbury-Meir? The earnest one with the horn-rimmed glasses?"

"He seems to be having a good time," Seth said. "Your friend Vanessa is out front, making nice with the paparazzi and the new male model on the Times Square billboard. Emily was just here to make an appearance, so she left over an hour ago, as soon as the paparazzi recognized her. Strange how you girls work. Can't get enough of the cameras until you get famous, then you'll do anything to stay out of their range. Not me. I'm a simple man. I love the camera," he said before bending close to her. "And it loves me!"

"What happened to the other girls?"

"Wendy was showing off her humps to some Latino guy in front of the DJ. And the last time I saw Vicky, she was headed off to the ladies room with some glorious redhead!"

The sound of Vicky's name made Allie's skin cover with goose flesh. She didn't want to think about Vicky. She didn't want to think about dancing naked in a movie. She didn't want to think about anything.

The bartender handed Allie her cocktail.

"Pay the man, Seth," she said coyly.

Seth pulled out a twenty from a roll in his pocket and gave it to the bartender as Allie begin to drain the glass.

"So, the new movie star going to dance with the leading man? Or is she just too, too cool for that?"

"You couldn't keep up with me," she teased. "I'm *a professional!*"

"Prove it. Dance with me."

Allie drained the glass quickly, grabbed Seth by the hand and pulled him onto the dance floor amongst all of the gyrating bodies. The lights were flashing around them and the music was fast. It fit the mood perfectly and she made the most of the beat.

He wasn't a bad dancer, she thought, dancing just a bit too close to Seth. And he had a great ass, she thought, as she twirled around him.

"So, what do you think," she said. "Can Will pick a dancer or can Will pick a dancer?"

The music slowed and Seth pulled her toward him. They began to move in unison.

"I don't know anything Will's ability to pick dancers," he whispered in her ear. "But he certainly understands beauty."

Allie felt her legs give way slightly and Seth's arms tighten around her.

"You're a beautiful girl, Allie. And you can be anything that you want to be."

🍁 🍁 🍁

"Allie. Allie! Wake up."

The sun was just coming up. It was too early. She wanted to sleep.

"Allie. Get up! Get up now!"

It was a male voice.

What was a man doing in the dorm, she thought, dazed and confused?

"Allie."

She felt someone shaking her and opened her eyes as much as she could. She was laying in bed. In a big bed. In a huge room. And Marc Hanson was standing over her.

"Where am I?"

"You're at my place. Don't you remember? Don't you remember last night?"

She remembered parts of last night.

She remembered making the movie. And going to club with Will and the cast and crew. And meeting her friends there. And drinking way too much.

But it all got a bit fuzzy after the first few drinks.

"I was at Boomers, I think."

"No shit! With Will and his crowd. What the hell did you think you were doing?"

"I was dancing. I remember I was dancing. With Seth Madden. The actor. From Will's movie. Were you at Boomers?"

"God, what a mess. Get out of bed. Now!"

Allie suddenly realized she didn't have any clothes on underneath the bed covers.

"Where … where are my clothes?"

"Well, we'll just have to ask Mr. Madden, I guess," he said, gesturing toward the naked man passed out on the floor beneath the room's huge bay window.

"OH MY GOD! What did I do?"

"For starters, you dropped your knickers for Mr. Madden there. Then, let's see. Oh, yeah. And you just loved posing for all of those photographers out in front of Boomers when you left there this morning, Mr. Madden in tow. No wait. That wasn't the best part. No I think the best part was getting yourself filmed in the fucking nude in a fucking movie. Yeah, I think that was the best part!" he said, venting his anger with every word.

"Oh, Marc. Don't tell Scott," she said. It was all she could think to say.

"Not to worry Allie. I don't think I am going to have to tell Scott anything. Get your ass out of bed. Now!" he said, grabbing her arm.

Allie tried to pull a sheet up around her to cover herself as best she could as Marc dragged her from the bed.

"Marc, you're hurting me! You're hurting my arm!" she protested as he pulled her along, out of the bedroom, down the hallway and into his room.

"Sit down."

Marc pulled out a chair in front of his computer desk.

"So, let's start out with the New York Times. Shall we? I think you will find the photos in the living section on page 3 especially entertaining."

He shoved a Sunday Times at Allie and she opened the paper to page 3.

There she was. Her short red dress just a little too short. Katrina on one side. Vicky on the other. Both of them kissing her as Seth embraced the three of them. It had all of their names under the picture. All of them but hers. She was described merely as "Seth's companion" in the caption.

"'Seen about Town' I think they call this section," Marc's voice overly loud. "I'll say. Seen about all over the fucking country. Seen about everywhere the Times gets delivered today."

Maybe it wasn't too bad, she thought.

Scott didn't read the Times. At least not the society pages. But his friends might, she thought.

"Oh, and that's not the best of it," Marc continued, pushing her aside and typing frantically on the computer keyboard.

"Oh no. You mean the pictures on the internet, as well?"

"No. The picture isn't on the internet. That would have been a pleasant surprise next to this," he said, pointing the curser to a small thumbnail on the screen and clicking the mouse.

It was on the internet.

She was on the internet.

A video clip of her on the internet.

Dancing.

Naked!

She covered her face in shame.

"Turn it off! Turn if off!" she pleaded.

She heard the music in the background. It was the music from the movie set. The clip was from Will's movie.

"Stupid girl! God, you are so stupid. What do you think the Repertory is going to do if anyone there sees this clip."

Allie uncovered her eyes.

The clip was still running. She was still dancing. Still naked.

"I'm ruined. It's all over for me. Everything. It's all over," she sobbed.

The music coming from the computer finally came to an end.

"I can fix the clip," Marc said. "It will take me a couple of hours to get the video pulled. But I can't do anything about the downloads from the time it was put up until they take it down. That's something you will have to figure out for yourself."

Marc spun Allie around to face him.

"And I can deal with Mr. Madden," he paused. "But the Times. Well, the Times is on the street, baby. And there ain't nobody fixing that one!"

"Oh, Marc. What have I done?" she sobbed.

CHAPTER 24

Phillips sat his morning tea down on a coaster next to his computer. He put his right thumb on the biometric keypad and entering his password with his left hand. He thumbed through the Times as the machine booted up.

He liked Sunday mornings. He liked the quietness of Sunday mornings. All of the young teenagers still asleep, sleeping late. No official duties. His time to catch up, he thought.

As the computer screen finally stabilized, he clicked through to the digital folder he was looking for, entered the final password, and launched the media player with nervous anticipation. That was the thing about technology, he thought. Sometimes it worked. Sometimes it didn't. Not at all something you could depend upon. Just a tool. That was all. Just a tool.

The file folder opened, displaying a short list of file names that were nothing more than dates and times. He looked specifically for Friday. For Friday evening.

There it was. 0621.2214. Friday evening. 10:14.

He was so clever.

Installing the digital cameras in the small cottage on Academy property had been easy. He had just waited until that dreadful French women had gone on holiday in the spring.

But figuring out a way to sort through all of the video feed from her residence. That had been the clever part.

After all, he was no "peeping Tom." He could care less about what the women did in her own home. And he certainly had no prurient interest in her.

His interest was very specific.

And his solution had been so insightful.

Rig the cameras.
Digitally monitor the feed 24x7.
Date and time stamp the recordings into files.
But which recordings?
That was simplicity itself, he thought.
A single woman living alone in the cottage.
The answer was obvious.
Start caching the video when the toilet seat was raised!
He laughed.

It had all been so simple. The nerdy college student out of Boston never asking any questions. Just installing the new lighting fixtures and cameras. Rigging the toilet seat switch out of sight. Installing the software on Phillips computer and testing the system. A day's work. Well worth the $500 he had paid the boy for his work, for his silence.

Friday evening. 10:14. He launched the file.

A mosaic popped up on the computer screen. One square for each room in the house. Hunter Hanson caught in all of his glory, relieving himself in the bathroom. The horrid French woman in her bed.

Phillips let the file run, watching Hunter as he disappeared out of range of the bathroom camera and appeared in the bedroom. That was the footage he needed to save to archive, Phillips thought, entering the computer commands. He maximized the bedroom thumbnail and watched intently as Hunter and the woman began their typical routine.

So easy, he thought, watching them roughly fumble about in bed with each other.

He let the video spool to archive and went back to the other files in the folder.

Odd, he thought, looking at a file from Saturday evening. Hunter had left on Saturday morning. So who would have been in the cottage Saturday evening? Who would have raised the toilet seat then?

Phillips opened the file.

In the thumbnail, the young Greenwood boy stood in front of the toilet in the cottage's bathroom.

Greenwood! What was he doing there?

Phillips let the file run, watching as the boy moved back to the living room. Conversation for a few minutes. Then he and the French woman moving from the living room camera to the hallway. Then to the bedroom!

This was just too good, Phillips thought with glee. The Greenwood boy and the French woman. Caught in the act!

As he had the thought, the boy and the woman appeared in the bedroom camera frame. He quickly maximized the frame. The lighting was low, but he could still see them distinctly.

The boy, turning back the bed.

The woman, unbuttoning her dress and letting it fall to the floor, her hand outstretched to the boy.

The boy sweeping the naked woman off her feet and laying her into the bed.

Ah, I have them both! Hunter would never stand for it. From either the boy or the woman!

But then all the boy in the video did was cover the woman up and leave the cottage.

Phillips rewound the video.

He was sure he had the two of them.

But then, nothing. Nothing happened.

How bizarre, he thought. Without audio, he had no clue what was actually happening. It certainly looked like the woman was preparing for a frolic with the boy. But then, nothing happened.

How bizarre, Phillips thought.

Had one of them declined the other's offer?

Had the woman passed out?

Was the boy too frightened?

He couldn't tell.

No matter, he thought. He had enough video that he could edit it into whatever he needed. And there would be no conclusion left from the edited footage but that the boy and the woman had been engaged in the type of inappropriate behavior that would seal their respective doom.

A good morning, Phillips thought. Hunter's video. The video of the woman the next night with the boy. Either would have been sufficient. Having both was just too good.

Phillips closed down the surveillance application. He had what he needed, he thought, turning back to his Sunday Times. More than what he needed, he thought.

🍁　　🍁　　🍁

Scott spent Sunday resting. And continuously calling the Repertory number trying to get in touch with Allie.

They should have planned better, he thought. If they had known they were going to be apart so long, almost a month now, they would have made other plans.

And neither of them having access to email or computers didn't help. And no cellphones? What was up with that?

Rules, he thought. Academy rules. Repertory rules. Too many rules.

He tried again and again. All day. Always a busy signal.

How had the movie gone, he wondered? Did she do well? Was she really going to be in a movie? He smiled. His girlfriend, a big time movie star!

She was pretty enough, he thought.

Why didn't she call him, he wondered? None of the boys ever used the phone in his dorm. It would be so much easier if she just called him.

🍁　　🍁　　🍁

"What were you up to this weekend, Marc?" Scott asked as he threw the football back to him. "You just kind of disappeared Saturday night."

Marc fumbled the catch and went running after the ball.

"I ... I had to run into New York," Marc said, picking up the ball.

Marc threw a wobbly spiral to Scott.

"Nothing special," Marc said.

"Did you see any of your friends? Did anyone say anything about Allie?" Scott said, catching and then throwing the ball back.

"Oh. Sure. I saw some of the guys."

"Who'd you see?"

"I saw Vanessa, of course. She is always hanging around."

"Yeah. I think your Mom wants you to hook up with Vanessa!" he teased.

"Yeah. Probably."

"Who else? See anybody else?"

"Oh. I saw Vicky. She was at a club I went to. Boomers. You remember Boomers?"

"Sure. Did Vicky say anything about Allie?"

"I'm sure Allie's fine, Scott."

"Yeah. Sure. It's just that I haven't talked to her in a while. I can never get through on the phone in the Repertory dorm and that's about the only way we have to communicate these days."

"She's fine, Scott. Let it go, man. She's fine."

They continued to toss the ball back and forth as the other players straggled onto the practice field.

"Did anyone say anything about the movie? Will's movie? Allie said she was going to dance in one of Will's movies. You would think she would call me and tell me about that. About how that went."

"Oh. The movie. Yeah. I ran into Will at Boomers. He said it went fine. He said Allie did good," Marc stumbled again and muffed the catch. "Only, you know, he wasn't sure he was going to use the film of her. It was just something he was going to film to see if it worked in the movie," Marc said, throwing a hard pass straight at Scott's stomach.

"Sure. I know. It's not like she's a movie star or anything. She was just doing a bit part."

What was Marc so fired up about, he wondered? Too much talk about Allie, maybe?

🍁   🍁   🍁

The scrimmage started like it always did. The first series of plays were routine. But Marc kept fumbling the snap from the center. Then, the linebacker started shooting the gap between the center and the guard every time he smelled a pass play. He almost took Marc's head off a couple of times. After over an hour of practice, the offense had yet to make a first down.

"Shit!" Marc screamed as he called the offense back into the huddle. "What the fuck is going on! Let's get some blocking on the line, damn it!

Scott trotted out to the sideline. A cornerback moved up opposite him.

Marc was losing it, Scott thought. Marc needed to be a leader in the huddle, he thought, listening for the cadence. Not screaming at everyone like that. Marc needed to lead, not bitch at everyone, he thought.

Scott sprinted forward the very instant the ball was centered. By the time Marc had dropped back two steps, Scott was already past the defender and headed for the sidelines. Scott glanced back over his shoulder just in time to see the linebacker sack Marc five yards deep. He pulled up at the sidelines just in time to see Marc tear off his helmet and throw it at the linebacker as he shouted profanities. Lindsey stepped in and prevented the linebacker from taking a swing at Marc.

The camp was turning ugly, Scott thought as he hurried back to pull Marc away from the linebacker. He had seen it happen before. The coaches standing back, waiting for someone to take charge of the respective teams.

Everyone was trying to impress the growing number of college coaches that had descended on the Academy. Everyone was focused on showing off. It was everyone for themselves. All egos. No teamwork.

❦   ❦   ❦

Scott went looking for Marc right after dinner. He found him sitting under a tree at the edge of The Academy next to the boathouse, lost in thought.

"Tough practice today," he remarked, falling onto the ground next to Marc. "A lot different when you have someone ready to take your head off every play."

Marc eyed him suspiciously.

"The line sucks," Marc quipped. "No blocking," he sneered. "How the hell am I supposed to run an offense if the line won't block?"

He tossed an acorn into the stream.

"You want my advice," he began. "Or do you just want me to listen to you bitch for a while?" he asked earnestly.

"Bitching will help me," Marc chuckled. "But I guess it won't do anything to help the blocking, will it?"

"No. Not likely to help the blocking," he agreed. "Want to screw with the defense?"

Marc turned toward Scott.

"Yeah," Marc smiled. "Let's screw with the defense."

"OK!" he jumped up. "Three things. First, you are giving the play away to the defense. You always set your right foot in the direction of the play. See, if the play is going right, you plant your right foot pointed in that direction," he said, demonstrating. "If the play is going left, your right foot turns left, slightly," he said, demonstrating again. "A good linebacker will catch that after the first series of downs. Now, you could just even your foot up. That would work. Or, you could screw with the linebacker. See if he reads the give, then reverse it."

Marc took the ball that Scott always seemed to be carrying with him these days and went through a couple of mock snaps. He watched how he placed his foot. Scott was right, as usual.

"OK, that's one," Marc agreed. "I can change that. What's two?"

"You pass with your upper body," Scott instructed, taking the ball back. "See, when you drop back to pass, you may look left and then right. But you keep your feet planted. A lot of quarterbacks who are good runners do that," he assured Marc, making an offhanded compliment to his running abilities. "They like a solid base under them. But, if you are really going to pass, you have to keep your feet moving. Little jumps, like this," he demonstrated, bouncing on the ball's of his feet as he looked left and then right, ready to pass the ball. "Defense won't know which direction you are going and when you deliver the ball, chances are your entire body will be aligned in the direction of the ball's flight, so you are always following through," he said. "Takes some practice. Some coaches call it 'having happy feet'. Looks good on the tapes and actually works."

Marc took the ball, placed it over his shoulder in a passing position and bounced lightly.

"Go out for a pass," Marc instructed him.

As he sprinted away toward the banks of the creek, Marc continued to bounce, looking left and right before delivering the pass. It spiraled neatly in a tight arc right into Scott's hands, who turned and trotted back to Marc's side.

"Happy feet," Marc chuckled. "OK. That's two. What's three?"

"When you come up to the line, you always know which play you are going to run. Right?" Scott quizzed.

"Sure. The one I called in the huddle," Marc answered assuredly.

"Wrong. That's the play you would like to run. But you should never decide which play to run until you come to the line and see how the defense is set up."

"Well, sure," Marc came to his own defense. "I can always call an audible if I want to change the play."

"Yeah, you can," he agreed. "But how often do you do that?"

Marc thought. He didn't like audibles. Too many chances for a mistake. Too much noise, usually, for everyone to hear the change in play. Too many ways for it to go badly.

"Look," Scott said. "You have to be the leader of the team. The players have to believe in you. You can't just always do what the coach tells you to do, always run the play coach tells you to run. Coach isn't the one that's going to get his head taken off by some blitzing linebacker. This is your team, Marc. They want to be your team. But, they all have to feel like you know what you are doing. Right now, they don't. That's why you are only getting fifty percent from them.

They are just doing what they are told to do and trying to look good to the recruiters doing it."

"The guys don't like me very much," Marc's gaze shifted to the ground.

"Who gives a fuck whether they like you or not!" he exclaimed. "All you want them to do is play for you."

"But they're supposed to play for me. I'm the quarterback," Marc replied indignantly.

"Being quarterback isn't an honorary position," he measured his advice to Marc. "You can't expect them to play for you just because you're a quarterback," he replied. "Just like you can't expect people to like you just because you're rich."

Marc's eyes flashed angrily at Scott for an instant. But all Marc saw was concern in Scott's face. Genuine concern. No malice or contempt.

"So, how do I get them to play for me? Exactly?"

"Stop bitching so much in the huddle. And start being a little rowdy and complimentary. Sounds lame, but the linemen get creamed on every play. Just telling them in the huddle that you know they are working hard for you makes them try all that much harder. And then, not always running what the coach tells you to run will help. They all need to know that you are the one leading the team. Not the coach. Oh, and make some of the linemen heroes every now and then."

"Heroes?"

"Yeah," he smiled. "Look, my quarterback in Texas used to do something that drove the defense crazy and turned the center into his best friend. Get down like you are going to center the ball to me," Scott instructed, tossing Marc the ball and coming up behind him to take a snap. "When you come up to the line, you check out the defense," Scott said, looking from side to side. "Everyone is paying attention now, because even your own team isn't sure what play you're going to run—the one you called in the huddle or an audible. So your team is on edge. That's good. Now, if the middle linebacker is lined up a bit too much to the right of center ..."

"Like when he is going to blitz my ass," Marc's voice was equal part humor and anger.

"Yeah, like when he is going to come after you on a pass play. Then what you do is to have a sign set up with the center for a special play. The whole line runs the play you call and fakes off the defense, but you and the center screw with everyone and run your own play."

"What play?" Marc stood up and turned at the waist to face Scott.

"A quarterback sneak," he smiled impishly. "Get down like you're the center. When you see the linebacker to the right, you put your left hand on the center's butt as you are looking over the defense."

"I'm not putting my hand on anybody's butt!" Marc protested in boyish discomfort.

"No, really. You just kind of brush the left ass of the center, like this," he demonstrated on a reluctant Marc. "Then, on the snap, the center blocks to his right and you come forward between the center and guard on the left side. If the linebacker reads a play to the left, you just reverse the signal. Brush the center on the right side and run to the right. Guaranteed five yards every play you run it."

Marc stood up and faced Scott again.

"Five yards? Really?"

"The quarterback on my team in Texas ran the play at least three times every game. It wasn't until the sixth game of the season that the opposing coaches picked up on it. And the defenses could never read it," Scott assured. "I think that one play made the difference in winning the state championship."

"Really?"

"Yeah, really," Scott replied, grabbing Marc by the shoulder. "Let's get back to the dorm. I have to study."

"You're always studying," Marc accused as he fell into pace with Scott. Then his voice more serious. "You really like Allie don't you?"

Scott saw a cloud descend over Marc.

"Sure. She's my girlfriend. Of course I like her."

"You know, girls. Sometimes they get. Well sometimes they get crazy."

He just stood there listening to Marc.

"It's just their way. Sometimes they just get so whacked out. There's really no telling. Sometimes they don't even know what they are going to do."

"What are you saying, Marc? Are you talking about Allie?"

"No. Not specifically about Allie. Just about girls. You know. In general."

Was Marc having girl problems, he wondered. Some problem with Vanessa, perhaps.

"Sure. Unpredictable. Allie's like that sometimes. She doesn't mean anything by it. Sometimes you just can't figure out what's going on in her head. Girls. They're like that."

"Yeah," Marc laughed, slapping Marc on the back. "Sometimes they just drive you absolutely crazy."

"Yeah. Sometimes," he smiled, as the walked back to the dorm.

❧   ❧   ❧

"I-32, split. On two. I-32, split. On two," Marc repeated the coaches call in the huddle.

"Break!" the team cried in unison as they broke from the huddle and began their walk to the line.

Marc waited for the offense to get set in their positions before walking slowly up behind the center. He glanced over the defense. They knew the play he had called, he thought. He could tell by the way the linebacker was moving in between the center and the guard, just waiting to lay Marc on his back when the ball was snapped. A sure indication that the linebacker was going to blitz and try to take his head off.

He casually laid his left hand momentarily on the center's left buttocks as he glanced from side to side and barked out the cadence for I-32, split. He felt the center shift uncomfortably, putting more weight on his left foot in preparation for a push to his right.

"Hut! Hut!" he yelled.

As soon as he felt the football come into contact with his fingertips, he lowered his shoulder and surged forward and to the left as the center pushed right, taking two defensive linemen to the ground with him. The linebacker came charging through from the right, but his speed only carried him further into the backfield. Marc planted his left foot, spun completely around the remaining defensive players at the line and then accelerated down the field. He let Scott bump the safety out of bounds and Marc danced into the end-zone for a touchdown.

His first impulse was to showboat, to celebrate his run. But he remembered Scott's conversation. Make the linemen heroes, he thought, somewhat reluctantly as he jumped up and ran back toward his offense.

"Great block Hawk!" he yelled, helping the huge center up off the ground. "Fucking sick!"

Hawkins looked blankly at Marc's unusual enthusiasm.

"Yeah," the overweight center muttered, somewhat embarrassed at his newfound attention. "Ah, good run, man," Hawkins stammered as he walked slowly back to the huddle.

Before the offense could get back to the huddle, Jim was screaming at the defense.

"What the hell was that! Linebacker. You think you need to blitz on every fucking play? What playbook were you reading last night, son?" he yelled at the bewildered linebacker.

"But coach," the linebacker tried to defend himself. "That was a pass play."

"Obviously not, son," Jim retorted, turning his back in disgust and walking away. "Obviously not!"

The entire offense enjoyed the dress down the defense was getting from Jim. And they enjoyed getting the better of the defense after the last few scrimmages.

"What was that play?" Josh McGuiness asked as the team got back into the huddle. "I thought we were running I-32, split."

"Yeah, me too," Lindsey Quinlan looked confused.

"Come on guys," he chuckled. "Just because I call it in the huddle, doesn't mean we are going to run it when we get to the line," he continued, then patting the center on the shoulder pads. "That was just a little something Henry Hawkins and I worked out to confuse the blitz. Anyone have a problem with Henry roughing up the defense every now and then?"

The whole offense looked at Henry. No one wanted to get on the bad side of someone that large.

"All right then. Let's run it again. I-32, split. I-32, split." he repeated.

CHAPTER 25

Scott eased his old Buick onto the short entrance ramp from the service plaza and then pressed hard on the accelerator.

"You ever think about your future?" Marc's voice was more of a shout in its effort to overpower the noise from the old car's engine compartment and the wind that whistled through the car from the open windows. "About what you're going to do?"

It was a tough question for Scott to answer. He was already in a future he had never imagined.

"I have," Marc continued in answer to his rhetorical question. "I think about it all the time. About going to Harvard next year. About Harvard law after that. About living in New York."

Scott just nodded his head. He knew he had enough gas to make it to Marc's apartment in New York. He knew he would sleep in Marc's apartment tonight. And he knew he would finally get to see Allie. That was the future for him, he thought. After a month, he would finally get to spend some time with her.

"You know my dad was a double Harvard," Marc continued his monologue. "He did the business school, of course. I guess that's why I want to go to Harvard Law," his voice full of reflection. "So I can do something different than what my father did."

Scott popped open his root beer and took a long drink from the can. It was so cold that there were small slivers of ice floating in the can when he drank. He liked that. He liked the icy texture of a freshly opened root beer.

"I mean," Marc starred straight through the windshield toward the tree-covered stretch of parkway in front of them. "I feel like I don't really have a life of my own. It's like I am living my father's life all over again."

Scott bit through the plastic tubing on his Slim Jim and spit the small slice of plastic into the brown paper bag on the front seat before tearing off a couple of inches of the spicy beef stick.

"Like at The Academy," Marc was nodding his head now in self-agreement. "The same prep school. The same classes. My God, I even have some of the same teachers he had. And football. I mean, I like playing football. And I like being quarterback. But that's just like my father, too," he paused, swallowing hard. "Only he was better than I am. At school. His SATs. Even his football record."

Scott took another drink of the cold soda and wiped the condensation from the can off on his jeans.

"It's like … I'm just never good enough for him," Marc finally admitted. "At anything."

Scott waited for Marc to continue, but sensed that he had already said what was on his mind. Maybe it had been his father's visit to The Academy last weekend that had caused this unusual self-reflection in Marc, Scott thought. Maybe Marc knew, he thought. About his father and Virginia Simone. After all, Hunter had spent only a few minutes with Marc on Friday after the scrimmage. Scott had seen them shouting at each other at the back of the gym. He had seen them both walk away from each other in anger. Scott wondered if Marc realized that his father had stayed in town that night. With Virginia.

"The spring I turned fourteen my father and I had been working on speed drills," Scott began. "Like what you and I did before football camp started," he explained. "At the end of every session he and I would line up at the start line and my mother would fire a starter's pistol and we would race each other. A hundred yard dash. Every day."

He took another bite of his Slim Jim, chewed it for a few seconds and then washed it down with more soda.

"On April 3rd, when I was fourteen, I beat my father in the hundred yard dash for the first time," he said simply. "April 3rd. I still remember the date. It had been raining in the morning and there were puddles at the edge of the track. We all went out to the track around four, after my mom and dad had finished at school. My sister sat in the stands the whole session, reading a new book of French poetry my mother had gotten for her birthday. She was wearing blue jeans and … a blue blouse. My mother still had on her school dress. It was white, with pastel flowers on it. And funny, short heeled shoes that she always used to teach in. My father had on a pair of gray sweat pants and a T-shirt that was about ten years old. I remember as a kid when he bought it in

Puerto Rico when we lived there. And these nasty old sneakers that he kept fishing out of the trash after my mother would throw them away," he smiled as he spoke.

Marc was looking blankly at Scott.

"When we finished, my father came over and shook my hand and said 'Good run'. That was all he said," Scott spoke slowly. "I don't think my sister even looked up from her book. And my mom was already putting things away in the gym bag, so my father just jogged back down the track to where she was and started helping her. I'm not sure if my Mom even saw the end of the race."

"So?" Marc finally asked. "Is there a point you are trying to make?"

"That was the last time my father ever raced me," Scott said. "I didn't understand immediately, either. But don't you see, Marc? After I beat him that once he knew that running against him would never be the same challenge again. So there wasn't any point in him racing me. We both knew I would win. Maybe not every race. Maybe not every day. But, eventually, I would win. So there wasn't any point in us racing, anymore."

Marc pursed his lips and nodded his head.

Scott used another drink of the warming soda to rinse down the lump that was forming in his throat in recounting the story.

Marc slid down in the seat slightly and let his head fall back against the rolled and pleated upholstery. He closed his eyes.

"So, maybe. Maybe I'm better than he was?" Marc asked through closed eyes.

"It doesn't really matter, does it? Whether he was better, I mean. The fact is, you're the quarterback now. All he has are memories. You're the quarterback now."

Scott watched Marc's face out of the corner of his eyes. Scott noticed that some of the tension had gone out of the muscles of Marc's jaw. He glanced sideways and saw a slight smile form on Marc's face.

It didn't matter, Scott thought, that Marc would never know that day, April 3rd, had been one of the saddest days of Scott's life to that point. Sure, there had been a brief moment of triumph. A rush of joy as he had crossed the finish line just inches in front of his father. And a moment of pride as his father had acknowledged Scott's accomplishment with a manly handshake.

But, then, slowly, Scott realized that things would never be the same between them again.

His father was no longer the omnipotent master that Scott had imagined.

He was beatable.

He was only human, Scott had come to understand.

And humans die, Scott thought bitterly.

Just like his father, he thought, finishing off the last of the soda.

❦ ❦ ❦

Scott threw his bag on the bed and picked up the phone. He glanced at the old grandfather clock at the far end of the room. Almost four o'clock, he thought as he walked over to the window of the third-floor bedroom and dialed the Repertory dorm number again.

"Third floor door," a youthful female voice answered.

"I'm looking for Allie Regis," he said. "Is she there? Has she gotten back yet?"

"Is this Scott? This is Katrina, Scott. Didn't you recognize me?" the female's voice was high pitched and liquid.

"Oh, Katrina, hi. I ... of course I recognized you ... I was just."

"Scott. You are such a terrible liar. You didn't recognize me. I'm hurt," Katrina tried to make her voice into a pout.

"OK," he admitted. "Maybe I didn't recognize you at first. But it's been a month since we talked."

"Too long between conversations, Scott," Katrina taunted. "Are you in New York? Marc told Wendy and Wendy told Heather and Heather told me that you were going to be in New York this weekend."

"I'm staying at Marc's," he began.

"Well, Allie isn't here," Katrina said. "She left a note for you that said she would be back at two. But I guess she must have gotten ... busy."

"Do you know where she is? Does the note say where she is?"

"No. The note doesn't say," Katrina said, thinking through her options. "I'm sure its all very innocent."

Innocent, he thought. What did she mean by that?

"Look, Vanessa and I were going to stop by Marc's before dinner," Katrina's voice became sultry. "So ... I guess I will see you there in a little while."

"Ah, sure. I'll be here. Look, will you leave a message on the board for Allie. Let her know that I called. Tell her she should just call Marc's place when she gets back. Okay? Let her know we're having dinner at Marc's tonight."

"Of course, Scott. I would do anything for you," Katrina offered.

"Thanks. Well ... guess I'll see you in a little while."

"I'm looking forward to it."

Scott hung up the phone before the conversation could go much further. He liked Katrina, he guessed. And she was wicked gorgeous. Maybe a better body than even Allie. But every time he was around her, she kept coming on to him. And Allie was especially jealous of her for some reason.

Where was Allie, he thought? What was she up to? He was sure she knew that he was coming in this weekend. He had left at least a dozen messages for her at the Repertory.

❦   ❦   ❦

Katrina rushed back to her room and started rummaging through her closet for just the right dress. Nothing slutty, she thought. That would be just too too obvious. No, something sophisticated. And tight!

She found a pair of dangerously high black pumps at the back of the closet and a small black cocktail dress hanging on thin straps, still in the plastic dry cleaning bag.

Perfect, she thought. Some pearls. A little makeup. She would be perfect.

Allie stuck her head into Katrina's room.

"Was that Scott? On the phone? Did he call? I thought maybe he might come into the city this weekend. I left him messages at his dorm that I didn't have anything to do. But I haven't gotten any messages on the board all week."

"Scott?" Katrina tried to sound completely innocent. "No. I don't think so. I didn't see a note on the board," her comment truthful and totally inaccurate. "But, I'm sure he will call you," Katrina smiled.

"Yeah. I guess. Are you going out? So early?"

"Oh, I just thought I might meet Vanessa for drinks. And maybe Vicky," Katrina made the remark sound off-handed.

The mention of Vicky's name sent an involuntary shutter over Allie's body.

"Well, I guess I'll see you later, then. Maybe at Boomers or something," Allie smiled weakly as she walked out of the room.

"Yeah, later girlfriend," Katrina said, turning back to her makeup mirror smiling.

❦   ❦   ❦

Scott tried to be polite and conversational during dinner. But he kept thinking about Allie. What had happened to Allie? Where was she?

Marc's mother had seated Katrina next to him at the table. Every now and then he would catch her scent between courses. It didn't make anything better. She smelled like Allie. Probably wearing the same perfume, he thought. Girls did that. Wore the same perfume, sometimes.

"Well, Scott, I was very impressed with the way you and young Marc played during the scrimmage last week," Hunter kept coming back to the same subject—the few minutes of the scrimmage that he had seen. "I think the two of you would certainly do well playing for the same team. What do you think Marc?"

"Yes, father," Marc replied formally. "I think we work well together."

"You know, The Academy provides an excellent educational experience for a young man," Hunter shifted his focus. "I think it has been great for Marc. Isn't that right Marc?"

"Yes, father," Marc obediently replied. "An excellent experience."

"Have you ever thought about going to The Academy, Scott? During the regular school year, I mean? Next year, perhaps?"

The question took Scott by surprise and distracted him. It wasn't the only thing that was distracting. Katrina kept moving her chair closer to him and her bare knee kept brushing, ever so slightly, against his.

"No sir," Scott looked at Marc, whose expression offered no clue as to the context for this conversation, then turned toward the head of the table to address Hunter. "I … don't think I could afford The Academy, sir," he offered in full explanation of his personal circumstances. Surely Hunter was aware of that, he thought.

"Well, The Academy has always been generous in its efforts to educate exceptional young men, Scott. Regardless of their circumstances. I am sure that if you had an interest in The Academy, if you wanted to play football next season, for example, something could be arranged to provide whatever you needed in the way of support," Hunter got to the point quickly as he inconspicuously glanced at his watch. "Don't you think Marc?"

"Yes father," Marc was more enthusiastic in his reply, but still reserved in his manner. "I am sure that The Academy could provide whatever was needed, Scott."

Marc smiled weakly, but assuredly at Scott.

"We could play on the same team, Scott," Marc offered. "Next season. You and I could kick some ass!" he let his enthusiasm get the best of his discretion.

"Marc!" Ms. Hanson exclaimed. "Watch your language at the table, please!"

Katrina giggled nervously, then put her hand softly on Scott's leg under the table.

"I actually agree with Marc, Scott," Hunter placed his napkin on the table. "I think the two of you could definitely 'kick some ass.'"

Hunter's use of the phrase evoked another girlish giggle from Katrina, whose hand slid, very discretely, further up Scott's leg.

"Well, I haven't given much thought to it, really, sir," he had not allowed himself such thoughts. "I was just there at The Academy to help Jim and Marc this summer, you know."

"Well you should give some thought to it, Scott. I could make a few calls if you're interested," Hunter said, offhandedly.

"Sure, I guess," he said, trying to move away from the table a bit, away from Katrina's hand.

It wouldn't be so bad, he thought. He could play football with Marc, for Jim. He might even be able to take French with Ms. Simone. He liked living in the dorm and having friends for a change. And its not like he had any place to go after the summer session ended.

Hunter rang the dinner bell for Jaffrey, who immediately refilled the large wine glasses from a new bottle.

How do these people drink so much, Scott wondered? He could hold a few beers or a couple of glasses of wine. But at the Hanson's dinner table, the glasses never seemed to empty. Jaffrey always there to keep them full. No matter how much you drank. He was beginning to feel a bit warm. Perhaps he should slow down on the wine, he thought.

The dinner just went on and on. One course after the next. New wine with each new course. Entirely too much wine for him, he thought, catching himself staring a bit to long at Katrina's long, bare expanse of leg next to him.

Where was Allie, he wondered?

He caught Katrina removing one of her high heels under the table. Her feet were so small. The nails so perfectly painted.

She smiled at him. Then turned slightly toward him and rubbed her bare foot against his leg, her toes against his bare skin.

God, she was such a tease, he thought. Picking at her food, slowly, as if she was toying with it. Pursing her lips at him. Tilting her head back and forth whenever he spoke to her.

But then so was Vanessa, he reasoned, watching her fawn all over Marc across the table.

Maybe New York girls were just like that. Overly … friendly, he thought.

Vanessa and Katrina seemed to be carrying on a number of conversations at once. With each other about a modeling contract Vanessa had just gotten for Katrina. With Marc's mom about some Broadway show. With Marc's dad about the stock market and where to put their trust money. But regardless of what they were talking about or who they were talking to, each girl seemed to be totally attentive to the boy next to her. Katrina's attentions to him including a lot of physical contact under the tablecloth, with fingers that just kept going a bit further up his leg each time she touched him, ever so slightly.

And then it was over. Dessert served. Wine glasses emptied. The meal completed.

"Shall we go dear, I think our theater tickets are for eight," Hunter collected Anna from her position and made his exit. "You kids have a good time," he waived over his shoulder.

The four young people stood and waited patiently for Marc's parents to make their graceful exit from the dining room.

Scott looked to Marc. He wasn't sure what was supposed to happen now. Now that just the two girls, he and Marc were left alone in the house. All he knew is that he was too drunk to do much of anything … and that Katrina's hand had finally found what it had been groping for all night.

Katrina tiptoed out of the bedroom as quietly as possible. Usually she didn't like to share. But this was just too good, she thought, rummaging through her bag for her pink cellphone and hitting the speed-dial.

"Vicky," she whispered into the phone. "Where are you?"

"I'm outside of Boomers. I thought you guys were coming over after dinner to the club."

"Girl, you have to get yourself over to Marc's house A-S-A-P! Seriously!"

"Are you guys still having dinner? This late?"

"No, sweetheart. We finished dinner a long time ago. I've just been having dessert for the last hour or so," Katrina giggled.

"Dessert? Are you drunk?"

"How fast can you get over here?"

"I can get a cab and be there in five minutes. Why? What are you guys doing? What are you doing?"

"Let's just say I have been enjoying a little Texas cuisine, served very, very rare!"

"You slut! You're with that Texas boy. You actually did it. You actually hooked up with him!"

"Of course I'm with that Texas boy. And stop being so judgmental," Katrina said. "After all, I am willing to share," she giggled.

"I'll be there in five minutes!"

CHAPTER 26

Did he know, Allie wondered?

Did Scott know about her? Had he seen the video of her on the internet? Had he seen her picture in the Times last Sunday with Seth and Vanessa?

Is that why he hated her, she thought?

Is that why he hated her so much he would just blow her off entirely? Not call? Not come to see her after he had promised?

It's not like she didn't deserve it, she admitted.

The video. Well, it wasn't supposed to be like that. It was supposed to be a movie. On the big screen. A real movie. Not some stupid, grainy video on the internet that made her look like some kind of porn star.

The picture in the Times, too. She really didn't remember how that happened. And it wasn't like it was anything other than just the gossip page.

He could have seen them, though. Or found out about them.

Either way he had a right to be mad about either of them, she guessed.

But that wasn't the worst of it.

The worst it.

Well, there was no way he would ever know the worst of it. She was sure of that.

Marc would never tell about Seth.

And Vicky.

Her stomach tightened.

Scott could just never know about Vicky. Ever!

No one could know about Vicky, she shuddered.

Allie heard a door close down the hallway of the deserted dorm.

It was creepy in the old dormitory building when all of the other girls were gone. On Sunday morning when no one was there. No one but her, she thought, getting up out of bed, tentatively, peeking around her doorway to see who had come back to the dorm.

She made her way slowly down the hallway, looking into each room.

Heather's room was empty. Just the stupid lava-lamp glowing in the darkness of the interior room.

Rosalyn was still out, her room empty. Probably still recovering from the 'coming out' party for her younger sister in Stamford.

Justine's room, the only one with a window, even if it did only look out into an airshaft, vacant. Clothes thrown across the floor. Makeup all over her table.

"Is anyone here?" Allie asked, trying to make her voice carry to the far end of the hallway. "Whose here?"

Allie heard footsteps on the third floor and climbed the stairs. The light was on in the bathroom and she heard the sound of water running.

"Whose there? Heather? Is that you?"

She crept up to the bathroom door and stuck her head just around the corner.

"Katrina! Thank God! I thought I heard someone come in, but then when you didn't answer when I called, I wasn't sure who it was."

"Just me," Katrina smiled back at her, brushing her teeth, the toothpaste spilling out of her mouth as she spoke.

"So, did you guys go out last night? You and Wendy? Did you guys go clubbing?"

"Yeah. Sort of. We went out for a while," Katrina said, spitting toothpaste out in the sink. "Then I got tired. So," she paused, "I spent the night with a friend."

Katrina seemed so happy. So pleased with herself.

"Well I'm glad you had a good time," she said.

"Oh, I had a great time!"

"Good. I'm glad," Allie said, noticing the boys' boxers Katrina was wearing. "Katrina, I haven't seen you wear those boxers before. Scott has a pair just like them. How funny!"

"Really? He has a pair just like them? That is funny," Katrina said, turning on the shower and pulling off her t-shirt. "I've never seen anything like these boxers before here in the City until last night. I thought I probably had the only pair. Wonder where Scott got his pair?"

"Probably in Texas," she said.

Katrina dropped the boxers and stepped into the shower.

"Yeah. He probably got his in Texas," Katrina said, giggling as the water ran over her.

❧   ❧   ❧

"Marc! Let's go! Come on man!" Scott shouted toward the top of the spiral staircase from the foyer of Marc's brownstone.

All he wanted to do was get out of the City.

"Coming. I'm coming," Marc shouted back.

Scott paced back and forth waiting at the bottom of the stairs. He kept looking through the windows next to the front door for some sign of Jaffrey pulling the old Buick up to the sidewalk.

"Really Marc. Let's get moving. It's going to be dark by the time we get back."

Not that driving in the dark meant anything. Scott just wanted out.

Marc came bounding down the stairs, two at time, his gym bag thrown over one shoulder, holding up his pants, trying to fasten his belt. He slipped on the marbled floor in the foyer and almost slid into Marc.

"Goodbye Marc," Vanessa shouted down from the banister on the second floor, a bed sheet loosely wrapped around her.

God, Scott thought! How could he have been so stupid last night? How could Marc have let him get so drunk? Why hadn't Marc done something about Katrina?

"She's hot!" Marc said, smiling broadly. "Nothing like a little sex in the city!"

"Jez, Marc. Maybe for you. But not for me," he said, shaking his head. "I'm in deep shit."

"Yeah. You are. Aren't you?" Marc smiled.

Why was Marc smiling? Didn't he know how badly Scott felt about last night? About Katrina?

A loud honk came from the curb. It was Jaffrey with the Buick.

"Let's roll, man," Marc said, running toward the door. "Before you get yourself in any more trouble than you are already in."

Scott ran after Marc, jumped in the car, pumped the accelerator, and speed east down the street toward the FDR. Ten minutes and he was across the Triboro Bridge. Thirty minutes and he was on the Merritt Parkway. Away from the city. Running away from the responsibility he felt for screwing things up so badly.

It wasn't until they passed Hartford that Marc said anything.

"So. How'd it go last night?"

"I was drunk."

"Yeah. Me, too."

Marc's next words didn't come until they had reached the Mass Turnpike.

"So. When did Vicky come over?"

"Yeah. I forgot to tell you about Vicky. She came over later," he grudgingly admitted. "I think Katrina must have called her."

Marc chuckled under his breath.

"Katrina. And Vicky."

Scott didn't respond.

"I hear they are very close friends," Marc laughed. "Very close."

"They seem to like each other," Scott tried to smile.

"So. Any details you want to share, my friend?"

Scott honestly couldn't remember many of the details. Well, he remembered Katrina. He had no excuses about her. But Vicky? That wasn't his fault, really. That was Katrina's doing.

"No. No details. Can't really remember."

"Bullshit! You can't tell me you spent the night with them and don't remember. No way!"

"It all got a little … a little confusing after Vicky came over."

"Yeah. I bet it did," Marc said, laughing loudly.

"Confusing," Scott reiterated.

"Sure. I understand completely. Confusing!"

Scott watched Marc's apparent delight with his dilemma.

"You … you don't think Katrina would say anything to Allie, do you? I mean, you know her. She promised me she wouldn't. But you know her. She wouldn't, would she? Not if she promised."

"I think your secret is safe with Katrina, Scott. She's not the kind to get into a catfight with another girl … especially after she's already won."

"And Vicky? What about Vicky?"

"Vicky? Well, she's more of a bitch. But she's certainly not going to do anything to make Katrina mad at her. Remember what close friends they are, after all," Marc laughed. "And I think Vicky has some secrets of her own that she might be a little concerned about. So Vicky. Not to worry. She's not telling Allie anything about you. Or Katrina."

Scott felt relieved. He knew he shouldn't be. He knew he should feel just as bad. Even if Allie never found out. But he couldn't help it. He couldn't help it if he didn't want Allie to find out about last night.

What was he going to tell Allie, Scott thought? What lie was he going to tell her?

"So, what would you do, if you were me?" Scott asked. "I mean, Allie's going to know I was in the City. I told her I was coming into the City. What do I tell her? About why I didn't call her? About why I didn't see her?"

They drove in silence through the toll as they turned north on to 495.

"I'll tell her you were with me," Marc said flatly. "End of story. I'll tell her you were with me. That we went into Boston. That I needed you to come into Boston with me."

The story sounded plausible to Scott. That he and Marc might go into Boston. At the last minute. And since Allie said she never got any of his phone messages, he could just say he called. She wouldn't be able to prove that he hadn't called. In Boston with Marc.

"OK. That's the story. I was in Boston with you," he nodded.

They finally turned off the interstate onto the back road leading to the Academy.

"What were we doing in Boston? I mean, exactly?"

Marc laughed.

"We went to the opera, I guess! How the hell do I know?"

"I don't think she would believe that. I don't think she would believe that you and I went to the opera together."

"It was a joke, Scott," Marc said shaking his head. "God, man. Lighten up. You aren't the first person in a relationship to have cheated. Or to have gotten by with it. Just tell her we went to a Red Sox game. They played Saturday at Fenway. Tell her we went to the game."

"Yeah. The Red Sox game. Good idea."

Good lie, Scott thought.

"Allie, is that you?" Scott asked.

"Where were you Scott? I thought you were coming in this weekend."

"Sorry. I had to go into Boston. With Marc."

"Is he OK? Was it an emergency or something?"

"No. No emergency," he said, suddenly realizing that going to see a Red Sox game instead of coming to see Allie wasn't such a good lie after all. "It was his father," he tried to embellish a bit. "His father insisted that we come into Boston to go to the game with him."

"Oh, yeah. I guess he doesn't get to see his dad that much. Must have been something special."

"It was great! We got to sit in a big corporate sky box and they had all of this food," he said, beginning to panic a bit. "Marc was glad I was there with him. You know, a guy thing."

"Sure. I understand."

She didn't sound like she understood, he thought.

"So, what's going on with you? We haven't talked in forever! I keep calling and leaving messages. But you don't ever seem to be around the dorm."

"Messages? I only got two messages this week."

"Only two? I must have called a dozen times this week and left a message every time. And then called a dozen more when the phone was busy."

"Really Scott?"

She sounded hurt. Or mad. Or something.

"Really," he said, panicking again. "Katrina answered a bunch of times," he blurted out without thinking.

Shit! Why did he mention her? He needed to change the subject, quickly.

"She said you were out with friends. You always seem to be out with friends. You must have made a lot of friends in New York," he tried to put her on the defensive.

There was a long pause.

"I guess. I know a few people. Some of the friends Marc introduced us to."

"Some of the movie people?"

There was another long pause.

"I see Will every now and then."

"No, I mean do you guys hang around together. You guys go out with the actors?"

Silence.

"What do you mean?"

Why was she being so evasive, he thought? He was the one with the guilty conscience.

"I just mean, do you guys hang out together. Marc said you finished the movie with Will and that there was some sort of 'wrap party' at Boomers. I thought that you might have met some people from the movie."

Allie coughed into the receiver.

"You OK? You sound like you have a cold or something. Like your nose is all stopped up."

"I'm fine, Scott."

More silence.

"What else did Marc tell you? About the movie?"

"Not much. He said you finished your scenes. I just thought that since you were such a big shot these days rubbing shoulders with all the actors that you might party with them."

"Look. I went out to Boomers. OK? I went out to Boomers after the movie. There were a lot of people there. Emily Ros even showed up. We were all just hanging out at Boomers. And then there were all of these photographers and they kept taking pictures of everyone. You know Marc's friends. They're all so rich. Even the girl whose father owns all of those hotels. She was there."

"Really! That must have been exciting. Did you get to see any of the pictures?"

"Are you toying with me, Scott? Because if you are, it isn't very nice."

What did that mean, Scott thought? He was just trying to make her feel special ... famous.

"I was just wondering if you got your picture taken with anyone famous. You know. A picture that you could send me, maybe."

"You want me ... to send you ... a picture? Of me? With people from the movie?"

"Sure. I'll put in on my wall. Show off my famous, movie-star girlfriend. The guys will get a kick out of it."

"Sure. Sure. I'm sorry," she sobbed slightly. "It's just that there is so much pressure here. And nothing has worked out the way I planned it."

Scott knew how that felt.

"Don't worry Allie. It will all work out. You're a great dancer. And you have all of these great opportunities in the City that you would never get here. I'm glad. I'm glad you're taking advantage of all of the opportunities. Really. I miss you. But you have to be having fun. Right. Even with all of the hard work. Aren't you having fun?"

"Scott. I need you to come see me. I need you to come in next weekend. Please. Promise me you'll come in next weekend."

He was feeling guilty again. Listening to her beg him to come to see her. After what he had done.

"Sure. Next weekend. I'll come back into the City to see you."

"What do you mean, 'come back into the City'?"

Shit!

"You know. Come back into the City. To see you," he struggled. "Like when we came in with Marc in the limo. Only I'll bring the Buick in. I'll drive this time."

"I have a recital on Saturday afternoon. Can you be here by two? Next Saturday?"

"That would be great! I haven't seen you dance in a long time."

There was a long pause.

"Allie? Allie? Are you still there?"

"I have to go now. Someone else needs to use the phone. I have to go now."

"Next Saturday. Two o'clock. I'll be there!"

Ben turned on the color photo printer in his darkened office. Only the glow of the computer monitor lit the room. He sat down and tried to toggle back and forth through the first video feed until he could get a clear shot of Greenwood's face. A clear shot of his face, with the French woman standing behind him.

He had only installed three cameras in the bedroom of the cottage. But he could really only use the one positioned next to the window, because it had to appear that someone had taken the photos from outside the house. That was critical. It wasn't worth revealing the cameras just yet.

He froze a couple of frames that clearly showed Virginia without clothing standing behind the boy. But they were useless without a clear shot of the boy's face in them.

He would just have to settle, he guessed. For one of the earlier frames. From some of the footage where she was still taking off her dress. The camera from the headboard of the bed clearly showed the boy's face as he was turning back the covers, Virginia in the background. The lighting wasn't as good on her. But you could definitely tell she was undressing.

Ben froze the frame and printed it.

He spent a few more minutes on the footage.

There was a pretty good one with the boy carrying her in his arms. You could tell she didn't have any clothes on. And it would be obvious to anyone inspecting the scene that it was in her bedroom. He printed that one as well.

The first one was the better of the two. More incriminating, he thought. The one with the woman in the boy's arms was just too … innocent, somehow. It didn't seem to matter that she was naked, he thought, closely inspecting the printout. The boy's expression was just … too innocent.

He placed the two photos in a large envelope, sealed the envelope with tape, weighed the package, and put the correct number of stamps in the upper right hand corner. He took a felt tip pen and scribbled the address so as to disguise the handwriting. Alexandra Regis, c/o New York Repertory Company, Summer Session. Then filled in the address from his rolodex.

He printed two more copies and went through the ritual with a second envelope. This one he didn't have to address. This one he could hand deliver, he thought, dropping it into a clear plastic sleeve and removing the latex gloves he had been wearing.

Ben smiled.

The pills in the boy's soda had just been a prank. Perhaps a bit overdone, Ben thought. But a prank, none the less. He had never intended the boy any real physical harm. He just wanted the boy out.

Now, the photos. They were a bit different.

They might do the trick!

CHAPTER 27

One of the nice things about being rich, Marc thought, is that the rules that applied to everyone else just didn't apply to you. He had learned that much from his father. And it had served him well.

It was surprising, really. Surprising how little money it really took. To break the rules, as it were.

For example, he thought smugly, tampering with the federal mail was a federal crime. But for a thousand dollars a month, he could pay off the mail room guy at the Academy to screen every piece of mail that left Ben Phillips' office. It wasn't really tampering with the mail, after all, he had convinced the middle-aged man with five kids to feed. It wasn't really mail until the mailman picked it up. Until then, it was just like the thousands of Academy memos that he delivered throughout the year. And there was nothing special about them. No federal offense with respect to them. All the man needed to do was tell Marc *before* the mail got into the hands of the postman.

It was a trivial distinction. A thousand dollar a month distinction. But it gave Marc incalculable pleasure. Removing Phillips' credit card payments so that he got overdue notices. Misdirecting confidential internal memos to members of the board of directors. Throwing away the continuous string of correspondence that Phillips kept writing to the local paper, knowing from the man's character how much being ignored in the local community news upset him.

And every now and then, something really important.

Like the parcel addressed to one "Alexandra Regis" that was brought to Marc's attention. Worth the extra hundred dollar tip, Marc thought.

Worth more, probably, he thought, as he opened the package and saw the photos of Scott and Virginia Simone. Photos he hid in his room all week, trying to think through the situation.

A private investigator, perhaps? Had old Ben Phillips stooped low enough to hire a PI to lurk outside Virginia's cottage and take snapshots of the bedroom.

Unlikely, Marc thought. Ben would be afraid of involving someone else. A PI would be too hard to control in a blackmail situation.

He kept studying the photos throughout the day on Tuesday, during breaks, behind his locked door.

Did Phillips take the pictures? Had he hidden in the bushes with a camera, lurking there in the dark outside the bedroom?

Even more unlikely than the PI, he thought. Phillips didn't have the balls for such antics. He would be too afraid he might be discovered and labeled a pervert or worse.

By Tuesday afternoon, though, all he could think about was why there were only two photos. If he was going to blackmail someone, he would certainly send more than two lousy pictures. And they would certainly be more incriminating than these two pictures.

He wanted to ask Scott. But then, that would mean he would have to let Scott see the pictures. And then that might lead to a discussion of where they came from and how Marc came into their possession. No, he couldn't ask Scott directly.

And even if Marc burned the prints he had intercepted, Phillips could have the negatives and make more copies he reasoned. There could be more photos, worse than these, he thought. But more probably, and this is what worried Marc the most, the two pictures were really trivial in the grand scheme of things. Scott wasn't that important to Phillips. Scott was just an irritation. Same with Virginia. Marc knew Phillips detested her. But it seemed unlikely that Phillips would go to all of this trouble just for her.

And that's when the puzzle began to make sense. Tuesday night, after study hall. That's when he stopped looking at the pieces of the puzzle and tried to understand the bigger picture.

Scott and Virginia were merely walk-ons in this bigger picture. Minor players. Distractions.

The photos were taken at the cottage.

The cottage belonged to the Academy.

The Academy belonged to Phillips, or so Phillips thought.

It was an easy puzzle, once you had the bigger picture.

The cameras weren't outside of the cottage.

The cameras were inside of Virginia's house!

After you figured that out, it was easy to see in the photos. The pictures weren't taken from the outside, through the window. They were taken from inside the bedroom.

Which meant hidden cameras.

Phillips had installed hidden cameras in the cottage.

Not for Scott. But for Virginia. Scott had just wandered into the scene. A mere fortuitous event for Phillips.

No, wait, he thought. Not for Virginia, either! Well, only incidentally for Virginia.

The bigger picture, he reasoned, laying in his bed Thursday night after lights out. What was the bigger picture?

It came in his sleep. As he tossed and turned in troubled sleep Thursday night.

And it was so cruelly obvious.

A suspicion he had for a long time. More than a suspicion, he had finally admitted to himself.

Finally confirmed. In his dream.

Phillips was hunting for the biggest game possible. The only game worth the risk of the hidden cameras.

Marc saw it clearly in his dream.

Phillips was after his father. Phillips was after T. Hunter Hansen.

How clever, Marc admitted the next morning. How clever of Ben Phillips. Laying in wait for the biggest game when it was in its most vulnerable moment. When the hunted least expected it. When the prey was most comfortable that it was beyond the gaze, beyond the grasp, of everyone.

Marc had never really understood how malevolently clever Phillips was until that moment, as he brushed his teeth and stared into the bathroom mirror on Friday morning.

Nor had Marc realized until that moment how much danger his father was in.

Scott ran all the way from the dorm to Virginia's cottage. She had sounded so upset over the phone. Crying. So upset that it was hard for him to understand exactly what she was saying. Something about some pictures. Of the two of them. But he didn't remember her taking any pictures of them. Maybe he just forgot.

She was waiting for him at the door. Holding a large brown envelope in her hand. Crying.

"Oh, my little rabbit! What am I to do? What am I to do?"

"What is it Virginia?" he called her by her first name, trying to calm her. "What's wrong?"

"You must come into the house, I think. Quickly!"

She pushed him through the front door rather roughly and toward the sofa in the front parlor.

"I don't know," she said. "I just don't know," she said, handing him the envelope. "I don't remember. Anything, my little rabbit. Was I … did I do something, my little rabbit? Please tell me I didn't. You are my friend. Please tell me that."

Scott took the package and opened it.

"Of course we are friends. Best friends. You're like … like family."

Virginia laid her head on his shoulder, looking over it as he scanned the photos.

"I … I just don't remember," she said, sobbing.

It was the two of them. From the night he had eaten dinner with Virginia. When she had gotten drunk and he had to put her to bed.

Why … how did she take these pictures, he wondered?

"It's from the night we had dinner together. You had too much to drink. And I put you to bed."

"And that is all, my little rabbit? That is all that happened?"

"Oh course that's all that happened! You had so much wine you couldn't even stand on your own. So I walked you back to your bedroom, turned down the covers, and then laid you in bed. You passed out. You had gotten so sad and you drank too much wine. That was all. That's what happened. Then I left."

"But the pictures? I think they are not good. For either of us, I think. I think someone, perhaps is up to, how you say it 'no good' for us."

Who took the pictures, he wondered? And why?

"And they were just inside your door when you woke up? Just laying under the door?"

"Yes. Just there," she pointed to the door. "Oh, what shall we do my little rabbit? I think this is not so good if someone else were to see these pictures."

"No shit!"

"What does 'no shit' mean? I do not understand it, this 'no shit'."

"It means I don't know what to do about the pictures either. But I have a friend who will know," he said, stuffing the pictures back into the envelope and running out of the house. "I'll call you later. After I figure this all out," he shouted back at Virginia.

Where would he be, Scott thought?

Where would Marc be at this time of day?

Scott checked the practice fields as he ran back toward the Academy. A few boys were still there, the younger boys, picking up the trash from the earlier scrimmage.

He checked the Circle. A couple of parents. A few teachers leaving the library to go home.

Too early for dinner, Scott thought. That only left the dorm.

He ran up the stairs of Smith dorm to the third floor, to the large triple where Marc roomed, an exact replica of Scott's own room in Hanover, Marc's on the west end of Smith, Scott's on the east end of Hanover, their respective rooms facing each other across the narrow walkway between the buildings.

"Have you seen Marc?" he asked John Webb.

"Yeah. He headed out to see Jim," John replied. "What's up with Marc this week, anyway? He's been holed up in his room all week."

"Can't talk," Scott shouted back, running as fast as he could down the stairs and out the side door of Smith toward the gym. A steady stream of boys were walking back to their dorms, waving at him, calling him. But he didn't have time now for them.

Scott ran down the incline through the basement door and straight past the cage toward Jim's office. The door was closed, but he didn't bother to knock.

Marc was sitting across the desk from Jim. Both of them with troubled expressions.

"I need to talk to Marc!" he said, pulling the envelope out of his pocket.

"We're kind of busy right now, Scott," Jim said. "Can it wait for a few minutes?"

Marc looked at Scott strangely, then quickly pulled some papers out of Jim's hands and stuffed them into his backpack.

"Ah, Jim, why don't you give Scott and I a second. OK? You and I can finish up later."

Jim looked at Scott, at the envelope in his hand.

"Sure. Sure. I'll just check on Lindsey's ankle. See how the sprain is," Jim said, quickly leaving the room and closing the door behind him.

"I have a problem," Scott said, offering the envelope to Marc. "I need your help."

Scott watched Marc take the envelope, open it, and flip through the two photographs quickly. For some reason Marc didn't seem too surprised. He just put the photos back in the envelope and sat there, his hand cupping his chin, lost in thought.

Then Marc started laughing. Just a little at first. Then holding his stomach as he laughed.

Scott felt his anger inside of him. Rising inside of him. Uncontrollable. He had come to Marc for help. He had come to Marc as a friend. He clenched his fists. He hated being laughed at. More than the disdain. More than the pity. Scott hated being laughed at worst of all, he thought, taking a step closer to Marc as he pulled his right hand back to strike.

Marc saw him coming and tipped his chair back sufficiently to put the corner of Jim's desk between the two of them.

"Scott! Wait a minute man! I'm not laughing at you," Marc shouted, trying to put on a serious face. "I get it! I understand. I'm not laughing *at you*!"

Scott tried to hold himself back. To keep his fist behind him.

"You stupid ass Texan!" Marc laughed. "It's Phillips. It's Ben Phillips. I already have this one figured out."

Phillips, Scott thought?

How was Phillips involved?

What did Phillips have to do with the two photos?

Marc reached around Scott, gingerly, and pulled an envelope out of his backpack along with the sheets of paper he had pulled out of Jim's hands earlier.

It was the same type of envelope, Scott realized. Marc already had another set of the photographs!

Marc handed his envelope to Scott.

Scott looked at the scribbled address.

Alexandra Regis, c/o New York Repertory Company, Summer Session.

Scott slumped into the chair that Marc had vacated.

Allie! Allie was going to see the photos.

Marc stood over him, placing his hand on Scott's shoulder.

"Like I said, Scott, I already have this one figured out," Marc offered, smiling. "Do you trust me, man?"

Scott sat silently.

He wasn't sure who he could trust anymore. But Marc seemed the best bet right now. His only chance, perhaps, Scott thought.

"Sure," Scott said. "I trust you."

❧   ❧   ❧

Scott rubbed the black makeup over his face, pulled on the black sock hat that Marc had given him and glanced at the clock. Almost three in the morning. Almost time, he thought, as he crept down the hallway toward Lindsey Quinlan's room. He opened the door slowly. Lindsey was sitting at his desk, smearing the same black makeup over his neck and arms. Wearing the same black knit hat. The room illuminated only by a small headlamp strapped to Lindsey's head. When Lindsey turned around, all Scott could see was the glare of the light and a row of very white teeth against Lindsey's blackface. He looked ridiculous, Scott thought. Like some politically incorrect caricature.

"It's time," Scott whispered. "Let's go. And get rid of that stupid headlamp!"

The two boys walked slowly, quietly out of the dorm, sneaking behind the bushes toward Smith hall. At the corner of the building they met up with Marc, Andrew Synesi, and Hawk Hawkins. All of the in black shirts, black pants, black caps, and black face.

"OK. Listen up. It's zero three hundred hours," Marc said, trying not to laugh. "Synchronize watches. Operation Mini-Cooper is commencing."

It had been a legend, Marc had told them. An urban legend and a prep-school myth. Dating from the 1950's or 1960's. It was rumored there were pictures, but no one had ever actually seen them. It had sounded preposterous when Marc had first described it to Scott. But it had just enough truth to it to be believable.

Smart teenage boys living together, day in and day out in the prep school dorms.

Too much time on their hands.

Just looking for a way to blow off a little steam.

The legend was that it happened at Stratham Prep. There had even been an article about it in their alumni magazine. That's how Marc found out how to do it, he had told Scott. One of Marc's mother's roommates at college had married a Stratham graduate who had apparently been in on the prank. The grandest prank in the annals of the prep school league. Unmatched in over half a century. Marc had met the Stratham alumnus on the Cape last summer. He had brought the man a bottle of his father's best cognac. And the two of them had set on the beach, in front of fire, the man drinking the cognac until he had finally told Marc how they had done it.

The man had been clear. It wasn't original. It had actually been done before at Stratham. In the late 1800's. Only then, before automobiles, the Stratham students had used the school's sailboat.

So when he had done it, in the 1960's, it was really just duplicating the feat. Only with the headmaster's Volkswagen in place of the sailboat.

It was so simple, Marc had explained to the other boys as they had plotted over dinner in Scott's room. Once you knew how to do it.

The boys followed Marc around the edge of the Circle, from bush to bush, seeking cover wherever they could, dashing between the buildings when there was no cover. Making their way slowly, steadily in the darkness of the early morning, toward the private parking spaces at the side of the headmaster's housing. Toward the brand new, bright red Mini-Cooper that Phillips had just bought for his wife.

❦ ❦ ❦

Ben tried to clear the cobwebs from his brain and grabbed the phone next to his bed after the second ring. It was just getting light outside.

"Mr. Phillips? This is Charlie in maintenance. I think we might have a little problem," the voice over the telephone said, chuckling.

"What sort of problem? With the plumbing, again?" he asked.

"I would say … a different kind of problem."

"Where?"

"I think you need to come to the auditorium, Mr. Phillips. It's a little hard to describe over the phone."

These simpleton's, Phillips thought. What kind of a problem was it that one couldn't describe and that would require his attention so early, he thought.

"Fine. I'll be there in a few minutes."

Phillips tried to get out of bed without waking his wife, groping for the robe that matched his pajamas and his new calf-skin slippers. No time to get dressed or freshened up, he thought. He would inspect the problem, tell maintenance how to deal with, then get back to his routine, he thought.

He padded softly out the front door of his residence in the mist of the early morning, around the walkway of the Circle so as not to allow the dampness laying on the grass to ruin his slippers, straight toward the auditorium. He hoped it wasn't much of a problem. Today was assembly. Some of the parents and trustees were actually going to show up. A photo op he had informed the local paper of last week by post. He hoped he could fix the problem before the assembly.

No one was waiting at the front doors, so he keyed the lock himself and walked into the foyer. The lights were on in the auditorium and he hurried down the corridor on the right side to the front, where the noise seemed to be coming from. Laughter? What were they laughing about? If there was a problem, the maintenance crew should be fixing it. Not standing around and joking with each other.

He reached the private entrance at the side of the auditorium, pushing through the oak doors to stand below the stage, stage right.

Looking from the floor of the auditorium, up onto the elevated stage, now fully lighted.

Looking at the maintenance men, the whole staff, standing there on stage, snickering.

His new Mini-Cooper, center stage of the comedy.

Two envelopes, one with an address clearly visible on it, stuck in between the wiper blades and the front window of the car.

CHAPTER 28

Marc paced frantically in the front parlor of Virginia's cottage, listening intently to the chatter on the maintenance band of the Academy's communication system. His distraction had worked. All of the maintenance department had rushed to the auditorium once the Mini-Cooper had been found on stage. In fact, everyone associated with the Academy seemed to have migrated to the other side of the campus to inspect the feat that they had accomplished.

"Naveed," Marc called softly. "We need to hurry. We are only going to have about another half hour."

The slight Indian boy was toying with electrical equipment and wires that seemed to hang from almost every lighting and electrical fixture in the house.

"Ah, yes, dude. I am working very hard here," Naveed replied. "Please to not distract me."

Scott sat on the sofa next to Virginia, watching Andrew guard the front door through the bay window.

"Got anything else to eat?" Lindsey asked, coming back into the parlor from the kitchen, a sandwich in each hand.

"Shut up!" Marc yelled. "We're on a schedule here."

"OK, dude," Naveed finally sighed. "I have switched the radio frequencies of the transmitters. And here is the solenoid that I wired from the toilet," he said, handing a switch to Marc. "It was most clever wiring. I only know of one boy in Boston who does such a thing," he said, his British and Indian accent thick overtones to the words. "He is an Indian boy," he said, smiling. "From Delhi!"

"So it's all switched out? All of them? You found all of the cameras and switched all of the transmitters?"

"Most assuredly!" Naveed said with a large smile, climbing down from the ladder. "After all, dude, I am a genius, you know."

The boy, normal sized, was dwarfed by Lindsey as he passed him, retrieving a large control panel set with switches and lights.

"This controls all of it, now," Naveed assured Marc. He plugged a small video monitor into the panel and threw one of the switches. A grainy black and white video of them all in the parlor appeared on the monitor's screen.

"Now you see it," Naveed said, then flipping the switch. "Now you don't!"

The monitor now showed an empty dorm room.

"And all of them are like that? You just flip the switch on each one?" Marc asked.

"Oh, most certainly. As simple as that!" Naveed said, handing the control panel to Marc.

"Phase 2, World's Worst Videos, complete!" Marc said. "On to Phase 3!"

"What was Phase 3, again?" Lindsey stared blankly at Marc.

"Its' 'The Trojan Horse'. But you're not involved in Phase 3, Lindsey. You and Andrew are supposed to put all of the wire and lights back like they were. Can you handle that? Can you and Andrew handle that much, as least, without me to babysit the two of you?"

"I don't need no babysitter," Andrew said as he walked through the front door. "But I could use something to eat. You got anything else to eat?" he said, chugging the rest of the milk from the yellow gallon container.

Virginia tried to smile.

"I think perhaps the football makes my young men very hungry, yes?" she said.

"All right. Feed the two of them first, then. Naveed and Scott and I have to go," Marc addressed the group. "Now remember, no one says anything. You don't know anything. Regardless of what anyone asks you about anything. Got it? You're just stupid jocks. You guys understand that?"

There was a pause.

"Me, too, dude?" Naveed asked, tilting his head and smiling broadly.

What was the saying, Ben thought?

Revenge is best when served cold?

Well, he had a nice cold serving in store for the Greenwood boy!

It had taken Ben all day and a full maintenance crew to extract the automobile from the auditorium, finally removing a door frame to get it outside the building.

Ben had moved the assembly into the chapel.

Little good it did, he thought.

Everyone on campus knew about the prank.

Even the trustees who had showed up for the assembly were laughing at him.

Ben wasn't sure how the boy had done it. How the boy had made a fool of him. But Ben was sure that the Greenwood boy was the only one that could have put the automobile on the auditorium stage. The only one who could have had both of those envelopes in his possession.

Ben didn't have proof, other than the envelopes.

But the story behind the envelopes he couldn't actually disclose to anyone.

And to single the boy out as the responsible party would only make him legend.

Phillips would never do such a thing.

The boy needed to be an example. But not that kind of example. Not some impish prankster duplicating a prank that only occurred once or twice a century.

God, Phillips thought. The boy wasn't even original with his pranks. He merely took his cue from his betters at one of the finest prep schools in the world. A not-so-subtle imitation of the type of disruptive behavior Ben had never condoned. Even among his own classmates when he was a student at Stewart.

The boy was going to be an example, all right.

Ben was going to make him an example of him for the whole community, Academy and town as well, he thought, as he unlocked the safe in his office, pulled out the interior lockbox, keyed it, and extracted a large test-tube sealed tightly with a rubber stopper. He flicked the test-tube slightly with his forefinger to free the small white rocks inside.

He would make an example out of the boy.

Scott threw his clothes into his gym bag hurriedly. He was running late. He had promised Allie that he would meet her in the City mid-afternoon. But Phillips had called a special assembly in the chapel that morning. Trying to get one of the boys to confess to the prank, to putting his car on the stage of the auditorium. He had lectured them. And then when no one said anything, he had just left them sitting there in the auditorium all morning. Until Jim had showed up and sent them all on their way.

Now he was late.

Had he forgotten anything, he wondered as he quickly went through his bags?

Bad enough to be late. He didn't need to screw up and forget something stupid. Like his socks. Or his boxers, he thought, remembering one of the many mistakes he had already made that summer.

He grabbed his keys and bag, ran down the stairs, and jumped into the Buick.

Please start, he begged, turning the engine over a couple of times. You can do it, he thought, encouraging the old car to life.

The engine revved and he stuffed the gear shift into drive, causing the tires to squeal slightly as he tore out of the parking area.

He looked as his watch.

1:10.

He was going to be in trouble, again.

He was going to be so late.

He stopped short at the gates to the Academy, looked both ways, then peeled out onto the main road, heading toward town. Within seconds he saw the flashing lights behind him.

"Shit!" he cursed aloud. "Just what I fucking need. A ticket."

He had come to a complete stop before pulling onto the road. He was sure of it.

Maybe he had accelerated a bit too quickly, burning a little rubber in the process.

But he had been below the ridiculously low speed limit that the town had posted on the two-lane road between the Academy and the interstate.

Didn't the local sheriff have anything better to do than ticket him for that, he wondered, pulling over to the edge of the road, turning off the engine, and putting both hands firmly on the wheel in full view as he had been taught in driver's education class?

Another police car suddenly appeared in front of him and swung across the road, blocking the Buick. Two officers jumped out of the squad car, weapons drawn, pointing them at him!

"Hands on the steering wheel!"

"Let me see your hands!"

A half dozen officers now, swarming the Buick from all directions. Screaming at him.

He froze. Hands in place on the wheel. Afraid to move a muscle.

"Out of the car!" a burly officer shouted, opening the door and pulling him roughly to the ground.

"Hands behind your back! Now!" another one shouted, pinning him, face down, to the ground as he wrenched Scott's arms around behind him.

"You have the right to remain silent," one of the policemen started the Miranda statement, as Scott felt the handcuffs clamp down tightly against his wrists.

What was going on, Scott wondered, too dazed to say anything? What the hell was going on, he wondered, seeing boys running down the road from the Academy out of the corner of his eye.

"Do you understand these rights?" the officer finally said.

"We have a warrant to search this vehicle and its contents," another officer waived a large sheet of official looking paper in front of Scott's face. "Do you have anything in your pockets? Any needles? Any weapons? Any sharp objects?" he asked beginning to run his hands over Scott while his partner held Scott over the back of the Buick.

"No. None of that," Scott managed as they finished turning his pockets inside out, spilling his coins onto the pavement.

Some of the boys from Hanover dorm were standing at the edge of the road, one of the officers motioning them back from the highway.

"I came to a complete stop. Really. I stopped. And I wasn't speeding. Honestly!" he protested as he watched the other officers begin searching through his car, his bag.

Scott saw Andrew and Lindsey running across the practice field, jumping the fence next to the stream, headed toward him.

Suddenly one of the officers stood up next to the opposite side of the Buick.

"Found it!" the officer said, holding up some sort of test tube and smiling in a self-satisfactory way.

All of the boys were just standing there looking at him. Staring at him.

"You're under arrest for the possession of a controlled substance," the officer behind him said, tightening his grip on Scott and forcing him sideways toward the back door of one of the police cruisers.

❦   ❦   ❦

Allie waited in the wings of the small recital hall at the Repertory.

It was obvious he wasn't coming, she thought.

It was obvious that he didn't care about her anymore, she thought.

Concentrate, Allie. Concentrate, she thought.

He's just a boy. Just another boy. Don't blow it over him. This is your big chance. What you have waited for all of your life. To dance the lead in New York.

The lights went down in the house and the shuffling and talking hushed as the small chamber group began to play.

She was so stupid, she thought.

She had almost thrown it all away.

She had almost lost her chance.

Sneaking out at night. The drinking. The movie. And worse.

She had lost sight of her goal.

It has started with Scott, she reasoned. She had been focused before she met him. He had been her first distraction.

And then it was this City, she thought, subconsciously counting the cadence of the music as the curtains opened and the ensemble began to whirl onto the stage to the applause of the small gathering of Repertory members, ballet company talent scouts, and press.

It was this City, she thought, and what it did to the people in it. What it did to her.

She had lost focus.

But that was over.

She knew what she wanted.

She wanted to be a dancer, she thought, readying herself.

A dancer!

Everything else, even Scott, was just a distraction, she thought, going to pointe and making her grand entrance, for the first time, as a lead in a New York ballet.

❦   ❦   ❦

Scott sat in the small cell at the edge of the bed, unable to stop his body from shaking.

It was all just a bad dream. That's what it had to be. A bad dream. He would wake up soon. Back in his dorm. Back in his own room. On his own bed.

He shivered uncontrollably again, listening to the sound of rough men he could not see. His other inmates in the town's jail.

They had taken his belt. And his shoe laces.

They had smeared black ink across his hands when they were fingerprinting him.

At least he finally had the cuffs off, he thought, rubbing his chaffed wrists.

Drugs. They had found drugs in his car.

Where did they come from?

They all kept asking him that question.

If they weren't his drugs, then where did they come from, they asked?

Why were the drugs in his car, they asked?

Scott wasn't sure what would happen next. It wasn't at all like what he had seen on TV. It was worse. So much worse. Losing all control. Everyone telling you what to do. Not having any rights at all, apparently.

Except one.

The right to remain silent.

He remembered that one.

Like Marc had told him, don't say anything to anybody.

Marc called the number his father had told him to use if he ever got into trouble at the Academy. It was a beeper number. He entered in the number to the cellphone he had stashed in his dorm room against Academy rules. And waited.

It took less than five minutes to get a call back.

"This is Judge Castignoli. You paged me."

Judge Castignoli, Marc chuckled to himself. Definitely the right man to call if you were in trouble in Massachusetts.

"This is Marc Hanson. T. Hunter's son."

"Marc. Why yes. How are you my boy? It's been what, almost a year since we've seen each other? At the fund-raiser in Boston that your father was nice enough to arrange on my behalf during the Presidential campaign. How is your father?"

"He's fine, sir," Marc spoke respectfully. Castignoli had been a long shot for the nomination, like all Massachusetts candidates since Kennedy. But Marc knew the man had been his father's favorite teacher during his MBA program in Cambridge. And, he knew that his father had pumped millions into the campaign on Castignoli's behalf, standing by him until the old judge had finally conceded.

Castignoli was definitely the right man for this job, Marc thought.

"I need to ask for your help, sir," Marc said respectfully. After all, Marc thought, the man deserved his respect. Marc had never met anyone like Castignoli. No one, not even his own father, came close.

"Why, of course Marc. Anything. What can I do to help?"

CHAPTER 29

She was perfect.

The dance was perfect.

Everything about the recital was … well, perfect, Allie thought, wiping away the stage makeup from her face as all of the other girls came by to compliment her performance.

It was exactly what she had imagined. Being center stage. Dancing the lead before an audience of real critics, people familiar enough with dance to know how superlative she had been. Taking her curtain calls as the roses were thrown onto the small stage at her feet.

"Great job!" Justine gushed, hugging her. "You were so beautiful!"

She was beautiful, she thought, looking at her reflection in the mirror.

Finally transformed into the swan that she had always hoped was there inside of her, just waiting to escape.

Not even Natasha could find fault with her performance! The highest of all praise, Allie thought.

"Well, you certainly captured the day, today, girlfriend," Katrina said, standing in Allie's doorway.

Allie thought the comment was a compliment. But she was never sure these days what Katrina meant by anything that she said. Maybe Katrina was just being catty. She had been that way all week. Jealousy, Allie surmised. Katrina was just jealous that Allie had captured the lead for the big recital, that Allie was the better dancer.

Allie had become increasingly annoyed with Katrina, she thought. Perhaps it was the stupid pair of boys boxer shorts that Katrina had insisted wearing all week. Perhaps it reminded Allie too much of Scott. Reminded Allie so much of

Scott that she could almost smell his scent on Katrina when she wore the boxers.

"Thanks," she said politely, trying to bring a quick end to the conversation.

"No, really," Katrina continued. "You did well. I was surprised."

Again, Allie wasn't sure if Katrina's comment was intended as a compliment or a dig.

"So, I didn't see Scott today," Katrina said, walking into Allie's room and sitting down opposite her.

Those stupid box shorts, Allie thought, Scott's scent in her nose.

"He was supposed to come," she offered. "But he didn't. His loss."

Katrina just sat next to her smiling coyly.

"I saw Seth in the audience," Katrina said. "He came to see you dance," she said, toying with the small envelope stuck in the vase of long stemmed roses that had been delivered to Allie right before the recital. "These from him?" she asked, prying into the card. "They are. They are from him. *Love, Seth*. How absolutely adorable," she said, dropping the card into the vase.

"Guess that means you're not just his companion, anymore?" Katrina said, walking out of the room.

Jealousy. The green-eyed monster. It was a bitch in gender, Allie thought.

She finished cleaning off her face, pulled back her hair, and headed upstairs to shower before the reception that the Repertory had planned for that evening. She spent a few minutes stretching out her muscles under the hot water as she lathered the scented bath gel over herself. Her legs were sore. Both of her feet had blisters. And the bruise on her back from Natasha's ruler earlier in the week was clearly visible in the mirror now that the water had washed away the last of Allie's body makeup.

Just part of it, Allie guessed, toweling dry and throwing on the short silk robe that Emily Ros had sent her. The robe Emily had used during the movie.

She trotted back to her room through the empty halls of the dormitory. She had taken a long time in the shower, in no particular hurry, savoring the feeling of success. The other girls could rush. She was going to take her time, she thought, tidying up her room, smelling the roses, combing out her hair.

There was knock at her door.

"Allie?"

It was Seth.

"Are you in here?" he said, walking through the doorway.

She tried to pull the robe closed around her quickly before he came in.

"Ah, you got my flowers, I see."

"I'm not dressed, Seth," she protested.

"I've seen you undressed, Allie," he teased, pushing away the junk at the bottom of her bed and sitting down.

She blushed, slightly.

"I have to get dressed Seth. You have to leave so I can get dressed for the reception."

"Yes. Dressed for the reception," he smiled. "My little ballerina," he said, holding out a large colorful shopping bag. "For you, Allie. For the reception."

Her flushed face deepened in color.

She looked inside the bag, filled with various size boxes, all with expensive designer names on them.

"Well, aren't you going to open them up?"

She sat the bag in the chair and took out the shoe box first. Inside, black pumps. Very Italian and very tall black pumps. In her size.

Next, a small purse. Black. Expensive.

Next, a French name. A courtier name. A ultra-short, ultra-skinny, black dress. Mere wisps of cloth, delicately stitched together.

And jewelry. Box after box of jewelry. A necklace. Earrings. Bracelets. She took a long time, putting on each piece as it came out of the box.

"The jewelry is on loan, I'm afraid," Seth said, noticing her enthusiasm. "Like Cinderella, it disappears after midnight. Well, not at midnight. I just have to take it back on Monday. Do you have any idea how much jewelry you are wearing right now?"

Allie looked at herself in the full length mirror inside her closet door. Standing there in her short silk robe with all the sparkling jewelry.

"More than I have ever worn before?"

"No, I mean guess how much it's worth. All of the jewelry?"

It sound crass to Allie to put a price tag on things so beautiful.

"A hundred thousand," Seth smiled. "More than that, and they make you use a body guard," he explained. "And we wouldn't want that, now would we?"

She was wearing a hundred thousand dollars. And a short, second-hand, silk robe.

"Well, try on the dress! I know its your size," Seth beamed.

What the hell, she thought. He's seen me before, she thought, dropping the robe to the floor and trying to squeeze herself into the tiny dress.

❦   ❦   ❦

Marc waited patiently in front of the desks in the small room just outside of the huge iron door that separated the jail cells from the rest of the world.

"You must have some very important friends, son," the huge state trooper standing next to him said.

A corpulent man with big glasses in a three piece suit and carrying a huge leather briefcase was talking to one of the arresting officers in a loud voice. Loud enough for Scott to hear all the way across the hall.

"Probable cause! Probable cause! Someone you can't identify calls from a number you can't trace and gives you an anonymous tip to watch for a four-door Buick with a Texas license plate transporting drugs at one o'clock Saturday afternoon from one of the finest college preparatory schools in the world?" the old man laughed. "This warrant isn't worth the paper its written on! One phone call to the Essex County office and its gone. Like that! And then where do you stand? False imprisonment, I think, at least. Perhaps a bit of overly enthusiast arrest behavior caught on several dashboard cameras, which by the way I will want impounded," he said, as he lay a very formal looking paper on the sheriff's desk, "along with all of the cars that were involved in the arrest until we clear this up."

"But, we used all of our cars. You can't impound all of our cars."

"Watch me. And the Academy parents. Exactly how much revenue do you think they pump into the local economy here each year? Exactly how much money do you think your constituency here in town will lose when the word gets out that you are roughing up sons and daughters of Academy parents. Exactly how much tax revenue do you think the Academy pumps into this town? A shame to lose that revenue, really. Just think what that would do to the property taxes here."

"Drugs. We found drugs. Don't forget about the drugs."

"Simple possession. And that's only if that mysterious substance is controlled, which by the way I will want to confirm with my own laboratory," the man said, pulling another official looking document from his briefcase and laying it on the sheriff's desk. "And then, of course, that's only if the warrant holds up, which it won't."

"Well, what the hell do you want me to do? Just let him go?"

The old man's cellphone rang and he answered it.

"Let's see if this phone call will help you decide the best course of action to take in this matter," the old man said, handing his cellphone to the sheriff.

"Sheriff Repucci here. Who am I talking to?" he asked gruffly. Then his tone immediately changed. "Yes sir. Certainly I know who you are. Voted for you in the last primary, sir."

There was a dead silence in the small constabulary.

"Yes sir. Yes sir. I understand, your honor. Yes sir. Yes, that was just being explained to me," the sheriff said, nodding at the old man in the three piece suit. "No sir. No sir, we wouldn't want that to happen. No sir. Absolutely not."

The sheriff stood up and started to pace behind his desk.

"Yes, sir. And a good day to you sir."

The sheriff handed the old man back his cellphone.

"Maybe we were mistaken," the sheriff offered. "Perhaps we acted on misleading information, that … well, that resulted in some mistakes being made."

The sheriff opened a locked drawer in his desk and pulled out the mysterious glass vial they had retrieved from Scott's car.

The old man in the three piece suit laughed.

"Chain of custody issues, I see, as well," he said, pulling yet another of the formal papers from his briefcase and laying it on the sheriff's table.

The sheriff looked in Scott's direction.

Then he looked around his office. At all of the other officers trying desperately to blend into the khaki-colored walls.

Then the sheriff took all of the papers that the old man had laid on his desk, straightened them into a neat stack, put the glass vial on top of them, and very meticulously rolled the papers around the vial, as if rolling a huge cigar. When he was finished, the sheriff handed the roll of papers, and their contents, to the old man in the three piece suit. Along with a small file that sat at the edge of the sheriff's desk.

"It's all there. All the paperwork," the sheriff said to the old man. "That's all the documentation."

"And the video from the patrol cars and the audio tape from the arrest?" the sly old man asked.

"Unfortunately, that equipment was malfunctioning today," the sheriff offered. "There are no records of any arrest occurring this afternoon."

"Yes. I would say you have some very important friends," the state patrolman smiled at Scott.

❦   ❦   ❦

All Scott wanted to do was leave. All he wanted to do was get in the Buick and drive off. All he wanted to do was get to New York and see Allie. Leave all of his problems at the Academy, in the small town, behind him.

But Marc wouldn't let him.

As soon as the highway patrol cars had escorted Scott and his Buick back to the Academy, Marc had corned Scott, dragging him back to Marc's room in Smith dorm.

"You're too late for the recital," Marc chided. "Allie will be going to the Repertory reception. It's a big deal. She will be there. Talking to the press, probably. It's a celebrity thing."

"But she's expecting me. I told her I would come to the recital to see her dance. I promised."

"Well, we all make promises. And break them," Marc offered.

Scott had broken a few promises lately. A promise to his father, no longer a vow that made sense. His commitment to Allie, that night in Marc's brownstone with Katrina. Suddenly, breaking the promise to come to Allie's recital didn't seem quite so fatal a mistake.

"Besides," Marc offered. "You won't want to miss this."

"Yeah, I know. Phase 3. The Trojan Horse."

Marc pulled back the huge packing box he used to hide the flat screen TV in his room. He had the controller that Naveed had given him plugged into this computer and the computer plugged into the TV.

Marc closed the door, pulled the curtains and flipped one of the switches on the controller. The TV screen began to glow in the darkening room. On screen, Scott's dorm room.

"You put a camera in my room? Why did you have Naveed do that, you pervert?"

"Wait for it," Marc said, scrolling through the video feed with his computer mouse. "Wait for it. Wait for it. Bingo!"

It wasn't a real time image they were watching, Scott finally realized. It was getting dark outside now. But in the video feed the sun was shining through the window in his dorm room. That only happened in the morning. They were watching tape from this morning.

A figure moved cautiously from the doorway of Marc's room into the center of the frame. It was Phillips. Looking over his shoulder. Sneaking around in Scott's room.

"Look familiar?" Marc asked.

"It's my dorm room. This morning. What's he doing in there?"

"Patience."

Phillips was going through Scott's closet. He pulled out Scott's gym bag. Then he took something from his pocket. A glass vial. And put it in the gym bag.

"Phillips planted the drugs on me? But … but why … why would he do that?"

"You're not from around here, are you?" Marc asked, mockingly. "Don't look so shocked. He hates your guts. And besides," Marc continued. "You're not that special, as it turns out. It's not the first time he's done anything like this. My father calls its 'spring cleaning'. Apparently Phillips does something like this every year in the spring. To the special needs kids. The ones that he doesn't want to 'ask back'. Sometimes its dope. Sometimes its alcohol. One time he even planted a switchblade in the room of a Hispanic kid from the Bronx, just because the kid would have lowered the average SAT scores if he had graduated with the class."

"I'm going to kill that guy," Scott said. And he meant it.

"Hold on cowboy! No reason for physical violence. I have a better way."

Marc fiddled with the switches on the control panel and his computer mouse.

"First, we embed a special executable file in this SouthPark clip."

The image of Cartman with the video coming across loud and clear.

"Respect my Authority! Respect my Authority! Respect my Authority!"

Over and over again on the screen, as the cartoon character's mouth opened and closed.

"When the Cartman plays, the executable searches the host computer for all other video files and then wipes them out."

"I don't get it. What do you mean, host computer?"

"Where do you think those photos of you and Virginia came from?"

Phillips! It had to be Phillips! The drugs. The photos. Probably even the root-beer episode.

"Smart boy," Marc smiled at him. "And where there are photos, there are digital files. That's what we have to wipe out. We have to wipe out all of the video files on Phillips' computer," he said. "So, we switch the feed from the cameras by alternating the radio frequency."

"Naveed!"

"Exactly. Then," he said, clicking the mouse one more time, "we substitute Cartman with the executable file embedded in him. Feed comes into Phillips computer. Cartman displays on the screen. The executable erases Phillips video archive."

It was brilliant, Scott thought. So simple in concept. So incredibly complex in execution.

"So the Mini-Cooper stunt? That was just a distraction so that we could rewire everything," he tried to follow the progression. "And the rewire. That was so we could get rid of the pictures of Virginia and me."

Close enough to the truth, Marc thought.

"Well, really all of his video from the cameras in the cottage. Everything. Wiped clean."

"And you knew that Phillips would think that I pulled the Mini-Cooper prank. That he would try to get back at me. So I get the camera in my room. But what are you going to do with that footage? The footage of Phillips in my room. Are we going to give it to the police?"

"You have to be one of the dumbest smart guys I have ever met," Marc snorted at him.

"Not the police," Scott said. "If not the police, then who?" he paused. "I get it!"

Marc shifted another of the switches and the video of Phillips planting the drugs downloaded into the computer, then slipped away into the ether.

"It should be quite a surprise, don't you think?" Marc laughed. "Oh, and I had Naveed make a few more adjustments to Phillips computer in the executable."

"So am I dismissed now, sensai?" he asked.

"Yes, grasshopper," Marc laughed. "Now, away with you. To the City!"

CHAPTER 30

Allie sat at a corner table and sipping on cranberry juice from her cocktail glass. No alcohol tonight, she thought, tugging down on the tiny black dress that Seth had given her.

The heels were tall and her feet were too blistered to do any dancing. Or walking for that matter.

So she just sat in the corner, watching all of the society set party. Talking to the journalists and posing for the photographers when they came by her table. Trying to enjoy herself.

This was what she had waited for. Worked for.

A small town girl. In the City. Tonight at the center of the City.

It was nice, she had to admit.

Being driven and escorted around town. Much nicer than the bus and subway rides she had become accustomed to as a concession to her meager Repertory stipend.

Having nice clothes to wear. What little she was wearing, she thought, trying to pull the top of the dress just a little bit higher.

Everyone wanting to talk to her. Sitting there, holding court, she thought, waiting for people to come and introduce themselves.

But she had imagined it differently.

A bit more glamorous, perhaps?

More fulfilling, somehow.

A photographer brought one of the ensemble over to her table, posed the two girls together, and snapped a couple of pictures. Allie didn't even remember the girl's name. But she smiled and put her arm around the girl, making them seem closer than they were.

Why was it so empty?

The recital. It had been everything that she expected it to be. The hushed audience watching her every move. The music washing over her. The movements she had practiced hundreds, thousands, of times, coming so easily to her on stage.

And the applause afterwards. Everyone calling her name. Gracefully collecting all of the flowers that had been thrown on the stage for her.

That had been intoxicating.

But it had been so brief.

A few minutes on stage. A few more to savor the audience response. A curtsy. Then back to the same cluttered dorm that she shared with all of the other girls.

Seth brought one of his female co-stars from his new television series over to the table. A gaggle of photographers followed, shouting instructions to the three of them.

"Seth, move closer to Ms. Regis!"

"Cameron, can you lean in a bit!"

"Allie, this way! Look this way!"

She was almost blinded by all of the flashes from the cameras.

"Cameron and I are going to cut out, Allie," Seth whispered as the last of the photographers finished. "You want to come?"

He had spent most of the night with Cameron. Once the two of them had gotten out of his limo, once they made it past the red carpet and photographers out side, he had left her. And hooked up with Cameron. Just left her sitting at the table while he danced with her and bought her drinks and fawned over her.

"No thanks! I'm staying."

"I'll send someone over for the jewelry tomorrow. Make sure you put it somewhere safe tonight. Locked away."

He was more interested in the jewelry now. And Cameron.

Allie undid her necklace.

"I don't want to have to worry about it," she said, handing him the necklace, then sliding off the bracelets and handing those to him. "You deal with this stuff," she said, removing the earrings and handing them over to him.

Seth took the jewelry without protest. He even handed the necklace to Cameron.

"You might as well wear it the rest of the night, sweetie," Seth said to her.

Allie thought about giving him back the shoes and the dress and the handbag. Right there. In front of everyone. Then she thought better of that idea. She actually liked the clothes. Not comfortable for her at all. But comfort wasn't their purpose. They were just for show. Like the borrowed jewelry. Like her, she thought, as Seth and Cameron left her alone again at the table.

Allie tried to make it last as long as she could, thinking that it might just take time to feel like it should at the reception. She tried to get as comfortable as she could. She tried to smile at everyone. She tried to relax and just enjoy it.

Two more couples, friends of Marc's parents, stopped by. Complimenting her performance. One of the men, an accountant he said, handed her his business card for some reason.

She hadn't asked her own parents to come. It would have been a long drive for them. And expensive for them to stay in the City overnight. They wouldn't have enjoyed all of the fuss. And she couldn't imagine her father in a tux.

She tried to discretely remove one of the high heels under the table and massage her foot. It was starting to cramp from being on pointe all day. First for the dance. Now for fashion. When another photographer came over to the table, she had to pull the bare foot up under her body, sitting on it. Trying to lean into the camera and smile, as he asked. Lean in even closer when he asked Allie her name and what she did.

It was all going by her so fast. People who had been at the recital had started to leave. In small groups and in couples. Now the room was filling with people she didn't know. And who didn't know her.

Soon she was just another pretty girl, sitting in the corner table, alone. She had been at the center of the City only a few minutes ago. Now, it seemed to her that she was at its periphery, an outsider looking in.

It had been in the back of her mind all day. A thought she wouldn't let herself have.

It was over. The first session of the Repertory for the summer was over.

Now what was she supposed to do?

Go back to her home?

Go back to serving pizza?

Just pack her things and leave?

This time when the cocktail waitress came around Allie ordered a Cosmopolitan.

All of her work. All of that time and effort and pain. For one night. For a few minutes on stage. A few fleeting hours of notoriety.

"You look a little distressed, Ms. Regis."

She had been looking down at the table, fumbling with the hem of her dress, again. She hadn't seen him approach. He was just there. At her table. Holding out her cocktail.

"Jaffrey! What are you doing here?" she said, excited to see a familiar face.

"May I sit down, Ms. Regis?"

He always called her Ms. Regis. Even when she had been at Marc's house. Even when it was just the two of them. Even now.

He didn't wait for an answer.

"I understand that you had quite a performance this afternoon. Very grand, I think they would say."

She laughed at his formality and English accent.

"Yes. It went well. I think I did OK."

He sat there quietly, letting her sip on her drink.

"Jaffrey, how long have you worked with Hansons?"

"Oh, Ms., that would be almost my whole life. I've worked for T. Hunter for twenty-five years. Before that, I was with his father. The elder Mr. Hanson."

Allie giggled. She was trying to imagine an elder Mr. Hanson more elder than T. Hunter.

"Something funny, Ms.?"

"No, not really. I was just thinking that you've worked with the Hansons longer than I have been alive," she said, finishing the cocktail.

"Well, yes, Ms. Much longer, I would think."

He just sat there. Staring over the heads of everyone there. Looking toward the door.

It seemed to be a younger crowd now in the bar. Rougher. More rowdy. Jaffrey looked singularly out of place in his neatly pressed black suit and bowtie.

"You came to get me, didn't you Jaffrey?"

He waited a moment, as if reflecting on the question. Then smiled.

"Yes, Ms. Regis. The young Mr. Hanson requested that I see to you. In case you needed an escort. Him knowing how these type of events are, you see."

The young Mr. Hanson. Marc Hanson.

"So what happens now, Jaffrey?"

"When you're ready Ms. Regis I have the car waiting for us. I think the plan is for me to escort you back to the Repertory for you to gather your things and then to offer you the hospitality of the house this evening."

So, it was really over, she thought. A man-in-waiting come to summon her back to reality.

"One more drink, I think Jaffrey. Then we can go."

❦   ❦   ❦

Things hadn't turned out as Ben had planned. The sheriff had called him late in the afternoon on his cellphone, interrupting a perfectly good day of sailing. Cursing at him about the Greenwood boy. Telling Ben about the phone call he had received that afternoon from Beacon Hill. Ben had tried to reassure the man. But he seemed inconsolable. Using particularly base language, in the process.

The call had cut the sail short. He had left his wife on the island and headed back to the Academy just to make sure things were as they should be. As he had left them.

There were still a few of the boys out lounging in the evening air in the Circle. But most of them had retired to the common rooms and their vulgar video games and DVDs.

Ben pulled the Mini-Cooper into the reserved space next to the residence.

He would just check on things and then retire early tonight, he thought, walking through the residence into his study, turning on the lights as he went.

He moved the mouse in circles to bring his computer to life, then put his thumb on the biometric pad, and keyed in his password. He checked email quickly. Nothing particularly interesting. Word of a new fund raising event by the ten year class. A sale at Harrod's Knightsbridge. A few personal notes.

He noticed the open video application at the bottom of his screen and maximized it. He keyed in the secondary password and brought up the file folder for the last few days. He hadn't expected to see anything. But there were two video files there. One time-stamped last night. One this morning.

Interesting, he thought. Who was the terrible French woman entertaining now?

He clicked last night's file and the computer seemed to explode with sound.

"RESPECT MY AUTHORITY, RESPECT MY AUTHORITY."

The sound blared out at him in the quiet of the house at full volume, a dreadfully drawn pudgy cartoon character mouthing the words at Ben from the computer screen. He fumbled for the volume control and tried to shut off the sound. But regardless of what he did, the phrase just kept repeating itself, full volume. Finally, he closed the file and was greeted with merciful quietness. The computer kept making fast whirring sounds that were unfamiliar. But at least the shouting had stopped.

Technology, he scoffed! The more complicated the machine, the more ways it could malfunction, he reasoned. He had his suspicions from the beginning that the Boston boy he had hired to wire the system wasn't particularly sure about the radio frequency transmission applications. This just proved the point, Ben thought. Errant TV signals of some obscene cartoon show finding its way into his "secure" system.

The whirring and clicking continued from his computer as he launched the second file, the file time-stamped this morning. The file didn't immediately open. Damn computer, he thought. With all of the new applications on it, it kept getting slower and slower. He clicked the file name once more, impatiently.

The file opened, haltingly, stuttered and then began to play.

What was this, he wondered looking at the video image? He didn't remember a room in the cottage like the image. The image looked more like one of the Academy dorm rooms.

But there was something familiar about the image. What was it? Why did he seem to remember this particular dorm room?

On the screen the door to the room opened and he saw himself enter.

Suddenly his heart was racing and he pushed himself back away from the computer monitor.

Why was that video of him in the Greenwood boy's room on his computer? How did it get there?

Ben tried to stop the video, but in the process hit the other video file and the dreadful yelling of the cartoon character started all over again. He kept hitting keys on the keyboard and try to click out of the applications, but now they were both there, on his monitor. The horrid, screaming cartoon character and the awful video of him leaning over and placing the vial in the gym-bag, over and over and over again.

Finally he hit control-alt-delete and the shouting stopped. The video of the dorm room disappeared.

He rebooted the computer, but kept getting error messages about files that had been deleted.

The dreadful videos. Now a virus. What more calamities, he wondered, awaited him?

As if in answer to his question, his office phone rang. His private number.

"Benjamin Franklin Phillips."

"Ben, this is Hunter."

"Hunter, what a pleasure," Phillips gushed. "I just got back from sailing. Beautiful day on the water. Gorgeous."

"I haven't got much time."

"Of course. I know how busy your schedule must be," Phillips was being too eager. His voice was slightly tremulous.

There was a long silence.

"I want the Texas boy in school there next year," Hunter's words came out not so much a request as a statement of fact. "I want him to play football next term with Marc."

"Well …" Phillips shifted uncomfortably. "I know that Marc has developed a certain … affection for the Texas boy," Phillips tried to make the relationship between the two boys sound suspect. "But … the boy … he's not … really our type, now. Is he?"

Dead silence on the phone.

"I mean …" Phillips stammered. "The boy … he didn't even go to school last year, apparently."

"I didn't say you had to graduate him, Ben," Hunter's voice seemed distant, distracted. "I just want him at the Academy next year."

Again, a long silence between the two of them.

Was it worth it? Was it worth Ben playing his Ace of Spades with Hunter? Just to keep the boy out of the school? Was it time to use the videos of Hunter and the French woman?

"Of course, if that is a problem, I can always make … other accommodations," Hunter's voice was no longer distracted. It seemed … angry.

Phillips thought quickly through the options. Quickly through what 'other accommodations' might mean. It sounded like a threat to him. It sounded like Hunter was threatening him. It was a quick change of circumstances. Hunter was never one to bluff, as Ben had observed on numerous times in the past, as Ben had watched Hunter's adversaries fall by the wayside.

Did Hunter already know about the videos in the cottage? Had his plan to use them against Hunter somehow backfired? The video of him in the Greenwood boy's room and the strange behavior of his computer. Did those have anything to do with this very unusual, late night conversation?

Too much for coincidence, Ben decided.

Fuck the boy, he thought.

His own job as headmaster might be at stake.

"Well, of course I would be glad to consider admitting the boy on your recommendation, Hunter," Phillips offered weakly. "If his academics are up to par and we can find the necessary aid I am sure he will need. Being an orphan, like he is," Phillips cautioned.

"He's in, Ben. Next term. I want you to make that happen. Understood?"

"Well, yes, I could start working on that on Monday, I suppose," Phillips muttered, swallowing his distaste for the task.

"Make it happen Ben. I will be at the Academy again next month to support you on the board matters we discussed. I want it done by then."

Phillips quickly made the connection. It was a trade. The boy for Hunter's support with the Board.

"Yes, we should be able to get everything squared away by next month on the boy, I think," he offered weakly.

"And Ben. I heard that there was an incident in town earlier today. Involving the police. I want to make sure that's not repeated, Ben. Bad press, you know, for the Academy. Bad for all of us. Understood?"

Damn Hunter Hanson, he thought.

Damn all of his kind, the kind that had made Ben feel so small and insignificant all of his life.

And damn that impertinent Texas boy.

Damn the Texas boy for being just like them.

"Understood," he finally said.

CHAPTER 31

It started raining as Scott turned onto the Turnpike. Then he hit Saturday night traffic outside of Worchester and again when he drove through Hartford. So it was almost one in the morning before he arrived at Marc's brownstone and Jaffrey let him in, directing him to the third floor guest suite, sneaking him up the back stairs through the kitchen in order to avoid the elder Hansons.

Scott could smell her as he entered the room. It was the coconut bath gel that he had given her. She smelled so good when she used it. She smelled like … summer.

The lights were dim in the room, but as he let his eyes adjust to the darkness, he saw her outline in the bed, under the covers, her breathing regular and deep.

There was another smell in the room. Alcohol.

Allie was smashed, he thought, noticing the two empty martini glasses on the nightstand next to the bed.

He chuckled softly. It must have been quite a day for her. He felt badly he had missed it. He felt badly that he had missed her. For so long.

He just hoped she had missed him.

He just hoped after all of her success here in the City that she could still care about a poor Texas orphan boy.

He just hoped that she knew nothing of the night he had spent in this same room with Katrina. Ever.

Allie moaned briefly.

What were her dreams these days, he wondered?

She was restless in the bed and started mumbling in her sleep. Nonsense words. And names. He thought he heard the her say Vicky's name. It sent a shudder through him to hear the name again in this room.

It must be a nightmare, he reasoned, to cause her to sleep so poorly, to carry on like that.

He knew how to handle her nightmares, he thought, pulling off his jeans and t-shirt and sliding under the covers with her.

She grunted at him as if in protest.

"No," she moaned, pushing at him in her sleep. Then mumbled more names.

She was so out of it, Scott thought. The two cocktails must have gotten to her, he thought.

Then she said his name.

"Scott," she called out in her sleep. "Scott," she mumbled his name.

"It's OK Allie. I'm here," he said. "Just like I promised" he said, snuggling up against her, their bodies touching each other after so many weeks.

She smiled a sleepy smile and threw her arm around him, almost slapping him in the face, pulling herself up as close as she could to him. Never waking.

"It's OK Allie. I'm here now," he reassured her as he brushed an errant strand of blonde hair away from her face. "I'm here."

He lay in the huge bed on the crisp, clean sheets. Feeling her body next to his. Listening to her breathe. Conscious of even the small twitches in the leg she had draped over him. Not wanting to sleep, himself. Enjoying this time, this quiet time, with her.

She stirred after an hour or so. Never fully awake. Still a little too drunk. Startled to find him there next to her in the bed. Saying his name. Touching his face. Kissing him, sloppily. Holding him. Holding him tightly. More tightly than he ever remembered. Too sleepy, too drunk to talk. Holding him, kissing him. Sobbing on his shoulder.

She had missed him, he thought, watching her clumsily trying to hold back her tears. Brushing them away, trying to smile at him through the tears. Girls were like that. They cried a lot. They cried when they were sad or upset. And then sometimes they cried when they were happy. Like now. Because she was so happy to see him, he thought.

He never truly slept. It felt too good to be there with her after all of the time apart. He didn't want to miss a single minute of time, now that they were together, again. Now that they were a couple, again.

His body next to hers. Listening to the wind and the rain against the bedroom window as the street sounds faded away in the small hours of Sunday morning.

She was so small, he thought, as she finally began to come out of her dazed sleep and pulled him on top of her toward dawn. So small and fragile, he thought, as they made love, quietly, never saying a word, and gently, as gently as he could as he wiped away tears from her face.

Girls were like that, he thought Sometimes they cried when they were happy.

🍁   🍁   🍁

"Do you have everything, Allie?" Scott asked as he began stacking the bags and boxes she had crudely stuffed her belongings into next to the dumb waiter. "Is this everything?"

She had been so quiet.

Understandably last night. Probably she was too wasted to remember much of that, he thought.

But so quiet this morning. Unusually quiet.

Scott knew she was glad to see him. She had demonstrated that. But she seemed a little sad, as well. Perhaps sad over having to leave the City, over the end of the Repertory classes, he speculated as he began to load the clothes and shoes and ballet accessories into the dumb waiter.

She had so much stuff, he thought. It seemed that she was going home with over twice as much baggage as she had when he had dropped her off in the City at the first of the summer. Where did she get all of this stuff? How did she afford it all?

"That's it," Allie smiled at him, dropping a new pair of ballet slippers into the last box.

"Do you want to put that bag in as well?" he asked, reaching for the colorful shopping bag she carried.

"No. I'll just carrying this one with me."

She kissed him on the cheek and started down the back stairs as he closed the door to the dumb waiter and sent the parcels down to the garage in the basement for Jaffrey to pack away in the trunk of the old Buick.

He followed, as quietly as he could, trying not to wake any of the Hansons that might be in the house. Or any of their friends.

By the time they reached the basement, Jaffrey had finished the loading and was standing at attention next to the car. It was an odd sight to see the formally dressed Englishman next to the old Buick. Perhaps equally as odd, Scott thought, for Jaffrey to be catering to someone like him.

Allie kissed Jaffrey on the cheek, like she would her father, and whispered something in his ear. He had been a good friend to them, Scott thought, shaking hands with Jaffrey. To both of them.

Now it was time for Allie and Scott to leave the City. To leave Jaffrey, to leave the people that they had allowed into their lives there, behind.

The rain was still falling as he pulled the Buick out onto the street from the garage.

"Do you want to drive by the Repertory one more time, Allie?"

"No. I have everything. No need," she said, still facing the window of the car, looking out of the window.

He tried to get her to talk to him. About the recital. About the Repertory. About the friends she had made. But she was in one of her quiet moods, answering in one word sentences.

Perhaps still hung over a bit, he thought. Perhaps just sad to leave.

The old car's air conditioner was no match for the city's summer heat and the humidity from the rain shower. The windows fogged on the inside and what little air that circulated through the Buick left a sticky feeling against his skin. There was little traffic this early on Sunday morning. Even at the tolls.

What was she thinking, he wondered, as they sped along the Merritt? She acted so differently since she had come to New York, since she had started with the Repertory.

Maybe she was just growing up too quickly. Kids did that when they were on their own. Trying to figure life out. Trying to figure out where they fit in. Maybe that had happened to her during the summer in the City, he thought.

She pulled back her hair and laid her head against the car window listening to her iPod through earphones, responding to his questions but never initiating any conversation. Napping, occasionally.

He finally ran out of questions and concentrated on the slippery road as they turned off of the Merritt and onto the confusing interchanges in Hartford that would take them to the Mass Pike.

He was getting tired. And sleepy. And hungry.

He pulled the Buick off the highway at the huge truckstop northeast of Hartford to get gas and try and wake up a bit before getting on the Turnpike. To get some coffee to wake him up and something to eat.

Allie went to the restroom and browsed through the store while he filled up the car and waited in line for doughnuts and coffee.

"You look tired," she said as they walked out of the TOA store. "You want me to drive for a while?"

"Would you? I just can't seem to keep my eyes open," he said, tossing her the keys and climbing in on the passenger side. He fumbled with the seatbelt for a while, trying to readjust it from where Allie had it tangled, then gave up. He was just too tired to deal with it.

Usually he didn't like for anyone to drive the old Buick. It was temper-mental at best. A lumbering behemoth of sheet metal with an oversized steering wheel that dwarfed the more fuel efficient mini-cars on the road. And he hadn't maintained it like he should have this summer. Just too many things happening, too many other things to do. He would have the oil changed when he got back, he thought, settling into the passenger seat as Allie gunned the engine and accelerated down the entrance ramp to the Interstate. And get the transmission and tires checked, he thought, trying to settle his coffee into one of the makeshift cup-holders he had installed. Too tired to eat more than a couple of bites of doughnut he closed the sack and threw it on the seat between them.

It was an uneasy sleep for him. Allie's tendency to over steer the car, changing in and out of lanes, waking him often. Waking him from dreams about his family.

Dreams about his mother. How she had loved him, in the little ways a boy remembers. A new toothbrush before he had to ask for one. His favorite soup on rainy days. The new pair of football cleats he knew they couldn't afford that had suddenly appeared when she started tutoring French students at the high school.

Dreams about his sister. Teaching him how to ride his bicycle without the training wheels. Taking the blame for the new lamp he had broken. Keeping his secrets.

About his father. All of the practices his father had come to, good weather or bad. The pancakes with Scott's initials meticulously laced in them on Saturday mornings. About his father's final days in the hospital when the emaciated man could no longer express that love.

The ancient pneumatic wipers on the old Buick were having a tough time keeping pace with the rain and labored when Allie pushed the car to pass other traffic. The huge eighteen-wheelers threw up sheets of water at them. He started to ask Allie to slow down, but then thought better of it. She never appreciated his comments about her driving.

He was sleeping when she took the Academy exit, slowing the car on the rain soaked two-lane road that led into town. Waking slightly when he noticed she took the back road to avoid having to go through the center of town. Looking at the small stream that ran along the roadbed. It had just begun to flood its banks. They must have gotten a lot of rain here, he thought.

Allie made the last curve before Federal Street and Scott caught a flash of light out of the corner of his eye. A car, spinning like a top, and headed straight for them. Everything in slow motion, it seemed.

He heard the horrible, sickening sound of the metal as the two cars met and felt the tremor as the Buick's frame began to crumple.

The front windshield shattered. An odd, spider's web in front of him, he thought, surprised that there wasn't more pain when he crashed through it.

The sky and ground began spiraling around him.

He felt the rain against him.

He sensed the change in the direction of his flight as he careened off of the telephone pole at the side of the road.

He felt the pain in his shoulder as his arm slipped out of the joint.

He finally landed, rag doll style, in mud, at the side of the road, water from the stream running over him.

Laying in the water, trying to breathe.

Watching the flashing lights.

Feeling the darkness and cold descend upon him, the taste of his own blood in his mouth.

CHAPTER 32

Scott lay shivering in the cold bluish light.
They kept moving him, forcing him first one way, then another on the small bed.
It hurt.
It hurt so badly.
Why did they have to shout so much?
They were all so loud.
All he longed for was quiet.
He just wanted the pain to go away.
"Scott! Scott! Stay with us, Scott!"
Why did they have to shout at him?
Didn't they see it was just too hard?
Just too hard to stay awake, he thought before the darkness came.

He was laying in the grass. Short green grass. Grass that had been recently mown.
The sky was blue. Incredibly blue.
The sun was so warm on his skin.
He heard birds in the distance. And the sounds of water close to him.
It was so nice. Just to lay there in the grass, basking in the sun.
It smelled so nice. So fresh.
It smelled like summer.

He was thirsty.
That was his first thought.
That he needed something to drink.
Then came the pain.
Then came the darkness, again.

He kept running from door to door.
They were all locked.
He would try one door, find it locked, then run to the next.
Trying to get out.
Frightened more than he had ever been before.
Gasping for air.
He needed to get out.
But the doors were all locked.
Just a long hallway.
Doors on each side.
All of them locked.
He couldn't breathe, the hallway closing in on him.
He had to get out!

He was talking when he woke up. He wasn't sure what he had just said, but the woman in the white nursing uniform was shaking her head up and down in affirmation, encouraging him.

He stopped talking when he woke up.

He was having trouble moving.

And he was cold.

"I'm cold."

The nurse lay a recently heated cotton blanket on him, the warmth sinking through the covers of the bed, before she hurried out of the room.

He closed his eyes and enjoyed the warmth a few seconds.

His body felt strange. And some parts he couldn't feel at all.

He opened his eyes to a hospital room.
He was laying in a hospital bed.
The accident!
Someone had hit the car when they turned onto Federal Street. A car had hydroplaned into the Buick. And hit them.
Hit them, he thought, his heart beginning to race!
The monitors next to his bed went off and he heard the terrible single tone in his ears.
Hit them, he thought!
Where was she?
Where was Allie, he thought, struggling to raise himself in bed?
"Allie!" he shouted.
Bodies in white began to surround the bed and he struggled with them.
"Allie!" he shouted.
They were holding him down.
He had to get up.
He had to find Allie.

❧   ❧   ❧

"Scotty."
He smiled.
He loved the sweetness of the voice.
"Scotty, are you awake?"
Not yet. He wasn't awake yet.
"Wake up, Scotty."
He didn't want to wake up. He just wanted to listen to that voice. Calling his name.
But it was too late.
He was waking up, he thought, as he opened his eyes.
Allie was standing next to the bed. She had a bandage on her head. And small stitches holding together cuts on the right side of her face. Her jaw was swollen. She looked so tired. And scared.
"Are you OK? I was worried about you," he said.
She smiled down at him, tears in her eyes.
"You were worried about me," she said, choking on her words. "I've been worried about you. Do you remember anything? Do you remember what happened?"

"Can I have some water. I'm so thirsty. But I don't seem to be able to move."

Allie held a small glass of water and let him sip water through its straw. It tasted so good to him.

"A car hit us. We had a wreck," he said, taking another sip of water. "Are you OK?"

"I'm fine. A few cuts and bruises. That's all. I was wearing my seat belt and you know that old Buick. It's a tank of a car."

He smiled.

The old Buick was a tank.

"What happened? To me?"

She was trying to smile, trying to appear cheerful. She wasn't very good at acting, though, he thought.

"You went through the windshield. Do you remember that?"

He did. He remembered. He remember slowly flying through the air. And hitting the telephone pole.

Suddenly his shoulder began to throb and his monitor went off again.

He moved his left hand up to his right shoulder, but couldn't touch it. His right shoulder was encased bandages.

"Your shoulder got banged up. You dislocated it when you hit the telephone pole," Allie said softly, taking his left hand and trying to hold it. "Lay still, Scotty. Lay still for minute. You have a lot of stitches. From where you crashed through the window."

A nurse walked in and started pushing bottoms on the monitor and tending to the tubes that ran under the sheet into his body.

"You need anything for pain, sweetie?" she asked.

Pain, he thought. He hurt all over. He felt like he had been hit by a truck! He tried to laugh at his own joke, but the pain in his chest hit him.

"Yes, please," he said, then turning to Allie. "But you're all right?"

"I'm going to be fine, Scott. Just banged up."

"Am I OK?"

The tears welled in her eyes.

"Here's your pain medication," the nurse interrupted, injecting cold liquid into the tube that ran into his free arm.

"You'll be fine," Allie said, unconvincingly. "You have to be," she said, sobbing as the darkness overcame him again.

❦   ❦   ❦

Macy was standing next to the bed.

He thought he would never see her again.

He thought she hated him.

For hitting her.

For killing her only brother.

She was smiling.

It must be a dream, he thought. Another of the strange dreams he kept having about his family.

"Scott?"

It was her voice. It was Macy's voice.

Maybe he wasn't dreaming.

"You gave me quite a scare," she said. "I thought I had lost you," she said smiling at him, taking his left hand and holding it tightly.

She actually looked a lot like his father, Scott thought. The way she smiled.

"I thought you hated me," he said. "For hitting you," he said.

"I don't hate you, Scott. You're my family. The only family I have left. I … I was scared … I was just scared of you," she said. "I didn't know what else to do."

"I thought you hated me," he said. "You know. Because of Dad," he said.

"Oh, Scott," she said, leaning over and kissing him on his forehead. "You couldn't help that. It wasn't your fault. Any more than your accident was Allie's fault. Bad things like that just happen. I was mad," she offered, stroking his hand. "But not at you. I was mad about losing my brother," she said. "And scared … about having to take care of you," she said. "I can't even seem to take care of myself, these days. And, I'm afraid I did a terrible job as far as you're concerned."

Allie was standing at the door. Waiting patiently. Trying not to disturb the two of them.

"You don't hate me, do you Scott?" Macy asked earnestly.

"I tried to," he admitted. "I tried to hate you. But, I couldn't. Not really. Really, I hated myself."

"You don't hate me, do you Scott?" Allie said, joining them by the bed.

She looked so serious, he thought. Both of them with such serious expressions. It almost made him laugh.

Neither of their faces were designed for sorrow, for guilt, for regret.

Their faces were made for joy.

For smiles.

Kind faces, from which loved just seemed to flow.

"Of course not! I love you Allie," he said.

"*I love you, Allie*," Andrew Synesi mimicked his tone of voice from the doorway. "*I want to marry you*," he continued in the same tone, smacking his lips to make fake kissing sounds.

"Oh, my little rabbit!" Virginia said, pushing past Andrew. "*You are going to be all right, I am thinking?*"

The French, the distinctive accent of Virginia so hauntingly similar to his mother's, brought Scott out of his reflections and back to the reality of the hospital room.

"*I have just heard of the tragedy. Again you are here in the hospital. It is not possible. You have none of the good luck at all. Only the tragedy,*" her words full of compassion.

Allie and Macy stared vacantly at Scott, waiting for the translation.

"She said that she's glad I am going to be OK."

It was the first time he had really had the thought, himself.

"I am going to be OK? Right?"

"Well you sure as hell aren't going to be playing any football for the rest of the summer," Andrew said.

Macy pushed Andrew back away from the bed, giving him a disapproving expression.

"What? What did I say?" Andrew asked, shrugging his shoulders.

"The doctor says you are going to be fine. Just fine. It will take a few weeks for the broken bones to heal. But you're going to be as good as new."

Broken bones, he thought. Plural.

"What's broken?" he asked trying to raise himself from the bed.

"You broke a couple of ribs, man," Andrew said shaking his head. "No big deal, man. Happened to me. No big deal. Feels like shit for a few weeks, is all."

So that's why he had so much trouble moving around in the hospital bed, Scott thought.

"Well, aren't we having a little party in here," the nurse chimed in as she brought in a lunch tray. "I guess those hospital rules about no more than two visitors in here at any one time just don't apply to you people?"

The overly large nurse crowded everyone else out, as she pushed her way through to the monitors.

"We got rules here, you know. You people got to get out of here. You people have to let this boy rest, now, if you want him out of here any time soon."

He was getting tired, he thought. And the pain was coming back. In his shoulder. In his chest. Where the stitches across his face pulled against the skin when he tried to talk.

"You people get out of here now. All of you. Everyone but you, sweetie," the nurse said, grabbing Allie by the arm. "I think you should stay, sweetie," she smiled. "What do you think, young man?" she said, sticking a machine in Scott's mouth to take his temperature.

He tried to answer the nurse, but the words came out garbled over the machine in his mouth.

"Didn't understand you, son," she smiled, toying with him. "I asked if you wanted this pretty young lady friend of yours to stay here a little longer," she said, taking the machine out of his mouth. "If she might improve your condition a bit."

"Yes, please," he said. "Allie can you stay with me a little longer?"

"As long as you want me," Allie answered, taking his hand again. "As long as you want me."

The others left the room, in single file, each with their own parting comments.

Then it was just the two of them, Allie and Scott, in the room.

"Oh, Scott, I'm so sorry. I'm so sorry. There wasn't anything I could do. The other car. It just hit us. Head-on."

Now it was Scott's turn to reassure Allie.

"You couldn't help it. It wasn't your fault," he said, taking her hand.

It wasn't her fault.

It wasn't his fault, he finally realized, for the first time.

Marc was the first one to visit Scott when Macy and Allie moved him out of the hospital and into the Victorian, into the huge room downstairs so that he could watch the big screen TV. He was carrying a large leather briefcase and had a particularly pleased expression on his face.

"Who wants presents?" he asked as the three of them settled in for an afternoon of baseball.

"Me, Me, Me," Allie shrieked with delight. "Me, first!"

She was such a little girl at times, Scott thought. Such an absolutely adorable little girl.

Marc rummaged through the briefcase, shuffling things around.

"Come on Marc! Don't tease!" Allie pleaded.

"These are for you, Allie," he said, handing Allie two small video cassettes.

Allie had a blank expression on her face.

"These are the originals from the dance sequence Will shot," Marc said. "There are no copies."

Allie grabbed the tapes and put them in her jeans.

"Will ... well, Will said to tell you he was sorry but he couldn't use the tapes he made of you dancing in his movie."

"How ... how did you get the tapes?" Allie asked furtively glancing in Scott's direction.

Scott sensed anxiety in Allie's voice. She must be disappointed, he thought. Thinking that she was going to be in movie, then Will deciding against using her tape. The tape of her dancing.

"Will isn't a bad guy, Allie. He's just obsessed with making movies. So, we traded," Marc said. "I gave him a new camera. He gave me the tapes. I thought you might want to have them. As a memento of your short-lived movie career."

Marc and Allie were just staring at each other. Not saying a word.

"Now me," Scott tried to catch Marc's attention. "What's my present?"

Marc went rummaging again in his briefcase, producing a thin letter with the Academy seal on it.

"What's that?" Scott asked, reaching for the letter.

"Open it. Find out."

Scott tore open the envelope and began reading the single page that was inside of it.

"What is it, Scott? What's the letter all about?"

Scott couldn't believe what he was reading.

How had Marc done it?

"Well, don't keep her waiting. Give her the good news," Marc encouraged him.

"It's from the Academy. From the Director of Admissions. Asking me to come to the Academy next year. As a student. All expenses paid."

"That's great," Allie said, throwing her arms around him, lightly, so as not to hurt his shoulder. "I can't believe it. You're going to be a prep!"

"Well technically, he's going to be a lower. That's what we call a sophomore at the Academy."

"But … what about Phillips?" Scott asked.

"I don't think Phillip should be a particular problem," Marc said, pulling a second tape from this briefcase. "I brought a tape I made at the Academy for you, too. Thought it might come in handy," Marc said, handing a cassette to Scott.

"What's on his tape?" Allie asked. "Is it you and Scott playing football? Is that how he got in? Is he on a football scholarship or something?"

"Yeah," Marc chuckled. "It's a practice tape we made. At the Academy. Maybe you and Scott could swap tapes sometimes and watch each other," he said, maliciously. "Seriously, they don't give athletic scholarships at the Academy, Scott. It's just an offer to come to school there. But if you want to play, if you want to come to the Academy and play football with me, then you can. I mean as soon as you rehab your shoulder. I talked to Jim. It's not that bad. A month of rehab, tops. And as an Academy student, the insurance covers it all. Rehab at the best sports medical clinic in Boston."

"Any more surprises?" Allie asked.

"Maybe," Marc offered, sticking his hand back into the briefcase. "Oh, I heard that Vicky was going abroad. With Katrina. Both of them will be abroad the rest of the year."

That was a surprise, Scott thought. A pleasant surprise. Allie looked relieved, as well. She had never liked Katrina, Scott thought. With good reason, he thought.

"Yes, one more surprise," he said, pulling out another envelope. "For Allie!"

Allie grabbed the letter from Marc's hand and tore it open.

"Oh, my God! It's from the Boston company!" Allie shouted. "One of their scouts saw the Repertory recital. They want me to join the Boston company!" she shouted, jumping up and down in front of them. "I'm going to dance in Boston!"

Scott looked at Marc.

If a scout had seen Allie and recommended her to the Boston company, then why did Marc have the offer letter, Scott wondered?

"Well, didn't that work out grandly," Marc said. "Scott at the Academy. Allie in Boston. All of us together next year."

Scott knew he was dreaming. But it seemed so real.

They were all together, again.

His mother was smiling at him as she carefully ironed his favorite shirt. Hanging it next to his other clothes on the hook on the family room door. His boxers and T-shirts and socks all laid out on the couch as if ready to pack.

He must be going away, Scott thought. She was getting his clothes together to pack them for a trip.

His sister was on the floor giggling as she talked on the telephone with one of her girlfriends. They were talking about Scott. The girlfriend wanting to know when Scott would be back. His sister taunting her with threats to reveal her older friend's attraction for Scott.

Scott's father was in his favorites chair. Reading. A travel book. Scott tried to make out the title of the book. But the cover of the book wasn't clear. His father looked up and nodded his approval to Scott. "Sounds interesting," his father said. "Different. But a place you might like," his father offered before immersing himself once again in the book.

It all seemed so normal.

So real.

Not like a dream at all.

There was a knock at the door. His mother, his sister, his father all looked up in unison. Not at the door. But at Scott. They were all smiling at him.

The dream began to fade away as quickly as it had come.

"Wait!" Scott called out. "I don't want you to go!" he yelled in the dream.

"It's time to go, Scott," his mother said, handing him a bag, already packed with the clean clothes.

"Goodbye, Scott. I'll miss you, little brother."

Then one final glimpse of his father.

Patting Scott on his back, gently.

Lovingly.

Telling Scott how he needed to be brave now.

Telling Scott to be strong.

Telling Scott how proud he was of him.

He didn't want the dream to end.

He wanted to hear what his father was telling him.

Just a few more words.

But, it was too late.

He was awake.

Laying next to Allie in bed.

In Macy's house.

He lay there, looking out of the window of the big first floor room, looking out on to the lawn on Federal Street.

It seemed strange to Scott.

He had been on his own. Since his family had died.

Now he had Allie. And he had Macy, again. And he had Marc for a friend.

Maybe it was time to go on with his life, he thought. Maybe that was what the dream was all about. Time to stop thinking about the past.

Not that he wanted to forget his family. He never wanted to do that.

It's just that it was time for him to move on.

It was time for him to find his own place in the world.

A separate place.

Just for him.

And for those that he allowed to share it with him.

978-0-595-34218-1
0-595-34218-3

Printed in the United States
82147LV00003B/266